THE TREE OF APPOMATTOX
A STORY OF THE CIVIL WAR'S CLOSE

By
JOSEPH A. ALTSHELER

The Tree Of Appomattox
A Story Of The Civil War's Close

by **Joseph A. Altsheler**

Copyright © 2023

All Rights reserved.
No part of this publication may be reproduced, stored in a retrieval system, or transmitted in any form or by any means, electronic, mechanical, photocopying or Otherwise, without the written permission of the publisher.

The author/editor asserts the moral right to be identified as the author/editor of this work.

ISBN: 978-93-57485-52-4

Published by

DOUBLE 9 BOOKS

2/13-B, Ansari Road, Daryaganj
New Delhi – 110002
info@double9books.com
www.double9books.com
Tel. 011-40042856

This book is under public domain

ABOUT THE AUTHOR

Joseph A. Altsheler was born on April 29, 1862, in Three Springs, Hart County, Kentucky, to Joseph and Louise Altsheler. He was a newspaper reporter, editor, and author of popular juvenile historical fiction. He wrote fifty novels and at least fifty-three short stories. Seven of his novels were in sequence. He worked as an editor at the Louisville Courier-Journal in 1885. In 1892, he started to work for New York World and then as the editor of the World's tri-weekly magazine. He wrote children's stories due to a lack of suitable stories. On May 30, 1880, Altsheler married Sarah Boles and had a son named Sidney. In 1914, during World War I Altsheler and his family were in Germany and they were forced to remain there. Altsheler died at the age of 57, on June 5, 1919, in New York. His wife, Sarah Boles died after 30 years. Their bodies are buried at the Cave Hill Cemetery in Louisville, Kentucky. Although each of the thirty-two novels constitutes an independent story, Altsheler suggested reading in sequence for each series (that is, he numbered the volumes). You can read the remaining eighteen novels in any order.

CONTENTS

CHAPTER I — THE APPLE TREE 7

CHAPTER II — THE WOMAN AT THE HOUSE 19

CHAPTER III — OVER THE HILLS 38

CHAPTER IV — THE FIGHT AT THE CROSSWAYS 49

CHAPTER V — AN OLD ENEMY 64

CHAPTER VI — THE FISHERMEN 76

CHAPTER VII — SHERIDAN'S ATTACK 88

CHAPTER VIII — THE MESSENGER FROM RICHMOND 106

CHAPTER IX — AT GRIPS WITH EARLY 121

CHAPTER X — AN UNBEATEN FOE 132

CHAPTER XI — CEDAR CREEK 149

CHAPTER XII — IN THE COVE 161

CHAPTER XIII — DICK'S GREAT EXPLOIT 178

CHAPTER XIV — THE MOUNTAIN SHARPSHOOTER 190

CHAPTER XV — BACK WITH GRANT 204

CHAPTER XVI — THE CLOSING DAYS 217

CHAPTER XVII — APPOMATTOX 228

CHAPTER XVIII — THE FINAL RECKONING 245

CHAPTER I
THE APPLE TREE

Although he was an officer in full uniform he was a youth in years, and he had the spirits of youth. Moreover, it was one of the finest apple trees he had ever seen and the apples hung everywhere, round, ripe and red, fairly asking to be taken and eaten. Dick Mason looked up at them longingly. They made him think of the orchards at home in his own state, and a touch of coolness in the air sharpened his appetite for them all the more.

"If you want 'em so badly, Dick," said Warner, "why don't you climb the tree and get 'em? There's plenty for you and also for Pennington and me."

"I see. You're as anxious for apples as I am, and you wish me to gather 'em for you by making a strong appeal to my own desires. It's your clever New England way."

"We're forbidden to take anything from the people, but it won't hurt to keep a few apples from rotting on the ground. If you won't get 'em Pennington will."

"I understand you, George. You're trying to play Frank against me, while you keep yourself safe. You'll go far. Never mind. I'll gather apples for us all."

He leaped up, caught the lowest bough, swung himself lightly into the fork, and then climbing a little higher, reached for the reddest and ripest apples, which he flung down in a bountiful supply.

"Now, gluttons," he said, "satiate yourselves, but save a lot for me."

Then he went up as far as the boughs would sustain him and took a look over the country. Apple trees do not grow very tall, but Dick's tree stood on the highest point in the orchard, and he had a fine view, a view that was in truth the most remarkable the North American continent had yet afforded.

He always carried glasses over his shoulder, and lately Colonel Winchester had made him a gift of a splendid pair, which he now put into use, sweeping the whole circle of the horizon. With their powerful aid he was able to see the ancient city of Petersburg, where Lee had thrown himself across Grant's path in order to block his way to Richmond, the Southern capital, and had dug long lines of trenches in which his army lay. It was Lee who first used this method of defense for a smaller force against a larger, and the vast trench warfare of Europe a half century later was a repetition of the mighty struggle of Lee and Grant on the lines of Petersburg.

Dick through his glasses saw the trenches, lying like a brown bar across the green country, and opposite them another brown bar, often less than a hundred yards away, which marked where the Northern troops also had dug in. The opposing lines extended a distance of nearly forty miles, and Richmond was only twenty miles behind them. It was the nearest the Army of the Potomac had come to the Southern capital since McClellan had seen the spires of its churches, and that was more than two years away.

Warner and Pennington were lying on the ground, eating big red apples with much content and looking up lazily at Mason.

"You're curving those glasses about a lot. What do you see, Dick?" asked Pennington at length.

"I see Petersburg, an old, old town, half buried in foliage, and with many orchards and gardens about it. A pity that two great armies should focus on such a pleasant place."

"No time for sentiment, Dick. What else do you see?"

"Jets of smoke and flame from the trenches, an irregular sort of firing, sometimes a half-dozen shots at one place, and then a long and peaceful break until you come to another place, where they're exchanging bullets."

"What more do you see, Brother Richard?"

"I see a Johnny come out of his trench hands up and advance toward one of our Yanks opposite, who also has come out of his trench hands up."

"What are they trading?" asked Warner.

"The Reb offers a square of plug tobacco, and the Yank a bundle of newspapers. Now they've made the exchange, now they've shaken hands and each is going back to his own trench."

"It's a merry world, my masters, as has been said before," resumed Warner, "but I should add that it's also a mad wag of a world. Here we are face to face for forty miles, at some points seeking to kill one another in a highly impersonal way, and at other points conducting sale and barter according to the established customs of peace. People at home wouldn't believe it, and later on a lot more won't believe it, when the writers come to write about it. But it's true just the same. What else do you see from the apple tower, Brother Richard?"

"A long line of wagons approaching a camp some distance behind the Confederate trenches. They must be loaded pretty heavily, because the drivers are cracking their whips over the horses and mules."

"That's bad. Provisions, I suppose," said Warner. "The more these Johnnies get to eat the harder they fight, and they're not supposed to be receiving supplies now. Our cavalry ought to have cut off that wagon train. I shall have to speak to Sheridan about it. This is no way to starve the Johnnies to death. Seest aught more, Brother Richard?"

"I do! I do! Jump up, boys, and use your own glasses! I behold a large man on a gray horse, riding slowly along, as if he were inspecting troops away behind the trenches. Wherever he passes the soldiers snatch off their caps and, although I can't hear 'em, I know they're cheering. It's Lee himself!"

Both Warner and Pennington swung themselves upon the lower boughs of the tree and put their glasses to their eyes.

"It's surely Lee," said Warner. "I'm glad to get a look at him. He's been giving us a lot of trouble for more than three years now, but I think General Grant is going to take his measure."

"They're terribly reduced," said Pennington, "and if we stick to it we're bound to win. Still, you boys will recall for some time that we've had a war. What else do you see from the heights of the apple tree, Dick?"

"Distant dust behind our own lines, and figures moving in it dimly. Cavalry practicing, I should say. Have you fellows fruit enough?"

"Plenty. You can climb down and if the farmer hurries here with his dog to catch you we'll protect you."

"This is a fine apple tree," said Dick, as he descended slowly. "Apple trees are objects of beauty. They look so well in the spring all in white bloom, and then they look just as well in the fall, when the red or yellow apples hang among the leaves. And this is one of the finest I've ever seen."

He did not dream then that he should remember an apple tree his whole life, that an apple tree, and one apple tree in particular, should always call to his mind a tremendous event, losing nothing of its intensity and vividness with the passing years. But all that was in the future, and when he joined his comrades on the ground he made good work with the biggest and finest apple he could find.

"Early apples," he said, looking up at the tree. "It's not the end of July yet."

"But good apples, glorious apples, anyhow," said Pennington, taking another. "Besides, it's fine and cool like autumn."

"It won't stay," said Dick. "We've got the whole of August coming. Virginia is like Kentucky. Always lots of hot weather in August. Glad there's no big fighting to be done just now. But it's a pity, isn't it, to tear up a fine farming country like this. Around here is where the United States started. John Smith and Rolfe and Pocahontas and the rest of them may have roamed just where this orchard stands. And later on lots of the great Americans rode about these parts, some of the younger ones carrying their beautiful ladies on pillions behind them. You are a cold-blooded New Englander, Warner, and you believe that anyone fighting against you ought to burn forever, but as for me I feel sorry for Virginia. I don't care what she's done, but I don't like to see the Old Dominion, the Mother of Presidents, stamped flat."

"I'm not cold-blooded at all, but I don't gush. I don't forget that this state produced George Washington, but I want victory for our side just the same, no matter how much of Virginia we may have to tread down. Is that farm house over there still empty?"

"Of course, or we wouldn't have taken the apples. It belongs to a man named Haynes, and he left ahead of us with his family for Richmond. I fancy it will be a long time before Haynes and his people sleep in their own rooms again. Come, fellows, we'd better be going back. Colonel Winchester is kind to us, but he doesn't want his officers to be prowling about as they please too long."

They walked together toward the edge of the orchard and looked at the farm house, from the chimneys of which no smoke had risen in weeks. Dick felt sure it would be used later on as headquarters by some general and his staff, but for the present it was left alone. And being within the Union lines no plunderer had dared to touch it.

It was a two-story wooden house, painted white, with green shutters, all closed now. The doors were also locked and sealed until such time as the army authorities wished to open them, but on the portico, facing the Southern lines were two benches, on which the three youths sat, and looked again over the great expanse of rolling country, dotted at intervals by puffs of smoke from the long lines of trenches. Where they sat it was so still that they could hear the faint crackle of the distant rifles, and now and then the heavier crash of a cannon.

Dick's mind went back to the Wilderness and its gloomy shades, the sanguinary field of Spottsylvania, and then the terrific mistake of Cold Harbor. The genius of Lee had never burned more brightly. He had handled his diminishing forces with all his old skill and resolution, but Grant had driven on and on. No matter what his losses the North always filled up his ranks again, and poured forward munitions and supplies in a vast and unbroken stream. A nation had summoned all its powers for a supreme effort to win, and Dick felt that the issue of the war was not now in doubt. The genius of Lee and the bravery of his devoted army could no longer save the South. The hammer strokes of Grant would surely crush it.

And then what? He had the deepest sympathy for these people of Virginia. What would become of them after the war? Defeat for the South meant nearer approach to destruction than any nation had suffered in generations. To him, born south of the Ohio River, and so closely united by blood with these people, victory as well as defeat had its pangs.

Warner and Pennington rose and announced that they would return to the regiment which was held in reserve in a little valley below, but Dick, their leave not having run out yet, decided to stay a while longer.

"So long," said Warner. "Let the orchard alone. Leave apples for others. Remember that they are protected by strict orders against all wandering and irresponsible officers, but ourselves."

"Yes, be good, Dick," said Pennington, and the two went down the slope, leaving Dick on the portico. He liked being alone at times. The serious cast of mind that he had inherited from his famous great grandfather, Paul Cotter, demanded moments of meditation. It was peaceful too on the portico, and a youth who had been through Grant's Wilderness campaign, a month of continuous and terrible fighting, was glad to rest for a while.

The distant rifle fire and the occasional cannon shot had no significance and did not disturb him. They blended now with the breeze that blew among the leaves of the apple trees. He had never felt more like peace, and the pleasant open country was soothing to the eye. What a contrast to that dark and sodden Wilderness where men fought blindly in the dusk. He shuddered as he remembered the forests set on fire by the shells, and burning over the fallen.

A light step aroused him and a large man sat down on the bench beside him. Dick often wondered at the swift and almost noiseless tread of Shepard, with whom he was becoming well acquainted. He was tall, built powerfully and must have weighed two hundred pounds, yet he moved with the ease and grace of a boy of sixteen. Dick thought it must come from his trade.

"I don't want to intrude, Mr. Mason," said Shepard, "but I saw you sitting here, looking perhaps too grave and thoughtful for one of your years."

"You're most welcome, Mr. Shepard, and I was thinking, that is in a vague sort of way."

"I saw your face and you were wondering what was to become of Virginia and the Virginians."

"So I was, but how did you know it?"

"I didn't know it. It was just a guess, and the guess was due to the fact that I was having the same thoughts myself."

"So you regard the war as won?" asked Dick, who had a great respect for Shepard's opinion.

"If the President keeps General Grant in command, as he will, it's a certainty, but it will take a long time yet. We can't force those trenches down there. Remember what Cold Harbor cost us."

Dick shuddered.

"I remember it," he said.

"It would be worse if we tried to storm Lee's lines. After Cold Harbor the general won't attempt it, and I see a long wait here. But we can afford it. The South grows steadily weaker. Our blockade clamps like a steel band, and presses tighter and tighter all the time. Food is scarce in the Confederacy. So is ammunition. They receive no recruits, and every day the army of Lee is smaller in numbers than it was the day before."

"You go into Richmond, Mr. Shepard. I've heard from high officers that you do. How do they feel there with our army only about twenty miles away?"

"They're quiet and seem to be confident, but I believe they know their danger."

"Have you by any chance seen or heard of my cousin, Harry Kenton, who is a lieutenant on the staff of the Southern commander-in-chief?"

Shepard smiled, as if the question brought memories that pleased him.

"A fine youth," he said. "Yes, I've seen him more than once. I'm free to tell you, Lieutenant Mason, that I know a lot about this rebel cousin of yours. He and I have come into conflict on several occasions, and I did not win every time."

"Nobody could beat Harry always," exclaimed Dick with youthful loyalty. "He was always the strongest and most active among us, and the best in forest and water. He could hunt and fish and trail like the scouts of our border days."

"I found him in full possession of all these qualities and he used them against me. I should grieve if that cousin of yours were to fall, Mr. Mason. I want to know him still better after the war."

Dick would have asked further questions about the encounters between Harry and the spy, but he judged that Shepard did not care to answer them, and he forbore. Yet the man aroused the most intense curiosity in him. There were spies and spies, and Shepard was one of them, but he was not like the others. He was unquestionably a man of great mental power. His calm, steady gaze and his words to the point showed it. No one patronized Shepard.

"I should like to go into Richmond with you some dark night," said Dick, who hid a strong spirit of adventure under his quiet exterior.

"You're not serious, Lieutenant Mason?"

"I wasn't, maybe, when I began to say it, but I believe I am now. Why shouldn't I be curious about Richmond, a place that great armies have been trying to take for three years? Just at present it's the center of the world to me in interest."

"You must not think of such a thing, Mr. Mason. Detection means certain death."

"No more for me than for you."

"But I have had a long experience and I have resources of which you can't know. Don't think of it again, Mr. Mason."

"I was merely jesting. I won't," said Dick.

He involuntarily looked toward the point beyond the horizon where Richmond lay, and Shepard meanwhile studied him closely. Young Mason had not come much under his notice until lately, but now he began to interest the spy greatly. Shepard observed what a strong, well-built young fellow he was, tall and slender but extremely muscular. He also bore a marked resemblance to his cousin, Harry Kenton, and such was the quality of Shepard that the likeness strongly recommended Dick to him. Moreover, he read the lurking thought that persisted in Dick's mind.

"You mustn't dream of such a thing as entering Richmond, Mr. Mason," he said.

"It was just a passing thought. But aren't you going in again?"

"Later on, no doubt, but not just now. I understand that we're planning some movement. I don't know what it is, but I'm to wait here until it's over. Good-by, Mr. Mason. Since things are closing in it's possible that you and I will see more of each other than before."

"Of course, when I'm personally conducted by you on that trip into Richmond."

Shepard, who had left the portico, turned and shook a warning finger.

"Dismiss that absolutely and forever from your mind, Mr. Mason," he said.

Dick laughed, and watched the stalwart figure of the spy as he strode away. Again the singular ease and lightness of his step struck him. To the lad's fancy the grass did not bend under his feet. Upon Dick as upon Harry, Shepard made the impression of power, not only of strength but of subtlety and courage.

"I'm glad that man's on our side," said Dick to himself, as Shepard's figure disappeared among the trees. Then he left the portico and went down in the valley to Colonel Winchester's regiment, where he was received with joyous shouts by several young men, including Warner and Pennington, who had gone on before. Colonel Winchester himself smiled and nodded, and Dick saluted respectfully.

The Winchesters, as they loved to call themselves, were faring well at this particular time. Like the Invincibles on the other side, this regiment had been decimated and filled up again several times. It had lost heavily in the Wilderness and at Spottsylvania, but its colonel had escaped without serious hurt and had received special mention for gallantry and coolness. It had been cut up once more at Cold Harbor, and because of its great services and losses it was permitted to remain a while in the rear as a reserve, and obtain the rest it needed so sorely.

The brave youths were recovering fast from their wounds and exertions. Their camp was beside a clear brook and there were tents for the officers, though they were but seldom used, most of them, unless it should be raining, preferring to sleep in their blankets under the trees. The water was good to drink, and farther down were several deep pools in which they bathed. Food, as usual in the Northern army, was good and plentiful, and for the Winchesters it seemed more a period of play than of war.

"What did you see at the house, Dick?" asked Colonel Winchester.

"The spy, Shepard. I talked a while with him. He says the Confederacy is growing weaker every day, but if we try to storm Lee's lines we'll be cut to pieces."

"I think he's right in both respects, although I feel sure that some kind of a movement will soon be attempted. But Dick, a mail from the west has arrived and here is a letter for you."

He handed the lad a large square envelope, addressed in tall, slanting script, and Dick knew at once that it was from his mother. He seized it eagerly, and Colonel Winchester, suppressing the wish to know what was inside, turned away.

* * * *

I have not heard from my dearest boy since the terrible battles in the east [Mrs. Mason wrote], but I hope and pray that you have come safely through them. You have escaped so many dangers that I feel you must escape all the rest. The news reaches us that the fighting in Virginia has been of the most dreadful character, but when it arrives in Pendleton it has two meanings. Those of our little town who are for the Confederacy say General Grant's losses have been so enormous that he can go no farther, and that the last and greatest effort of the North has failed.

Those who sympathize with the Union say General Lee has been reduced so greatly that he must be crushed soon and with him the Confederacy. As you know, I wish the latter to be true, but I suspect that the truth is somewhere between the two statements.

But the truth either way brings me great grief. I cannot hate the Southern people. We are Southern ourselves in all save this war, and, although our dear little town is divided in feeling, I have received nothing but kindness from those on the other side. Dr. Russell often asks about you. He says you were the best Latin scholar in the Academy, and he expects you to have a great future, as a learned man, after the war. He speaks oftenest of you and Harry Kenton, and I believe that you two were his favorite pupils. He says that Harry's is the best mathematical mind he has ever found in his long years of teaching.

Your room remains just as it was when you left. Juliana brushes and airs it every day, and expects at any time to see her young Master Dick come riding home. She keeps in her mind two pictures of you, absolutely unlike. In one of these pictures you are a great officer, carrying much of the war's weight on your shoulders, consulted continually by General Grant, who goes wrong only when he fails to take your advice. In the other you are a little boy whom she alternately scolds and pets. And it may be that I am somewhat like Juliana in this respect.

The garden is very fine this year. The vegetables were never more plentiful, and never of a finer quality. I wish you were here for your share. It must be a trial to have to eat hard crackers and tough beef and pork day after day. I should think that you would grow to hate the sight of them. Sam, the colored man who has been with us so long, has proved as faithful and trustworthy as Juliana. He makes a most excellent farmer, and the yield of corn in the bottom land is going to be amazing.

They say that since the Federal successes in the West the operations of Skelly's band of guerrillas have become bolder, but he has not threatened Pendleton again. They say also that a little farther south a band of like character, who call themselves Southern, under a man named Slade, are ravaging, but I suppose that you, who see great generals and great armies daily, are not much concerned about outlaws.

Always keep your feet dry and warm if you can, and never fail to spread a blanket between you and the damp grass. Give my respects to Colonel Winchester. Tell him that we hear of him now and then in Kentucky and that we hear only good. Don't forget about the blanket.

* * * *

There was more, but it was these passages over which Dick lingered longest.

He read the letter three times — letters were rare in those years, and men prized them highly — and put it away in his strongest pocket. Colonel Winchester was standing by the edge of the brook, and Dick, saluting him, said:

"My mother wishes me to deliver to you her respects and best wishes."

A flush showed through the tan of the colonel's face, and Dick, noticing it, was startled by a sudden thought. At first his feeling was jealousy, but it passed in an instant, never to come again. There was no finer man in the world than Colonel Winchester.

"She is well," he added, "and affairs could go no better at Pendleton."

"I am glad," said Colonel Winchester simply. Then he turned to a man with very broad shoulders and asked:

"How are the new lads coming on?"

"Very well, sir," replied Sergeant Daniel Whitley. "Some of 'em are a little awkward yet, and a few are suffering from change of water, but they're good boys and we can depend on 'em, sir, when the time comes."

"Especially since you have been thrashing 'em into shape for so many days, sergeant."

"Thank you, sir."

An orderly came with a message for Colonel Winchester, who left at once, but Dick and the sergeant, his faithful comrade and teacher, stood beside the stream. They could easily see the bathers farther down, splashing in the water, pulling one another under, and, now and then, hurling a man bodily into the pool. They were all boys to the veteran. Many of them had been trained by him, and his attitude toward them was that of a school teacher toward his pupils.

"You have ears that hear everything, sergeant," said Dick. "What is this new movement that I've heard two or three men speak of? Something sudden they say."

"I've heard too," replied Sergeant Whitley, "but I can't guess it. Whatever it is, though, it's coming soon. There's a lot of work going on at a point farther down the line, but it's kept a secret from the rest of us here."

The sergeant went away presently, and Dick, going down stream, joined some other young officers in a pool. He lay on the bank afterward, but, shortly after dark, Colonel Winchester returned, gave an order, and the whole regiment marched away in the dusk. Dick felt sure that the event Sergeant Whitley had predicted was about to happen, but the colonel gave no hint of its nature, and he continued to wonder, as they advanced steadily in the dusk.

CHAPTER II
THE WOMAN AT THE HOUSE

The men marched on for a long time, and, after a while, they heard the hum of many voices and the restless movements that betokened the presence of numerous troops. Dick, who had dismounted, walked forward a little distance with Colonel Winchester, and, in the moonlight, he was able to see that a large division of the army was gathered near, resting on its arms. It was obvious that the important movement, of which he had been hearing so much, was at hand, but the colonel volunteered nothing concerning its nature.

The troops were allowed to lie down, and, with the calmness that comes of long experience, they soon fell asleep. But the officers waited and watched, and Dick saw other regiments arriving. Warner, who had pushed through some bushes, came back and said in a whisper:

"I've seen a half-dozen great mounds of fresh earth."

"Earth taken out to make a trench, no doubt," said Dick.

But Warner shook his head.

"There's too much of it," he said, "and it's been carried too far to the rear. In my opinion extensive mining operations have been going on here."

"For what?" asked Pennington. "Not for silver or gold. We're no treasure hunters, and besides, there's none here."

Warner shook his head again.

"I don't know," he replied, "but I'm quite sure that it has something to do, perhaps all to do, with the movement now at hand. To the right of us, regiments, including several of colored troops, are already forming in line of battle, and I've no doubt our turn will come before long."

"We must be intending to make an attack," said Dick, "but I don't suppose we'll move until day."

He had learned long since that night attacks were very risky. Friend was likely to fire into friend and the dusk and confusion invariably forbade victory. But the faculties that create anxiety and alarm had been dulled for the time by immense exertions and dangers, and he placidly awaited the event, whatever it might be.

"What time is it?" asked Pennington.

"Half past three in the morning," replied Dick, who was able to see the face of his watch.

"Not such a long wait then. Day comes early this time of the year."

"You lads can sit down and make yourselves comfortable," said Colonel Winchester. "It's desirable for you to be as fresh as possible when you're wanted. I'm glad to see the men sleeping. They'll receive a signal in ample time."

The young officers followed his suggestion, but they kept very wide awake, talking for a little while in whispers and then sinking away into silence. The noise from the massed troops near them decreased also and Dick's curiosity began to grow again. He stood up, but he saw no movement, nothing to indicate the nature of any coming event. He looked at his watch again. Dawn was almost at hand. A narrow band of gray would soon rim the eastern hills. An aide arrived, gave a dispatch to Colonel Winchester, and quickly passed on.

The men were awakened and stood up, shaking the sleep from their eyes and then, through habit, looking to their arms and ammunition. The thread of gray showed in the east.

"Whatever it is, it will come soon," whispered Warner to Dick.

The gray thread broadened and became a ribbon of silver. The silver, as it widened, was shot through with pink and red and yellow, the colors of the morning. Dick caught a glimpse of massed bayonets near him, and of the Southern trenches rising slowly out of the dusk not far away. Then the earth rocked.

He felt a sudden violent and convulsive movement that nearly threw him from his feet, and the whole world in front of him blazed with fire, as if a volcano, after a long silence, had burst suddenly into furious activity. Black objects, the bodies of men, were borne upon the mass of shooting flames, and the roar was so tremendous that it was heard thirty miles away.

Dick had been expecting something, but no such red dawn as this, and when the fires suddenly sank, and the world-shaking crash turned to echoes he stood for a few moments appalled. He believed at first that a magazine had exploded, but, as the dawn was rapidly advancing, he beheld in front of them, where Southern breastworks had stood, a vast pit two or three hundred feet long and more than thirty feet deep. At the bottom of it, although they could not be seen through the smoke, lay the fragments of Confederate cannon and Confederate soldiers who had been blown to pieces.

"A mine breaking the rebel line!" cried Warner, "and our men are to charge through it!"

Trumpets were already sounding their thrilling call, and blue masses, before the smoke had lifted, were rushing into the pit, intending to climb the far side and sever the Southern line. But Colonel Winchester did not yet give the word to his own regiment, and Dick knew that they were to be held in reserve.

Into the great chasm went white troops and black troops, charging together, and then Dick suddenly cried in horror. Those were veterans on the other side, and, recovering quickly from the surprise, they rushed forward their batteries and riflemen. Mahone, a little, alert man, commanded them, and in an instant they deluged the pit, afterward famous under the name of "The Crater," with fire. The steep slope held back the Union troops and from the edges everywhere the men in gray poured a storm of shrapnel and canister and bullets into the packed masses.

Colonel Winchester groaned aloud, and looked at his men who were eager to advance to the rescue, but it was evident to Dick that his orders held him, and they stood in silence gazing at the appalling scene in the crater. A tunnel had been run directly under the Confederates, and then a huge mine had been exploded. All that part was successful, but the Union army had made a deep pit, more formidable than the earthwork itself.

Never had men created a more terrible trap for themselves. The name, the crater, was well deserved. It was a seething pit of death filled with smoke, and from which came shouts and cries as the rim of it blazed with the fire of those who were pouring in such a stream of metal. Inside the pit the men could only cower low in the hope that the hurricane of missiles would pass over their heads.

"Good God!" cried Dick. "Why don't we advance to help them!"

"Here we go now, and we may need help ourselves!" said Warner.

Again the trumpets were sending forth their shrill call to battle and death, and, as the colonel waved his sword, the regiment charged forward with others to rescue the men in the crater. A bright sun was shining now, and the Southern leaders saw the heavy, advancing column. They were rapidly bringing up more guns and more riflemen, and, shifting a part of their fire, a storm of death blew in the faces of those who would go to the rescue.

As at Cold Harbor, the men in blue could not live before such a fire at close quarters, and the regiments were compelled to recoil, while those who were left alive in the crater surrendered. The trumpets sounded the unwilling call to withdraw, and the Winchester men, many of them shedding tears of grief and rage, fell back to their old place, while from some distant point, rising above the dying fire of the cannon and rifles, came the long, fierce rebel yell, full of defiance and triumph.

The effect upon Dick of the sight in the crater was so overwhelming that he was compelled to lie down.

"Why do we do such things?" he exclaimed, after the faintness passed. "Why do we waste so many lives in such vain efforts?"

"We have to try," replied Warner, gloomily. "The thing was all right as far as it went, but it broke against a hedge of fire and steel, crowning a barrier that we had created for ourselves."

"Let's not talk about it," said Pennington, who had been faint too. "It's enough to have seen it. I am going to blot it out of my mind if I can."

But not one of the three was ever able wholly to forget that hideous dawn. Luckily the Winchesters themselves had suffered little, but they were quite content to remain in their old place by the brook, where the next day a large man in civilian dress introduced himself to Dick.

"Perhaps you don't remember me, Mr. Mason," he said, "but in such times as these it's easy to forget chance acquaintances."

Dick looked at him closely. He was elderly, with heavy pouches under his eyes and a rotund figure, but he looked uncommonly alert and his pale blue eyes had a penetrating quality. Then Dick recalled him.

"You're Mr. Watson, the contractor," he said.

"Right. Shake hands."

Dick shook his hand, and he noticed that, while it was fat, it was strong and dry. He hated damp hands, which always seemed to him to have a slimy touch, as if their owner were reptilian.

"I suppose business is good with you, Mr. Watson," he said.

"It couldn't be better, and such affairs as the one I witnessed this morning mean more. But doubtless I have grieved over it as much as you. I may profit by the great struggle, but I have not wished either the war or its continuance. Someone must do the work I am doing. You're a bright boy, Lieutenant Mason, and I want you still to bear in mind the hint that I gave you once in Washington."

"I don't recall it, this instant."

"That to go into business with me is a better trade than fighting."

"I thank you for the offer, but my mind turns in other directions. I'm not depreciating your occupation, Mr. Watson, but I'm interested in something else."

"I knew that you were not, Lieutenant Mason. You have too much sense. Your kind could not fight if my kind did not find the sinews, and after the war the woods will be full of generals, and colonels and majors who will be glad to get jobs from men like me."

"I've no doubt of it," said Dick, "but what happened this morning made me think the war is yet far from over."

"We shall see what we shall see, but if you ever want a friend write to me in Washington. General delivery, there will do. Good-by."

"Good-by," said Dick, and, as he watched the big man walk away, he felt that he was beginning to understand him. He had never been interested greatly in mercantile pursuits. Public and literary life and the soil were the great things to him. Now he realized that the vast strength of the North, a strength that could survive any number of defeats, lay largely in her trade and commerce. The South, almost stationary upon the soil, had fallen behind, and no amount of skill and courage could save her.

Colonel Winchester gave the young officers who had been awake all night permission to sleep, and Dick was glad to avail himself of it. He still felt weak, and ill, and, with a tender smile, remembering his mother's advice about the blanket, he spread one in the shade of a small oak and lay down upon it.

Despite the terrible repulse of the morning most of the men had regained their usual spirits. Several were playing accordions, and the others were listening. The Winchesters were known as a happy regiment, because they had an able colonel, strong but firm, efficient and tactful minor officers. They seldom got into mischief, and always they pooled their resources.

One lad was reading now to a group from a tattered copy of "Les Miserables," which had just reached them. He was deep in Waterloo and Dick heard their comments.

"You wait till the big writers begin to tell about Chickamauga and Gettysburg and Shiloh," said one. "They'll class with Waterloo or ahead of it, and the French and English never fought any such campaign as that when Grant came down through the Wilderness. What's that about the French riding into the sunken road? I'm willin' to bet it was nothing but a skirmish beside Pickett's charge at Gettysburg."

"And both failed," said Warner. "There are always brave men on every side in any war. I don't know whether Napoleon was right or wrong—I suppose he was wrong at that time—but it always makes me feel sad to read of Waterloo."

"Just as a lot of our own people were grieved at the death of Stonewall Jackson, although next to Lee he was our most dangerous foe," said Pennington.

The reader resumed, and, although he was interrupted from time to time by question or comment, his monotone was pleasant and soothing, and Dick fell asleep. When he awoke his nerves were restored, and he could think of the crater without becoming faint again.

That night Colonel Hertford of the cavalry came to their camp and talked with Colonel Winchester in the presence of Dick and his comrades of the staff. The disastrous failure of the morning, so the cavalryman said, had convinced all the generals that Lee's trenches could not be forced, and the commander-in-chief was turning his eye elsewhere. While the deadlock before Petersburg lasted he would push the operations in some other field. He was watching especially the Valley of Virginia, where Early, after his daring raid upon the outskirts of Washington, was being pursued by Sheridan, though not hard enough in the opinion of General Grant.

"It's almost decided that help will be sent to Sheridan," said Hertford, "and in that event my regiment is sure to go. Yours has served as a mounted regiment, and I think I have influence enough to see that it is sent again as cavalry, if you wish."

Colonel Winchester accepted the offer gladly, and his young officers, in all eagerness, seconded him. They were tiring of inactivity, and of the cramped and painful life in the trenches. To be on horseback again, riding over hills and across valleys, seemed almost Heaven to them, and, as Colonel Hertford walked away, earnest injunctions to use his influence to the utmost followed him.

"It will take the sight of the crater from my mind," said Warner. "That's one reason why I want to go."

Dick, searching his own mind, concluded it was the chief reason with him, although he, too, was eager enough for a more spacious life than that of the trench.

"I'm going to wish so hard for it," said Pennington, "that it'll come true."

Whether Pennington's wish had any effect or not, they departed two days later, three mounted regiments under the general command of Hertford, his right as a veteran cavalry leader. All regiments, despite new men, had been reduced greatly by the years of fighting, and the three combined did not number more than fifteen hundred horse. But there was not one among them from the oldest to the youngest who did not feel elation as they rode away on the great curve that would take them into the Valley of Virginia.

"It's glorious to be on a horse again, with the world before you," said Pennington. "I was born horseback, so to speak, and I never had to do any walking until I came to this war. The great plains and the free winds that blow all around the earth for me."

"But you don't have rivers and hills and forests like ours," said Dick.

"I know it, but I don't miss them. I suppose it's what you're used to that you like. I like a horizon that doesn't touch the ground anywhere within fifteen or eighteen miles of me. And think of seeing a buffalo herd, as I have, that's all day passing you, a million of 'em, maybe!"

"And think of being scalped by the Sioux or Cheyennes, as your people out there often are," said Warner.

Pennington took off his cap and disclosed an uncommonly thick head of hair.

"You see that I haven't lost mine yet," he said. "If a fellow can live through big battles as I've lived through 'em he can escape Sioux and Cheyennes."

"So you should. Look back now, and you can see the armies face to face."

They were on the highest hill, and all the cavalry had turned for a last glance. Dick saw again the flashes from occasional rifle fire, and a dark column of smoke still rising from a spot which he knew to be the crater. He shuddered, and was glad when the force, riding on again, passed over the hill. Before them now stretched a desolated country, trodden under foot by the armies, and his heart bled again for Virginia, the most reluctant of all the states to secede, and the greatest of them all to suffer.

Colonel Hertford, Colonel Winchester, and the colonel of the third regiment, a Pennsylvanian named Bedford, rode together and their young officers were just behind. All examined the country continually through glasses to guard against ambush. Stuart was gone and Forrest was far away, but they knew that danger from the fierce riders of the South was always present. Just when the capital seemed safest Early's men had appeared in its very suburbs, and here in Virginia, where the hand of every man and of every woman and child also was against them, it was wise to watch well.

As they rode on the country was still marked by desolation. The fields were swept bare or trampled down. Many of the houses and barns and all the fences had been burned. The roads had been torn up by the passage of artillery and countless wagons. All the people seemed to have gone away.

But when they came into rougher and more wooded regions they were shot at often by concealed marksmen. A half-dozen troopers were killed and more wounded, and, when the cavalrymen forced a path through the brush in pursuit of the hidden sharpshooters, they found nothing. The enemy fairly melted away. It was easy enough for a rifleman, knowing every gully and thicket, to send in his deadly bullet and then escape.

"Although it's merely the buzzing and stinging of wasps," said Warner, "I don't like it. They can't stop our advance, but I hate to see any good fellow of ours tumbled from his horse."

"Makes one think of that other ride we took in Mississippi," said Dick.

"In one way, yes, but in others, no. This is hard, firm ground, and we're not persecuted by mosquitoes. Nor is the country suitable for an ambush by a great force. Ouch, that burnt!"

A bullet fired from a thicket had grazed Warner's bridle hand. Dick was compelled to laugh.

"You're free from mosquitoes, George," he said, "but there are still little bullets flying about, as you see."

A dozen cavalrymen were sent into the thicket, but the sharpshooter was already far away. Colonel Hertford frowned and said:

"Well, I suppose it's the price we have to pay, but I'd like to see the people to whom we have to pay it."

"Not much chance of that," said Colonel Winchester. "The Virginians know their own ground and the lurking sharpshooters won't fire until they're sure of a safe retreat."

But as they advanced the stinging fire became worse. There was no Southern force in this part of the country strong enough to meet them in open combat, but there was forest and thicket sufficient to shelter many men who were not only willing to shoot, but who knew how to shoot well. Yet they never caught anybody nor even saw anybody. A stray glimpse or two of a puff of smoke was the nearest they ever came to beholding an enemy.

It became galling, intolerable. Three more men were killed and the number of wounded was doubled. The three colonels held a consultation, and decided to extend groups of skirmishers far out on either flank. Dick was chosen to lead a band of thirty picked men who rode about a mile on the right, and he had with him as his second, and, in reality, as his guide and mentor in many ways, the trusty Sergeant Whitley. It was altogether likely that Colonel Winchester would not have sent Dick unless he had been able to send the wise sergeant with him.

"While you are guarding us from ambush," he said to Dick, "be sure you don't fall into an ambush yourself."

"Not while Whitley, here, is with us," replied Dick. "He learned while out on the plains, not only to have eyes in the back of his head, but to have 'em in the sides of it as well. In addition he can hear the fall of a leaf a mile away."

The sergeant shook his head and uttered an emphatic no in protest, but in his heart he was pleased. He was a sergeant who liked being a sergeant, and he was proud of all his wilderness and prairie lore.

Dick gave the word and the little troop galloped away to the right, zealous in its task and beating up every wood and thicket for the hidden riflemen who were so dangerous. At intervals they saw the cavalry force riding steadily on, and again they were hidden from it by forest or bush. More than an hour passed and they saw no foe. Dick concluded that the sharpshooters had been scared off by the flanking force, and that they would have no further trouble with them. His spirits rose accordingly and there was much otherwise to make them rise.

It was like Heaven to be on horseback in the pleasant country after being cramped up so much in narrow trenches, and there was the thrill of coming action. They were going to join Sheridan and where he rode idle moments would be few.

"Ping!" a bullet whistled alarmingly near his head and then cut leaves from a sapling beyond him. The young lieutenant halted the troop instantly, and Sergeant Whitley pointed to a house just visible among some trees.

"That's where it came from, and, since it hasn't been followed by a second, it's likely that only one man is there, and he is lying low, waiting a chance for another bullet," he said.

"Then we'll rout him out," said Dick.

He divided his little troop, in order that it could approach the house from all sides, and then he and the sergeant and six others advanced directly in front. He knew that if the marksman were still hidden inside he would not fire now, but would seek rather to hide, since he could easily observe from a window that the building was surrounded.

It was a small house, but it was well built and evidently had been occupied by people of substance. It was painted white, except the shutters which were green, and a brick walk led to a portico, with fine and lofty columns. There was nobody outside, but as the shutters were open it was probable that someone was inside.

Dick disliked to force an entrance at such a place, but he had been sent out to protect the flank and he could not let a rifleman lie hidden there, merely to resume his deadly business as soon as they passed on. They pushed the gate open and rode upon the lawn, an act of vandalism that he regretted, but could not help. They reached the door without any apparent notice being taken of them, and as the detachments were approaching from the other sides, Dick dismounted and knocked loudly. Receiving no answer, he bade all the others dismount.

"Curley, you hold the horses," he said, "and Dixon, you tell the men in the other detachments to seize anybody trying to escape. Sergeant, you and I and the others will enter the house. Break in the lock with the butt of your rifle, sergeant! No, I see it's not locked!"

He turned the bolt, and, the door swinging in, they passed into an empty hall. Here they paused and listened, which was a wise thing for a man to do when he entered the house of an enemy. Dick's sense of hearing was not much inferior to that of the sergeant, and while at first they heard nothing, they detected presently a faint click, click. He could not imagine what made the odd sound, and, listening as hard as he could, he could detect no other with it.

He pushed open a door that led into the hall and he and his men entered a large room with windows on the side, opening upon a rose garden. It was a pleasant room with a high ceiling, and old-fashioned, dignified furniture. A blaze of sunlight poured in from the windows, and, where a sash was raised, came the faint, thrilling perfume of roses, a perfume to which Dick was peculiarly susceptible. Yet, for years afterward, the odor of roses brought back to him that house and that room.

He thought at first that the room, although the faint clicking noise continued, contained no human being. But presently he saw sitting at a table by the open window a woman whose gray dress and gray hair blended so nearly with the gray colors of the chamber that even a soldier could have been excused for not seeing her at once. Her head and body were perfectly still, but her hands were moving rapidly. She was knitting, and it was the click of her needles that they had heard.

She did not look up as Dick entered, and, taking off his cap, he stood, somewhat abashed. He knew at once by her dress and face, and the dignity, disclosed even by the manner in which she sat, that she was a great lady, one of those great ladies of old Virginia who were great ladies in fact. She was rather small, Martha Washington might have looked much like her, and she knitted steadily on, without showing by the least sign that she was aware of the presence of Union soldiers.

A long and embarrassed silence followed. Dick judged that she was about sixty-five years of age, though she seemed strong and he felt that she was watching them alertly from covert eyes. There was no indication that anyone else was in the building, but it did not seem likely that a great lady of Virginia would be left alone in her house, with a Union force marching by.

He approached, bowed and said:

"Madame!"

She raised her head and looked at him slowly from head to foot, and then back again. They were fierce old eyes, and Dick felt as if they burned him, but he held his ground knowing that he must. Then she turned back to her knitting, and the needles clicked steadily as before.

"Madame!" repeated Dick, still embarrassed.

She lifted the fierce old eyes.

"I should think," she said, "that the business of General Grant's soldiers was to fight those of General Lee rather than to annoy lone women."

Dick flushed, but angry blood leaped in his veins.

"Pardon me, madame," he said, "but we have not come here to annoy a woman. We were fired upon from this house. The man who did it has had no opportunity to escape, and I'm sure that he's still concealed within these walls."

"Seek and ye shall—not find," she half quoted.

"I must search the house."

"Proceed."

"First question her," the sergeant whispered in the young lieutenant's ear.

Dick nodded.

"Pardon me, madame," he said, "but I must obtain information from you. This is war, you know."

"I have had many rude reminders that it is so."

"Where is your husband?"

She pointed upward.

"Forgive me," said Dick impulsively. "I did not intend to recall a grief."

"Don't worry. You and your comrades will never intrude upon him there."

"Perhaps you have sons here in this house?"

"I have three, but they are not here."

"Where are they?"

"One fell with Jackson at Chancellorsville. It was a glorious death, but he is not dead to me. I shall always see him, as he was when he went away, a tall, strong man with brown hair and blue eyes. Another fell in Pickett's charge at Gettysburg. They told me that his body lay across one of the Union guns on Cemetery Hill. That, too, was a glorious death, and like his brother he shall live for me as long as I live. The third is alive and with Lee."

She had stopped knitting, but now she resumed it, and, during another embarrassed pause, the click, click of the needles was the only sound heard in the room.

"I regret it, madame," resumed Dick, "but we must search the house thoroughly."

"Proceed," she said again in that tone of finality.

"Take the men and look carefully through every room," said Dick to the sergeant. "I will remain here."

Whitley and the troopers withdrew quietly. When the last of them had disappeared he walked to one of the windows and looked out. He saw his mounted men beyond the rose garden on guard, and he knew that they were as vigilant on the other sides of the house. The sharpshooter could not escape, and he was firmly resolved not to go without him. Yet his conscience hurt him. It was hard, too, to wait there, while the woman said not a word, but knitted on as placidly as if he did not exist.

"Madame," he said at last, "I pray that you do not regard this as an intrusion. The uses of war are hard. We must search. No one can regret it more than I do, in particular since I am really a Southerner myself, a Kentuckian."

"A traitor then as well as an enemy."

Dick flushed deeply, and again there was angry blood in his veins, but he restrained his temper.

"You must at least allow to a man the liberty of choice," he said.

"Provided he has the intelligence and honesty to choose right."

Dick flushed again and bit his lip. And yet he felt that a woman who had lost two sons before Northern bullets might well be unforgiving. There was nothing more for him to say, and while he turned back to the window the knitting needles resumed their click, click.

He waited a full ten minutes and he knew that the sergeant and his men were searching the house thoroughly. Nothing could escape the notice of Whitley, and he would surely find the sharpshooter. Then he heard their footsteps on a stairway and in another minute they entered the great room. The face of the sergeant clearly showed disappointment.

"There's nobody in the house," he said, "or, if he is he's so cleverly hidden, that we haven't been able to find him—that is so far. Perhaps Madame here can tell us something."

"I know nothing," she said, "but if I knew anything I would not tell it to you."

The sergeant smiled sourly, but Dick said:

"We must look again. The man could not have escaped with the guard that we've set around the house."

The sergeant and his men made another search. They penetrated every place in which a human being could possibly hide. They thrust their rifle barrels up the chimneys, and they turned down the bed covers, but again they found nothing. Dick meanwhile remained as before in the large room, covertly watching the woman, lest she give a signal to the rifleman who must be somewhere.

All the while the perfume of the roses was growing stronger and more penetrating, a light wind that had sprung up bringing it through the open window. It thrilled Dick in some singular manner, and the strangeness of the scene heightened its effect. It was like standing in a room in a dim old castle to which he had been brought as a prisoner, while the terrible old woman was his jailer. Then the click of the knitting needles brought him back to the present and reality, but reality itself, despite the sunshine and the perfume of the roses, was heavy and oppressive.

Dick apparently was looking from the window at the garden, brilliant with flowers, but in fact he was closely watching the woman out of the corner of his eye. He had learned to read people by their own eyes, and he had seen how hers burned when she looked at them. Strength of will and intent lie in the human eye. Unless it is purposely veiled it tells the mind and power that are in the brain back of it.

A fear of her crept slowly over him. Perhaps the fear came because, obviously, she had no fear at all of him, or of Whitley or of the soldiers. After their short dialogue she had returned to her old immobility. Neither her body nor her head moved, only her hands, and the motion was wholly from the wrists. She was one of the three Fates, knitting steadily and knitting up the destiny of men.

He shook himself. His was a sound and healthy mind, and he would allow no taint of morbidness to enter it. He knew that there was nothing supernatural in the world, but he did believe that this woman with the gray hair, the burning eyes and the sharp chin, looking as if it had been cut from a piece of steel, was the possessor of uncanny wisdom. Beyond a doubt she knew where the marksman was hidden, and, unless he watched her ceaselessly, she would give him a signal of some kind.

Perhaps he was hidden in the garden among the rose bushes, and he would see her hand, if it was raised ever so slightly. Maybe that was why the window was open, because the clearest glass even could obscure a signal meant to be faint, unnoticed by all except the one for whom it was intended. He would have that garden searched thoroughly when the sergeant returned, and his heart beat with a throb of relief when he heard the stalwart Whitley's footstep once more at the door.

"We have found nothing, sir," said the sergeant. "We've explored every place big enough to hide a cat."

"Search the garden out there," said Dick. "Look behind every vine and bush."

"You will at least spare my roses," said the woman.

"They shall not be harmed," replied the lieutenant, "but my men must see what, if anything, is in the garden."

She said no more. She had not even raised her head when she spoke, and the sergeant and his men went into the garden. They looked everywhere but they damaged nothing. They did not even break off a single flower for themselves. Dick had felt confident that after the failure to find the sharpshooter in the house he would be discovered there, but his net brought in no fish.

He glanced at the sergeant, who happened to glance at him at the same time. Each read the look in the eyes of the other. Each said that they had failed, that they were wasting time, that there was nothing to be gained by hunting longer for a single enemy, that it was time to ride on, as flankers on the right of the main column.

"Madame," said Dick politely, "we leave you now. I repeat my regret at being compelled to search your house in this manner. My duty required it, although we have found nobody."

"You found nobody because nobody is here."

"Evidently it is so. Good-by. We wish you well."

"Good-by. I hope that all of you will be shot by our brave troops before night!"

The wish was uttered with the most extraordinary energy and fierceness. For the first time she had raised her level tone, and the lifted eyes that looked into Dick's were blazing with hate. He uttered an exclamation and stepped back. Then he recovered himself and said politely:

"Madame, I do not wish any such ill to you or yours."

But she had resumed her knitting, and Dick, without another word, walked out of the house, followed by the sergeant and his men.

"I did not know a woman could be so vindictive," he said.

"Our army has killed two of her sons," said the sergeant. "To her we, like all the rest of our troops, are the men who killed them."

"Perhaps that is so," said Dick thoughtfully, as he remounted.

They rode beside the walk and out at the open gate. Dick carried a silver whistle, upon which he blew a signal for the rest of his men to join them, and then he and the sergeant went slowly up the road. He was deeply chagrined at the escape of the rifleman, and the curse of the woman lay heavily upon him.

"I don't see how it was done," he said.

"Nor I," said the sergeant, shaking his head.

There was a sharp report, the undoubted whip-like crack of a rifle, and a man just behind, uttering a cry, held up a bleeding arm. Dick had a lightning conviction that the bullet was intended for himself. It was certain also that the shot had come from the house.

"Back with me, sergeant!" he exclaimed. "We'll get that fellow yet!"

They galloped back, sprang from their horses, and rushed in, followed by the original little troop that had entered, Dick shouting a direction to the others to remain outside. The fierce little old woman was sitting as before by the table, knitting, and she had never appeared more the great lady.

"Once was enough," she said, shooting him a glance of bitter contempt.

"But twice may succeed," Dick said. "Sergeant, take the men and go through all the house again. Our friend with the rifle may not have had time to get back into his hidden lair. I will remain here."

The sergeant and his men went out and he heard their boots on the stairway and in the other rooms. The window near him was still open and the perfume of the roses came in again, strangely thrilling, overpowering. But something had awakened in Dick. The sixth, and even the germ of a seventh sense, which may have been instinct, were up and alive. He did not look again at the rose garden, nor did he listen any longer to the footsteps of his men.

He had concentrated all his faculties, the known, and the unknown, which may have been lying dormant in him, upon a single object. He heard only the click of the knitting needles, and he saw only the small, strong hands moving swiftly back and forth. They were very white, and they were firm like those of a young woman. There were none of the heavy blue veins across the back that betoken age.

The hands fascinated him. He stared at them, fairly pouring his gaze upon them. They were beautiful, as the hands of a great lady should be kept, and it was all the more wonderful then that the right should have across the back of it a faint gray smudge, so tiny that only an eye like his, and a concentrated gaze like his, could have seen it.

He took four swift steps forward, seized the white hand in his and held it up.

"Madame," he said, and now his tone was as fierce as hers had ever been, "where is the rifle?"

She made no attempt to release her hand, nor did she move at all, save to lift her head. Then her eyes, hard, defiant and ruthless, looked into his. But his look did not flinch from hers. He knew, and, knowing, he meant to act.

"Madame," he repeated, "where is the rifle? It is useless for you to deny."

"Have I denied?"

"No, but where is the rifle?"

He was wholly unconscious of it, but his surprise and excitement were so great that his hand closed upon hers in a strong muscular contraction. Thrills of pain shot through her body, but she did not move.

"The rifle! The rifle!" repeated Dick.

"Loose my hand, and I will give it to you."

His hand fell away and she walked to the end of the room where a rug, too long, lay in a fold against the wall. She turned back the fold and took from its hiding place a slender-barreled cap-and-ball rifle. Without a word she handed it to Dick and he passed his hand over the muzzle, which was still warm.

He looked at her, but she gave back his gaze unflinching.

"I could not believe it, were it not so," he said.

"But it is so. The bullets were not aimed well enough." Dick felt an emotion that he did not wholly understand.

"Madame," he said, "I shall take the rifle, and again say good-by. As before, I wish you well."

She resumed her seat in the chair and took up the knitting. But she did not repeat her wish that Dick and all his men be shot before night. He went out in silence, and gently closed the door behind him. In the hall he met Sergeant Whitley and said:

"We needn't look any farther. I know now that the man has gone and we shall not be fired upon again from this house."

The sergeant glanced at the rifle Dick carried and made no comment. But when they were riding away, he said:

"And so that was it?"

"Yes, that was it."

CHAPTER III
OVER THE HILLS

Dick and his little troop rode on through the silent country, and they were so watchful and thorough that they protected fully the right flank of the marching column. One or two shots were fired, but the reports came from such distant points that he knew the bullets had fallen short.

But while he beat up the forests and fields for sharpshooters he was very thoughtful. He had a mind that looked far ahead, even in youth, and the incident at the house weighed upon him. He foresaw the coming triumph of the North and of the Union, a triumph won after many great disasters, but he remembered what an old man at a blacksmith shop in Tennessee had told him and his comrades before the Battle of Stone River. Whatever happened, however badly the South might be defeated, the Southern soil would still be held by Southern people, and their bitterness would be intense for many a year to come. The victor forgives easily, the vanquished cannot forget. His imagination was active and vivid, often attaining truths that logic and reason do not reach, and he could understand what had happened at the house, where the ordinary mind would have been left wondering.

It is likely also that the sergeant had a perception of it, though not as sharp and clear as Dick's.

"When the war is over and the soldiers all go back, that is them that's livin'," he said, "it won't be them that fought that'll keep the grudge. It's the women who've lost their own that'll hate longest."

"I think what you say is true, Whitley," said Dick, "but let's not talk about it any more. It hurts."

"Me too," said the sergeant. "But don't you like this country that we're ridin' through, Mr. Mason?"

"Yes, it's fine, but most of it has been cropped too hard. I remember reading somewhere that George Washington himself said, away back in the last century, that slave labor, so careless and reckless, was ruining the soil of Virginia."

"Likely that's true, sir, but it won't have much chance to keep on ruinin' it. Wouldn't you say, sir, that was a Johnny on his horse up there?"

"I can soon tell you," said Dick, unslinging his glasses.

On their right was a hill towering above the rest. The slopes were wooded densely, but the crest was quite bare. Upon it sat a solitary figure on horseback, evidently watching the marching column.

Dick put his glasses to his eyes. The hill and the lone sentinel enlarged suddenly and came nearer. The pulses in his temples beat hard. Although he could not see the watcher's face clearly, because he too was using glasses, he knew him instantly. He would have known that heroic figure and the set of the shoulders and head anywhere. He felt astonishment at first, but it passed quickly. It was likely that they should meet again some time or other, since the field of battle had narrowed so much.

Sergeant Whitley, who invariably saw everything, had seen Dick's slight start.

"Someone you know, sir?" he asked.

"Yes, sergeant. It's my cousin, Harry Kenton. You've heard me talk of him often. A finer and braver and stronger fellow never lived. He's using glasses too and I've no doubt he's recognized me."

Dick suddenly waved his glasses aloft, and Harry Kenton replied in like manner.

"He sees and knows me!" cried Dick.

But the sergeant was very sober. He foresaw that these youths, bound by such ties of blood and affection, might come into battle against each other. The same thought was in Dick's mind, despite his pleasure at the distant view of Harry.

"We exchanged shots in the Manassas campaign," said Dick. "We were sheltered and we didn't know each other until several bullets had passed."

"Three more horsemen have joined him," said the sergeant.

"Those are his friends," said Dick, who had put the glasses back to his eyes. "Look how they stand out against the sun!"

The four horsemen in a row, at equal distances from one another, were enlarged against a brilliant background of red and gold. Their attitude was impressive, as they sat there, unmoving, like statues cut in stone. They were in truth Harry and Dalton, St. Clair and Happy Tom, and farther on the Invincibles were marching, the two colonels at their head, to the Valley of Virginia to reinforce Early, and to make headway, if possible, against Sheridan.

Harry was deeply moved. Kinship and the long comradeship of youth count for much. Perhaps for more in the South than anywhere else. Stirred by a sudden emotion he took off his cap and waved it as a signal of hail and farewell. The four removed their own caps and waved them also. Then they turned their horses in unison, rode over the hill and were gone from Dick's sight.

Sergeant Whitley was not educated, but his experience was vast, he knew men and he had the gift of sympathy. He understood Dick's feelings.

"All civil wars are cruel," he said. "The killing of one's own people is worst of all."

But as they went on, Dick's melancholy fell from him, and he had only pleasant recollections of the meeting. Besides, the continued movement and freedom were inspiriting in the highest degree to youth. Although it was August the day was cool, and the blue sky of Virginia was never brighter. A refreshing breeze blew from dim, blue mountains that they could see far ahead, and, as they entered a wide stretch of open country where ambush was impossible, the trumpets called in the flankers.

"We shall make the lower mountains about midnight, and we'd better camp then until dawn. Don't you think so, gentlemen?" asked Colonel Hertford of his associate colonels, Winchester and Bedford.

"The plan seems sound to me," replied Bedford, the Pennsylvanian. "Of course, we want to reach Sheridan as soon as possible, but if we push the horses too hard we'll break them down."

Dick had dropped back with Warner and Pennington, but he heard the colonels talking.

"We all saw General Sheridan at the great battles in the West," he said. "I particularly remember how he planted himself and the batteries at Perryville and saved us from defeat, but he seems to be looming up so much more now in the East."

"He's become the Stuart of our side," said Warner. "I've heard some of the people at Washington don't believe in him, but he has General Grant's confidence and that's enough for me. Not that I put military authority over civil rule, but war has to be fought by soldiers. I look for lively times in the Valley of Virginia."

"Anyway, the Lord has delivered me from the trenches at Petersburg," said Pennington. "Think of me, used to roaming over a thousand miles of plains, shut up between mud walls only four or five feet apart."

"I believe that, with Sheridan, you're going to have all the roaming you want," said Dick.

They passed silent farm houses, but took nothing from them. Ample provision was carried on extra horses or their own, and the three colonels were anxious not to inflame the country by useless seizures. Twilight came, and the low mountains sank away in the dusk. But they had already reached a higher region where nearly all the hills were covered with forest, and Colonel Hertford once more spread out the flankers, Dick and the sergeant, as before, taking the right with their little troop.

The night was fortunately clear, almost as light as day, with a burnished moon and brilliant stars, and they did not greatly fear ambush. Dick shrewdly reckoned that Early would need all his men in the valley, and, after the first day at sharpshooting, they would withdraw to meet greater demands.

Nevertheless he took a rather wide circuit and came into a lonely portion of the hills, where the forest was unbroken, save for the narrow path on which they rode. The sergeant dismounted once and examined the ground.

"Nothing has passed here," he said, "and the woods and thickets are so dense that men can't ride through 'em."

The path admitted of only two abreast, and the forest was so heavy that it shut out most of the moonlight. But they rode on confidently, Dick and the sergeant leading. If it had not been for the size of the trees, Dick would have thought that he was back in the Wilderness. They heard now and then the wings of night birds among the leaves, and occasionally some small animal would scuttle across the path. They forded a narrow but deep stream, its waters black from decayed vegetation, and continued to push on briskly through the unbroken forest, until the sergeant said in a low voice to Dick:

"I think I hear something ahead of us."

They pulled back on the reins so suddenly that those behind almost rode into them. Then they sat there, a solid, compact little group, while Dick and the sergeant listened intently.

"It's hoofbeats," said Dick, "very faint, because they are far away."

"I think you are right, sir," said the sergeant.

"But they're coming this way."

"Yes, and at a steady pace. No stops and no hesitation."

"Which shows that it's somebody who doesn't fear any harm."

"The beats are pretty solid. A heavy man on a heavy horse."

"About three hundred yards away, don't you think?"

"About that, sir."

"Maybe a farmer going home?"

"Maybe, but I don't think so, sir."

"At any rate, we'll soon see, because our unknown comes on without a break. There he is now!"

They had a comparatively clear view straight ahead, and the figure of a man and a horse emerged from the shadows.

The sergeant raised his rifle, but, as the man came on without fear, he dropped it again. Some strange effect of the moonlight exaggerated the rider and his horse, making both look gigantic, blending them together in such manner that a tremendous centaur seemed to be riding them down. In an instant or two the general effect vanished and as a clear beam fell upon the man's face Dick uttered an exclamation of relief.

"Shepard!" he said, and he felt then that he should have known before that it was Shepard who was coming. He, alone of all men, seemed to have the gift of omniscience and omnipresence. The spy drew his horse to a halt directly in front of him and saluted:

"Lieutenant Mason, sir?" he said.

"I'm glad it's you, Mr. Shepard," said Dick. "I think that in this wood we'll need the hundred eyes that once belonged to Argus, but which he has passed on to you."

"Thank you, sir," said Shepard.

But the man at whom he looked most was the sergeant, and the sergeant looked most at him. One was a sergeant and the other was a spy, but each recognized in the other a king among men. Eyes swept over powerful chests and shoulders and open, bold countenances, and signified approval. They had met before, but they were more than well met here in the loneliness and the dark, amid dangers, where skill and courage, and not rank, counted. Then they nodded without speaking, as an Indian chief would to an Indian chief, his equal.

"You were coming to meet us, Mr. Shepard?" said Dick.

"I expected to find you on this path."

"And you have something to tell?"

"A small Confederate force is in the mountains, awaiting Colonel Hertford. It is inferior to his in numbers, but it knows the country thoroughly and has the sympathy of all the inhabitants, who bring to it news of everything."

"Do you know these Confederate troops?"

"Yes, sir. Their corps is a regiment called in General Lee's army the Invincibles, but it includes two other skeleton regiments. Colonel Talbot who leads the Invincibles is the commander of them all. He has, I should say, slightly less than a thousand men."

"You know a good deal about this regiment called the Invincibles, do you not, Mr. Shepard?"

"I do, sir. Its colonel, Talbot, and its lieutenant-colonel, St. Hilaire, are as brave men as any that ever lived, and the regiment has an extraordinary reputation in the Southern army for courage. Two of General Lee's young staff officers are also with them now."

"Who are they?"

"Lieutenant Harry Kenton and Lieutenant George Dalton."

Dick with his troop rode at once to Colonel Hertford and reported.

Colonel Hertford listened and then glanced at Dick.

"Kenton is your cousin, I believe," he said.

"Yes, sir," replied Dick. "He has been in the East all the time. Once in the second Manassas campaign we came face to face and fired at each other, although we did not know who was who then."

"And now here you are in opposing forces again. With the war converging as it is, it was more than likely that you should confront each other once more."

"But I don't expect to be shooting at Harry, and I don't think he'll be shooting at me."

"Will you ride into the woods again on the right, Mr. Shepard?" said Colonel Hertford. "Perhaps you may get another view of this Confederate force. Dick, you go with him. Warner, you and Pennington come with me."

Dick and Shepard entered the woods side by side, and the youth who had a tendency toward self-analysis found that his liking and respect for the spy increased. The general profession of a spy might be disliked, but in Shepard it inspired no repulsion, rather it increased his heroic aspect, and Dick found himself relying upon him also. He felt intuitively that when he rode into the forest with Shepard he rode into no danger, or if by any chance he did ride into danger, they would, under the guidance of the spy, ride safely out of it again.

Shepard turned his horse toward the deeper forest, which lay on the left, and very soon they were out of sight of the main column, although the sound of hoofs and of arms, clinking against one another, still came faintly to them. Yet peace, the peace for which Dick longed so ardently, seemed to dwell there in the woods. The summer was well advanced and as the light winds blew, the leaves, already beginning to dry, rustled against one another. The sound was pleasant and soothing. He and Harry Kenton and other lads of their age had often heard it on autumn nights, when they roamed through the forests around Pendleton in search of the raccoon and the opossum. It all came back to him with astonishing vividness and force.

He was boy and man in one. But he could scarcely realize the three years and more of war that had made him a man. In one way it seemed a century, and in another it seemed but yesterday. The water rose in his eyes at the knowledge that this same cousin who was like a brother to him, one with whom he had hunted, fished, played and swum, was there in the woods less than a mile away, and that he might be in battle with him again before morning.

"You were thinking of your cousin, Mr. Kenton," said Shepard suddenly.

"Yes, but how did you know?" asked Dick in surprise.

"Because your face suddenly became melancholy—the moonlight is good, enabling me to read your look—and sadness is not your natural expression. You recall that your cousin, of whom you think so much, is at hand with your enemies, and the rest is an easy matter of putting two and two together."

"You're right in all you say, Mr. Shepard, but I wish Harry wasn't there."

Shepard was silent and then Dick added passionately:

"Why doesn't the South give up? She's worn down by attrition. She's blockaded hard and fast! When she loses troops in battle she can't find new men to take their places! She's short in food, ammunition, medicines, everything! The whole Confederacy can't be anything but a shell now! Why don't they quit!"

"Pride, and a lingering hope that the unexpected will happen. Yes, we've won the war, Mr. Mason, but it's yet far from finished. Many a good man will fall in this campaign ahead of us in the valley, and in other campaigns too, but, as I see it, the general result is already decided. Nothing can change it. Look between these trees, and you can see the Southern force now."

Dick from his horse gazed into a valley down which ran a good turnpike, looking white in the moonlight. Upon this road rode the Southern force in close ranks, but too far away, for any sound of their hoof beats to come to the watchers. The moon which was uncommonly bright now colored them all with silver, and Dick, with his imaginative mind, easily turned them into a train of the knights of old, clad in glittering mail. They created such a sense of illusion and distance, time as well as space, that the peace of the moment was not disturbed. It was a spectacle out of the past, rather than present war.

"You are familiar with the country, of course," said Dick.

"Yes," replied Shepard. "Our road, as you know, is now running parallel with that on which the Southern force is traveling, with a broad ridge between. But several miles farther on the ridge becomes narrower and the roads merge. We're sure to have a fight there. Like you, I'm sorry your cousin Harry Kenton is with them."

"It seems that you and he know a good deal of each other."

"Yes, circumstances have brought us into opposition again and again from the beginning of the war, but the same circumstances have made me know more about him than he does about me. Yet I mean that we shall be friends when peace comes, and I don't think he'll oppose my wish."

"He won't. Harry has a generous and noble nature. But he wouldn't stand being patronized, merely because he happened to be on the beaten side."

"I shouldn't think of trying to do such a thing. Now, we've seen enough, and I think we'd better go back to the colonels, with our news."

They rode through the woods again, and, for most of the distance, there was no sound from the marching troops. The wonderful feeling of peace returned. The sky was as blue and soft as velvet. The great stars glittered and danced, and the wind among the rustling leaves was like the soft singing of a violin. At one point they crossed a little brook which ran so swiftly down among the trees that it was a foam of water. They dismounted, drank hastily, and then let the horses take their fill.

"I like these hills and forests and their clear waters," said Dick, "and judging by the appearance it must be a fine country to which we're coming."

"It is. It's something like your Kentucky Blue Grass, although it's smaller and it's hemmed in by sharper and bolder mountains. But I should say that the Shenandoah Valley is close to a hundred and twenty miles long, and from twenty-five to forty miles wide, not including its spur, the Luray Valley, west of the Massanuttons."

"As large as one of the German Principalities."

"And as fine as any of them."

"It's where Stonewall Jackson made that first and famous campaign of his."

"And it's lucky for us that we don't have to face him there now. Early is a good general, they say, but he's no Stonewall Jackson."

"And we're to be led by Sheridan. I think he saved us at Perryville in Kentucky, but they say he's become a great cavalry commander. Do you know him, Mr. Shepard?"

"Well. A young man, and a little man. Why, you'd overtop him more than half a head, Mr. Mason, but he has a great soul for battle. He's the kind that will strike and strike, and keep on striking, and that's the kind we need now."

"Here are our own men just ahead. I see the three colonels riding together."

They went forward swiftly and told what they had seen, Shepard also describing the nature of the ground ahead, and the manner in which the two roads converged.

"Which column do you think will reach the junction first?" asked Colonel Hertford.

"They'll come to it about the same time," replied Shepard.

"And so a clash is unavoidable. It was not our purpose to fight before we reached General Sheridan, but since the enemy wants it, it must be that way."

Orders were issued for the column to advance as quietly as possible, while skirmishers were thrown out to prevent any ambush. Shepard rode again into the forest but Dick remained with Warner and Pennington. Warner as usual was as cool as ice, and spoke in the precise, scholarly way that he liked.

"We march parallel with the enemy," he said, "and yet we're bound to meet him and fight. It's a beautiful mathematical demonstration. The roads are not parallel in an exact sense but converge to a point. Hence, it is not our wish, but the convergence of these roads that brings us together in conflict. So we see that the greatest issues of our life are determined by mathematics. It's a splendid and romantic study. I wish you fellows would pay more attention to it."

"Mathematics beautiful and romantic!" exclaimed Pennington. "Why, George, you're out of your head! There's nothing in the world I hate more than the sight of an algebra!"

"The trouble is with you and not with the algebra. You were alluding in a depreciatory manner to my head but it's your own head that fails. When I said algebra was a beautiful and romantic study I used the adjectives purposely. Out of thousands of adjectives in the dictionary I selected those two to fit the case. What could be more delightful than an abstruse problem in algebra? You never know along what charming paths of the mind it will lead you. Moreover there is over it a veil of mystery. You can't surmise what delightful secrets it will reveal later on. What will the end be? What a powerful appeal such a question will always make to a highly intelligent and imaginative mind like mine! No poetry! No beauty! Why every algebraic problem from the very nature of its being is surcharged with it! It's like the mystery of life itself, only in this case we solve the mystery! And if I may change the metaphor, an algebraic formula is like a magnificent diamond, cutting its way through the thick and opaque glass, which represents the unknown! I long for the end of the war for many reasons, but chief among them is the fact that I may return to the romantic and illimitable fields of the mathematical problem!"

"I didn't know anyone could ever become dithyrambic about algebra," said Dick.

"What's dithyrambic?" asked Pennington.

"Spouting, Frank. But George, as we know, is a queer fellow. They grow 'em in Vermont, where they love steep mountains, deep ravines and hard mathematics."

They had been speaking in low tones, but now they ceased entirely. Shepard had come back from the forest, reporting that the junction of the roads was near, and the Confederate force was marching toward it at the utmost speed.

The hostile columns might be in conflict in a half hour now, and the men prepared themselves. Innumerable battles and skirmishes could never keep their hearts from beating harder when it became evident that they were to go under fire once more. After the few orders necessary, there was no sound save that of the march itself. Meanwhile the moon and stars were doing full duty, and the night remained as bright as ever.

CHAPTER IV
THE FIGHT AT THE CROSSWAYS

Colonel Hertford was near the head of the Union column, while the three youths rode a little farther back with Colonel Winchester, the regiment of Colonel Bedford bringing up the rear. Just behind Dick was Sergeant Whitley, mounted upon a powerful bay horse. The sergeant had shown himself such a woodsman and scout, and he was so valuable in these capacities that Colonel Winchester had practically made him an aide, and always kept him near for orders.

Dick noticed now that the sergeant leaned a little forward in his saddle and was using his eyes and ears with all the concentration of the great plainsman that he was. In that attitude he was a formidable figure, and, though he lacked the spy's subtlety and education, he seemed to have much in common with Shepard.

As for Dick himself his nerves had not been so much on edge since he went into his first battle, nor had his heart beat so hard, and he knew it was because Harry Kenton and those comrades of his would be at the convergence of the roads, and they would meet, not in the confused conflict of a great battle, when a face might appear and disappear the next second, but man to man with relatively small numbers. The moon was dimmed a little by fleecy clouds, but the silvery color, instead of vanishing was merely softened, and when Dick looked back at the Union column it, like the troop of the South, had the quality of a ghostly train. But the clouds floated away and then the light gleamed on the barrels of the short carbines that the horsemen carried. From a point on the other side of the forest came the softened notes of a trumpet and the great pulse in Dick's throat leaped. Only a few minutes more and they would be at the meeting of the ways.

Colonel Hertford sent a half dozen mounted skirmishers into the road, but the column moved forward at its even pace, still silvered in the moonlight, but ready for battle, wounds and death. Sergeant Whitley whispered to Dick:

"Other men than our own are moving in the forest. I can hear the tread of horses' hoofs on the dry leaves and twigs at the far edge. Our scouts should meet them in a moment or two."

It came as the sergeant had predicted, and Dick saw a tiny flash of fire, not much larger than a pink dot in the woods, heard the sharp report of a rifle and then the crack of another rifle in reply. Silence followed for an instant, but it was evident that the hostile forces were in touch and then in another moment or two the horses of the scouts crashed in the brush, as they rode back to the main column. They had seen enough.

Colonel Hertford gave the order and the entire Union force now advanced at a gallop. Through the woods, narrowing so rapidly, came the swift beat of hoofs on the other side, and it was apparent that coincidence would bring the two forces to the point of convergence at the same time. The moonlight seemed to Dick to grow so bright and intense that it had almost the quality of sunlight. Nature, in the absence of day, was making the field of battle as light as possible.

"What's the lay of the land at the point of meeting?" he whispered hurriedly to Shepard who had ridden up by his side.

"Almost level," came the quick response.

A few more rapid hoofbeats and the shrouding woods between disappeared. One column saw another column, both clad in the moonlight, in Dick's fancy, all in silver mail. The two forces wheeled and faced each other across the open space, their horses staring with red eyes, and the men looking intently at their opponents. Both were oppressed for an instant or two by a deep and singular silence.

Dick's eyes swept fearfully along the gray column of the South, and he saw the one whom he did not wish to see—at least not there—Harry Kenton himself, sitting on his bay horse with his friends around him. The two elderly men must be Colonel Leonidas Talbot and Lieutenant-Colonel Hector St. Hilaire, and the three youths beside Harry were surely St. Clair, Langdon and Dalton.

As he looked, Colonel Leonidas Talbot raised his sword, and at the same time came the sharp command of Colonel Hertford. Rifles and carbines flashed from either side across the open space, and two streams of bullets crossed. In an instant the silver of the moonlight was hidden by clouds of smoke through which flashed the fire from hundreds of rifles and carbines. All around Dick's ears was the hissing sound of bullets, like the alarm from serpents.

The fire at close range was so deadly to both sides that holes were smashed in the mounted ranks. The shrill screams of wounded horses, far more terrible than the cries of wounded men, struck like knife points on the drums of Dick's ears. He saw Shepard's horse go down, killed instantly by a heavy bullet, but the spy himself leaped clear, and then Dick lost him in the smoke. A bullet grazed his own wrist and he glanced curiously at the thin trickle of blood that came from it. Yet, forgetting it the next instant, he waved his saber above his head, and began to shout to the men.

Rifles and pistols emptied, the Southern horsemen were preparing to charge. The lifting smoke disclosed a long line of tossing manes and flashing steel. At either end of the line a shrill trumpet was sounding the charge, and the Northern bugles were responding with the same command. The two forces were about to meet in that most terrible of all combats, a cavalry charge by either side, when enemies looked into the eyes of one another, and strong hands swung aloft the naked steel, glittering in the moonlight.

"Bend low in the saddle," exclaimed the sergeant, "and then you'll miss many a stroke!"

Dick obeyed promptly and their whole line swept forward over the grass to meet the men in gray who were coming so swiftly against them. He saw a thousand sabers uplifted, making a stream of light, and then the two forces crashed together. It seemed to him that it was the impact of one solid body upon another as solid, and then so much blood rushed to his head that he could not see clearly. He was conscious only of a mighty crash, of falling bodies, sweeping sabers, that terrible neigh again of wounded horses, of sun-tanned faces, and of fierce eyes staring into his own, and then, as the red mist thinned a little, he became conscious that someone just before him was slashing at him with a long, keen blade. He bent yet lower, and the sword passed over him, but as he rose a little he cut back. His edge touched only the air, but he uttered a gasp of horror as he saw Harry Kenton directly before him, and knew that they had been striking at each other. He saw, too, the appalled look in Harry's eyes, who at the same time had recognized his opponent, and then, in the turmoil of battle, other horsemen drove in between.

That shiver of horror swept over Dick once more, and then came relief. The charging horsemen had separated them in time, and he did not think it likely that the chances of battle would bring Harry and him face to face more than once. Then the red blur enclosed everything and he was warding off the saber strokes of another man. The air was yet filled with the noise of shouting men, and neighing horses, of heavy falls and the ring of steel on steel. Neither gave way and neither could advance. The three Union colonels rode up and down their lines encouraging their men, and the valiant Talbot and St. Hilaire were never more valiant than on that night.

A combat with sabers cannot last long, and cavalry charges are soon finished. North and South had met in the center of the open space, and suddenly the two, because all their force was spent, fell back from that deadly line, which was marked by a long row of fallen horses and men. They reloaded their rifles and carbines and began to fire at one another, but it was at long range, and little damage was done. They fell back a bit farther, the firing stopped entirely, and they looked at one another.

It was perhaps the effect of the night, with its misty silver coloring, and perhaps their long experience of war, giving them an intuitive knowledge, that made these foes know nothing was to be gained by further combat. They were so well balanced in strength and courage that they might destroy one another, but no one could march away from the field victorious. Perhaps, too, it was a feeling that the God of Battles had already issued his decree in regard to this war, and that as many lives as possible should now be spared. But whatever it was, the finger fell away from the trigger, the saber was returned to the scabbard, and they sat on their horses, staring at one another.

Dick took his glasses from his shoulder and began to scan the hostile line. His heart leaped when he beheld Harry in the saddle, apparently unharmed, and near him three youths, one with a red bandage about his shoulder. Then he saw the two colonels, both erect men with long, gray hair, on their horses near the center of the line, and talking together. One gestured two or three times as he spoke, and he moved his arm rather stiffly.

The three Union colonels were in a little group not far from Dick, and they also were talking with one another. Dick wondered what they would do, but he was saved from long wonderment by the call of a trumpet from the Southern force, and the appearance of a horseman not older than himself riding forward and bearing a white flag.

"They want a truce," said Colonel Hertford. "Go and meet them, Mason."

Dick, willing enough, turned his horse toward the young man who, heavily tanned, was handsome, well-built and dressed with scrupulous care in a fine gray uniform.

"My name is St. Clair," he said, "and I'm an officer on the staff of Colonel Leonidas Talbot, who commands the force behind me."

"I think we've met once before," said Dick. "My name is Mason, Richard Mason, and I am with Colonel Arthur Winchester, who commands one of the regiments that has just been fighting you."

"It's so! Upon my life it's so, and you're the same Dick Mason that's the cousin of our Harry Kenton, the fellow he's always talking about! He's on General Lee's staff, but he's been detached for temporary duty with us. He's over there all right. But I've come to tell you that Colonel Talbot, who commands us, offers a flag of truce to bury the dead. He sees that neither side can win, that to continue the battle would only involve us in mutual destruction. He wishes, too, that I convey to your commander his congratulations upon his great skill and courage. I may add, myself, Mr. Mason, that Colonel Talbot knows a brave man when he sees him."

"I've no doubt the offer will be accepted. Will you wait a moment?"

"Certainly," replied St. Clair, giving his most elegant salute with his small sword.

Dick went back to the Union colonels, and they accepted at once. That long line of dead and wounded, and the mournful song of the wind through the trees, affected the colonels on both sides. More flags of truce were hoisted, and the officers in blue or gray rode forward to meet one another, and to talk together as men who bore no hate in their hearts for gallant enemies.

The troopers rapidly dug shallow graves with their bayonets in the soft soil, and the dead were laid away. The feeling of friendship and also of curiosity among these stern fighters grew. They were anxious to see and talk a little with men who had fought one another so hard more than three years. Nearly all of them had lost blood at one time or another, and the venom of hate had gone out with it.

Dick found Harry dismounted and standing with a group of officers, among whom were St. Clair and Langdon. The two cousins shook hands with the greatest warmth.

"Well, Dick," said Harry, "we didn't think to meet again in this way, did we?"

"No, but both of us at least have come out of it alive, and unwounded. I'm sorry to see that your friend there is hurt."

"It's nothing," said Langdon, whose left arm was in a hasty bandage. "A scratch only. I'll be able to use my arm as well as ever three days from now."

"Your force," said St. Clair, "was marching to reinforce General Sheridan in the Valley of Virginia. I'm not asking for information, which of course you wouldn't give. I'm merely stating the fact."

"And yours," said Dick, "was marching to reinforce General Early in the same valley. I, like you, am just making a statement."

"We've met, but you haven't been able to stop us."

"Nor have you been able to stop _us_."

"And so it's checkmate."

"Checkmate it is."

"Why don't you fellows give up and go home?" exclaimed Dick, moved by an irresistible impulse. "You know that your armies are wearing out, while ours are growing stronger!"

"We couldn't think of such a thing," replied St. Clair, in a tone of cool assurance. "My friend Langdon here, has taken an oath to sleep in the White House. We also intend to make a triumphal march through Philadelphia, and then down Broadway in New York. You would not have us break our oaths or change our purposes."

"It's true, Dick," said Harry, "we can't do either. We'd like to oblige you Yankees, but we must make those triumphal parades through Philadelphia and New York."

"I should have known that I couldn't reason with you Johnny Rebs," said Dick, smiling, "but I hope that none of you will get killed, and here and now I make you a promise."

"What is it, Dick?" asked Harry.

"When you suffer your final defeat, and all of you become my prisoners, I'll treat you well. I'll turn you loose in a Blue-grass pasture, and you can roam as you please within its limits."

"Thank you," said Happy Tom, "but I'm no Nebuchadnezzar. I can't live on grass. If I become a prisoner at any time I demand the very best of food, especially as you Yankees already have more than your share."

"There go the trumpets recalling us," said St. Clair. "The men have finished the gruesome task. I want you to know, Mr. Mason, that we bear you no animosity, and we're quite sure that you bear us none."

He extended his hand and Dick's met it in a warm grasp. Langdon also shook hands with him, and as his eyes twinkled he said:

"Don't fail to notice my haughty bearing when I march at the head of a triumphal troop down Broadway!"

"I promise," said Dick. Then he and Harry gave each other the final clasp. But with the pride of the young they strove not to show emotion.

"Take care of yourself, Dick, old man!" said Harry. "Don't get in the way of bullets and shell. Remember they're harder than you are."

"The same to you, Harry. It's not worth while to take any more risks than necessary."

Then, obeying the call of the trumpets, they mounted and rode to their own commands. There was something strange in this brief half hour of friendship, when they buried the dead together. Blue and gray formed again in long lines facing one another, but midway between was another long line of fresh earth, and it rose up suddenly, an impassable barrier to a charge by either force.

"We can't beat them and they can't beat us. That's been proved," said Colonel Hertford to Colonel Winchester and Colonel Bedford.

"So it has," said Colonel Winchester, "and I'd like to march from here. I don't care for any more fighting on this spot."

"Nor I. Hark, they've decided it for us!"

The Southern trumpet sounded another call, and the line of men in gray, turning away, began to march into the southwest. Colonel Hertford promptly gave an order, the Union trumpet sounded also, and the men in blue, curving also, rode toward the northwest.

Dick and his comrades were silent a long time. Their feelings were perhaps the same. To youth a year is a long time, and two years are almost a life time. Three years and more of it had made war to them a normal state. They had not thought much before of an end to the great struggle between North and South, and of what was to come after. Now they realized that peace, not war, was normal, and that it must return.

The moonlight faded and then the stars were dimmed, as the darkness that precedes the dawn came. The silvery veil that had been thrown over them vanished and the column became a ghostly train riding in the dusk. But the road into which Shepard guided them led over a pleasant land of hills and clear streams. Although the scouts on their flanks kept vigilant watch, many of the men slept soundly in their saddles. Dick himself dozed awhile, and slept awhile, and, when he roused himself from his last nap, the dawn was breaking over the brown hills and the column was halting for food and a little rest.

It was August, the time of great heat in Virginia, but they were already building fires to cook the breakfast and make coffee, and most of the men had dismounted. Dick sprang down also and turned his horse loose to graze with the others. Then he joined Warner and Pennington and fell hungrily to work. When he thought of it afterward he could scarcely remember a time in the whole war when he was not hungry.

The sense of unreality disappeared with the brilliant dawn, though the night itself with the battle in the moonlight seemed to be almost a dream. Yet the combat had been fought, and he had met Harry Kenton and his friends. The empty saddles proved it.

"I see a great country opening out before us," said Warner. "I suppose it's this Valley of Virginia, of which we've all heard and seen so much, and in which once upon a time Stonewall Jackson thumped us so often."

"It's a branch of it," said Pennington, "but Stonewall Jackson is gone, God rest his soul—I say that from the heart, even if he was against us—and I've an idea that instead of getting thumped we're going to do the thumping. There's something about this man Sheridan that appeals to me. We've seen him in action with artillery, but now he's a cavalry commander. They say he rides fast and far and strikes hard. People are beginning to talk about Little Phil. Well, I approve of Little Phil."

"He'll be glad to hear of it," said Dick. "It will brace him up a lot."

"He may be lucky to get it," replied Pennington calmly. "There are many generals in this war, and two or three of them have been commander-in-chief, of whom I don't approve at all. I think you'll find, too, that history will have a habit of agreeing with me."

"But don't make predictions," said Dick. "There have been no genuine, dyed-in-the-wool prophets since those ancient Hebrews were gathered to their fathers, and that was a mighty long time ago."

"There you're wrong, Dick," said Warner, earnestly. "It's all a matter of mathematics, the scientific application of a romantic and imaginative science to facts. Get all your premises right, arrange them correctly, and the result follows as a matter of course."

The trumpet sounded boots and saddles, and cut him short. In a few more minutes they were all up and away, riding over the hills and across the dips toward the main sweep of the famous valley which played such a great part in the tactics and fighting of the Civil War. It had already been ravaged much by march and battle and siege, but its heavier fate was yet to come.

But Dick did not think much of what might happen as he rode with his comrades across the broken country and saw, rising before them, the dim blue line of the mountains that walled in the eastern side of the valley. The day was not so warm as usual, and among the higher hills a breeze was blowing, bringing currents of fresh, cool air that made the lungs expand and the pulses leap. The three youths felt almost as if they had been re-created, and Pennington became vocal.

"Woe is the day!" he said. "I lament what I have lost!"

"If what you have lost was worth keeping I lament with you," said Dick. "O, woe is the day!"

"O, woe is the day for me, too!" said Warner, "but why do we utter cries of woe, Frank?"

"Because of the narrow, little, muddy little, ugly little, mean little trench we've left behind us! O, woe is me that I've left such a trench, where one could sit in mud to the knees and touch the mud wall on either side of him, for this open, insecure world, where there is nothing but fresh air to breathe, nothing but water to drink, nothing but food to eat, and no world but blue skies, hills, valleys, forests, fields, rivers, creeks and brooks!"

"O, woe is me!" the three chanted together. "We sigh for our narrow trench, and its muddy bottom and muddy sides and foul air and lack of space, and for the shells bursting over our heads, and for the hostile riflemen ready to put a bullet through us at the first peep! Now, do we sigh for all those blessings we've left behind us?"

"Never a sigh!" said Dick.

"Not a tear from me," said Pennington.

"The top of the earth for me," said Warner.

Their high spirits spread to the whole column. So thoroughly inured were they to war that their losses of the night before were forgotten, and they lifted up their voices and sang. Youth and the open air would have their way and the three colonels did not object. They preferred men who sang to men who groaned.

"Do you know just where we're going, and where we expect to find this Little Phil of yours?" asked Warner.

"I've heard that we're to report to him at Halltown, a place south of the Potomac, and about four miles from Harper's Ferry," replied Dick.

"As that's a long distance, we'll have a long ride to reach it," said Warner, "and I'm glad of it. I'm enjoying this great trail, and I hope we won't meet again those fire-eating friends of yours, Dick, who gave us so much trouble last night."

"I hope so too," said Dick, "for their sake as well as ours. I don't like fighting with such close kin. They must be well along on the southwestern road now to join Early."

"There's no further danger of meeting them, at least before this campaign opens," said Warner. "Shepard has just come back from a long gallop and he reports that they are now at least twenty miles away, with the distance increasing all the time."

Dick felt great relief. He was softening wonderfully in these days, and while he had the most intense desire for the South to yield he had no wish for the South to suffer more. He felt that the republic had been saved and he was anxious for the war to be over soon. His heart swelled with pride at the way in which the Union states had stood fast, how they had suffered cruel defeats, but had come again, and yet again, how mistakes and disaster had been overcome by courage and tenacity.

"A Confederate dollar for your thoughts," said Warner.

"You can have 'em without the dollar," replied Dick. "I was thinking about the end of the war and after. What are all the soldiers going to do then?"

"Go straight back to peace," replied Warner promptly. "I know my own ambition. I've told you already that I intend to be president of Harvard University, and, barring death, I'm bound to succeed. I give myself twenty-five years for the task. If I choose my object now and bend every energy toward it for twenty-five years I'm sure to obtain it. It's a mathematical certainty."

"I'm going to be a great ranchman in Western Nebraska with my father," said Pennington. "He's under fifty yet, and he's as strong as a horse. The buffalo in Western Nebraska must go and then Pennington and Son will have fifty thousand fine cattle in their place. And you, Dick, have you already chosen the throne on which you're going to sit?"

"Yes, I've been thinking about it for some time. I've made up my mind to be an editor. After the war I'm going to the largest city in our state, get a place on a newspaper there and strive to be its head. Then I'll try to cement the reunion of North and South. That will be my greatest topic. We soldiers won't hate one another when the war is over, and maybe the fact that I've fought through it will give weight to my words."

"I'll tell you what I'll do," said Warner. "When I'm president of Harvard I'll invite the great Kentucky editor, Richard Mason, to deliver the annual address to my young men. I like that idea of yours about making the Union firmer than it was before the war. Since the Northern States and the Southern States must dwell together the more peace and brotherly love we have the better it will be for all of us."

"When you give me that invitation, George, you'd better ask my cousin, Harry Kenton, at the same time, because it's almost a certainty that he will then be governor of Kentucky. His great grandfather, the famous Henry Ware, was the greatest governor the state ever had, and, as I know that Harry intends to study law and enter politics, he's bound to follow in his footsteps."

"Of course I'll ask him," said Warner in all earnestness, "and he shall speak too. You can settle it between you who speaks first. It will be an exceedingly effective scene, the two cousins, the great editor who fought on the Northern side and the great governor who fought on the Southern side, speaking from the same stage to the picked youth of New England. Pennington, the representative of the boundless West, shall be there too, and if the owner of fifty thousand fine cattle roaming far and wide wants to make an address he shall do so."

"I don't think I'd care to speak, George," said Pennington. "I'm not cut out for oratory, but I certainly accept right now your invitation to come. I'll sit on the stage with Dick and the Johnny Reb, his cousin Harry, and I'll smile and smile and applaud and applaud, and after it's all over I'll choose a few of your picked youth of New England, take 'em out west with me, teach 'em how to rope cattle, how to trail stray steers and how to take care of themselves in a blizzard. Oh, I'll make men of 'em, I will! Now, what is that on the high hill to the south?"

The three put their glasses to their eyes and saw a man on horseback waving a flag. The head of the horse was turned toward some hill farther south, and the man was evidently making signals to another patrol there.

"A Johnny," said Pennington. "I suppose they're sending the word on toward Early that we're passing."

"From hill to hill," said Dick. "A message can be sent a long way in that manner."

"I don't think it will interfere with us," said Warner. "They're merely telling about us. They don't intend to attack us. They haven't the men to spare."

"No, they won't attack, they know I'm here," said Pennington.

The three colonels did not stop the column, but they watched the signals as they rode. Nobody was able to interpret them, not even Shepard, but they felt that they could ignore them. Colonel Hertford, nevertheless, sent off a strong scouting party in that direction, but as it approached the horseman on the hill rode over the other side and disappeared.

All that day they advanced through a lonely and hostile country. It was a region intensely Southern in its sympathies, and it seemed that everybody, including the women and children, had fled before them. Horses and cattle were gone also and its loneliness was accentuated by the fact that not so long before it had been a well-peopled land, where now the houses stood empty and silent. They saw no human beings, save other watchmen on the hills making signals, but they were far away and soon gone.

By noon both horses and men showed great fatigue. They had slept but little the night before, and, toughened as they were by war, they had reached the limit of endurance. So the trumpet sounded the halt in a meadow beside a fine stream, and all, save those who were to ride on the outskirts and watch for the enemy, dismounted gladly. A vast drinking followed. The water was clear, running over clean pebbles, and a thousand men knelt and drank again and again. Then the horses were allowed to drink their fill, which they did with mighty gurglings of satisfaction, and the men cooked their midday meal.

Meanwhile they talked of Sheridan. All expected battle and then battle again when they joined him, and they looked forward to a great campaign in the valley. That valley was not so far away. The blue walls of the mountains that hemmed its eastern edge were very near now. Dick looked at them through his glasses, not to find an enemy, but merely for the pleasure of bringing out the heavy forests on their slopes. It was true that the leaves were already touched by the summer's heat, but in the distance at least the mass looked green. He knew also that under the screen of the leaves the grass preserved its freshness and there were many little streams, foaming in white as they rushed down the steep slopes. It was a marvelously pleasing sight to him, and, as the wilderness thus called, he was once more deeply grateful that he had escaped from the muddy trench.

"We'll pass through a gap, sir, tomorrow morning," said Sergeant Whitley, "and go into the main valley."

"The gap would be the place for the Southern force to meet us."

But Sergeant Whitley shook his head.

"There are too many gaps and too few Southern troops," he said. "I think we'll find this one clear. Besides, Colonel Hertford is sure to send a scouting party ahead tonight. But if you don't mind taking a little advice from an old trooper, sir, I'd lie on the grass and sleep while we're here. An hour even will do a lot of good."

Dick followed his advice gladly and thanked him. He was always willing to receive instruction from Sergeant Whitley, who had proved himself his true friend and who in reality was able to teach men of much higher rank. He lay down upon the brown grass, and despite all the noise, despite all the excitement of past hours, fell fast asleep in a few minutes. He slept an hour, but it seemed to him that he had scarcely closed his eyes, when the trumpets were calling boots and saddles again. Yet he felt refreshed and stronger when he sprang up, and Sergeant Whitley's advice, as always, had proved good.

The column resumed its march before mid-afternoon, continuing its progress through a silent and empty country. The blue wall came closer and closer and Dick and his comrade saw the lighter line, looking in the distance like the slash of a sword, that marked the gap. Shepard, who rode a very swift and powerful horse, came back from another scouting trip and reported that there was no sign of the enemy, at least at the entrance to the gap.

Later in the afternoon, as they were passing through a forest several shots were fired at them from the covert. No damage was done beyond one man wounded slightly, and Dick, under orders, led a short pursuit. He was glad that they found no one, as prisoners would have been an incumbrance, and it was not the custom in the United States to shoot men not in uniform who were defending the soil on which they lived. He had no doubt that those who had fired the shots were farmers, but it had been easy for them to make good their escape in the thickets.

He thought he saw relief on Colonel Hertford's face also, when he reported that the riflemen had escaped, and, after spreading out skirmishers a little farther on either flank, the column, which had never broken its march, went on at increased pace. It was growing warm now, and the dust and heat of the long ride began to affect them. The blue line of the mountains, as they came close, turned to green and Dick, Warner and Pennington looked enviously at the deep shade.

"Not so bad," said Warner. "Makes me think a little of the Green Mountains of Vermont, though not as high and perhaps not as green."

"Of course," said Dick. "Nothing outside of Vermont is as good as anything inside of it."

"I'm glad you acknowledge it so readily, Dick. I have found some people who would not admit it at first, and I was compelled to talk and persuade them of the fact, a labor that ought to be unnecessary. The truth should always speak for itself. Vermont isn't the most fertile state in the Union and it's not the largest, but it's the best producer of men, or I should say the producer of the best men."

"What will Massachusetts say to that? I've read Daniel Webster's speech in reply to Hayne."

"Oh, Massachusetts, of course, has more people, I'm merely speaking of the average."

"Nebraska hasn't been settled long," said Pennington, "but you just wait. When we get a population we'll make both Vermont and Massachusetts take a back seat."

"And that population, or at least the best part of it," rejoined the undaunted Warner, "will come from Vermont and Massachusetts and other New England states."

"Sunset and the gap together are close at hand," said Dick, "and however the mountains of Virginia may compare with those of Vermont, it's quite certain that the sun setting over the two states is the same."

"I concede that," said Warner; "but it looks more brilliant from the Vermont hills."

Nevertheless, the sun set in Virginia in a vast and intense glow of color, and as the twilight came they entered the gap.

CHAPTER V
AN OLD ENEMY

Despite the brilliant sunset the night came on very dark and heavy with damp. The road through the gap was none too good and the lofty slopes clothed in forest looked menacing. Many sharpshooters might lurk there, and the three colonels were anxious to reach Sheridan with their force intact, at least without further loss after the battle with Colonel Talbot's command.

The column was halted and it was decided to send out another scouting party to see if the way was clear. Twenty men, of whom the best for such work were Shepard and Whitley, were chosen, and Dick, owing to his experience, was put in nominal command, although he knew in his heart that the spy and the sergeant would be the real leaders, a fact which he did not resent. Warner and Pennington begged to go too, but they were left behind.

Shepard had received a remount, and, as all of them rode good horses, they advanced at a swift trot through the great gap. The spy, who knew the pass, led the way. The column behind, although it was coming forward at a good pace, disappeared with remarkable quickness. Dick, looking back, saw a dusky line of horsemen, and then he saw nothing. He did not look back again. His eyes were wholly for Shepard and the dim path ahead.

The aspect of the mountains, which had been so inviting before they came to them, changed wholly. Dick did not long so much for green foliage now, as a chill wind began to blow. All of them carried cloaks or overcoats rolled tightly and tied to their saddles, which they loosed and put on. The wind rose, and, confined within the narrow limits of the pass, it began to groan loudly. A thin sheet of rain came on its edge, and the drops were almost as cold as those of winter.

Dick's first sensation of uneasiness and discomfort disappeared quickly. Like his cousin, Harry, he had inherited a feeling for the wilderness. His own ancestor, Paul Cotter, had been a great woodsman too, and, as he drew on the buckskin gauntlets and wrapped the heavy cloak about his body, his second sensation was one of actual physical pleasure. Why should he regard the forest with a hostile eye? His ancestors had lived in it and often its darkness had saved them from death by torture.

He looked up at the dark slopes, but he could see only the black masses of foliage and the thin sheets of driven rain. For a little while, at least, his mind reproduced the wilderness. It was there in all its savage loneliness and majesty. He could readily imagine that the Indians were lurking in the brush, and that the bears and panthers were seeking shelter in their dens. But his own feeling of safety and of mental and physical pleasure in the face of obstacles deepened.

"I've been just that way myself," said Sergeant Whitley, who was riding beside him and who could both see and read his face. "On the plains when we were so well wrapped up that the icy winds whistling around us couldn't get at us then we felt all the better. But it was best when we were inside the fort and the winter blizzard was howling."

"A lot of us were talking a little while back about what they were going to do after the war. What's your plan, sergeant, if you have any?"

"I do have a plan, Mr. Mason. I was a lumberman, as you know, before I entered the regular army, and when the fighting's done I think I'll go back to it. I can swing an axe with the best of 'em, but I mean after a while to have others swinging axes for me. If I can I'm going to become a big lumberman. I'd rather be that than anything else."

"It's a just and fine ambition, sergeant, I feel sure that you're going to become a man of money and power. Mr. Warner means to become president of Harvard, twenty or twenty-five years from now, and my cousin Harry Kenton, a reconstructed rebel, is going to deliver an address there to the new president's young men, while Mr. Pennington and I, as the president's guests, are going to sit on the stage and smile. Right now, and with authority from Mr. Warner, I'm going to invite you as the lumber king of the Northwest to sit on the stage with us on that occasion, as the guest of President Warner, and smile with us."

"If I become what you predict I'll accept," said the sergeant.

The chances were a thousand to one against the prophecy, but it all came true, just as they wished.

The rain increased a little, although it was not yet able to penetrate Dick's heavy coat, but they were compelled to go more slowly on account of the thickening darkness. They reached very soon the crest of the pass and halted there a little while to see or hear any sign of a human being. But no sound came to them and they resumed the scout in the darkness, riding now down the slope which would end before long in a great valley.

The ground softened by the rain deadened the footsteps of their horses, and they made little noise as they rode down the narrow pass, examining as well as they could the dripping forest on either side of the road. Shepard was a bit ahead, and Dick and the sergeant, riding side by side, came next. Behind were the troopers, a small picked band, daring horsemen, used to every kind of danger.

They did not really anticipate the presence of an enemy in the pass. They knew that Colonel Talbot's command had turned toward the southwest. All the other Confederate forces must be gathering far up the valley to meet Sheridan, and the South was too much reduced to raise new men. Yet after a half hour's moderate riding down the slope Dick became sure that some one was in the narrow belt of forest on their right, where the slope was less steep than on their left.

At first it seemed to be an intuition, merely a feeling brought on waves of air that men, enemies, were in the wood. Then he knew that the feeling was due to sounds as of someone moving lightly through a wet thicket, but unable to keep the boughs from giving forth a rustle. He was about to call to Shepard, but before he could do so the spy stopped. Then all the others stopped also.

"Did you hear it?" Dick whispered to Sergeant Whitley.

"Yes," replied the sergeant. "Men are moving in the thicket on our right. I couldn't hear much, but they must be as numerous as we are. They're enemies or they'd have come out. They're on foot, too, as they couldn't manage horses in those deep woods. Likely they've left their mounts with a guard on top of a ridge, as men on foot wouldn't be abroad at such a time on such a night."

"Then it's an ambush!" said Dick, and he added in a sharp voice:

"Pull away to the left, men, under cover!"

Shepard was the first to turn and all the others followed instantly. Three jumps of the horses and they were among the bushes and trees on the left. It was lucky for them that they had heard the sound of the wet bushes rustling together, as a dozen rifles flashed in the dusk on the other side of the road. Bullets cut the leaves about them. Two or three buried themselves with a plunk in the trunks of trees, one killed a horse, the trooper springing clear without hurt, and one man was wounded slightly in the arm.

"Take cover," called Dick, "but don't lose your horses!"

They dismounted and concealed themselves behind the trunks of trees. Some hastily tethered their horses to bushes, but others hung the bridle over an arm. They knew that if a combat was to occur it must be fought on foot, but, for the present, they were compelled to wait. Yet if their enemy was hidden from them they also were hidden from him. All the conditions of an old Indian battle in darkness and ambush were reproduced, and Dick was deeply grateful that he had at his elbow two redoubtable champions like Whitley and Shepard. They were peculiarly fitted for such work as that which lay before them, and he was ready and willing to take advice from either.

"It's a small party," whispered Shepard, "probably not much larger than ours. They must have expected to make a complete ambush, but we heard them too soon."

"It's surely not a part of Colonel Talbot's command," said Dick. "If so, Harry Kenton and his friends would certainly be there and I shouldn't like to be in battle with them again."

"Never a fear of that," said Sergeant Whitley. "It's more likely to be some guerrilla band, roaming around as it pleases. The condition of the country and these mountains give such fellows a chance. I'm going to lie down and creep forward as we used to do on the plains. I want to get a sight of those fellows, that is, if you say so, sir."

"Of course," said Dick, "but don't take too big risks, sergeant. We can't afford to let you be shot."

"Never fear," said the sergeant, dropping almost flat upon his face, and creeping slowly forward.

The dusky figure worming itself through the bushes heightened the illusion of an old Indian combat. The sergeant was a scout and trailer feeling for the enemy and he reminded Dick of his famous ancestor, Paul Cotter. Several more shots were fired by the foe, but they did not hurt anybody, all of them flying overhead. Dick's men were anxious to send random bullets in reply into the thickets, but he restrained them. It would be only a waste, and while it was annoying to be held there, it could not be helped. Some of the horses reared and plunged with fright at the shots, but silence soon came.

Dick still watched the sergeant as he edged forward, inch by inch. Had not his eyes been following the dusky figure he could not have picked it out from the general darkness. But he still saw it faintly, a darker blur against the dark earth. Yielding a little to his own anxiety, he handed the bridle of his horse to his orderly, and moved toward the edge of the woodland strip, bending low, and using the tree trunks for shelter.

At the last tree he knelt and looked for those on the other side. The sergeant was already beyond cover, but he lay so low in the grass that Dick himself could scarcely discern him.

The wind was still driving the thin sheets of rain before it, and was keeping up a howling and whistling in the pass, a most sinister sound to one not used to the forest and darkness, although Dick paid no attention to it.

Twice the clouds parted slightly and showed a bit of moonlight, but the gleam was so brief that it was gone in a second or two. Nevertheless at the second ray Dick saw crouched beside a tree at the far side of the road a small hunched figure holding a rifle, the head crowned by an enormous flap-brimmed hat. His imagination also made him see small, close-set, menacing red eyes, and he knew at once that it was Slade, the same guerrilla leader who had once pursued him with such deadly vindictiveness through the Mississippi forest and swamps. He had heard that he had come farther north and had united his band with that of Skelly, who pretended to be on the other side. But one could never tell about these outlaws. When they were distant from the regular armies nobody was safe from them.

"Did you see?" whispered Dick to the sergeant who had crept to his side.

"Yes, I caught a glimpse of him. It was Slade, who tried so hard to kill you down there in the Vicksburg campaign. If we get another ray of the moonlight I'll pick him off, that is if you say so, sir."

"I've no objection, sergeant. Such a man as Slade cumbers the earth. Besides, he'll do everything he can now to kill us."

The sergeant knelt, carbine raised, and waited for the ray of moonlight. He was a dead shot, and he believed that he would not miss, but when the ray came at last Slade was not there. Whitley uttered a low exclamation of disgust.

"A good chance gone," he said, "and it may never come again. I'd have saved the lives of a lot of good men."

But a flash came from the thicket, and the sergeant from the grass replied. A cry followed his shot, showing that some one had received his bullet, but Dick knew instinctively that it was not Slade, the crafty leader he was sure now being safe behind the trunk of a tree.

Presently the sergeant fired from another point, and then crept hastily away lest the flash of his rifle betray him. A dozen shots were fired by Slade's band, but no harm was done, and then, the sergeant coming back, Dick held a consultation with his two lieutenants and advisers.

"Perhaps we may flank them," he said. "We can divide our force, and taking them by surprise drive them out of the wood."

But Sergeant Whitley, wary and weatherwise, was against it.

"The risk would be too great, sir," he said. "We can afford to wait while they can't. Our whole column will be up in time, while it's not likely that anybody can come to help Slade. It's true too, sir, that this rain is going to stop. The clouds are beginning to clear away, and when there's light we'll have a fair chance at 'em."

"I think," said Dick, "that it will be best for Mr. Shepard to return and hurry up a relieving column. What do you say?"

"I think so too, sir," said Shepard. "I can lead my horse back some distance through the forest, then mount and gallop up the road. They may be gone before I come again, but if they are not we can soon drive them away."

"We'll cover you with our rifles against any rush made by Slade's men," said Dick.

But it did not become necessary to fire. Shepard was able to lead his horse through the woods without noise, until he was at least three hundred yards on the return journey. Then he mounted and galloped at great speed up the pass. Dick heard the distant thud of hoofs growing fainter and fainter until they died away altogether, and he knew that Slade must have heard them too. And a man as acute and experienced as the guerrilla chief would easily divine their meaning.

The rain ceased, and the moaning and whistling of the wind in the pass became a murmur. The clouds parted and sank away toward every horizon, leaving the full dome of the sky, shot with a bright moon and millions of dancing stars. A silvery light over the woods and thickets drove away the deep darkness, and when Sergeant Whitley crept forward again to spy out the enemy he found that they were gone. He trailed them up the lofty slope and discovered, as he had surmised, that they had left their horses there while they attempted the ambush. He was sure now that they were far away, and he returned with his story, just as Shepard arrived with the vanguard of the column, led by Colonel Winchester.

"And so it was Slade!" said the Colonel.

"Undoubtedly, sir," said Dick. "I saw him plainly, and so did Sergeant Whitley."

"I'm not sorry he's here," said Colonel Winchester thoughtfully, "and I hope the story that he and Skelly have joined bands is true, because if they are in this region they're so far away from Pendleton that your people are safe from mischief at their hands."

"I hadn't thought of it in that way, sir, but it's just as you say. I'd rather have to fight them here than have them attacking our innocent people at home. In the early part of the war Skelly called himself a Unionist, did he not?"

"Yes, and he may do so yet, but names are nothing to him. He'd rob, and murder, too, with equal zest under either flag."

"It's so," said Dick, and he felt the full truth as he thought of Pendleton, and his beautiful young mother, alone in her house, save for the gigantic and faithful Juliana. But Juliana was an armed host herself, and Dick smiled at the recollection of the strong and honest black face that had bent over him so often. He prayed without words that these ruthless guerrillas, no matter what flag they bore, should never come to Pendleton.

"I don't think our column on its present march need fear anything from Slade and his band," said Colonel Winchester. "Such as he can operate only from ambush, and so far as Virginia is concerned, in the mountains. Shepard says we'll be out of the pass in another hour, and by that time it will be day. I'll be glad, too, as the cold rain and the darkness and the long ride are beginning to affect the men."

The column resumed its march, Dick rode by the side of Colonel Winchester. Time, propinquity, genuine esteem, and a fourth influence which Dick did not as yet suspect, were fast knitting these two, despite the difference in age, into a friendship which nothing could break. The meeting with Slade was forgotten quickly, by all except those concerned, and by most of those too, so vast was the war and so little space did it afford for the memory of brief events. Yet it lingered a while with Dick. Twice now he had met Slade and he felt that he would meet him yet again at points far apart.

Dawn came slow and gray in a cloudy sky, but the sun soon broke through. The heat returned and the earth began to dry. The three colonels felt it necessary to give their men rest and food, and let them dry their uniforms, which had become wet in many cases, despite their overcoats and heavy cloaks.

They were now in a deep cove of the great Valley of Virginia, with the steep mountains just behind them, and far beyond the dim blue outline of other mountains enclosing it on the west. As the fires blazed up and the men made coffee and cooked their breakfasts, Dick's heart leaped. This was the great valley once more, where so much history had been made. Lee and Grant were deadlocked in the trenches before Petersburg, but here in the valley history would be made again. It was the finest part of Virginia, the greatest state of the Confederacy, and Dick knew in his heart that some heavy blows would soon be struck, where fields already had been won and lost in desperate strife.

But the men were very cheerful. The little band of skirmishers or sharpshooters under Slade had been brushed aside easily, and now that they were in the valley they did not foresee any further attempt to stop their march to Sheridan. The three colonels shared in the view, and when the men had finished breakfast and dried themselves at their fires they remounted and rode away gaily. High spirits rose again in youthful veins, and some lad of a mellow voice began to sing. By and by all joined and a thousand voices thundered out:

> "Oh, share my cottage, gentle maid,
>   It only waits for thee
> To give a sweetness to its shade
>   And happiness to me.
>
> "Here from the splendid, gay parade
>   Of noise and folly free
> No sorrows can my peace invade
>   If only blessed with thee.
>
> "Then share my cottage, gentle maid,
>   It only waits for thee
> To give a sweetness to its shade
>   And happiness to me."

Colonel Hertford made no attempt to check them as they rode across the fields, yet green here, despite the summer's heat.

"They're bravest when they sing," he said to Colonel Winchester.

"It encourages them," said Colonel Winchester, "and I like to hear it myself. It's a wonderful effect, a thousand or more strong lads singing, as they sweep over the valley toward battle."

Dick, Pennington and Warner had joined in the song, but the youth some distance ahead of them was leader. They finished "Gentle Maid" and then, with the same lad leading them, swung into a song that made Dick start and that for a moment made other mountains and another valley stand out before him, sharp and clear.

> "Soft o'er the fountain, ling'ring falls the Southern moon
> Far o'er the mountain, breaks the day too soon.
> In thy dark eyes' splendor, where the warm light loves to dwell,
> Weary looks, yet tender, speak their fond farewell.
> Nita! Juanita! Ask thy soul if we should part,
> Nita! Juanita! Lean thou on my heart.
>
> "When in thy dreaming moons like these shall shine again,
> And daylight beaming prove thy dreams are vain,

Wilt thou not, relenting, for thy absent lover sigh?
In thy heart consenting to a prayer gone by!
Nita! Juanita! Let me linger by thy side.
Nita! Juanita! Be my own fair bride."

They put tremendous heart and energy into the haunting old song as they sang, and Dick still saw Sam Jarvis, the singer of the hills, and his valley, where the paths of Harry Kenton and himself had crossed, though at times far apart.

"Now!" shouted the young leader, "The last verse again!" and with increased heart and energy they thundered out:

"When in thy dreaming moons like these shall shine again,
And daylight beaming prove thy dreams are vain,
Wilt thou not, relenting, for thy absent lover sigh?
In thy heart consenting to a prayer gone by!
Nita! Juanita! Let me linger by thy side.
Nita! Juanita! Be my own fair bride."

The mighty chorus sank away and the hills gave it back in echoes until the last one died.

"It's sung mostly in the South," said Dick to Warner and Pennington.

"True," said Warner, "but before the war songs were not confined to one section. They were the common property of both. We've as much right to sing Juanita as the Johnnies have."

All that day they rode and sang, going north toward Halltown, where the forces of Sheridan were gathering, and the valley, although lone and desolate, continually unfolded its beauty before them. The mountains were green near by and blue in the distance, and the fertile floor that they enclosed, like walls, was cut by many streams. Here, indeed, was a region that had bloomed before the war, and that would bloom again, no matter what war might do.

They found inhabited houses now and then, but all the men of military age were gone away and the old men, the women and the children would answer nothing. The women were not afraid to tell the Yankees what they thought of them, and in this war which was never a war on women the troopers merely laughed, or, if they felt anger, they hid it.

On they went through night and day, and now they drew near to Sheridan. Scouts in blue met them and the gallant column shook their sabers and saluted. Yes, it was true, they said, that Sheridan was gathering a fine army and he and all of his men were eager to march, but Colonel Hertford's force, sent by General Grant to help, would be welcomed with shouts. The fame of its three colonels had gone on before.

It was bright noon when they approached the northern end of the valley, and Dick saw a horseman followed by a group of about twenty men galloping toward them. The leader was a short, slender man, sitting firmly in his saddle.

"General Sheridan!" exclaimed Shepard.

Colonel Hertford instantly ordered his trumpeter to sound a signal, and the troopers, stopping and drawing up in a long line, awaited the man who was to command them, and who was coming on so fast. Again Dick examined him closely through his glasses, and he saw the young, tanned face under the broad brim of his hat, and the keen, flashing eyes. He noticed also how small he was. Sheridan was but five feet five inches in height and he weighed in the momentous campaign now about to begin, only one hundred and fifteen pounds! As slight as a young boy, he gave, nevertheless, an impression of the greatest vigor and endurance.

He reined in his horse a score of yards in front of the long line and was about to speak to Colonel Hertford, who sat his saddle before it, Colonel Winchester and Colonel Bedford on either side of him, but there was a sudden interruption.

Fifteen hundred sabers flashed aloft, the blazing sunlight glittering for a moment on their broad blades. Then they swept in mighty curves, all together, and from fifteen hundred throats thundered:

"Sheridan! Sheridan! Sheridan!"

The sabers made another flashing curve, sank back into their scabbards, and the men were silent.

Sheridan's tanned face flushed deeply, and a great light leaped up in his eyes, as he received the magnificent salute. His own sword sprang out, and made the salute in reply. Then, riding a little closer, he said in a loud, clear tone that all could hear:

"Men, I have been looking for you! I have come forward to meet you! I knew that you were great horsemen, gallant soldiers, but I see that you are even greater and more gallant men than I had hoped. The Army of the Potomac has sent its best as a gift to the Army of the Shenandoah. Men, I thank you for this welcome, the warmest I have ever received!"

Again the sabers flashed aloft, made their glittering curve, and again from muscular throats came the thunderous cheer:

"Sheridan! Sheridan! Sheridan!"

Then the young general shook hands heartily with the three colonels, the young aides were introduced, and with Sheridan himself at their head the whole column swept off toward the north, and to the camp of the Army of the Shenandoah which lay but a little distance away.

CHAPTER VI
THE FISHERMEN

The welcome that the column found in Sheridan's camp was as warm as they had hoped, and more. Fifteen hundred sabers such as theirs were not to be valued lightly, and Sheridan knew well the worth of three such colonels as Hertford, Winchester and Bedford, with all three of whom he was acquainted personally, and with whose records he was familiar. Dick, Pennington and Warner also came in for his notice, and he recalled having seen Dick at the fierce battle of Perryville in Kentucky, a fact of which Dick was very proud.

"Now don't become too haughty because he remembers you," said Warner reprovingly. "Bear in mind that trifles sometimes stick longer in our minds than more important things."

"It's just jealousy on your part," said Dick. "You New Englanders are able people, but you can't bear for anybody else to achieve distinction."

"We don't have to feel that jealousy often," said Warner calmly.

"Merit like charity begins with you at home."

"And modesty can't keep us from admitting it, but you Kentuckians do fight well—under our direction."

"Don't talk with him, Dick," said Pennington. "Against his wall of mountainous conceit wisdom breaks in vain."

"I'm glad to see you expressing yourself so poetically, Frank," said Warner. "The New England seed planted in Nebraska will flower into bloom some day."

Sergeant Whitley came at that moment and asked them to go and see the new horses provided for them, and the three went with him, friends bound to one another by hooks of steel. The horses given to them by special favor of Sheridan in place of their worn-out mounts, were splendid animals, and Sergeant Whitley himself had prepared them for their first appearance before their new masters.

"They'll do! They'll do!" said Dick with enthusiasm. "Grand fellows! They ought to carry us anywhere!"

"Upon this point I must confess myself somewhat your inferior," said Warner in his precise manner. "The mountainous character of our state keeps us from making horses a specialty. You, I believe, in Kentucky, pay great attention to their breeding, and so I ask you, young Mr. Mason, if the horse chosen for me is all that he should be."

"He asks it as a matter of condescension, Dick, and not as a favor," said Pennington.

"It's all right any way you take it," laughed Dick. "Yes, George, your horse has no defect. You can always lead the charge on him against Early."

"If I'm not at the very front I expect to be somewhere near it," said Warner. "But don't you like the looks of this camp, boys? It shows order, method and precision. Everything has been done according to the best algebraic formulae. I call it mathematics, charged with fire. Our Little Phil is a great commander. One can feel his spirit in the air all about us."

Dick himself had noticed the military workmanship and that, too, of a high order, and he understood thoroughly that Sheridan had gathered a most formidable army. It was not much short of thirty thousand men, veteran troops, and he had with him Wright, Emory, Crook, Merritt, Averill, Torbert, Wilson and Grover, all able generals. Nor had Sheridan neglected to inform himself of the country over which he intended to march. With his lieutenant of engineers, Meigs, a man of great talent, he had spent days and nights studying maps of the valley. Now he knew all the creeks and brooks and roads and towns, and he understood the country as well as Early himself, who faced him with as large a Confederate force as he could gather.

Dick and his comrades expected immediate action, but it did not come. They lingered for days, due, they supposed, to orders from Washington, but they did not bother themselves about it, as they liked their new camp and were making many new friends. September days passed and they saw the summer turning into autumn. The mountains in the distance looked blue, but, near at hand, their foliage had turned brown. The great heat gave way to a crisper air and the lads who had come from the trenches before Petersburg enjoyed for a little while the luxury of early autumn and illimitable space.

They rode now and then with the cavalry outposts. Early and his men stretched across the valley to oppose them, and often Northern and Southern pickets were in touch, though they seldom fired upon one another. Dick, whenever he rode with the advanced guard, watched for Harry Kenton, St. Clair and Langdon, but it was nearly a week before he saw them. Then they rode with a small group, headed by two elderly but very upright men, whom he knew to be Colonel Leonidas Talbot and Lieutenant Colonel Hector St. Hilaire.

He felt genuine gladness, and, shouting at the top of his voice, he waved his hand. They recognized him, and all waved a welcome in return. He saw the two colonels studying him through their glasses, but he knew that no attack would be made upon him and the little party with which he rode. It was one of those increasing intervals of peace and friendship between battles. The longer the war and the greater the losses the less men troubled themselves to shoot one another save when real battle was joined.

They were about four hundred yards apart and Dick used his glasses also, enabling him to see that the young Southern officers were unwounded—Langdon's slight hurt had healed long since—and were strong and hearty. He thought it likely that they, as well as he, had found the brief period of rest and freedom from war a genuine luxury.

He waved his hand once more, and they waved back as before. Then the course of the two little troops took them away from each other, and the Southerners were hid from his view by a belt of forest. But he was very glad that he had seen them. It had been almost as if there were no war.

Dick rode back to the camp, gave his horse to an orderly, and, walking toward his tent, was met by Warner and Pennington, carrying long slender rods on their shoulders—Warner in fact carrying two.

"What's this?" he exclaimed.

"We're going fishing," replied Warner. "We've permission for you also. There's a fine stream about a half mile west of us, running through the woods, and it's been fished in but little since the war started. Here, take your rod! You don't expect me to carry it for you any longer do you? It has a good hook and line and it's easy for us to find bait under a big stone on soft soil."

"Thank you, George," said Dick happily. "You couldn't keep me from going with you two. Do you know, I haven't been fishing in more than three years, and me not yet of age?"

"Well, now's your chance, and you may not have another until after the war is over. They say it's a fine stream, though, of course, it's not like the beautiful little rivers of Vermont, that come dashing down from the mountains all molten silver, where they're not white foam. Splendid fish! Splendid rivers! Splendid sport! Dick, do you think I'm facing now in the exact direction of Vermont?"

He had turned about and was gazing with a rapt look into the northeast.

"I should say," said Dick, "that if your gaze went far enough it would strike squarely upon the Green Mountains of Vermont."

Warner's hand rose in a slow and majestic salute.

"Great little state, mother of men, I salute thee!" he said. "Thou art stern and yet beautiful to the eye and thy sons love thee! I, who am but one among them, love all thy rocks, and clear streams, and noble mountains and green foliage! Here, from the battle fields and across the distance I salute thee, O great little state! O mother of men!"

"Quite dithyrambic," said Dick, "and now that your burst of rhetoric is over let's go on and catch our fish. Will you also use your romantic science of mathematics in fishing? By the way, what has become of that little algebra book of yours?"

"It's here," said Warner, taking it from the breast pocket of his tunic. "I never part with it and I most certainly expect to use its principles when I reach the fishing stream. Let x express my equipment and myself, let y equal skill and patience; x we shall say also equals the number 7, while y equals the number 5. Now the fish are represented by z which is equal to 12. It is obvious even to slow minds like yours and Pennington's that neither x nor y alone can equal z, the fish, otherwise 12, but when combined they represent that value exactly, that is x plus y equals 12. So, if I and my equipment coordinate perfectly with my skill and patience, which most certainly will happen, the fish are as good as caught by me already. The rest is a mere matter of counting."

"Best give in, Dick," said Pennington. "He'll always prove to you by his algebra that he knows everything, and that everything he does is right. Of course, he's the best fisherman in the world!"

"I'd have you to know, Francis Pennington," said Warner, with dignity, "that I was a very good fisherman when I was five years old, and that I've been improving ever since, and that Vermont is full of fine deep streams, in which one can fish with pleasure and profit. What do you know, you prairie-bred young ruffian, about fishing? I've heard that your creeks and brooks are nothing but strips of muddy dew. The Platte River itself, I believe, is nearly two inches deep at its deepest parts. I don't suppose there's another stream in America which takes up so much space on the map and so little on the ground."

"The Platte is a noble river," rejoined Pennington. "What it lacks in depth it makes up in length, and I'll not have it insulted by anybody in its absence."

While they talked they passed through the brown woods and came to the creek, flowing with a fine volume of water down from the mountains into one of the rivers of the valley.

"It's up to its advertisements," said Warner, looking at it with satisfaction. "It's clear, deep and it ought to have plenty of good fish. I see a snug place between the roots of that oak growing upon the bank, and there I sit."

"There are plenty of good places," said Dick, as they seated themselves and unwrapped their lines, "and I've a notion that our fishing is going to prove good. Isn't it fine? Why, it's like being back home!"

"Time's rolled back and we're just boys again," said Pennington.

"Don't try to be poetic, Frank," said Warner. "I've told you already that a man who has nothing but muddy streaks of dew to fish in can't know anything about fishing."

"Stop quarreling, you two," said Dick. "Don't you know that such voices as yours raised in loud tones would scare away the boldest fish that ever swam?"

The three cast their lines out into the stream. They were of the old-fashioned kind, a hook, a lead sinker, and a cork on the line to keep it from sinking too far. Dick had used just such an equipment since he was eight years old, in the little river at Pendleton, and now he was anxious to prove to himself that he had not lost his skill. All three were as eager to catch a fish as they were to win a battle, and, for the time, the war was forgotten. It seemed to Dick as he sat on the brown turf between the enclosing roots of the tree, and leaning against its trunk, that his lost youth had returned. He was just a boy again, fishing and with no care save to raise something on his hook. The wood, although small, was dense, and it shut out all view of the army. Nor did any martial sounds come to them. The rustle of the leaves under the gentle wind was soothing. He was back at Pendleton. Harry Kenton was fishing farther up the stream, and so were other boys, his old friends of the little town.

The bit of forest was to all intents a wilderness just then, and it was so pleasant in the comfortable place between the supporting roots of the tree that Dick fell into a dreamy state, in which all things were delightful. It was perhaps the power of contrast, but after so much riding and fighting he felt a sheer physical pleasure in sitting there and watching the clear stream flow swiftly by. He smiled too at the way in which his cork bobbed up and down on the water, and he began to feel that it would not matter much whether he caught any fish or not. It was just enough to sit there and go through all the motions of fishing.

A shout from a point twenty yards below and he looked up, startled, from his dream.

"A bite!" exclaimed Warner, "I thought I had him, but he slipped off the hook! I raised him to the surface and I know he was two feet long!"

"Nine inches, probably," said Dick. "Allow at least fifteen inches for your imagination, George."

"I suppose you're right, Dick. At least, I have to do it down here. If it were a Vermont river he'd be really two feet long."

Dick heard his line and sinker strike the water again, and then silence returned to the little wood, but it did not endure long. From a point beyond Warner came a shout, and this was undeniably a cry of triumph. It was accompanied by a swishing through the air and the sound of an object striking the leaves.

"I got him! I got him! I got him!" exclaimed Pennington, dancing about as if he were only twelve years old.

Dick stood up and saw that Pennington, in truth, had caught a fine fish, at least a foot long, which was now squirming over the leaves, its silver scales gleaming.

"It seems to me," said Dick, "that the very young Territory of Nebraska has scored over the veteran State of Vermont."

"A victor merely in a preliminary skirmish," said Warner serenely. "The fish happened to be there. Frank's baited hook was close by. The fish was hungry and the result was a mathematical certainty. Frank is entitled to no credit whatever. As for me, I lure my fish within the catching area."

As Dick resumed his seat he felt a sharp pull at his own line, and drawing it in smartly he drew with it a fish as large as Pennington's, a fact that he announced with pride.

"I think, Frank," he called, "that this is not good old Vermont's day. Either we're more skillful or the fish like us better than they do Warner. Which do you think it is?"

"It's both, Dick."

"On second thought, I don't agree with you, Frank. The fish in this river are entirely new to us. They've never seen us before, and they know nothing about us by hearsay and reputation. It's a case of skill, pure skill, Frank. We've got Mr. Vermont down, and we're going to hold him down."

Warner said nothing, but Dick rose up a little and saw his face. It was red, the teeth clenched tightly, and the mouth drawn down at the corners. His eyes were fixed eagerly on his cork in the hope of seeing it bob for a moment and then be drawn swiftly under.

"Good old George," said Dick, under his breath. "He hates to be beaten—well, so do we all."

Pennington caught another fish and then Dick drew in his second. Warner did not have a bite since his first miss and his two comrades did not spare him. They insinuated that there were no fish in Vermont, and they doubted whether the state had any rivers either. In any event it was obvious that Warner had never fished before. For several minutes they carried on this conversation, the words, in a way, as they went back and forth, passing directly by his head. But Warner did not speak. He merely clenched his teeth more tightly and watched his floating cork. Meanwhile Dick caught his third fish and then Pennington equaled him. Now their taunts, veiled but little, became more numerous.

Warner never spoke, nor did he take his eyes from his cork. He had heard every word, but he would not show annoyance. He was compelled to see Dick draw in yet another fine fellow, while his own cork seemed to have all the qualities of a lifeboat. It danced and bobbed around, but apparently it had not the slightest intention of sinking. Why did he have such luck, or rather lack of it? Was fortune going to prove unkind to the good old rock-ribbed Green Mountain State?

There came a tremendous jerk upon the line! The cork shot down like a bullet, but Warner, making a mighty pull and snap with the rod, landed a glorious gleaming fish upon the bank, a full two feet in length, probably as large as any that had ever been caught in that stream. He detached the hook and looked down at his squirming prize, while Dick and Pennington also came running to see.

"I've been waiting for you, my friend," said Warner serenely to the fish. "Various small brothers of yours have come along and looked at my bait, but I've always moved it out of reach, leaving them to fall a prey to my friends who are content with little things. I had to wait for you some time, O King of Fishes, but you came at last and you are mine."

"You can't put him down, Dick, and it's not worth while trying," said Pennington, and Dick agreeing they went back to their own places.

The fishing now went on with uninterrupted success. Dick caught a big fellow too, and so did Pennington. Fortune, after wavering in her choice, decided to favor all three about equally, and they were content. The silvery heaps grew and they rejoiced over the splendid addition they would make to their mess. The colonels would enjoy this fine fresh food, and they were certainly enjoying the taking of it.

They ran out of chaff and fell into silence again, while they fished industriously. Dick, who was farthest up the stream, noticed a small piece of wood floating in the center of the current. It seemed to have been cut freshly. "Loggers at work farther up," he said to himself. "May be cutting wood for the army."

He caught another fish and a fresh chip passed very near his line. Then came a second, and a third touched the line itself. Dick's curiosity was aroused. Loggers at such a time would not take the trouble to throw their chips into the stream. He lifted his line, caught an unusually large white chip on the hook and drew it to the land. When he picked it up and looked at it he whistled. Someone had cut upon its face with a sharp penknife these clear and distinct words:

Yankees Beware
This is our River
Don't Fish in It
These Fish are Ours.
JOHNNY REBS.

"Well, this is surely insolence," said Dick, and calling his comrades he showed them the chip. Both were interested, but Warner had admiration for its sender.

"It shows a due consideration for us," he said. "He merely warns us away as trespassers before shooting at us. And perhaps he's right. The river and the fish in it really belong to them. We're invaders. We came down here to crush rebellion, not to take away property."

"But I'm going to keep my fish, just the same," said Pennington. "You can't crush a rebellion without eating. Nor am I going to quit fishing either."

"Here comes another big white chip," said Dick.

Warner caught it on his hook and towed it in. It bore the inscription, freshly cut:

Let our river alone
Take in your lines
You're in danger,
As you'll soon see.

It was unsigned and they stared at it in wonder.

"Do you think this is really a warning?" said Pennington, "or is it some of the fellows playing tricks on us?"

"I believe it's a warning," said Warner soberly. "Probably a farmer a little distance up the stream has been cutting wood, and these chips have come from his yard, but he didn't send them. Dick, can you tell handwriting when it's done with a knife?"

Dick looked at the chip long and critically.

"It may be imagination," he said, "but the words cut there bear some resemblance to the handwriting of Harry Kenton. He makes a peculiar L and a peculiar A and they're just the same way on this chip. The writing is different on the other chip, but on this one I believe strongly that it's Harry's."

"It looks significant to me," said Warner thoughtfully. "A mile or two farther up, this stream, so I'm told, makes an elbow, and beyond that it comes with a rush out of the mountains. Its banks are lined with woods and thickets and some of the enemy may have slipped in and launched these chips. I've a sort of feeling, Dick, that it's really your cousin and his friends who have done it."

"I incline to that belief myself," said Dick. "You know they're ready to dare anything, and they don't anticipate any great danger, because we don't care to shoot at one another, until the campaign really begins."

"At least," said Warner, "it's best to apply to the problem a good algebraic formula. Here we are in a wood, some distance from our main camp. Messages, bearing a warning either in jest or in earnest, have come floating down from a point which may be within the enemy's country. One of the facts is x and the other is y, but what they amount to is an unknown quantity. Hence we are left in doubt, and when you're in doubt it's best to do the safe thing."

"Which means that we should go back to the camp," said Dick. "But we'll take our fish with us, that's sure."

They began to wind up their lines, but knowing that departure would be prudent they were yet reluctant to go in the face of a hidden danger, which after all might not be real.

"Suppose I climb this tree," said Pennington, indicating a tall elm, "and I may be able to get a good look over the country, while you fellows keep watch."

"Up you go, Frank," said Dick. "George and I will be on guard, pistols in one hand and fish in the other."

Pennington climbed the elm rapidly and then announced from the highest bough able to support him that he saw open country beyond, then more woods, a glimpse of the stream above the elbow, but no human being. He added that he would remain a few minutes in the tree and continue his survey of the country.

Dick's eyes had followed Frank's figure until it disappeared among the brown leaves, and he had listened to him carefully, while he was telling the result of his outlook, but his attention now turned back to the river. No more chips were floating down its stream. Nothing foreign appeared upon the clear surface of its waters, but Dick's sharp vision caught sight of something in a thicket on the far shore that made his heart beat.

It was but little he saw, merely the brown edge of an enormous flap-brimmed hat, but it was enough. Slade and his men undoubtedly were there—practically within the Union lines—and he was the danger! He called up the tree in a fierce sibilant whisper that carried amazingly far:

"Come down, Frank! Come down at once, for your life!"

It was a call so alarming and insistent that Pennington almost dropped from the tree. He was upon the ground, breathless, in a half minute, his fish in one hand and the pistol that he had snatched from his belt in the other.

"What is it?" exclaimed Warner, who had not yet seen anything.

"Slade and his men are in the bush on the other side of the river. The warning was real and I've no doubt Harry sent it. They've seen Frank come down the tree! Drop flat for your lives!"

Again his tone was so compelling that the other two threw themselves flat instantly, and Dick went down with them. They were barely in time. A dozen rifles flashed from the thickets beyond the stream, but all the bullets passed over their heads.

"Now we run for it!" exclaimed Dick, once more in that tone of compelling command. All three rose instantly, though not forgetting their fish and their fishing rods, and ran at their utmost speed for fifty or sixty yards, when at Dick's order they threw themselves flat again. Three or four more shots were fired from the thickets, but they did not come near their targets.

"Thank God for that little river in between us!" said Pennington, piously and sincerely. "Rivers certainly have their uses!"

Then they heard a sharp, shrill note blown upon a whistle.

"That's Slade recalling his men," said Dick. "I heard him use the same whistle in Mississippi and I know it. His wicked little scheme to slaughter us has failed and knowing it he prudently withdraws."

"For which, perhaps, we have a chip to thank," said Warner. "Shall we rise and run again?"

"Yes," said Dick. "I think they've gone, but fifty yards farther and nobody in those thickets can reach us."

They stooped as they ran, and they ran fast, but, when they dropped down again, it was behind a little hill, and they knew that all danger had passed. The thumping of their hearts ceased, and they looked thankfully at one another.

"Our lives were in danger," said Warner proudly, "but I didn't forget my fish. See, the silver beauties!"

"And here are mine too!" said Pennington, holding up his string.

"And mine also!" said Dick.

"I don't like the way we had to run," said Warner. "We were practically within our own lines and we were compelled to be undignified. I've been insulted by that flap-brimmed scoundrel, Slade, and I shall not forget it. If he hangs upon our flank in this campaign I shall make a point of it, if I am able, to present him with a bullet."

The sound of thudding hoofs came, and Colonel Winchester and a troop galloped up.

"We heard shots!" he exclaimed. "What was it?"

Dick held up his fish.

"We've been fishing, sir," he replied, "and as you can see, we've had success, but we were interrupted by the guerrilla Slade, whom I met in Mississippi, and his men. We got off, though, unhurt, and brought our fish with us."

Colonel Winchester's troop numbered more than a hundred men, and crossing the river they beat up the country thoroughly, but they saw no Confederate sign. When he came back Dick told him all the details of the episode, and Colonel Winchester agreed with him that Harry had sent the warning.

"You'd better keep it to yourself," he said. "It's too vague and mysterious to make a peg upon which to hang anything. Since we've cleared the bush of enemies we'll go eat the fish you and your friends have caught."

Sergeant Whitley cooked them, and, as Dick and a score of others sat around the fire and ate fish for supper, they were so exuberant and chaffed so much that he forgot for the time all about Slade.

CHAPTER VII
SHERIDAN'S ATTACK

More days passed and the army of Sheridan lay waiting at the head of the valley, apparently without any aim in view. But Dick knew that if Little Phil delayed it was with good cause. As Colonel Winchester was high in the general's confidence Dick saw the commander every day. He soon learned that he was of an intensely energetic and active nature, and that he must put a powerful rein upon himself to hold back, when he had such a fine army to lead.

Many of the younger officers expressed impatience and Dick saw by the newspapers that the North too was chafing at the delay. Newspapers from the great cities, New York, Philadelphia and Boston, reached their camp and they always read them eagerly. Criticisms were leveled at Sheridan, and from the appearance of things they had warrant, but Dick had faith in their leader. Yet another period of depression had come in the North. The loss of life in Grant's campaign through the Wilderness had been tremendous, and now he seemed to be held indefinitely by Lee in the trenches before Petersburg. The Confederacy, after so many great battles, and such a prodigious roll of killed and wounded, was still a nut uncracked, and Sheridan, who was expected to go up the valley and turn the Southern flank, was resting quietly in his camp.

Such was the face of matters, but Dick knew that, beneath, great plans were in the making and that the armies would soon stir. The more he saw of Sheridan the more he was impressed by him. He might prove to be the Stonewall Jackson of the North. Young, eager, brave, he never fell into the fault some of the other Union commanders had of overestimating the enemy. He always had a cheery word for his young officers, and when he was not poring over the maps with his lieutenant of engineers, Meigs, he was inspecting his troops, and seeing that their equipment and discipline were carried to the highest pitch. He was the very essence of activity and the army, although not yet moving, felt at all times the tonic of his presence.

Cavalry detachments were sent out on a wider circle. Slade and his men had no opportunity to come so close again, but Shepard informed Dick that he was in the mountains hemming in the valley on the west, and that the statement of his having formed a junction with a band under Skelly from the Alleghanies was true. He had seen the big man and the little man together and they had several hundred followers.

Shepard in these days showed an almost superhuman activity. He would leave the camp, disguised as a civilian, and after covering a great distance and risking his life a dozen times he would return with precious information. A few hours of rest and he was gone again on a like errand. He seemed to be burning with an inward fire, not a fire that consumed him, but a fire of triumph. Dick, who had formed a great friendship with him and who saw him often, had never known him to speak more sanguine words. Always cautious and reserved in his opinions, he talked now of the certainty of victory. He told them that the South was not only failing in men, having none to fill up its shattered ranks, but that food also was failing. The time would come, with the steel belt of the Northern navy about it and the Northern armies pressing in on every side, when the South would face starvation.

But a day arrived when there were signs of impending movements in the great Northern camp. Long columns of wagons were made ready and orders were issued for the vanguard of cavalry to start at an appointed time. Then, to the intense disappointment of the valiant young troops, the orders were countermanded and the whole army settled back into its quarters. Dick, who persistently refused to be a grumbler, knew that a cause must exist for such an action, but before he could wonder about it long Colonel Winchester told him, Warner and Pennington to have their horses saddled, and be ready to ride at a moment's notice.

"We're to be a part of General Sheridan's escort," he said, "and we're to go to a little place called Charlestown."

The three were delighted. They were eager to move, and above all in the train of Sheridan. The mission must be of great importance or the commander himself would not ride upon it. Hence they saddled up in five minutes, hoping that the call would come in the next five.

"Did Colonel Winchester tell you why we were going to ride?" asked Warner of Dick.

"No."

"Then perhaps we're going to receive the surrender of Early and all his men."

Dick laughed.

"I've heard that old Jube Early is one of the hardest swearers in the Southern army," he said, "and I've heard, too, that he's just as hard a fighter. I don't think he'll be handing us his surrender on a silver platter at Charlestown or anywhere else."

"I know it," said Warner. "I was only joking, but I'm wondering why we go."

In ten minutes an orderly came with a message for them and they were in the saddle as quickly as if they intended to ride to a charge. Sheridan himself and his staff and escort were as swift as they, and the whole troop swept away with a thunder of hoofs and the blood leaping in their veins. It was now almost the middle of September, and the wind that blew down from the crest of the mountains had a cool breath. It fanned Dick's face and the great pulse in his throat leaped. He felt that this ride must portend some important movement. Sheridan would not gallop away from his main camp, except on a vital issue.

It was not a long distance to Charlestown, and when they arrived there they dismounted and waited. Dick saw Colonel Winchester's face express great expectancy and he must know why they waited, but the youth did not ask him any questions, although his own curiosity increased.

An hour passed, and then a short, thickset, bearded man, accompanied by a small staff, appeared. Dick drew a deep breath. It was General Grant, Commander-in-Chief of all the armies of the Union, and Sheridan hastened forward to meet him. Then the two, with several of the senior officers, went into a house, while the younger men remained outside, and on guard.

"I knew that we were waiting for somebody of importance," said Warner, "but I didn't dream that it was the biggest man we've got in the field."

"Didn't your algebra give you any hint of it?" asked Dick.

"No. An algebra reasons. It doesn't talk and waste its time in idle chatter."

The young officers with their horses walked back and forth a long time, while Grant and Sheridan talked. Dick, surprised that Grant had left the trenches before Petersburg and had come so far to meet his lieutenant, felt that the meeting must be momentous. But it was even more crowded with the beginnings of great events than he thought. Grant, as he wrote long afterward, had come prepared with a plan of campaign for Sheridan, but, as he wrote, "seeing that he was so clear and so positive in his views I said nothing about this and did not take it out of my pocket." It was a quality of Grant's greatness, like that of Lee, to listen to a lieutenant, and when he thought his plan was better than his own to adopt the lieutenant's and put his own away.

In that memorable interview, from which such stirring campaigns dated, Grant was impressed more and more by the earnestness and clearness of the famous Little Phil, and, when they parted, he gave him a free rein and an open road. Sheridan, when they rode away from the conference, was sober and thoughtful. He was to carry out his own plan, but the full weight of the responsibility would be his, and it was very great for a young man who was not much more than thirty.

But Dick and his comrades felt exultation, and did not try to hide it. Now that Grant himself had come to see Sheridan the army was bound to move. Pennington looked toward the South and waved his hand.

"You've been waiting for us a long time, old Jube," he said, "but we're coming. And you'll see and hear our resistless tread."

"But don't forget, Frank," said Warner soberly, "that we'll have a big bill of lives to pay. We don't ride unhurt over the Johnnies."

"Don't I know it?" said Pennington. "Haven't I been learning it every day for three years?"

Action was prompt as the young officers had hoped. The very next day after the meeting with his superior, Sheridan prepared to march, and the hopes of Dick and his friends rose very high. They did not know that daring Southern spies had learned of the meeting of Grant and Sheridan, and Early, judging that it portended a great movement against him, was already consolidating his forces and preparing to meet it. And Jubal Early was an able and valiant general.

Dick did not sleep that night. All had received orders to hold themselves in readiness for an instant march, and his blood tingled with expectancy. At midnight the Winchester regiment rode off to the left to join the cavalry under Wilson which was to lead the advance, moving along a pike road and then crossing the little river Opequan.

Dick rode close behind Colonel Winchester and Warner and Pennington were on either side of him. Not far away from them was Sergeant Whitley, ready for use as a scout. Shepard had disappeared already in the darkness. They joined Wilson's command and waited in silence. At three o'clock in the morning the word to advance was given and the whole division marched forward in the starlight.

They had not gone far before Shepard rode back telling them that the crossing of the Opequan was guarded by Confederate troops. The cavalry increased their speed. After the long period of inaction they were anxious to come to grips with their foe. Dick still rode knee to knee with Warner and Pennington, as they went on at a rapid pace in the starlight, the fields and strips of forest gliding past. Men on horseback talk less at night than in the day and moreover these had little to say. Their part was action, and they were waiting to see what the little Opequan would disclose to them.

"Do you think they'll have a big force at the river?" asked Pennington.

"No," replied Dick. "I fancy from what we've heard of Early's army that he won't have the men to spare."

"But we can look for a brush there," said Warner.

The night began to darken as a premonition of the coming dawn, a veil of vapor was drawn before the stars, trees blended together and the air became chill. Then the vapor was pierced in the east by a lance of light. The rift widened, and the pale light of the first dawn appeared over the hills. Dick, using his glasses, saw a flash which he knew was the Opequan. And with that silvery gleam of water came other flashes of red and rapid crackling reports. The Southern sharpshooters along the stream were already opening fire.

A great shout went up from the cavalry. All the forces restrained so long in these young men burst forth. The dawn was now deepening rapidly, its pallor turning to silver, and the river, for a long length, lay clear to view before them. Trumpets to right and left and in the center sounded the charge, the mellow notes coming back in many echoes.

The horsemen firing their own carbines and swinging aloft their sabers, galloped forward in a mighty rush. The beat of hundreds of hoofs made a steady sound, insistent and threatening. The yellow light of the sun, replacing the silver of the first dawn, gilded them with gold, glittering on the upraised blades and tense faces. The bullets of the Southern sharpshooters, in the bushes and trees along the Opequan, crashed among them, and horses and men went down, but the mighty sweep of the mass was not delayed for an instant.

Dick was flourishing the cavalry saber that he now carried and was shouting with the rest. Nearer and nearer came the belt of clear water, and the fire of the Southern skirmishers increased in volume and accuracy. No great Southern force was there, but the men were full of courage and activity. Their rifle fire emptied many of the Northern saddles. A bullet went through the sleeve of Dick's tunic and grazed the skin, but he only felt a slight burning touch and then soon forgot it.

Then the whole column started together, as they swept into the Opequan, driving before them through sheer weight of mass the skirmishers and sharpshooters, who were hidden among the trees and thickets. The water itself proved but little obstacle. It was churned to foam by hundreds of trampling hoofs, and Dick felt it falling upon him like rain, but the drops were cool and refreshing.

Still at a gallop, they emerged from the river, wet and dripping, so much water had been dashed up by the beating hoofs, and charged straight on, driving the scattered Southern riflemen before them. Dick's exultation swelled, and so did that of Warner and Pennington. The young Nebraskan was compelled to give voice to his.

"Hurrah!" he shouted. "We'll gallop the whole length of the valley! Nothing can stop us!"

But Warner, naturally cautious, despite his rejoicings, would not go so far.

"Not the whole length of the valley, Frank!" he exclaimed. "Only half of it!"

"All or nothing!" shouted Pennington, carried away by his enthusiasm. "Hurrah! Hurrah!"

Before them now lay a small earthwork, from which field pieces began to send ugly gusts of fire, but so great was the sweep of the cavalry that they charged directly upon it. The defenders, too few to hold it, withdrew and retreated in haste, and in a few minutes the Northern cavalry were in possession.

"Didn't I tell you," exclaimed Pennington, "that we were going to gallop the whole length of the valley! We've taken a fort with horsemen!"

"Yes," said Warner, "but we'll stop here a while. Listen to the trumpets sounding the halt, and yonder you can see the main lines of the Johnnies."

It was obvious that it was unwise to go farther until the whole army came up, as they heard other trumpets calling now, and they were not their own but those of their enemies. Early had not been caught napping. The dark lines of his infantry were advancing to retake the little fort. The cavalry was reduced in an instant from the offensive to the defensive, and dismounting and sending their horses to the rear, where they were held by every tenth man, they waited with carbines ready, the masses of men in gray bearing down upon them. Dick wondered if the Invincibles were there before him. Second thought told him that it was unlikely, as the advancing troops were infantry, and he knew that the Invincibles were now mounted.

"Now, lads," said Colonel Winchester, going down the ranks, "ready with your rifles!"

The Southern infantry came on to the steady beating of a drum somewhere, but as they drew near the fort a sheet of bullets poured upon them, and drove them back, leaving the ground sprinkled with the fallen. Again and again they reformed and returned to the charge always to meet the same fate.

"Brave fellows!" exclaimed Warner, "but they can't retake this fort from us!"

After the last repulse Colonel Winchester drew out his men, mounted them, and charging the infantry in flank sent them far down the road toward Winchester, where heavy columns came to their support. But the Winchester men had time to breathe, and also to exult, as they had suffered but little loss. While they remained at the captured fort, awaiting further orders, they watched the battle elsewhere, flaring in a long irregular line across the valley.

The rifle fire was heavy and the big guns of Early were sweeping the roads with shell and grapeshot. As well as Dick could see through his glasses, the only success yet achieved was that of the cavalry at the fort. Sheridan himself had not yet appeared, and the hopes of the three sank a little. They had seen so many triumphs nearly achieved and then lost that they could believe in nothing until it was done.

But the morning was yet very young. While the east had long been full of light, the golden glow was just enveloping the west. The rifles crashed incessantly and the heavy thunder of the cannon gave the steady sound a deeper note. The fire of the defending Southern force made a red stream across the hills and fields.

"It's too early to have a battle," said Warner, looking at the sun, which was not yet far above the horizon.

"Too early for us or too early for the Johnnies?" said Pennington. "I think, Dick, I see those rebel friends of yours. Turn your glasses to the right, and look at that regiment of horses by the edge of the grove. I see at the head of it two men with longish hair. Apparently they are elderly, and they must be Colonel Talbot and Lieutenant Colonel St. Hilaire."

Dick turned his glasses eagerly and the officers of the Invincibles were at once recognizable to his more familiar eye. He could not mistake Colonel Leonidas Talbot and Lieutenant Colonel Hector St. Hilaire, both of whom were watching the progress of the battle through glasses, and he knew that the four young men who sat their horses just behind them were Harry, St. Clair, Dalton and Langdon.

As no further attack was made on the fort, and Colonel Winchester's troop remained stationary for the time, Dick kept his glasses bearing continually upon the Invincibles. The glasses were powerful and they told him much. He inferred from the manner in which the men were drawn up that they would charge soon. Near them a battery of four Confederate guns was planted on a hill, and it was firing rapidly and effectively, sending shell and shrapnel into advancing lines of blue infantry.

A singular feeling took hold of him, one of which he was not then conscious. He knew six of the officers who sat in the front of the Invincibles, and one of them was his own cousin, almost his brother. He did not know a soul in the blue columns advancing upon them, and his hopes and fears centered suddenly around that little group of six.

The wood was filled with Southern infantry, as it was now spouting flame, and the battery continued to thunder as fast as the men could reload and fire. The Invincibles who carried short rifles, much like the carbines of the North, raised them and pulled the triggers. Many in the blue column fell, but the others went on without faltering.

Dick knew from long experience what would follow, and he watched it alike with the eye and the mind that divines. Either his eye or his fancy saw the Invincibles lean forward a little, fasten their rifles, shake loose the reins with one hand, and drop the other hand to the hilt of the saber. It was certain that in the next minute they would charge.

He saw a trumpeter raise a trumpet to his lips and blow, loud and shrill. Then the column of the Invincibles leaped forward, the necks of the horses outstretched, the men raising their sabers and flashing them above their heads. Dick drew deep breaths and his pulses beat painfully. Had he realized what his wishes were then he would have considered himself a traitor. In those swift moments his heart was with the Invincibles and not with the blue columns that stood up against them.

He saw the gray horsemen sweep forward into a cloud of fire and smoke, in which he caught the occasional flash of a saber. The combat behind the veil lasted only a minute or two, though it seemed an hour to Dick, and then he saw the blue infantry reeling back, their advance checked by the charge of the Invincibles. A cheer rose in Dick's throat, but he checked it, and then, remembering, he trembled in a brief chill, as if shaken by the knowledge that for a few moments at least he had not been true to the cause for which he fought.

"A gallant charge those Johnnies made," said Warner, "and it's been effective, too. Our men are falling back, while the Johnnies are returning to their place near the wood."

Dick was straining his eyes through the glasses to see whether any one of the five whom he knew had fallen, but as the Invincibles returned from their victorious charge in a close mass it was impossible for him to tell. A number of saddles had been emptied, as riderless horses were galloping wildly over the plain. He sighed a little and replaced his glasses in their case.

"Here come more of our cavalry!" said Warner.

They heard the heavy beat of many hoofs and in an instant many horsemen swarmed about them. It was Sheridan himself who led them, his face flushed and eager and his eyes blazing. He was a little man, but he was electric in his energy, and his very presence seemed to communicate more spirit and fire to the troops. The officers crowded about him, and, while he swept the field with his glasses, he also gave a rapid command.

The Southern resistance, despite inferior numbers, was valiant and enduring. Their heavy guns were pouring a deadly fire upon the Northern center. Beyond the taking of the fort by the cavalry the Army of the Shenandoah had made no progress, and the Southern troops were rapidly concentrating at every critical point. Old Jube Early, mighty swearer, was proving himself a master of men.

Dick could not watch Sheridan long, as the cavalry were quickly sent off to the left to clear away skirmishers, and let the infantry and artillery get up on that front. There were many groups of trees, and from every one of these the Southern riflemen sent swarms of bullets. It seemed to Dick that he was preserved miraculously. Many a bullet coming straight for his head must have turned aside at the last moment to seek a target elsewhere. To him at least these bullets were merciful that morning.

But they cleared the ground, though some of their own saddles were emptied, and the infantry and the artillery came up behind them. The big guns were planted and began to reply to those of the South. Yet the Confederate lines still held fast. Clouds of smoke floated over the field, but whenever they lifted sufficiently Dick saw the gray army maintaining all its positions. He looked for the Invincibles again but could not find them. Doubtless they were hid from his view by the hills.

"It's anybody's fight," said Warner, surveying the field with his cool, mathematical eye. "We have the greater numbers but our infantry are coming up slowly and, besides, the enemy has the advantage of interior lines."

"And the morning wanes," said Dick. "I thought we'd make a grand rush and sweep over 'em!"

"Oh, these Johnnies are tough. They have to be. There's not much marching over the other by either side in this war."

A heavy battle of cannon and rifles, with no advantage to either side, went on for a long time. Dick saw Sheridan galloping here and there, and urging on his troops, but the reserves were slow in coming and he was not yet able to hurl his full strength upon his enemy. Noon came, the battle already having lasted four or five hours, and Sheridan had no triumph to show, save the little fort that the cavalry had seized early in the morning.

"Do you think we'll have to draw off?" asked Pennington.

"Maybe we'll have to, but we won't," replied Dick. "Sheridan refuses to recognize necessities when they're not in his favor. You'll now see the difference between a man and men."

Colonel Winchester's regiment was sent off further to the left to prevent any flanking movement, but they could still see most of the field. For the moment they were not engaged, and they watched the thrilling and terrific panorama as it passed before them.

Colonel Winchester himself suddenly broke from his calm and pointed to the rear of the Union lines.

"Look!" he exclaimed. "All our reserves of artillery and infantry are coming up! The whole army will now advance!"

They saw very clearly the deepening of the lines in the center. Sheridan was there massing the new troops for the attack, and soon the trumpets sounded the charge along the whole front. The Northern batteries redoubled their fire, and the South, knowing that a heavier shock of battle was coming, replied in kind.

"Here we go again!" cried Pennington, and the horsemen rode straight at their enemy. It seemed to Dick that the Southern regiments came forward to meet them and a battle long, fierce and wavering in its fortunes ensued. The wing to which the Winchesters belonged pressed forward, driving their enemy before them, only to be caught when they went too far by a savage flanking fire of artillery. Early had brought in his reserve guns, and so powerful was their attack that at this point the Northern line was almost severed, and a Southern wedge was driven into the gap.

But Sheridan did not despair. He had a keen eye and a collected mind, infused with a fiery spirit. Where his line had been weakened he sent new troops. With charge after charge he drove the Confederates out of the gap and closed it up. A whole division was then hurled with its full weight against the Southern line and broke it, although the gallant general who led the column fell shot through the heart.

But Early formed new lines. It was only a temporary success for Sheridan. An important division of cavalry sent on a wide flanking movement had not yet arrived, and he wondered why. Perhaps the thought came into his own dauntless heart that he might not succeed at all, but, if so, he hid it, and called up fresh resources of strength and courage. It was now far into the afternoon but he resolved nevertheless to win victory before the day was over. Everywhere the call for a new charge was sounded.

The Winchesters had a good trumpeter, a deep-chested young fellow who loved to blow forth mellow notes, and now as his brazen instrument sang the song that summoned men to death the young men unconsciously tightened the grip of the knee on their horses, and leaned a little forward, as if they would see the enemy more closely. To the right the fire grew heavier and heavier, and most of the field was hidden by a thick veil of smoke.

Dick saw other cavalry massing on either side of the Winchester regiment, and he knew their charge was to be one of great weight and importance.

"I feel that we're going to win or lose here," he said to Warner.

"Looks like it," replied the Vermonter, "but I think you can put your money on the cavalry today. It's Sheridan's great striking arm."

"It'll have to strike with all its might, that's sure," said Dick.

He did not know that the force in front of him was commanded by a general from his own state, Breckinridge, once Vice-President of the United States and also high in the councils of the Confederacy. Breckinridge was inspiring his command with the utmost vigor and already his heavy guns were sweeping the front of the Union cavalry, while the riflemen stood ready for the charge.

The great mass of Northern horsemen were eager and impatient. A thrill of anticipation seemed to run through them, as if through one body, and when the final command was given they swept forward in a mighty, irresistible line. In Dick's mind then anticipation became knowledge. He was as sure as he was of his own name that they were going to win.

Again he was knee to knee with Warner and Pennington, and with these good comrades on his right and left he rode into the Southern fire, among the shell and shrapnel and grapeshot and bullets that had swept so often around him. In spite of the most desperate courage, the Southern troops gave way before the terrific onset — they had to give ground or they would have been trampled under the feet of the horses. Cannon and many rifles were taken, and the whole Confederate division was driven in disorder down the road.

Warner's stern calm was broken, and he shouted in delight "We win! We win!" Then Dick and Pennington shouted with him: "We win! We win!" and as the smoke of their own battle lifted they saw that the Union army elsewhere was triumphant also. Sheridan along his whole line was forcing the enemy back toward Winchester, raking him with his heavy guns, and sending charge after charge of cavalry against him. Unable to withstand the weight hurled upon them the Southern troops gave ground at an increased rate.

Yet Early and his veterans never showed greater courage than on that day. His brave officers were everywhere, checking the fugitives and, his best division turning a front of steel to the enemy, covered the retreat. Neither infantry nor cavalry could break it, although every man in the Southern command knew that the battle was lost. Yet they were resolved that it should not become a rout, and though many were falling before the Union force they never shrank for a moment from their terrible task.

The Invincibles were in the division that covered the retreat, and they were exposed at all times to the full measure of the Union attack. Dalton had joined them that morning, but the bullets and shells seemed resolved to spare the four youths and the two colonels, or at least not to doom them to death. Nearly every one of them bore slight wounds, and often men had been killed only a few feet away, but the valiant band, led by its daring officers, fought with undimmed courage and resolution.

"I fear that we have been defeated, Hector," said Colonel Leonidas Talbot.

"Don't call it a defeat, Leonidas. It's merely a masterly retreat before superior numbers, after having inflicted great loss upon the enemy. As you see, we are protecting our withdrawal. Every attack of the enemy upon our division has been beaten back, and we will continue to beat him back as long as he comes."

"True, true, Hector, and the Invincibles are bearing a great part in this glorious feat of arms! But the Yankee general, Sheridan, is not like the other Yankee generals who operated in the valley earlier in the war. We're bound to admit that."

"We do admit it, Leonidas, and alas! we have now no Stonewall Jackson to meet him, brave and capable as General Early is!"

The two colonels looked at the setting sun, and hoped that it would go down with a rush. The division could not hold forever against the tremendous pressure upon it that never ceased, but darkness would put an end to the battle. The first gray of twilight was already showing on the eastern hills, and Early's men still held the broad turnpike leading into the South. Here, fighting with all the desperation of imminent need, they beat off every effort of the Northern cavalry to gain their ground, and when night came they still held it, withdrawing slowly and in good order, while Sheridan's men, exhausted by tremendous marches and heavy losses, were unable to pursue. Yet the North had gained a great and important victory.

* * * *

Darkness closed over a weary but exultant army. It had not destroyed the forces of Early, and it had been able to pursue only three miles. It had lost five thousand men in killed and wounded, but the results, nevertheless, were great and the soldiers knew it. The spell of Southern invincibility in the famous valley, where Jackson had won so often, was broken, and the star of Sheridan had flashed out with brilliancy, to last until the war's close. They knew, too, that they now held all of the valley north of Winchester, and they were soon to know that they would continue to hold it. They commanded also a great railway and a great canal, and the South was cut off from Maryland and Pennsylvania, neither of which it could ever invade again.

Although a far smaller battle than a dozen that had been fought, it was one of the greatest and most complete victories the North had yet won. After a long and seemingly endless deadlock a terrible blow had been struck at the flank of Lee, and the news of the triumph filled the North with joy. It was also given on this occasion to those who had fought in the battle itself to know what they had done. They were not blinded by the dust and shouting of the arena.

Dick with his two young comrades sat beneath an oak and ate the warm food and drank the hot coffee the camp cook brought to them. They had escaped without hurt, and they were very happy over the achievement of the day. The night was crisp, filled with starshine, and the cooking fires had been built along a long line, stretching away like a series of triumphant bonfires.

"I felt this morning that we would win," said Dick.

"I've felt several times that we would win, when we didn't," said Pennington.

"But this time I felt it right. They say that Stonewall Jackson always communicated electricity to his men, and I think our Little Phil has the same quality. Since we first came to him here I haven't doubted that we would win, and when I saw him and Grant talking I knew that we'd be up and doing."

"It's the spirit that Grant showed at Vicksburg," said Warner, seriously. "Little Phil—I intend to call him that when I'm not in his presence, because it's really a term of admiration—is another Grant, only younger and on horseback."

"It's fire that does it," said Dick. "No, Frank, I don't mean this material fire burning before us, but the fire that makes him see obstacles little, and advantages big, the fire that makes him rush over everything to get at the enemy and destroy him."

"Well spoken, Dick," said Warner. "A bit rhetorical, perhaps, but that can be attributed to your youth and the region from which you come."

"It's a great pity, George, about my youth and the region from which I come. If so many youths in blue didn't come from that same region the whole Mississippi Valley might now be in the hands of the Johnnies."

"Didn't I tell you, Dick, not to argue with him?" said Pennington. "What's the use? New England has the writers and when this war is ended victoriously they'll give the credit of all the fighting to New England. And after a while, through the printed word, they'll make other people believe it, too."

"Then you Nebraskans and Kentuckians should learn to read and write. Why blame me?" said Warner with dignity.

Colonel Winchester joined them at that moment, having returned from a brief council with Sheridan and his officers. Dick, without a word, passed him a plate of hot ham and a tin cup of sizzling coffee. The colonel, who looked worn to the bone but triumphant, ate and drank. Then he settled himself into an easy place before one of the fires and said:

"A messenger has gone to General Grant with the news of our victory, and it will certainly be a most welcome message. The news will also be sent to the nearest telegraph station, and then it will travel on hundreds of wires to every part of the North, but while it's flashing through space we'll be riding forward to new battle."

"I expected it, sir," said Dick. "I suppose we advance again at dawn."

"And maybe a little sooner. Now you boys must rest. You've had eighteen hours of marching and fighting. I've been very proud of my regiment today, and fortunately we have escaped without large losses."

"And you sleep, too, sir, do you not?" said Warner, respectfully. "If we've been marching and fighting for eighteen hours so have you."

"I shall do so a little later, but that's no reason why the rest of you should delay. How that coffee and ham refreshed me! I didn't know I was so nearly dead."

"Here's more, Colonel!"

"Thank you, Dick. I believe I will. But as I say, go to sleep. I want all my regiment to sleep. We don't know what is before us tomorrow, but whatever it is it won't be easy. Now you boys have had enough to eat and drink. Into the blankets with you!"

He did not wait to see his order obeyed, but strode away on another hasty errand. But it was obeyed and that, too, without delay. The young warriors rolled themselves in their blankets and hunted a soft place for their heads. But their nerves were not yet quiet, and sleep did not come for a little while. The long lines of fires still glowed, and the sounds of an army came to them. Dick looked up into the starshine. He was still rejoicing in the victory, not because the other side had lost, but because, in his opinion, it brought peace much nearer. He realized as he lay there gazing into the skies that the South could never win as long as the North held fast. And the North was holding fast. The stars as they winked at him seemed to say so.

He propped himself upon his elbow and said:

"George, does your little algebra tell you anything about the meaning of this victory?"

Warner tapped his breast.

"That noble book is here in the inside pocket of my tunic," he replied. "It's not necessary for me to take it out, but tucked away on the 118th page is a neat little problem which just fits this case. Let x equal the Army of Northern Virginia, let y equal the army of Early here in the valley, and let x plus y equal a possibly successful defense by the South. But when y is swept away it's quite certain that x standing alone cannot do so. My algebra tells you on the 118th page, tucked away neatly in a paragraph, that this is the beginning of the end."

"It sounds more like a formula than a problem, George, but still I'm putting my faith in your little algebra book."

"George's algebra is all right," said Pennington, "but it doesn't always go before, it often comes after. It doesn't show us how to do a thing, but proves how we've done it. As for me, I'm pinning my faith to Little Phil. He won a great victory today, when all our other leaders for years have been beaten in the Valley of Virginia, and sometimes beaten disgracefully too."

"Your argument is unanswerable, Frank," said Dick. "I didn't expect such logic from you."

"Oh, I think I'm real bright at times."

"Despite popular belief," said Warner.

"I don't advertise my talents," said Pennington.

"But you ought to. They need it."

Dick laughed.

"Frank," he said, "I give you your own advice to me. Don't argue with him. With him the best proof that he's always right is because he thinks he is."

"I think clearly and directly, which can be said of very few of my friends," rejoined Warner.

Then all three of them laughed and lay down again, resting their heads on soft lumps of turf.

They were under the boughs of a fine oak, on which the leaves were yet thick. Birds, hidden among the leaves, began to sing, and the three, astonished, raised themselves up again. It was a chorus, beautiful and startling, and many other soldiers listened to the sound, so unlike that which they had been hearing all day.

"Strange, isn't it?" said Pennington.

"But fine to hear," said Warner.

"Likely they were in the tree this morning when the battle began," said Dick, "and the cannon and the rifles frightened 'em so much that they stayed close within the leaves. Now they're singing with joy, because it's all over."

"A good guess, I think, Dick," said Warner, "but isn't it beautiful at such a time and such a place? How these little fellows must be swelling their throats! I don't believe they ever sang so well before."

"I didn't think today that I'd be sung to sleep tonight," said Dick, "but it's going to happen."

When his eyes closed and he floated away to slumberland it was to the thrilling song of a bird on a bough above his head.

CHAPTER VIII
THE MESSENGER FROM RICHMOND

It seemed that Dick and his comrades were to see an activity in the valley under Sheridan much like that which Harry and his friends had experienced under Stonewall Jackson earlier in the war. All of the men before they went to sleep that night had felt confirmed in the belief that a strong hand was over them, and that a powerful and clear mind was directing them. There would be no more prodigal waste of men and supplies. No more would a Southern general have an opportunity to beat scattered forces in detail. The Union had given Sheridan a splendid army and a splendid equipment, and he would make the most of both.

Their belief in Sheridan's activity and energy was justified fully, perhaps to their own discomfort, as the trumpets sounded before dawn, and they ate a hasty breakfast, while the valley was yet dark. Then they were ordered to saddle and ride at once.

"What, so early?" exclaimed Pennington. "Why, it's not daylight yet. Isn't this new general of ours overdoing it?"

"We wanted a general who would lead," said Warner, "and we've got him."

"But a battle a day! Isn't that too large an allowance?"

"No. We've a certain number of battles to fight, and the sooner we fight them the sooner the war will be over."

"Here comes the dawn," said Dick, "and the bugles are singing to us to march. It's the cavalry that are to show the way."

The long line of horsemen rode on southward, leaving behind them Winchester, the little city that had been beloved of Jackson, and approached the Massanuttons, the bold range that for a while divided the valley into two parts. The valley was twenty miles wide before they came to the Massanuttons, but after the division the western extension for some distance was not more than four miles across, and it was here that they were going. At the narrower part, on Fisher's Hill, Early had strong fortifications, defended by his finest infantry, and Colonel Winchester did not deem it likely that Sheridan would make a frontal attack upon a position so well defended.

It was about noon when the cavalry arrived before the Southern works. Dick, through his glasses, clearly saw the guns and columns of infantry, and also a body of Southern horse, drawn up on one flank of the hill. He fancied that the Invincibles were among them, but at the distance he could not pick them from the rest.

The regiment remained stationary, awaiting the orders of Sheridan, and Dick still used his glasses. He swept them again and again across the Confederate lines, and then he turned his attention to the mountains which here hemmed in the valley to such a straitened width. He saw a signal station of the enemy on a culminating ridge called Three Top Mountain, and as the flags there were waving industriously he knew that every movement of the Union army would be communicated to Early's troops below.

Yet the whole scene despite the fact that it was war, red war, appealed to Dick's sense of the romantic and beautiful. The fertile valley looked picturesque with its woods and fields, and on either side rose the ranges as if to protect it. Mountains like trees always appealed to him, and the steep slopes were wooded densely. Lower down they were brown, with touches of green that yet lingered, but higher up the glowing reds and golds of autumn were beginning to appear. The wind that blew down from the crests was full of life.

Sheridan arrived and, riding before the center of his army, looked long and well at the Southern defenses. Then he called his generals, and some of the colonels, including Winchester, and held a brief council.

"It means," said Warner, while the colonel was yet away at the meeting, "that we won't fight any this afternoon, but that we'll do a lot of riding tonight. That position is too strong to be attacked. It would cost us too many men to take it straight away, but having seen a specimen of Little Phil's quality we know that he'll try something else."

"You mean get on their flank," said Dick. "Maybe we can make a passage along the slopes of the mountains."

"As the idea has occurred to me I take it that it will occur to Little Phil also," said Warner.

"Are you sure that he hasn't thought of it first?"

"My politeness forbids an answer. I am but a lieutenant and he is our commander."

The rest of the day was spent in massing the troops across the valley, the Winchester regiment being sent further west until it was against the base of the Massanuttons. Here Shepard came in the twilight and conferred with Colonel Winchester, who called Dick.

"Dick," he said, "Mr. Shepard thinks he can obtain information of value on the mountain. He has an idea that some fighting may occur, and so it's better for a small detachment to go with him. I've selected you to lead the party, because you're at home in the woods."

"May I take Lieutenant Warner and Lieutenant Pennington with me? It would hurt their feelings to be left behind."

"Yes. Under no circumstances must the feelings of those two young men be hurt," laughed Colonel Winchester.

"And Sergeant Whitley, too? He's probably the best scout in our army. He can follow a trail where there is no trail. He can see in the pitchy dark, and he can hear the leaves falling."

"High recommendations, but they're almost true. Take the sergeant by all means. I fancy you'll need him."

The whole party numbered about a dozen, and Shepard was the guide. It was dismounted, of course, as the first slope they intended to carry was too steep for a horse to climb. They were also heavily armed, it being absolutely certain that Southern riflemen were on Massanutton Mountain.

Dick and Shepard were in the lead, and, climbing up at a sharp angle, they quickly disappeared from the view of those below. It was as if night and the wilderness had blotted them out, but every member of the little party felt relief and actual pleasure in the expedition. Something mysterious and unknown lay before them, and they were anxious to find out what it was.

Shepard whispered to Dick of the care that they must take against their foes, and Warner whispered to Pennington that the mountain was really fine, although finer ridges could be found in Vermont.

Two hundred yards up, and Shepard, touching Dick's shoulder, pointed to the valley. The whole party stopped and looked back. Although themselves buried in brown foliage they saw the floor of the valley all the way to the mountains on the other side, and it was a wonderful sight, with its two opposing lines of camp fires that shot up redly and glowed across the fields. Now and then they saw figures of men moving against a crimson background, but no sound of the armies came to them. Peace and silence were yet supreme on the mountain.

"It makes you feel that you're not only above it in the body, but that you are not a part of it at all," said Shepard.

Dick was not surprised at his words. He had learned long since that the spy was an uncommon man, much above most of those who followed his calling.

"It gives me a similar feeling of detachment," he said, "but we know just the same that they're going to fight again tomorrow, and that we'll probably be in the thick of it. I hope, Mr. Shepard, that our victory yesterday marks the beginning of the end."

"I think it does, Mr. Mason. If we clean up the valley, and we'll do it, Lee's flank and Richmond will be exposed. He'll have to come out of his trenches then, and that will give Grant a chance to attack him with an overwhelming force. The Confederacy is as good as finished, but I've never doubted the result for a moment."

"I've worried a little at times. It seemed to me now and then that all those big defeats in Virginia might make our people too weary to go on. Why is that light flaring so high on Fisher's Hill?"

"It may be a signal. Possibly the Southerners are replying to it with another fiery signal on this mountain. We can't see the crest of Massanutton from this slope."

"You seem to know every inch of the ground in this region. How did you manage to learn it so thoroughly?"

"I was born in the valley not far from here. I've climbed over Massanutton many a time. Not far above us is a grove of splendid nut trees, and along the edge of it runs a ravine. I mean to lead the way up the ravine, Mr. Mason. It will give us shelter from the scouts and spies of the enemy."

"Shelter is what we want. I've no taste for being shot obscurely here on the side of the mountain."

"Then keep close behind me, all of you," said Shepard. "We're above the steepest part now, and I know a little path that leads to the ravine. Don't stumble if you can help it."

The path was nothing more than a trace, but it sufficed to give them a surer footing, and in eight or ten minutes they reached the ravine which ran in a diagonal line across the face of the mountain, gradually ascending to the summit. The ravine itself was not more than three or four feet deep, but as its banks were thickly lined with dwarfed cedar they were completely hidden unless they should chance to meet the Southern riflemen, coming down the mountain by the same way.

The ravine at one point led out on a bare shoulder of the slope, and looking over the little pines they clearly saw a fire blazing on the crest and waving flags silhouetted before its glow. Far below, at Fisher's Hill, flags were waving also.

"Quite a lively talk," whispered Shepard. "I suppose the lookouts are telling a lot about our army."

"But it won't make much difference," said Dick. "By the time they've spelled out from the flags what Sheridan is doing he'll be doing something else."

They resumed their climb and the ravine led again into dense forest. Sergeant Whitley had moved up by the side of Shepard, as they were now near the enemy, and his great scouting abilities were needed. It was a wise precaution, as presently he held up his hand, and then, at a signal from him, the whole party climbed softly out of the ravine, and crouched among the little cedars.

Now Dick himself heard what the sergeant had heard perhaps a half minute earlier, that is, the footsteps of two men coming swiftly down the ravine. In another minute they came in sight, Confederate troopers, obviously scouting. Luckily, the ravine being stony and the light bad, they did not see any trail, left by Shepard's troop, and they went on down the ravine.

"Shall we go on?" asked Dick.

"Not yet, sir," replied Shepard. "They don't suspect that we're up here, and it's likely they're trying for a good view of our army. But I fancy they'll be returning in a few minutes. We'd best be very quiet, sir."

Dick cautioned the men, and they lay as still as wild animals in their coverts. In about ten minutes the two riflemen came back up the ravine, and the hidden troopers could hear them talking.

"We'll try some other part of the slope, Jack," said one.

"Yes, that was a bad view," rejoined the other. "We couldn't tell a thing about the Yankee movements from down there. We can leave the ravine higher up, and I know a path that leads toward the north."

"There's not much good in finding out about 'em anyway. That fellow Sheridan is going to press us hard, and they have everything, numbers, arms, food, while we have next to nothing."

"But we'll fight 'em anyhow. Still, I wish old Stonewall was here."

"But he ain't here, and we'll have to do the best we can without him."

Their voices were lost, as they passed up the ravine and disappeared. Then Dick and his little party came out cautiously, and followed.

"I gather from what those two said that Early's men are depressed," said Dick.

"They've a right to be," replied Shepard. "Their army is in bad shape, besides being small, and now that we have a real leader we are, I think, sure to clean up the valley."

"But there'll be plenty of hard fighting."

"Yes. We'll have to win what we get."

The ravine widened and deepened a little, and they stopped. Sergeant Whitley in his capacity of chief scout and trailer climbed up the rocky side and looked about a little, while the others waited. He returned in two or three minutes, and Dick saw, by the moonlight, that his face expressed surprise.

"What is it, sergeant?" asked Dick.

"A woman is on the mountain. She passed by the ravine not long since, perhaps not a half hour ago."

"A woman at such a time? Why, sergeant, it's impossible!"

"No, sir, it isn't. See here!"

He opened his left hand. Within the palm lay a tiny bit of thin gray cloth.

"There may not be more than a dozen threads here," he said, "but I found 'em sticking to a thorn bush not twenty yards away. A half hour ago they were a part of a woman's dress. A thorn bush grows among the cedars above. She was in a hurry, and when her dress caught in it she jerked it loose."

"But how do you know it was only a half hour or less ago?" asked Dick.

"Because she broke two 'or three of the thorns when she jerked, and it was so late that their wounds are still bleeding, that is, a faint bit of sap is oozing out at the fractures."

"That sounds conclusive," said Dick, "but likely it was a mountain woman who lives somewhere along the slope."

The sergeant shook his head.

"No, sir, it was no mountain woman," he said. "When I found the cloth on the thorns I knelt and looked for a trail. It's hard ground mostly, but I thought I might find the trace of a footstep somewhere. I found several, and not one of them was made by the flat, broad shoe that mountain women wear. I found small rounded heel prints which the shoes worn by city women make."

"If any city woman is on this mountain she's a long way from home," said Warner.

"But I'm quite sure of what I say, sir," said the sergeant.

"And so am I," said Shepard, who had been listening with the keenest attention. "Will you mind letting me lead the way for a little while, sir?"

"Go ahead, of course," said Dick. "In such work as this we rely upon the sergeant and you."

"Then I'd like to take a look at those heel prints also."

Dick thought he detected a quiver of excitement or emotion in the voice of Shepard, always so calm and steady hitherto, and he wondered. Nevertheless he asked no questions as he led the way out of the ravine.

The sergeant showed the heel prints to Shepard, and beyond question they had been made by a woman. By careful scrutiny they found a half dozen more leading in a diagonal direction up the side of the mountain, but beyond that the ground was so hard and rocky that they could discover no further traces.

"You agree with me that the tracks have just been made?" said the sergeant to Shepard.

"I do," replied the spy, his voice showing growing excitement, "and I think I know who made them. I didn't believe it at first. It seemed incredible. I want to try a little experiment. Will all of you remain perfectly still?"

"Of course," said Dick.

He took a small whistle from his pocket and blew upon it. The sound was not shrill like that of Slade's whistle, but was very low, soft and musical. He blew only a few notes. Then he took the whistle from his lips and waited. Dick saw that his excitement was growing. It showed clearly in the spy's eyes, and he felt his own excitement increasing, too. He divined that something extraordinary was going to happen.

Out of the cedars to their right and a little higher up the slope came the notes of a whistle, exactly similar, low, soft and musical.

"Ah, I knew it!" breathed Shepard. He waited perhaps half a minute and then blew again, notes similar and just the same in number. In a few moments came the reply, a precise duplicate.

"We'll wait," said Shepard. "She'll be here in a minute or two."

Dick and his comrades looked eagerly toward the point from which the sound of the second whistle had come. This was something amazing, something beyond their experience, but the excitement of Shepard seemed to have passed. His face had become a mask once more, and he was waiting with certainty.

Dick's sharp ear caught the sound of a light footstep approaching them, evidently coming straight and with confidence. He realized that until now he had not really believed, despite the footprints, despite everything, that a woman was on the mountain. But he knew at last. He even heard the swish of her skirts once or twice against the bushes. Then she came through the dwarfed cedars, stepping boldly, and stood before them.

The stranger stood full in the moonlight, and Dick saw her very clearly. She was thin, small and elderly, clothed in a gray riding suit, and with a sort of small gray turban on her head. But despite her smallness and thinness and years there was nothing insignificant in her appearance. As she stood there looking at them, she showed a pair of the brightest and most intelligent eyes that Dick had ever seen. Her small, pointed chin had the firmness of steel, and figure, manner and appearance alike betokened courage and resolution in the highest degree.

All these impressions were made upon Dick in a single instant, as if in a flash of light, and he also noticed in her face a resemblance to some one, although he could not recall, for a moment, who it was. But the silence that endured for a half minute, while the men regarded the woman and the woman regarded the men, was broken by Shepard, who uttered a low cry and strode forward.

"Henrietta," he exclaimed, "you here at such a time!"

He put his arms around her and kissed her.

She returned his kiss, laughed a little, and the two turned toward the others. Then Dick saw whom she resembled. As they stood side by side the likeness was marked, the same eyes, the same nose, the same mouth, the same chin, only hers were in miniature, in comparison with his, and in addition she was eight or ten years older.

"Mr. Mason," said Shepard, addressing himself directly to their nominal leader. "This is my sister. She also serves as I do, and for her, hardships and dangers are not less than mine for me. She works chiefly in Richmond itself. But as you see, she has now come alone into the mountains, and also into the very fringe of the armies."

"Then," said Dick, "she must come on a mission of great importance and it is for us to honor so brave a messenger."

He and all the others took off their caps in silence. They might have cheered, but every one knew that the foe was not far away in the thickets. There was sufficient light for him to see a little flush of pride appear for a moment on the face of the woman. Strange as her position was, she seemed easy and confident, lightly swinging in her hand a small riding whip.

"I'll not ask you for the present, Henrietta, how you come to be here," said Shepard, "but I'll ask instead what you've brought. These young men are Lieutenant Mason, Lieutenant Warner and Lieutenant Pennington. As I've indicated already, Lieutenant Mason leads us."

"I bring information," she replied, "information that you will be glad to carry to General Sheridan. As a woman I could go where men could not, and you remember, Brother William, that I know the country."

"Almost as well as I do," said Shepard. "As a girl you rode like a man and were afraid of nothing. Nor do you fear anything today."

"Tell General Sheridan," she said, turning to Dick, "that the Confederate numbers are even less than he thinks, that a large area at the base of Little North Mountain is wholly unoccupied."

"And if we get there," exclaimed Dick, eagerly, "we can crash in on the flank of Early."

"I'm not a soldier," she said, "but that plan was in my mind. A large division could be hidden in the heavy timber along Cedar Creek, and then, if the proper secrecy were observed, reach the Confederate flank tomorrow night, unseen."

"And that's on the other side of the valley," said Dick.

"But at this point it's only four or five miles across."

"I wasn't making difficulties, I was merely locating the places as you tell them."

"I've drawn a map of the Confederate position. It's in pencil, but it ought to help."

"It will be beyond price!" exclaimed Dick. "You will give it to me?"

"Of course! But you must wait a minute! Until I heard my brother's whistle I didn't know whether it was North or South that I was going to meet on the mountain."

She disappeared in the bushes, and Dick heard a light rustling, but in a few moments she returned and held out a broad sheet of heavy paper, upon which a map had been drawn with care and skill.

He had divined already its great value, and now his opinion was confirmed.

"I can't thank you," he said, as he took it, "but General Sheridan and General Grant can. And I've no doubt they'll do it when the time comes."

Again the light flush appeared in her cheeks and she looked actually handsome.

"Since my present task is finished," she said, "I'd better go."

"Where did you leave your horse?" asked Shepard.

"He's tethered in the bushes about a hundred yards farther down the side of the mountain. I'll mount and ride back in the direction of Richmond. I know all the roads."

Sergeant Whitley, who had gone a little higher up and who was watching while they talked, whistled softly. Yet the whistle, low as it was, was undoubtedly a signal of alarm.

"Go at once, Henrietta," whispered Shepard, urgently. "It's important that you shouldn't be held here, that you be left with a free hand."

"It's so," she said.

He stooped and kissed her on the brow, and, without another word, she vanished among the cedars on the lower slope. Dick thought he heard a moment later the distant beat of hoofs and he felt sure she was riding fast and far. Then he turned his attention to the danger confronting them, because a danger it certainly was, and that, too, of the most formidable kind. But, first, he gave the map to Shepard to carry.

Sergeant Whitley came down the slope and joined them.

"I think we'd better lie down, all of us," he said.

Now the real leadership passed to the sergeant, scout, trailer and skilled Indian fighter. It passed to him, because all of them knew that the conditions made him most fit for the place. They knelt or lay but held their weapons ready. The sergeant knelt by Dick's side and the youth saw that he was tense and expectant.

"Is it a band of the Johnnies?" he whispered.

"I merely heard 'em. I didn't see 'em," replied the sergeant, "but I'm thinkin' from the way they come creepin' through the woods that it's Slade and his gang."

"If that's so we'd better look out. Those fellows are woodsmen and they'll be sure to see signs that we're here."

"Right you are, Mr. Mason. It's well the lady left so soon, and that we're between them and her."

"It looks as if this fellow Slade had set out to be our evil genius. We're always meeting him."

"Yes, sir, but we can take care of him. I don't specially mind this kind of fighting, Mr. Mason. We had to do a lot of it in the heavy timber on the slopes of some of them mountains out West, the names of which I don't know, and generally we had to go up against the Sioux and Northern Cheyennes, and them two tribes are king fighters, I can tell you. Man for man they're a match for anybody."

"Slade's men don't appear to be moving," said Shepard, who was on the other side of the sergeant.

"Not so's you could hear 'em," said Sergeant Whitley. "They heard us and they're creeping now so's to see what we are and then fall on us by surprise. Guess them that's kneeling had better bend down a little lower."

Warner, who had been crouched on his knees, lay down almost flat. He did not understand forests and darkness as Dick did, nor did he have the strong hereditary familiarity with them, and he felt uncomfortable and apprehensive.

"I don't like it," he said to Pennington. "I'd rather fight in the open."

"So would I," said Pennington. "It's awful to lie here and feel yourself being surrounded by dangers you can't see. I guess a man in the African wilderness stalked at night by a dozen hungry lions would feel just about as I do."

"I'm going to creep a little distance up the slope again," said the sergeant, "and try to spy 'em out."

"A good idea, but be very careful."

"I certainly will, Mr. Mason. I want to live."

He slid among the bushes so quietly that Dick did not hear the noise of him passing, nor was there any sound until he came back a few minutes later.

"I saw 'em," he whispered. "They're lying among the bushes, and they're not moving now, 'cause they're not certain what's become of us. It's Slade sure. I saw him sitting under a tree, wearing that big flap-brimmed hat, and sitting beside him was a great, black-haired, red-faced man, a most evil-looking fellow, too."

"Skelly! Bill Skelly, beyond a doubt!" said Dick.

"That's him! From what you said Skelly started out by being for the Union. Now, as we believed before, he's joined hands with Slade who's for the South."

"They're just guerrillas, sergeant. They're for themselves and nobody else."

"I reckon that's true, and they're expecting to get some plunder from us. But if you'll listen to me, Mr. Mason, we'll burn their faces while they're about it."

"You're our leader now, sergeant. Tell us what to do."

"Just to our right is a shallow gully, running through the cedars. We can take shelter in it, crawl up it, and open fire on 'em. They don't know our numbers, and if we take 'em by surprise maybe we can scatter 'em for the time."

"I suppose we'll have to. I'd like to get away with this map at once, but they'd certainly follow and force us to a fight."

"That's true. We must deal with 'em, now. I'll have to ask all of you to be very careful. Don't slip, and look out for the dead wood lying about. If a piece of it cracks under you Slade and Skelly will be sure to notice it, and it'll be all up with our surprise."

"You hear," whispered Dick to the others. "If you don't do as the sergeant says, very likely you'll get shot by Slade's men."

With life as the price it was not necessary to say anything more about the need of silence, and nobody slipped and no stick broke as they crept into the gully after the sergeant. The cedars and thickets almost met over the narrow depression, shutting out the moonlight, but every one was able to discern the man before him creeping forward like a wild animal. It was easy enough for Dick to imagine himself that famous great grandfather of his, Paul Cotter reincarnated, and that the days of the wilderness and the Indian war bands had come back again. He even felt exultation as he adapted himself so readily to the situation, and became equal to it. But Warner was grieved and exasperated. It hurt his dignity to prowl on his knees through the dark.

They advanced about two hundred yards in a diagonal course along the side of the mountain until they came to a point where the cedars thinned out a little. Then the sergeant whispered to the others to stop, rose from his knees, and Dick rose beside him.

"See!" he said, nodding his head in the direction in which he wished Dick to look.

Dick saw a number of dark figures standing among the trees. Two were in close conference, evidently trying to decide upon a plan. One, a giant in size, was Skelly, and the other, little, weazened and wearing an enormous flap-brimmed hat, could be none but Slade.

"A pretty pair," said Dick, "but I don't like to fire on 'em from ambush."

"Nor do I," said the sergeant, "but we've got to do it, or we won't get the surprise we need so bad."

But they were saved from firing the first shot as some one in the gully—they never knew or asked his name—stumbled at last. Slade and Skelly instantly sprang for the trees and Slade blew sharply upon his whistle. Twenty shots were fired in the direction of the gully, but they whistled harmlessly over the heads of its occupants.

It was Dick who gave the command for the return volley, and with a mighty shouting they swept the woods with their breech-loading rifles. They were not sure whether they hit anything, but as the gully blazed with fire they presented all the appearance of a formidable force that might soon charge.

"Cease firing!" said Dick, presently.

A cloud of smoke rose from the gully, and, as it lifted, they could see nothing in the woods beyond, but the sergeant announced that for an instant or two he heard the sound of running feet.

"It means they've gone," said Dick, "and that being the case we'll be off, too. I fancy we've a great prize in this map. Your sister, Mr. Shepard, must be a woman of extraordinary daring and ability."

"She's all that," replied the spy earnestly. "I think sometimes that God gave to me the size and physical strength of the family, but to her the mind. Think of her life there in Richmond, surrounded by dangers! She has done great service to our cause tonight, and she has done other services, equally as great, before."

Shepard was silent for a little while and then he began to chuckle to himself, almost under his breath, but Dick heard.

"What is it?" he asked.

"I was thinking of my sister," Shepard replied. "Your cousin, Harry Kenton, if you should ever meet him again—and I know that you will—could tell you a story of a dark night in Richmond, or at least a part of it, and he could also tell an interesting story, or a part of it, of another map, almost as valuable as this, which disappeared mysteriously from the house of a rich man in Richmond where he and other Southern officers were being entertained. It vanished almost from under their hands."

"Tell me now," said Dick, feeling great curiosity.

"I think I'd better wait, if you'll pardon me, sir," said Shepard.

"I'll have to wait anyhow," said Dick, "because I hear the tread of men coming toward us."

"But they're our own," said Sergeant Whitley, who was a little ahead, peering between the cedars.

"I suppose they heard the shots and are hurrying to our relief," said Dick. "But we routed the enemy, we did not lose a man, and we've brought away the prize."

The two forces joined and they were shortly back with Colonel Winchester, who fully appreciated the great value of the information obtained by such a remarkable coordination of effort.

"Dick," he said, "you and Mr. Shepard shall ride at once with me and this map to General Sheridan."

CHAPTER IX
AT GRIPS WITH EARLY

Dick felt great excitement and elation as he rode before dawn with Colonel Winchester and the spy to see Sheridan. They found him sitting by a small fire receiving or sending reports, and talking with a half-dozen of his generals. It was not yet day, but the flames lighted up the commander's thin, eager face, and made him look more boyish than ever.

Dick felt as he had felt before that he was in the presence of a man. He had had the same impression when he stood near Grant and Thomas. Did strong men send off electric currents of will and power which were communicated to other men, by which they could know them, or was it the effect of deeds achieved? He could not decide the question for himself, but he knew that he believed implicitly in their leader.

Colonel Winchester paused near Sheridan, but the general's keen eye caught him at once.

"Good morning, Colonel Winchester!" he exclaimed. "You bring news of value. I can tell it by your face!"

"I do, sir," replied the colonel, "but it was Mr. Shepard here, whom you know, and Lieutenant Mason who obtained it. Mr. Shepard, show General Sheridan the map."

It was characteristic of Colonel Winchester, a man of the finest feelings, that he should have Shepard instead of himself carry the map to General Sheridan. He wanted the spy to have the full measure of credit, including the outward show, for the triumph he had achieved with the aid of his sister. And Shepard's swift glance of thanks showed that he appreciated it. He drew the map from his pocket and handed it to the general.

Sheridan held it down, where the full glow of the flames fell upon it, and he seemed to comprehend at once the meaning of the lines. A great light sprang up in his eyes.

"Ah!" he exclaimed. "The location of the Confederate forces and the openings between them and the mountains! This is important! Splendid! Did you make it yourself, Mr. Shepard?"

"No, sir. It was made by my sister who came from Richmond. We met her on the mountain."

Sheridan looked at Shepard and the eyes of general and spy met in complete understanding.

"I know of her," the general murmured. "A noble woman! There are many such as she who have done great service to our cause that can never be repaid! But this is a stroke of fortune!"

"Look, Merritt, Averill and all of you," he said aloud. "Here lies our path! Mr. Shepard, you will go over the details of this with us and, Colonel Winchester, you and your aide remain also to help."

Dick felt complimented, and so did Colonel Winchester. Sheridan knew how to handle men. While the sentinels, rifle on shoulder, walked up and down a little distance away, a dozen eager faces were soon poring over the map, Shepard filling in details as to the last little hill or brook.

"Since we know where they are and how many they are," said Sheridan, "we'll make a big demonstration in front of Fisher's Hill, where Early's works are too strong to be carried, and while we keep him occupied there we'll turn his left flank with a powerful force, marching it just here into the open space that Mr. Shepard's map shows. Tomorrow—or rather today, for I see the dawn comes—will be a day of great noise and of much burning of powder. But behind the curtain of smoke we'll make our movements. Merritt with his cavalry shall go to the right and Averill will go with him. Crook shall take his two divisions and hold the north bank of Cedar Creek, and later on Crook shall be the first to strike. Gentlemen, we've won one victory, and I know that all of you appreciate the value of a second and a third. The opportunity of the war lies here before us. We can uncover the entire left flank of the Confederacy here in Virginia, and who knows what will follow!"

He looked up, his eyes glowing and his confidence was communicated to them all. They were mostly young men and they responded in kind to his burning words. Sheridan knew that he could command from them the utmost fidelity and energy, and he uttered a little exclamation of confidence.

"I shall consider the victory already won," he said.

The generals left for their commands, and Sheridan again thanked Colonel Winchester, Dick and Shepard.

"I recommend that all three of you take some rest," he said, "you won't have much to do this morning."

They saluted, mounted and rode back. "You take his advice, Dick, and roll yourself in your blanket," said Colonel Winchester, when they were on the way.

"I will, sir," said Dick, "although I know that great history is being made now."

"I feel that way, too," said the colonel. "Look, the sun is coming up, and you can see the Confederate outposts."

The thin, clear air of September was brilliant with morning light, and through glasses the Confederate outposts and works around Fisher's Hill were quite clear and distinct. Some of the Northern and Southern sentinels were already exchanging compliments with one another, and they heard the faint popping of rifles. But Dick well knew from Sheridan's words that this early firing meant nothing. It would grow much heavier bye and bye and it would yet be but the cover for something else.

He found Warner and Pennington already sound asleep, and wrapping himself in his blanket he lay down under a tree and fell asleep to the distant crackle of rifles and the occasional thud of great guns. He slept on through the morning while the fire increased, and great volumes of smoke rolled, as the wind shifted up or down the valley. But it did not disturb him, nor did he dream. His slumbers were as sound as if he lay in his distant bed in Pendleton.

While Dick and his comrades slept Sheridan was moving the men on his chess board. Young in years, but great in experience, he was never more eager and never more clear of mind than on this, one of the most eventful days of his life. He saw the opportunity, and he was resolved that it should not escape him. Two great reputations were made in the valley by men very unlike, Stonewall Jackson and Little Phil Sheridan. In the earlier years of the war the Union armies had suffered many disasters there at the hands of the leader under the old slouch hat, and now Sheridan was resolved to retrieve everything, not with one victory alone, but with many.

There was firing in the valley all day long, the crackling of the rifles, the thudding of the great guns, and the occasional charge of horsemen. The curtain of smoke hung nearly always. Sometimes it grew thicker, and sometimes it became thinner, but Sheridan's mind was not upon these things, they were merely the veil before him, while behind it, as a screen, he arranged the men on his chess board. When night came his whole line was pushed forward. His vanguard held the northern part of the little town of Strasburg, while Early's held the southern part, only a few hundred yards away. In the night the large force under Crook was moved into the thick forest along Cedar Creek, where it was to lie silent and hidden until it received the word of command.

All the next day the movements were continued, while Crook's force, intended to be the striking arm, was still concealed in the timber. Yet before dark there was a heavy combat, in which the Southern troops were driven out of Strasburg, enabling the Northern batteries to advance to strong positions. That night Crook's whole strength was brought across Cedar Creek, but was hidden again in heavy timber. To the great pleasure of its colonel and other officers the Winchester regiment was sent to join it as a cavalry support.

It was quite dark when they rode their horses across the creek and Shepard was again with them as guide. Although he concealed it, the spy felt a great exultation. The map that he had brought from his sister had proved invaluable. Sheridan was using it every hour, and Shepard was giving further assistance through his thorough knowledge of the ground. Dick was glad to ride beside him and whisper with him, now and then.

"I haven't known things to go so well before," Dick said, when they were across the creek.

"They're going well, Mr. Mason," said Shepard, "because everything is arranged. There is provision against every unlucky chance. It's leadership. The difference between a good general and a bad general is about fifty thousand men."

The entire division moved forward in the dusk at a fair pace, but so many troops with cavalry and guns could not keep from making some noise. Dick with Shepard and the sergeant rode off in the woods towards the open valley to see if the enemy were observing them. Dick's chief apprehensions were in regard to Slade and Skelly, but they found no trace of the guerrillas, nor of any other foes.

The night was fairly bright, and from the edge of the wood they saw far over hills and fields, dotted with two opposing lines of camp fires. A dark outline was Fisher's Hill, and lights burned there too. From a point in front of it a gun boomed now and then, and there was still an intermittent fire of skirmishers and sharpshooters.

"That hill will be ours inside of twenty-four hours," said Shepard. "We'll fall upon Early from three sides and he'll have to retreat to save himself. He hasn't numbers enough to stand against an army driven forward by a hand like that of General Sheridan."

* * * *

While Dick, the sergeant and the spy looked from the woods upon the lights of Fisher's Hill the Invincibles lay in an earthwork before it facing their enemy. Harry Kenton sat with St. Clair, Langdon and Dalton. The two colonels were not far away. For almost the first time, Harry's heart failed him. He did not wish to depreciate Early, but he felt that he was not the great Jackson or anything approaching him. He knew that the troops felt the same way. They missed the mighty spirit and the unfaltering mind that had led them in earlier years to victory. They were ragged and tired, too, and had but little food.

Happy Tom, who concealed under a light manner uncommonly keen perceptions, noticed Harry's depression.

"What are you thinking about, Harry?" he asked.

"Several things, Happy. Among them, the days when we rode here with Stonewall from one victory to another."

"We'll have to think of something else. Cheer up. Remember the old saying that the darkest hour is just before the dawn."

"Whose dawn?"

"That's not like you, Harry. You've usually put up the boldest front of us all."

"Happy's giving you good advice," said St. Clair.

"So he is," said Harry, as he shook himself. "We'll fight 'em off tomorrow. They can't beat us again. The spirit of Old Jack will hover over us."

"If we only had more men," said Dalton. "Then we could spread out and cover the slopes of the mountains on either side. I wish I knew whether those dark fringes hid anything we ought to know."

"They hide rabbits, squirrels, raccoons, birds and maybe a black bear or two," said Happy Tom. "When we shatter Sheridan's army and drive the fragments across the Potomac I think I'll come back here and do a little hunting, leaving to Lee the task of cleaning up the Army of the Potomac."

"I'd like to come with you," said St. Clair, "but I wouldn't bring any gun. I'd just roam through the woods for a week and disturb nothing. If I saw a bear I'd point my finger at him and say: 'Go away, young fellow, I won't bother you if you won't bother me,' and then he'd amble off peacefully in one direction, and I'd amble off peacefully in another. I wouldn't want to hear a gun fired during all that week. I'd just rest, rest, rest my nerves and my soul. I wouldn't break a bough or a bush. I'd even be careful how hard I stepped on the leaves. Birds could walk all over me if they liked. I'd drink from those clear streams, and I'd sleep in my blanket on a bed of leaves."

"But suppose it rained, Arthur?"

"I wouldn't let it rain in that enchanted week of mine. Nothing would happen except what I wanted to happen. It would be a week of the most absolute peace and quiet the world has ever known. There wouldn't be any winds, they would be zephyrs. The skies would all be made out of the softest and finest of blue satin and any little clouds that floated before 'em would be made of white satin of the same quality. The nights would be clear with the most wonderful stars that ever shone. Great new stars would come out for the first time, and twinkle for me, and the man in the most silvery moon known in the history of time would grin down at me and say without words: 'St. Clair, old fellow, this is your week of peace, everything has been fixed for you, so make the most of it.' And then I'd wander on. The birds would sing to me and every one of 'em would sing like a prima donna. Wherever I stepped, wild flowers would burst into bloom as I passed, and if a gnat should happen to buzz before my face I wouldn't brush him away for fear of hurting him. The universe and I would be at peace with each other."

"Hear him! O, hear him!" exclaimed Happy Tom. "Old Arthur grows dithyrambic and hexametrical. He fairly distills the essence of highfalutin poetry."

"I don't know that he's so far fetched," said sober Dalton. "I feel a good deal that way myself. I suppose, Thomas Langdon, that the colors of the world depend upon one's own eyes. What I call green may appear to you like the color of blue to me. Now, Arthur really sees all these things that he's telling about, because he has the eye of the mind with which to see them. I've quit saying that people don't see things, because I don't see 'em myself."

"Good for you, Professor," said Langdon. "That's quite a lecture you gave me, long though not windy, and I accept it. Those Elysian fields that Arthur was painting are real and he's going to have his enchanted week as he calls it. Arthur is a poet, sure enough."

"I have written a few little verses which were printed in the Charleston Mercury," said St. Clair.

"What's this? What's this?" asked a mellow voice. "Can it be possible that young gentlemen are discussing poetry between battles and with the enemy in sight?"

It was Colonel Leonidas Talbot, coming down the trench, and Lieutenant Colonel Hector St. Hilaire was just behind him. The young officers rose and saluted promptly, but they knew there was no reproof in Colonel Talbot's tone.

"We had to do it, sir," said Harry respectfully. "Something struck Arthur here, and like a fountain he gushed suddenly into poetry. He had a most wonderful vision of the Elysian fields and of himself wandering through them for a week, knee deep in flowers, and playing the softest of music on a guitar."

"He's put that in about the guitar," protested St. Clair. "I never mentioned such a thing, but all the rest is true."

"Well, if I had my way," said the colonel, "you should have a guitar, too, if you wanted it, and I like that idea of yours about a week in the Elysian fields. We'll join you there and we'll all walk around among the flowers, and Hector's relative, that wonderful musician, young De Langeais, shall play to us on his violin, and maybe the famous Stonewall will come walking to us through the flowers, and he'll have with him Albert Sidney Johnston, and Turner Ashby and all the great ones that have gone."

The colonel stopped, and Harry felt a slight choking in his throat.

"In the course of this lull, Leonidas and I had some thought of resuming our unfinished game of chess," said Lieutenant Colonel St. Hilaire, "but the time is really unpropitious and too short. It may be that we shall have to wait until the war is over to conclude the match. The enemy is pressing us hard, and I need not conceal from you lads that he will press us harder tomorrow."

"So he will," agreed Colonel Talbot. "There was some heavy and extremely accurate artillery fire from his ranks this afternoon. The way the guns were handled and the remarkable rapidity and precision with which the discharges came convinces me that John Carrington is here in the valley, ready to concentrate all the fire of the Union batteries upon us. It is bad, very bad for us that the greatest artilleryman in the world should come with Sheridan, and yet we shall have the pleasure of seeing how he achieves wonders with the guns. It was in him, even in the old days at West Point, when we were but lads together, and he has shown more than once in this war how the flower that was budding then has come into full bloom."

As if in answer to his words the deep boom of a cannon rolled over the hills, and a shell burst near the earthwork.

"That, I think, was John talking to us," said Colonel Talbot. "He was saying to us: 'Beware of me, old friends. I'm coming tomorrow, not with one gun but with many!' Well, be it so. We shall give John and Sheridan a warm welcome, and we shall try to make it so very warm that it will prove too hot for them. Now, my lads, there is no immediate duty for you, and if you can sleep, do so. Good-night."

They rose and saluted again as the two colonels went back to their own particular place.

"I hope those two will be spared," said St. Clair. "I want them to finish their chess game, and I'd like, too, to see their meeting after the war with their old friend, John Carrington."

"It will all come to pass," said Harry. "If Arthur is a poet as he seems to be, then I'm a prophet, as I know I am."

"At least you're an optimist," said Dalton.

"Go to sleep, all of you, as the colonel told you to do," said Harry. "If you don't stop talking you'll keep the enemy awake all night."

But Harry himself was the last of them to sleep. He could not keep from rising at times, and, in the starlight, looking at the fires of the foe and the dark slopes of the mountains. His glasses passed more than once over the forests along Cedar Creek, but no prevision, no voice out of the dark, told him that Dick was there, one of a formidable force that was lying hidden, ready to strike the fatal blow. His last dim sight, as he fell asleep, was a spectacle evoked from the past, a vision of Old Jack riding at the head of his phantom legions to victory.

* * * *

At dawn all of Crook's forces marched out of the woods along Cedar Creek, the Winchester men, Shepard at their head, leading, but they still kept to the shelter of the forest and wide ravines along the lower slopes of the mountain. The sun was not clear of the eastern hills before the heavy thudding of the great guns and the angry buzz of the rifles came from the direction of Fisher's Hill.

The demonstration had begun and it was a big one, big enough to make the defenders think it was reality and not a sham. Before Early's earthworks a great cloud of smoke was gathering. Dick looked over his shoulder at it. It gave him a curious feeling to be marching past, while all that crash of battle was going on in the valley. It almost looked as if they were deserting their general.

"How far are we going?" he asked Warner.

"I don't know," replied the Vermonter, "but I fancy we'll go far enough. My little algebra, although it remains unopened in my pocket, tells me that we shall continue our progress unseen until we reach the desired point. These woods have grown up and these gullies have been furrowed at a very convenient time for us."

The light was yet dim in the forests along the slopes, but the valley itself was flooded with the sun's rays. The echoes of the firing rolled continuously through the gorges and multiplied it. Despite the clouds about the earthworks and the hill, Dick saw continual flashes of light, and he knew now that the battle below was a reality and not a sham. Early and all his men would be kept too busy to see the march of Crook and his force on his flank, and Dick, like Warner, became sure that the great movement would be a success.

But their progress, owing to the nature of the ground and the need to keep under cover, was slow. It seemed to Dick that they marched an interminable time under the trees, while the battle flashed and roared in the plain. He saw noon pass and the sun rise to the zenith. He saw the brilliant light dim on the eastern mountains, and they were still marching through the forests.

The battle was now behind them and the sun was very low, but the command halted and turned toward the east. Nevertheless, they were still hidden by the woods and the low hills of the valley. Yet they lay behind and on the side of their enemy who would speedily be exposed where he was weakest, to their full weight. The long flanking movement had been a complete success so far.

Little of the day was left. The sun was almost hidden behind the eastern mountains but it still flamed in the west, glittering along the bayonets of the men in the forest, and showing their eager faces. Dick's heart throbbed. In that moment of anticipated victory he forgot all about Harry and his friends who were in the closing trap. Then trumpets sang the charge, and the cavalry thundered out of the wood, followed by the infantry and the artillery.

At the same time, another powerful division that had been moved forward by Sheridan, charged, while those in front increased their fire. The unfortunate Southern army was overwhelmed by troops who had moved forward in such complete unison. They were swept out of their earthworks, driven from their fortified hill, and those who did not fall or were not taken were sent in rapid flight down the valley.

The battle was short. Completeness of preparation and superiority in numbers and resources made it so. Early and what was left of his army had no choice but the flight they made. The sun had nearly set when the deadly charge issued from the wood, and, by the time it had set, the pursuit was thundering along the valley, the Winchester men in the very forefront of it. Long after dark it continued. Several miles from the field the fragments of the Invincibles and some others rallied on a hill, posted two cannon and made a desperate resistance. But the attack upon them was so fierce that they were compelled to retreat again, and they did not have time to take the guns with them.

It was a strange night to Dick, alike joyous and terrible. He believed that the army of the enemy was practically destroyed, and yet he had a great sympathy for some who were in it. He was in constant fear lest he should find them dead, or wounded mortally. But he had no time to look for them. Sheridan was pressing the pursuit to the utmost. Midnight did not stop it. Fugitives were captured continually. Here and there an abandoned cannon was taken. Rifles flashed all through the darkness, and the horses of the Union cavalry were driven to the utmost.

Neither Dick nor his companions felt exhaustion. Their excitement was too great, and the taste of triumph was too strong. They had seen no such victory before, and eager and willing they still led the advance. Midnight passed and the pursuit never ceased until it reached Woodstock, ten miles from Fisher's Hill. By that time Sheridan's infantry was exhausted, and as Early was beginning to draw together the remains of his force he would prove too strong for the cavalry alone.

At dawn the army of Sheridan stopped, the troopers almost falling from their horses in exhaustion, while Early used the opportunity to escape with what was left of his men, leaving behind many prisoners and twenty cannon. Yet the triumph had been great, and again, when the telegraph brought the news of it, the swell of victory passed through the North.

The Winchester regiment was drawn up near Woodstock, already dismounted, the men standing beside their horses. The camp cooks were lighting the fires for breakfast, but many of the young cavalrymen fell asleep first. Dick managed to keep awake long enough for his food, and then, at the order of the colonel, he slept on the ground, awaiting the command of Sheridan which might come at any moment.

CHAPTER X
AN UNBEATEN FOE

Dick's belief that he would not be allowed to sleep long was justified. In three or four hours the whole Winchester regiment was up, mounted and away again. Early and his army left the great valley pike, and took a road leading toward the Blue Ridge, where he eventually entered a gap, and fortified to await supplies and fresh men from Richmond, leaving all the great Valley of Virginia, where in former years the Northern armies had suffered so many humiliations, in the possession of Sheridan. It was the greatest and most solid triumph that the Union had yet achieved and Dick and the youths with him rejoiced.

After many days of marching and fighting they lay once more in the shadow of the mountains, within a great grove of oak and beech, hickory and maple. The men and then the horses had drunk at a large brook flowing near by, and both were content. The North, as always, sent forward food in abundance to its troops, and now, just as the twilight was coming, the fires were lighted and the pleasant aromas of supper were rising. Colonel Winchester and his young staff sat by one of the fires near the edge of the creek. They had not taken off their clothes in almost a week, and they felt as if they had been living like cave-men. Nevertheless the satisfaction that comes from deeds well done pervaded them, and as they lay upon the leaves and awaited their food and coffee they showed great good humor.

"Have you any objection, sir, to my taking a census?" said Warner to Colonel Winchester.

"No, Warner, but what kind of a census do you mean?"

"I want to count our wounds, separately and individually and then make up the grand total."

"All right, George, go ahead," said Colonel Winchester, laughing.

"Dick," said Warner, "what hurts have you sustained in the past week?"

"A bullet scratch on the shoulder, another on the side, a slight cut from a saber on my left arm, about healed now, a spent bullet that hit me on the head, raising a lump and ache for the time being, and a kick from one of our own horses that made me walk lame for a day."

"The kick from a horse, as it was one of our horses, doesn't go."

"I didn't put it forward seriously. I withdraw my claim on its account."

"That allows you four wounds. Now, Pennington, how about you?"

"First I had a terrible wound in the foot," replied the Nebraskan. "A bullet went right through my left shoe and cut the skin off the top of my little toe."

"Leave out the 'terrible.' That's no dreadful wound."

"No, but it burned like the sting of a wasp and bled in a most disgraceful manner all over my sock. Then my belt buckle was shot away."

"That doesn't count either. A wound's a wound only when you're hit yourself, not when some piece of your clothing is struck."

"All right. The belt buckle's barred, although it gave me a shock when the bullet met it. A small bullet went through the flesh of my left arm just above the elbow. It healed so fast that I've hardly noticed it, due, of course, to the very healthy and temperate life I've led. I suppose, George, it would have laid up a fellow of your habits for a week."

"Never mind about my habits, but go on with the list of your wounds. A great beauty of mathematics is that it compels you to keep to your subject. When you're solving one of those delightful problems in mathematics you can't digress and drag in irrelevant things. Algebra is the very thing for a confused mind like yours, Frank, one that doesn't coordinate. But get on with your list."

"When we were in pursuit my horse stumbled in a gully and fell so hard that I was thrown over his shoulder, giving my own shoulder a painful bruise that's just getting well."

"We'll allow that, since it happened in battle. What else now? Speak up!"

"That's all. Three good wounds, according to your own somewhat severe definition of a wound. I'm one behind Dick, but I believe that when I was thrown over my horse's head I was hurt worse than he was at any time."

"Frank Pennington, you're a good comrade, but you're a liar, an unmitigated liar."

"George, if I weren't so tired and so unwilling to be angry with anybody I'd get up and belt you on the left ear for that."

"But you're a liar, just the same. You're holding something back."

"What are you driving at, you chattering Green Mountaineer?"

"Why don't you tell something about the time the trooper fell from his horse wounded, and you, dismounting under the enemy's fire, helped him on your own horse, although you got two wounds in your body while doing it, and brought him off in safety? Didn't I say that you were a liar, a convicted liar from modesty?"

Pennington blushed.

"I didn't want to say anything about that," he muttered. "I had to do it."

"Lots of men wouldn't have had to do it. You go down for five good wounds, Frank Pennington."

"Now, then, what about yourself, George?" asked Dick.

"One in the arm, one on the shoulder and one across the ankle. I don't waste time in words, like you two, my verbose friends. That gives the three of us combined twelve wounds, a fair average of four apiece."

"And it's our great good luck that not one of the twelve is a disabling hurt," said Dick.

"But we get the credit for the full twelve, all the same," said Warner, "and we maintain our prestige in the army. Our consciences also are satisfied. But the last two or three weeks of battles and marches have fairly made me dizzy. I can't remember them or their sequence. All I know is that we've cleaned up the valley, and here we are ready at last to take a couple of minutes of well earned rest."

"Do you know," said Pennington, "there were times when I clear forgot to be hungry, and I've been renowned in our part of Nebraska for my appetite. But nature always gets even. For all those periods of forgetfulness memory is now rushing upon me. I'm hungry not only for the present but from the past. It'll take a lot to satisfy me."

The briskness of the night also sharpened Pennington's appetite. They were deep in autumn, and the winds from the mountains had an edge. The foliage had turned and it glowed in vivid reds and yellows on the slopes, although the intense colors were hidden now by the coming of night.

The wind was cold enough to make the fires feel good to their relaxed systems, and they spread out their hands to the welcome flames, as they had often done at home on wintry nights, when children. Beyond the trees the horses, under guard, were grazing on what was left of the late grass, but within the wood the men themselves, save those who were preparing food, were mostly lying down on the dry leaves or their blankets, and were talking of the things they had done, or the things they were going to do.

"I wonder what the bill of fare will be tonight," said Pennington, who was growing hungrier and hungrier.

"I had several engraved menus," said Warner, "but I lost them, and so we won't be able to order. We'll just have to take what they offer us."

"A month or so later they'll be having fresh sausage and spare ribs in old Kentucky," said Dick, "and I wish we had 'em here now."

"And a month later than that," said Pennington, "they'll be having a roasted bull buffalo weighing five thousand pounds for Christmas dinner in Nebraska."

"Nonsense!" exclaimed Warner. "No buffalo ever weighed five thousand pounds."

Pennington looked at him pityingly.

"You have no romance or poetry after all, George," he said. "Why can't you let me put on an extra twenty-five hundred or three thousand pounds for the sake of effect?"

"Besides, you don't roast buffaloes whole and bring them in on a platter!"

"No, we don't, but that's no proof that we can't or won't. Now, what would you like to have, George?"

"After twelve or fifteen other things, I'd like to finish off with a whole pumpkin pie, and a few tin cups of cider would go along with it mighty well. That's the diet to make men, real men, I mean."

"Any way," said Dick, raising a tin cup of hot coffee, "here's to food. You may sleep without beds, and, in tropical climates, you may go without clothes, but in whatever part of the world you may be, you must have food. And it's best when you've ridden hard all day, and, in the cool of an October evening, to sit down by a roaring fire in the woods with the dry leaves beneath you, and the clear sky above you."

"Hear! hear!" said Warner. "Who's dithyrambic now? But you're right, Dick. War is a terrible thing. Besides being a ruthless slaughter it's an economic waste,—did you ever think of that, you reckless youngsters?—but it has a few minor compensations, and one of them is an evening like this. Why, everything tastes good to us. Nothing could taste bad. Our twelve wounds don't pain us in the least, and they'll heal absolutely in a few days, our blood being so healthy. The air we breathe is absolutely pure and the sky over our heads is all blue and silver, spangled with stars, a canopy stretched for our especial benefit, and upon which we have as much claim of ownership as anybody else has. We've lived out of doors so much and we've been through so much hard exercise that our bodies are now pretty nearly tempered steel. I doubt whether I'll ever be able to live indoors again, except in winter."

"I'm the luckiest of all," said Pennington. "Out on the plains we don't have to live indoors much anyway. I've lived mostly in the saddle since I was seven or eight years old, but the war has toughened me just the same. I'll be able to sleep out any time, except in the blizzards."

"As soon as you finish devouring the government stores," said a voice behind them, "it would be well for all of you to seek the sleep you're telling so much about."

It was Colonel Winchester who spoke, and they looked at him, inquiringly.

"Can I ask, sir, which way we ride?" said Dick.

"Northward with General Sheridan," replied the Colonel.

"But there is no enemy to the north, sir!"

"That's true, but we go that way, nevertheless. Although you're discreet young officers I'm not going to tell you any more. Now, as you've eaten enough food and drunk enough coffee, be off to your blankets. I want all of you to be fresh and strong in the morning."

Fresh and strong they were, and promptly General Sheridan rode away, taking with him all the cavalry, his course taking him toward Front Royal. The news soon spread among the horsemen that from Front Royal the general would go on to Washington for a conference with the War Department, while the cavalry would turn through a gap in the mountains, and then destroy railroads in order to cut off General Early's communications with Richmond.

"We're to be an escort and then a fighting and destroying force," said Dick. "But it's quite sure that we'll meet no enemy until we go through the gap. Meanwhile we'll enjoy a saunter along the valley."

But when they reached Front Royal a courier, riding hard, overtook them. He demanded to be taken at once to the presence of General Sheridan, and then he presented a copy of a dispatch which read:

> To Lieutenant-General Early:
> Be ready to move as soon as my forces join you, and we will crush Sheridan.
> Longstreet, Lieutenant-General.

Sheridan read the dispatch over and over again, and pondered it gravely. The courier informed him that it was the copy of a signal made by the Confederate flags on Three Top Mountain, and deciphered by Union officers who had obtained the secret of the Confederate code. General Wright, whom he had left in command, had sent it to him in all haste for what it was worth.

The young general not only pondered the message gravely, but he pondered it long. Finally he called his chief officers around him and consulted with them. If the grim and bearded Longstreet were really coming into the valley with a formidable force, then indeed it would be the dance of death. Longstreet, although he did not have the genius of Stonewall Jackson, was a fierce and dangerous fighter. All of them knew how he had come upon the field of Chickamauga with his veterans from Virginia, and had turned the tide of battle.

His presence in the valley might quickly turn all of Sheridan's great triumphs into withered laurels.

But Sheridan had a great doubt in his mind. The Confederate signal from Three Top Mountain that his own officers had read might not be real. It might have been intended to deceive, Early's signalmen learning that the Union signalmen had deciphered their code, or it might be some sort of a grim joke. He did not believe that the Army of Northern Virginia could spare Longstreet and a large force, as it would be weakened so greatly that it could no longer stand before Grant, even with the aid of the trenches.

His belief that this dispatch, upon which so much turned, as they were to learn afterward, was false, became a conviction and most of his officers agreed with him. He decided at last that the coming of Longstreet with an army into the valley was an impossibility, and he would go on to Washington. But Sheridan made a reservation, and this, too, as the event showed, was highly important. He ordered all the cavalry back to General Wright, while he proceeded with a small escort to the capital.

It was Dick who first learned what had happened, and soon all knew. They discussed it fully as they rode back on their own tracks, and on the whole they were glad they were to return.

"I don't think I'd like to be tearing up railroads and destroying property," said Dick. "I prefer anyhow for the valley to be my home at present, although I believe that dispatch means nothing. Why, the Confederates can't possibly rally enough men to attack us!"

"I think as you do," said Warner. "I suppose it's best for the cavalry to go back, but I wish General Sheridan had taken me on to Washington with him. I'd like to see the lights of the capital again. Besides, I'd have given the President and the Secretary of War some excellent advice."

"He isn't jesting. He means it," said Pennington to Dick.

"Of course I do," said Warner calmly. "When General Sheridan failed to take me with him, the government lost a great opportunity."

But their hearts were light and they rode gaily back, unconscious of the singular event that was preparing for them.

* * * *

The army of Early had not been destroyed entirely. Sheridan, with all his energy, and with all the courage and zeal of his men could not absolutely crush his foe. Some portions of the hostile force were continually slipping away, and now Early, refusing to give up, was gathering them together again, and was meditating a daring counter stroke. The task might well have appalled any general and any troops, but if Early had one quality in preeminence it was the resolution to fight. And most of his officers and men were veterans. Many of them had ridden with Jackson on his marvelous campaigns. They were familiar with the taste of victory, and defeat had been very bitter to them. They burned to strike back, and they were willing to dare anything for the sake of it.

Orders had already gone to all the scattered and ragged fragments, and the men in gray were concentrating. Many of them were half starved. The great valley had been stripped of all its live stock, all its grain and of every other resource that would avail an army. Nothing could be obtained, except at Staunton, ninety miles back of Fisher's Hill, and wagons could not bring up food in time from such a distant place.

Nevertheless the men gleaned. They searched the fields for any corn that might be left, and ate it roasted or parched. Along the slopes of the mountains they found nuts already ripening, and these were prizes indeed.

Among the gleaners were Harry Kenton, the staunch young Presbyterian, Dalton, and the South Carolinians, St. Clair and Langdon. St. Clair alone was impeccable of uniform, absolutely trim, and Langdon alone deserved his nickname of Happy.

"Don't be discouraged, boys," he said as he pulled from the stalk an ear of corn that the hoofs of the Northern cavalry had failed to trample under. "Now this is a fine ear, a splendid ear, and if you boys search well you may be able to find others like it. All things come to him who looks long enough. Remember how Nebuchadnezzar ate grass, and he must have had to do some hunting too, because I understand grass didn't grow very freely in that part of the world, and then remember also that we are not down to grass yet. Corn, nuts and maybe a stray pumpkin or two. 'Tis a repast fit for the gods, noble sirs."

"I can go without, part of the time," said Harry, "but it hurts me to have to hunt through a big field for a nubbin of corn and then feel happy when I've got the wretched, dirty, insignificant little thing. My father often has a hundred acres of corn in a single field, producing fifty bushels to the acre."

"And my father," said Dalton, "has a single field of fifty acres that produces fifteen hundred bushels of wheat, but it's been a long time since I've seen a shock of wheat."

"Console yourself with the knowledge," said Harry, "that it's too late in the year for wheat to be in the stack."

"Or anywhere else, either, so far as we're concerned."

"Don't murmur," said Happy. "Mourners seldom find anything, but optimists find, often. Didn't I tell you so? Here's another ear."

Harry had approached the edge of the field and he saw something red gleaming through a fringe of woods beyond. The experienced eye of youth told him at once what it was, and he called to his comrades.

"Come on, boys," he said. "There's a little orchard beyond the wood. I know there is because I caught a glimpse of a red apple hanging from a tree. I suppose the skirt of forest kept the Yankee raiders from seeing it."

They followed with a shout of joy.

"Treasure trove!" exclaimed Happy.

"Who's an optimist now?" asked Harry.

"All of us are," said St. Clair.

They passed through the wood and entered a small orchard of not more than half an acre. But it was filled with apple trees loaded with red apples, big juicy fellows, just ripened by the October sun. A little beyond the orchard in a clearing was a small log house, obviously that of the owner of the orchard, and also obviously deserted. No smoke rose from the chimneys, and windows and doors were nailed up. The proprietor no doubt had gone with his family to some town and the apples would have rotted on the ground had the young officers not found them.

"There must be bushels and bushels here," said St. Clair. "We'll fill up our sacks first and then call the other men."

They had brought sacks with them for the corn, but the few ears they had found took up but little space.

"I'll climb the trees, and shake 'em down," said Harry. He was up a tree in an instant, all his boyhood coming back to him, and, as he shook with his whole strength, the red apples, held now by twigs nearly dead, rained down. They passed from tree to tree and soon their sacks were filled.

"Now for the colonels," said St. Clair, "and on our way we'll tell the others."

Bending under the weight of the sacks, they took their course toward a snug cove in the first slope of the Massanuttons, hailing friends on the way and sending them with swift steps toward the welcome orchard. They passed within the shadow of a grove, and then entered a small open space, where two men sat on neighboring stumps, with an empty box between them. Upon the box reposed a board of chessmen and at intervals the two intent players spoke.

"If you expect to capture my remaining knight, Hector, you'll have to hurry. We march tomorrow."

"I can't be hurried, Leonidas. This is an intellectual game, and if it's played properly it demands time. If I don't take your remaining knight before tomorrow I'll take him a month from now, after this campaign is over."

"I have my doubts, Hector; I've heard you boast before."

"I never boast, Leonidas. At times I make statements and prophecies, but I trust that I'm too modest a man ever to boast."

"Then advance your battle line, Hector, and see what you can do. It's your move."

The two gray heads bent so low over the narrow board that they almost touched. For a little space the campaign, the war, and all their hardships floated away from them, their minds absorbed thoroughly in the difficult game which had come in the dim past out of the East. They did not see anything around them nor did they hear Harry as he approached them with the heavy sack of apples upon his back.

Harry's affection for both of the colonels was strong and as he looked at them he realized more than ever their utter unworldliness.

He, although a youth, saw that they belonged to a passing era, but in their very unworldliness lay their attraction. He knew that whatever the fortunes of the war, they would, if they lived, prove good citizens after its close. All rancor—no, not rancor, because they felt none—rather all hostility would be buried on the battlefield, and the friend whom they would be most anxious to see and welcome was John Carrington, the great Northern artilleryman, who had done their cause so much damage.

He opened his sack and let the red waterfall of apples pour down at their feet. Startled by the noise, they looked up, despite a critical situation on the board. Then they looked down again at the scarlet heap upon the grass, and, powerful though the attractions of chess were, they were very hungry men, and the shining little pyramid held their gaze.

"Apples! apples, Harry!" said Colonel Talbot. "Many apples, magnificent, red and ripe! Is it real?"

"No, Leonidas, it can't be real," said Lieutenant Colonel Hector St. Hilaire. "It can't be possible in a country that Sheridan swept as bare as the palm of my hand. It's only an idle dream, Leonidas. I was deceived by it myself, for a moment, but we will not yield any longer to such weakness. Come, we will return to our game, where every move has now become vital."

"But it isn't a dream, sir! It's real!" exclaimed Harry joyfully. "We found an abandoned orchard, and it was just filled with 'em. Help yourselves!"

The colonels put away their chessmen, remembering well where every one had stood, and fell on with the appetites of boys. Other officers, and then soldiers who were made welcome, joined them. Harry and Dalton, after having eaten their share, were walking along the slope of the mountain, when they heard the sound of a shot. It seemed to come from a dense thicket, and, as no Northern skirmishers could be near, their curiosity caused them to rush forward. When they entered the thicket they heard Langdon's voice raised in a shout of triumph.

"I got him! I got him!" he cried. Then they heard a heavy sliding sound, as of something being dragged, and the young South Carolinian appeared, pulling after him by its hind legs a fine hog which he had shot through the head.

"It was fair game," he cried, as he saw his friends. "Piggy here was masterless, roaming around the woods feeding on nuts until he was fat and juicy! My, how good he will taste! At first I thought he was a bear, but bear or hog he was bound to fall to my pistol!"

Langdon had indeed found a prize, and he had robbed no farmer to obtain it. Harry and Dalton stood by for a half minute and gloated with him. Then they helped him drag the hog into the cove, where the colonels sat. A half dozen experts quickly dressed the animal, and the Invincibles had a feast such as they had not tasted in a long time.

"Didn't I tell you," said Happy as he gazed contentedly into the coals over which the hog had been roasted in sections, "that those who look hard generally discover, that is, 'seek and ye shall find.' It's the optimists who arrive. Your pessimist quits before he comes to the apple trees, or before he reaches the thicket that conceals the fine fat pig. As for me, I'm always an optimist, twenty-four carats fine, and therefore I'm the superior of you fellows."

"You're happier than we are because you don't feel any sense of responsibility," said Dalton. "I'd rather be unhappy than have an empty head."

"Oh, it's just jealous you are, George Dalton. Born with a sour disposition you can't bear to see me shedding joy and light about me."

Dalton laughed.

"It's true, Happy," he said. "You do help, and for that reason we tolerate you, not because of your prowess in battle."

"Has anybody seen that fellow Slade again?" asked St. Clair.

"I'm thankful to say no," replied Harry. "He came out of the Southwest promising big things, and he certainly does have great skill in the forest, but our officers don't like his looks. Nor did I. If there was ever a thorough villain I'm sure he's one. I've heard that he's drawn off and is operating with a band of guerrillas in the mountains, robbing and murdering, I suppose."

"And they say that a big ruffian from the Kentucky mountains with another band has joined him," said Happy.

"What's his name?" asked Harry with sudden interest.

"Skelly, I think, Bill Skelly."

"Why, I know that fellow! He comes from the hills back of our town of Pendleton, and he claimed to be on the Union side. He and his band fired upon me at the very opening of the war."

"If you are not careful he'll be firing upon you again. He may have started out as a Union man, but he's shifting around now, I fancy, to suit his own plundering and robbing forces. We'll hear of their operations later, and it won't be a pretty story."

They talked of many things, and after a while Harry and St. Clair were sent with a message to the crest of Three Top Mountain, where the Confederate signal station was located, and from which the Union officers had taken the dispatch about the coming of Longstreet with a strong force. Both were fully aware of the great movement contemplated by Early and their minds now went back to march and battle.

The climb up the mountain was pleasant to such muscles and sinews as theirs, and they stopped at intervals to look over the valley, now a great desolation, until nature should come again with her healing touch. Harry smothered a sigh as he recalled their early and wonderful victories there, and the tremendous marches with the invincible Stonewall. Old Jack, as he sat somewhere with Washington and Cromwell and all the group of the mighty, must feel sad when he looked down upon this, his beloved valley, now trodden into a ruin by the heel of the invader.

He resolutely put down the choking in his throat, and would not let St. Clair see his emotion. They reached the signal station, which at that hour was in charge of a young officer named Mortimer, but little older than themselves. They delivered to him their message and stood by, while he talked with flags to another station on the opposite mountain. Harry watched curiously although he could read none of the signals.

"This is our only newspaper and I can't read it," he said when Mortimer had finished. "What's the news?"

"There's a lot of it, and it's heavy with importance," replied Mortimer.

"Tell us a bit of it, can't you?"

"Sheridan has left his army and gone north. That's one bit."

"What?"

"It's so. We know absolutely, and we've signaled it to General Early. But we don't know why he has gone."

"That is important."

"It surely is, and he's taken his cavalry with him. Our men have seen the troops riding northward. Since Sheridan went away, the Union commander, whoever he is, has been strengthening his right, fearing an attack there, since he learned of our reappearance in the valley."

"Therefore General Early will attack on the left?"

"Correct. You can see now the value of signal stations like ours. We can look down upon the enemy and see his movements. Then we know what to do."

"And what have they on their left?" asked Harry. "Do you know that, too?"

"Of course. General Crook with two divisions is there. He has Cedar Creek in front of him, and on his own left the north fork of the Shenandoah. He's considerably in front of the main Union force, and they haven't posted much of a picket line."

"I suppose they're relying upon the natural strength of the ground."

"That's it, I take it, but we may give them a surprise."

Harry and Dalton used their glasses and far to the north they saw dim figures, not larger than toys. At first view they appeared to be stationary, but, as the eyes became used to the distance, Harry knew they were moving. Apparently they were infantry going toward the Union right, where danger was feared, and he felt a grim satisfaction in knowing that the real danger lay on their left. But could Early with his small numbers, with the habit now of defeat, make any impression upon the large Union armies flushed with victories?

Harry wondered if Dick was among those moving troops, but his second thought told him it was not likely. They had learned from spies that the Winchester regiment was mounted, and in all probability it was part of the cavalry that had gone north with Sheridan. But he thought again how strange it was that the two should have been face to face at the Second Manassas, and then after a wide separation, involving so many great battles and marches, should come here into the Valley of Virginia, face to face once more.

Mortimer and his assistants presently began to manipulate the flags again, and Confederate signalmen, on a far peak, replied. Harry and St. Clair watched them with all the curiosity that a mystery inspires.

"Can we ask again," said Harry, when they had finished, "what you fellows were saying?"

Mortimer laughed.

"It was a quick dialogue," he replied, "but it was intended for the Yankees down in the valley, who, we learn, have deciphered some of our signals. I said to Strother on the other peak: 'Six thousand?' He replied: 'No, eight thousand!' I said: 'In center or on their right flank?' He replied: 'On their right flank.' I said: 'Two thousand fresh horses?' He replied: 'Nearer twenty-five hundred.' I said: 'Five hundred fresh beeves from the other side of the Blue Ridge.' He replied: 'Great news, we need 'em!' I wish it was true, but it will set our Yankee friends to thinking."

"I see. Your talk was meant to fool the Yankees."

"Yes, and we need to fool 'em as much as we can. It's a daring venture that we're entering upon, but it's great luck for us to have Sheridan away. It looks like a good omen to me."

"And to me, too. We used to say that Old Jack was an army corps, and he was, two of them for that matter. Then Sheridan is worth at least ten thousand men to the Yankees. Good-by, we'd like to see more of your work with the flags, but down below they need Captain St. Clair, who is a terrible fighter. We can't hope to beat the Yankees with St. Clair away."

Mortimer smiled, waved them farewell, and, a few minutes later, was at work once more with the flags. Meanwhile, Harry and St. Clair were descending the mountain, pausing now and then to survey the valley with their glasses, where they could yet mark the movements of the Northern troops. When they reached the cove they found that the board and the chess men were put away, and the two colonels were inspecting the Invincibles to see that the last detail was done, while Early made ready for his desperate venture.

Harry and his comrades were fully conscious that it was a forlorn hope. They had been driven out of the valley once by superior numbers and equipment, directed by a leader of great skill and energy, but now they had come back to risk everything in a daring venture. The Union forces, of course, knew of their presence in the old lines about Fisher's Hill—Shepard alone was sufficient to warn them of it—but they could scarcely expect an attack by a foe of small numbers, already defeated several times.

Harry's thought of Shepard set him to surmising. The spy no longer presented himself to his mind as a foe to be hated. Rather, he was an official enemy whom he liked. He even remembered with a smile their long duel when Lee was retreating from Gettysburg, and particularly their adventure in the river. Would that duel between them be renewed? Intuition told him that Shepard was in the valley, and if Sheridan was worth ten thousand men the spy was worth at least a thousand.

The Invincibles were ready to the last man, and it did not require any great counting to reach the last. Yet the two colonels, as they rode before their scanty numbers, held themselves as proudly as ever, and the hearts of their young officers, in spite of all the odds, began to beat high with hope. The advance was to be made after dark, and their pulses were leaping as the twilight came, and then the night.

The march of the Southern army to deal its lightning stroke was prepared well, and, fortunately for it, a heavy fog came up late in the night from the rivers and creeks of the valley to cover its movements and hide the advancing columns from its foe. When Harry felt the damp touch of the vapor on his face his hopes rose yet higher. He knew that weather, fog, rain, snow and flooding rivers played a great part in the fortunes of war. Might not the kindly fog, encircling them with its protection, be a good omen?

"Chance favors us," he said to St. Clair and Langdon, as the fog grew thicker and thicker, almost veiling their faces from one another.

"I told you that the optimists usually had their way," said Happy. "We persisted and found that orchard of apples. We persisted and found that fat porker. Now, I have been wishing for this fog, and I kept on wishing for it until it came."

Harry laughed.

"You do make the best of things, Happy," he said.

The fog thickened yet more, but the Invincibles made their sure way through it, the different portions of the army marching in perfect coordination. Gordon led three divisions of infantry, supported by a brigade of cavalry across the Shenandoah River and marched east of Fisher's Hill. Then he went along the slope of the Massanuttons, recrossed the river, and silently came in behind the left flank of the Union force under Crook.

Early himself, with two divisions of infantry and all the artillery, marched straight toward Cedar Creek, where he would await the sound of firing to tell him that Gordon had completed his great circling movement. Then he would push forward with all his might, and he and Gordon appearing suddenly out of the fog and dark would strike sledge hammer blows from different sides at the surprised Union army. It was a conception worthy of Old Jack himself, although there was less strength with which to deal the blows.

The Invincibles were with Early, and they arrived in position before Cedar Creek long before Gordon could complete his wide flanking movement. Both artillery and infantry were up, and there was nothing for them to do but wait. The officers dismounted and naturally those who led the Invincibles kept close together. The wait was long. Midnight came, and then the hours after it passed one by one.

It was late in the year, the eighteenth of October, and the night was chill. The heavy fog which hung low made it chillier. Harry as he stood by his horse felt it cold and damp on his face, but it was a true friend for all that. Whether Happy wishing for the fog had made it come or not they could have found no better aid.

He could not see far, but out of the vapors came the sound of men moving, because they were restless and could not help it. He heard too the murmur of voices, and now and then the clank of a cannon, as it was advanced a little. More time passed. It was the hour when it would be nearly dawn on a clear day, and thousands of hearts leaped as the sound of shots came from a distant point out of the fog.

CHAPTER XI
CEDAR CREEK

The Winchester Regiment and the rest of the cavalry returned to the Union army, and, on the memorable night of the eighteenth of October, they were north of Cedar Creek with the Eighth Corps, most of the men being then comfortably asleep in tents. A courier had brought word to General Wright that all was quiet in front, and the same word was sent to Sheridan, who, returning, had come as far as Winchester where he slept that night, expecting to rejoin his command the next day.

But there were men of lower rank than Wright and Sheridan who were uneasy, and particularly so Sergeant Daniel Whitley, veteran of the plains, and of Indian ambush and battle. None of the Winchester officers had sought sleep either in the tents or elsewhere, and, in the night, Dick stood beside the suspicious sergeant and peered into the fog.

"I don't like it," said the veteran. "Fogs ain't to be taken lightly. I wish this one hadn't come at this time. I'm generally scared of most of the things I can't see."

"But what have we to be afraid of?" asked Dick. "We're here in strong force, and the enemy is too weak to attack."

"The Johnnies are never too weak to attack. Rec'lect, too, that this is their country, and they know every inch of it. I wish Mr. Shepard was here."

"I think he was detailed for some scout duty off toward the Blue Ridge."

"I don't know who sent him, but I make bold to say, Mr. Mason, that he could do a lot more good out there in the fog on the other side of Cedar Creek, a-spyin' and a-spyin', a-lookin' and a-lookin', a-listenin' and a-listenin'."

"And perhaps he would neither see nor hear anything"

"Maybe, sir, but if I may make bold again, I think you're wrong. Why, I just fairly smell danger."

"It's the fog and your fear of it, sergeant."

"No, sir; it's not that. It's my five senses working all together and telling me the truth."

"But the pickets have brought in no word."

"In this fog, pickets can't see more'n a few yards beyond their beats. What time is it, Mr. Mason?"

"A little past one in the morning, sergeant."

"Enough of the night left yet for a lot of mischief. I'm glad, sir, if I may make bold once more, that the Winchester men stay out of the tents and keep awake."

Warner joined them, and reported that fresh messengers from the front had given renewed assurances of quiet. Absolutely nothing was stirring along Cedar Creek, but Sergeant Daniel Whitley was still dissatisfied.

"It's always where nothin' is stirrin' that most is doin', sir," he said to Dick.

"You're epigrammatic, sergeant."

"I'm what, sir? I was never called that before."

"It doesn't depreciate you. It's a flattering adjective, but you've set my own nerves to tingling and I don't feel like sleeping."

"It never hurts, sir, to watch in war, even when nothing happens. I remember once when we were in a blizzard west of the Missouri, only a hundred of us. It was in the country of the Northern Cheyennes, an' no greater fighters ever lived than them red demons. We got into a kind of dip, surrounded by trees, an' managed to build a fire. We was so busy tryin' to keep from freezin' to death that we never gave a thought to Indians, that is 'ceptin' one, the guide, Jim Palmer, who knowed them Cheyennes, an' who kept dodgin' about in the blizzard, facin' the icy blast an' the whirlin' snow, an' always lookin' an' listenin'. I owe my life to him, an' so does every other one of the hundred. Shore enough the Cheyennes come, ridin' right on the edge of the blizzard, an' in all that terrible storm they tried to rush us. But we'd been warned by Palmer an' we beat 'em off at last, though a lot of good men bit the snow. I say again, sir, that you can't ever be too careful in war. Do everything you can think of, and then think of some more. I wish Mr. Shepard would come!"

They continued to walk back and forth, in front of the lines, and, at times, they were accompanied by Colonel Winchester or Warner or Pennington. The colonel fully shared the sergeant's anxieties. The fact that most of the Union army was asleep in the tents alarmed him, and the great fog added to his uneasiness. It came now in heavy drifts like clouds sweeping down the valley, and he did not know what was in the heart of it. The pickets had been sent far forward, but the vast moving column of heavy whitish vapor hid everything from their eyes, too, save a circle of a few yards about them.

Toward morning Dick, the colonel and the sergeant stood together, trying to pierce the veil of vapor in front of them. The colonel did not hesitate to speak his thought to the two.

"I wish that General Sheridan was here," he said.

"But he's at Winchester," said Dick. "He'll join us at noon."

"I wish he was here now, and I wish, too, that this fog would lift, and the day would come. Hark, what was that?"

"It was a rifle shot, sir," said the sergeant.

"And there are more," exclaimed Dick. "Listen!"

There was a sudden crackle of firing, and in front of them pink dots appeared through the fog.

"Here comes the Southern army!" said Sergeant Whitley.

Out of the fog rose a tremendous swelling cry from thousands of throats, fierce, long-drawn, and full of menace. It was the rebel yell, and from another point above the rising thunder of cannon and rifles came the same yell in reply, like a signal. The surprise was complete. Gordon had hurled himself upon the Union flank and at the same moment Early, according to his plan, drove with all his might at the center.

Dick was horrified, and, for a moment or two, the blood was ice in his veins.

"Back!" cried Colonel Winchester to him and the sergeant, and then after shouting, "Up men! Up!" he blew long and loud upon his whistle. All of his men were on their feet in an instant, and they were first to return the Southern fire, but it had little effect upon the torrent that was now pouring down upon them. Other troops, so rudely aroused from sleep, rushed from their tents, still dazed, and firing wildly in the fog.

Again that terrible yell arose, more distinct than ever with menace and triumph, and so great was the rush of the men in gray that they swept everything before them, their rifles and cannon raking the Union camp with a withering fire. The Winchesters, despite their quickness to form in proper order, were driven back with the others, and the whole corps, assailed with frightful force on the flank also, was compelled continually to give ground, and to leave long rows of dead and wounded.

"Keep close to me!" shouted Colonel Winchester to his young officers, and then he added to the sergeant, who stood beside him: "Whitley, you were right!"

"I'm sorry to say I was, sir," replied the sergeant. "It was a great ambush, and it's succeeding so far."

"But we must hold them! We must find some way to hold them!" cried the colonel.

He said more, but it was lost in the tremendous uproar of the firing and the shouting. All the officers were dismounted—their horses already had been taken by the enemy—and now, waving their swords, they walked up and down in front of the lines, seeking to encourage their own troops. Despite the surprise and the attack from two sides, the men in blue sustained their courage and made a stubborn fight. Nevertheless the attack in both front and flank was fatal. Again and again they sought to hold a position, but always they were driven from it, leaving behind more dead and wounded and more prisoners.

Dick's heart sank. It was bitter to see a defeat, after so many victories. Perhaps the fortunes of the South had not passed the zenith after all! If Sheridan were defeated and driven from the valley, and Lee's flank left protected, Grant might sit forever before him at Petersburg and not be able to force his trenches. All these thoughts and fears swept before him, vague, disconnected, and swift.

But he saw that Warner, Pennington and the colonel were still unhurt, and that the Winchesters, despite their exposed position, had not suffered as much loss as some of the other regiments. General Wright in the absence of Sheridan retained his head, and formed a strong core of resistance which, although it could not yet hold the ground, might give promise of doing so, if help arrived.

Dawn came, driving the fog away, and casting a red glow over the field of battle. The ground where the Union troops had slept the night before was now left far behind, and the Southern army, full of fire and the swell of victory, was pushing on with undiminished energy, its whole front blazing with the rapid discharge of cannon and rifles.

The terrible retreat lasted a long time, and the whole Union army was driven back a full five miles before it could make a permanent stand. Then, far in the morning, the regiments reformed, held their ground, and Dick, for the first time, took a long free breath.

"We've been defeated but not destroyed," he said.

"No, we haven't," said a voice beside him, "but the fact that the Johnnies were so hungry has saved us a lot."

It was Shepard, who seemed to have risen from the ground.

"I've got back from places farther north," he said. "Chance kept me away from here last night."

"What do you mean about the Southern hunger helping us?" asked Dick.

"I've been on the flank, and I saw that when they drove us out of our camps the temptation was too great for many of their men. They scattered, seizing our good food and devouring it. It was impossible for their officers to restrain them. They've suffered losses too, and they can drive us no farther."

Then Shepard spoke briefly with Colonel Winchester, and disappeared again. The fire had now died somewhat and the banks of smoke were rising, enabling Dick to see the field with a degree of clearness. Union batteries and regiments were in line, but behind them a mass of fugitives, who had not yet recovered from the surprise and who thought the defeat complete, were pouring along the turnpike toward Winchester. When Dick saw their numbers his fears were renewed. He believed that if the Southern army could gather up all its forces and attack once more it would win another success.

But while he looked at the long line of fire in front of them a sudden roar of cheering rose from the Union ranks. It became a shout, tremendous and thrilling. Dick turned in excitement and he was about to ask what it meant, when he distinguished a name thundered again and again:

"Sheridan! Sheridan! Sheridan!"

Then before them galloped their own Little Phil, seeming to bring strength, courage and victory with him. His hat was thrown back, his face flushed, and his eyes sparkling. Everywhere the men rallied to his call and the shouts: "Sheridan! Sheridan!" rolled up and down. The fugitives too came pouring back to swell the line of battle. Dick caught the enthusiasm at once, and felt his own pulses leaping. He and Pennington and Warner joined in the shouts: "Sheridan! Sheridan!" and snatching off their caps waved them with all their vigor.

It was an amazing transformation. A beaten and dispirited army, holding on from a sense of duty, suddenly became alive with zeal, and asked only to be led against the enemy by the general they trusted. One man alone had worked the miracle and as his enemies had truly said his presence was worth ten thousand men.

His coming had been dramatic. He had spent the night quietly at Winchester, but, early in the morning, he had heard the sounds of firing which steadily grew louder. Apprehensive, he rode at once toward the distant field, and, before he had gone two miles, he met the first stragglers, bringing wild tales that the army had been routed, and that the Southerners were hot on their heels. Sheridan rode rapidly now. He met thicker streams of fugitives, but turned them back toward the enemy, and when he finally came upon the field itself he brought with him all the retreating regiments.

Dick never beheld a more thrilling and inspiring sight than that which occurred when Sheridan galloped among them, swinging his hat in his hand.

"What troops are these?" he had asked.

"The Sixth Corps!" hundreds of voices shouted in reply.

"We are all right! We'll win!" cried Sheridan.

And then, as he galloped along the line he added:

"Never mind, boys, we'll whip 'em yet! We'll whip 'em yet! We'll sleep in their quarters tonight!"

The roar of cheering swept up and down the line again, and Sheridan and his officers began to prepare the restored army for a new battle. All the time the Union numbers swelled, and, as the Southern army was hesitating, Sheridan was able to post his divisions as he pleased.

The Winchester regiment was drawn up towards the flank. All the officers were still on foot, but they stood a little in front, ready to lead their men into the new battle. It was now about noon, and there was a pause in the combat, enabling the smoke to lift yet higher, and disclosing the whole field. Sheridan was still riding up and down the lines, cool, determined and resolved to turn defeat into victory. Wherever he went he spoke words of encouragement to his troops, but all the time his eye, which was the eye of a true general, swept the field. He put the gallant young Custer with his cavalry on the right, Crook and Merritt with their horse on the left, while the infantry were massed in the center. The Winchester men were sent to the right.

The doubts in the ranks of the South helped Sheridan. Early after his victory in the morning was surprised to see the Union army gather itself together again and show such a formidable front. Neither he nor his lieutenants could understand the sudden reversal, and the pause, which at first had been meant merely to give the troops opportunity for fresh breath, grew into a long delay. Here and there, skirmishers were firing, feeling out one another, but the masses of the army paid no attention to those scattered shots.

The Winchester men were elated. Colonel Winchester and the young officers knew that delay worked steadily for them. All the defeated troops of the morning were coming back into line, and now they were anxious to retrieve their disaster. Dick, through his glasses, saw that the Confederates so far from continuing the advance were now fortifying behind stone fences and also were spreading across the valley to keep from being flanked on either side by the cavalry. But he saw too that their ranks were scanty. If they spread far enough to protect their flanks they would become dangerously thin in the center. He handed his glasses to the sergeant, and asked him to take a look.

"Their surprise," said Whitley, "has spent its force. Their army is not big enough. Our general has seen it, and it's why he delays so long. Time works for us, because we can gather together much greater numbers than they have."

The delay lasted far into the afternoon. The smoke and dust settled, and the October sun gleamed on cannon and bayonets. Dick's watch showed that it was nearly four o'clock.

"We attack today surely," said Pennington, who was growing nervous with impatience.

"Don't you worry, young man," said Warner. "The two armies are here in line facing each other and as it would be too much trouble to arrange it all again tomorrow the battle will be fought today. The whole program will be carried out on time."

"I think," said Dick, "that the attack is very near, and that it's we who are going to make it. Here is General Sheridan himself."

The general rode along the line just before the Winchesters and nodded to them approvingly. He came so close that Dick saw the contraction of his face, and his eager burning look, as if the great moment had arrived. Suddenly, he raised his hand and the buglers blew the fierce notes of the charge.

"Now we go!" cried Pennington in uncontrollable excitement, and the whole right wing seemed to lift itself up bodily and rush forward. The men, eager to avenge the losses of the morning, began to shout, and their cheers mingled with the mighty tread of the charge, the thunder of the cannon and the rapid firing of thousands of rifles. They knew, too, that Sheridan's own eye was upon them, and it encouraged them to a supreme effort.

Infantry and cavalry swept on together in an overwhelming mass. Cannon and rifles sent a bitter hail upon them, but nothing could stop their rush. Dick felt all his pulses beating heavily and he saw a sea of fire before him, but his excitement was so intense that he forgot about danger.

The center also swung into the charge and then the left. All the divisions of the army, as arranged by Sheridan, moved in perfect time. The soldiers advanced like veterans going from one victory to another, instead of rallying from a defeat. The war had not witnessed another instance of such a quick and powerful recovery.

Dick knew, as their charge gathered force at every step, that they were going to certain triumph. The thinness of the Southern lines had already told him that they could not withstand the impact of Sheridan. A moment later the crash came and the whole Union force rushed to victory. Early's army, exhausted by its efforts of the morning, was overwhelmed. It was swept from the stone fences and driven back in defeat, while the men in blue, growing more eager as they saw success achieved, pressed harder and harder.

No need for bugle and command to urge them on now. The Southern army could not withstand anywhere such ardor and such weight. Position after position was lost, then there was no time to take a new stand, and the defeat became a rout. Early's army which had come forward so gallantly in the morning was compelled to flee in disorder in the afternoon. The brave Ramseur, fighting desperately, fell mortally wounded, Kershaw could save but a few men, Evans held a ford a little while, but he too was soon hurled from it. The Invincibles were driven on with the rest, cannon and wagons were lost, and all but the core of Early's force ceased to exist.

The sun set upon the Union army in the camps that it had lost in the fog of the morning. It had been driven five miles but had come back again. It had recovered all its own guns, and had taken twenty-four belonging to the South. It was the most complete victory that had yet been won by either side in the war, and it had been snatched from the very jaws of defeat and humiliation. Small wonder that there was great rejoicing in the ranks of northern youth! Despite their immense exertions and the commands of their officers they could not yet lie down and sleep or rest. Now and then a tremendous cheer for Little Phil who had saved them arose. Huge bonfires sprang up in the night, where they were burning the captured Confederate ambulances and wagons, because they did not have the horses with which to take them away.

Long after the battle was over, Dick's heart beat hard with exertion and excitement. But he shared too in the joy. He would not have been human, and he would not have been young if he had not. Warner and Pennington and he had collected four more small wounds among them, but they were so slight that they had not noticed them in the storm and fury of the battle. Colonel Winchester had not been touched.

When Dick was at last able to sit still, he joined his comrades about one of the fires, where they were serving supper to the victors. Shepard had just galloped back from a long ride after the enemy to say that they had been scattered to the winds, and that another surprise was not possible, because there were no longer enough Southern soldiers in the valley to make an army.

"They made a great effort," said Colonel Winchester. "We must give them credit for what they achieved against numbers and resources. They organized and carried out their surprise in a wonderful manner, and perhaps they would be the victors tonight if we didn't have such a general as Sheridan."

"It was a great sight," said Warner, "when he appeared, galloping before our line, calling upon us to renew our courage and beat the enemy."

"One man can influence an army. I've found out that," said Dick.

They rose and saluted as General Sheridan walked past with some of the higher officers. He returned the salutes, congratulated them on their courage and went on. After a long while the exhausted victors fell asleep.

* * * *

That night a band of men, a hundred perhaps, entered the woods along the slopes of the Massanuttons. They were the remains of the Invincibles. Throughout those fatal hours they had fought with all the courage and tenacity for which they had been famous so long and so justly. In the heat and confusion of the combat they had been separated from the other portions of Early's army, and, the Northern cavalry driving in between, they had been compelled to take refuge in the forest, under cover of darkness. They might have surrendered with honor, but not one among them thought of such a thing. They had been forced to leave their dead behind them, and of those who had withdrawn about a third were wounded. But, their hurts bandaged by their comrades, they limped on with the rest.

The two colonels were at the head of the sombre little column. It had seemed to Harry Kenton as they left the field that each of them had suddenly grown at least ten years older, but now as they passed within the deep shadows they became erect again and their faces grew more youthful. It was a marvelous transformation, but Harry read their secret. All the rest of the Invincibles were lads, or but little more, and they two middle-aged men felt that they were responsible for them. In the face of defeat and irretrievable disaster they recovered their courage, and refused to abandon hope.

"A dark sunset, Hector," said Colonel Talbot, "but a bright dawn will come, even yet."

"Who can doubt it, Leonidas? We won a glorious victory over odds in the morning, but when a million Yankees appeared on the field in the afternoon it was too much."

"That's always the trouble, Hector. We are never able to finish our victories, because so many of the enemy always come up before the work is done."

"It's a great pity, Leonidas, that we didn't count the Yankees before the war was started."

"It's too late now. Don't call up a sore subject, Hector. We've got to take care of these lads of ours, and try to get them across the mountain somehow to Lee. It's useless to seek Early and we couldn't reach him if we tried. He's done for."

"Alas! It's true, Leonidas! We're through with the valley for this autumn at least, and, since the organization of the army here is broken up, there is nothing for us to do but go to Lee. Harry, is this a high mountain?"

"Not so very high, sir," replied Harry Kenton, who was just behind him, "but I don't think we can cross it tonight."

"Maybe we don't want to do so," said Colonel Talbot. "You boys have food in your knapsacks, taken from the Union camps, which we held for a few short and glorious hours. At least we have brought off those valuable trophies, and, when we have climbed higher up the mountain side, we will sup and rest."

The colonel held himself very erect, and spoke in a firm proud tone. He would inspire a high spirit into the hearts of these boys of his, and in doing so he inspired a great deal of it into his own. He looked back at his column, which still limped bravely after him. It was too dark for him to see the faces of the lads, but he knew that none of them expressed despair.

"That's the way, my brave fellows," he said. "I know we'll find a warm and comfortable cove higher up. We'll sleep there, and tomorrow we'll start toward Lee. When we join him we'll whip Grant, come back here and rout Sheridan and then go on and take Washington."

"Where I mean yet, sir, to sleep in the White House with my boots on," said the irrepressible Happy.

"You are a youth frivolous of speech, Thomas Langdon," said Colonel Leonidas Talbot gravely, "but I have always known that beneath this superficiality of manner was a brave and honest heart. I'm glad to see that your courage is so high."

"Thank you, sir," said Happy sincerely.

Half way up the mountain they found the dip they wished, sheltered by cedars and pines. Here they rested and ate, and from their covert saw many lights burning in the valley. But they knew they were the lights of the victorious foe, and they would not look that way often.

The October winds were cold, and they had lost their blankets, but the dry leaves lay in heaps, and they raked them up for beds. The lads, worn to the bone, fell asleep, and, after a while, only the two colonels remained awake.

"I do not feel sleepy at all, Hector," said Colonel Leonidas Talbot.

"I could not possibly sleep, Leonidas," said Lieutenant Colonel St. Hilaire.

"Then shall we?"

"Why not?"

Colonel Talbot produced from under his coat a small board, and Lieutenant Colonel St. Hilaire took from under his own coat a small box.

They put the board upon a broad stone, arranged the chessmen, as they were at the latest interruption, and, as the moonlight came through the dwarfed pines and cedars, the two gray heads bent over the game.

CHAPTER XII
IN THE COVE

General Sheridan permitted the Winchester men to rest a long time, or rather he ordered them to do so. No regiment had distinguished itself more at Cedar Creek or in the previous battles, and it was best for it to lie by a while, and recover its physical strength — strength of the spirit it had never lost. It also gave a needed chance to the sixteen slight wounds accumulated by Dick, Pennington and Warner to heal perfectly.

"Unless something further happens," said Warner, regretfully, "I won't have a single honorable scar to take back with me and show in Vermont."

"I'll have one slight, though honorable, scar, but I won't be able to show it," said Pennington, also with regret.

"I trust that it's in front, Frank," said Dick.

"It is, all right. Don't worry about that. But what about you, Dick?"

"I had hopes of a place on my left arm just above the elbow. A bullet, traveling at the rate of a million miles a minute, broke the skin there and took a thin flake of flesh with it, but I'm so terribly healthy it's healed up without leaving a trace."

"There's no hope for us," said Warner, sighing. "We can never point to the proof of our warlike deeds. You didn't find your cousin among the prisoners?"

"No, nor was he among their fallen whom we buried. Nor any of his friends either. I'm quite sure that he escaped. My intuition tells me so."

"It's not your intuition at all," said Warner reprovingly. "It's a reasonable opinion, formed in your mind by antecedent conditions.

You call it intuition, because you don't take the trouble to discover the circumstances that led to its production. It's only lazy minds that fall back upon second sight, mind-reading and such things."

"Isn't he the big-word man?" said Pennington admiringly. "I tell you what, George, General Early is still alive somewhere, and we're going to send you to talk him to death. They say he's a splendid swearer, one of the greatest that ever lived, but he won't be able to get out a single cuss, with you standing before him, and spouting the whole unabridged dictionary to him."

"At least when I talk I say something," replied Warner sternly. "It seems strange to me, Frank Pennington, that your life on the plains, where conditions, for the present at least, are hard, has permitted you to have so much frivolity in your nature."

"It's not frivolity, George. It's a gay and bright spirit, in the rays of which you may bask without price. It will do you good."

"Do you know what's to be our next duty?"

"No, I don't, and I'm not going to bother about it. I'll leave that directly to Colonel Winchester, and indirectly to General Sheridan. When you rest, put your mind at rest. Concentration on whatever you are doing is the secret of continued success."

They were lying on blankets near the foot of the mountain, and the time was late October. The days were growing cold and the nights colder, but a fine big fire was blazing before them, and they rejoiced in the warmth and brightness, shed from the flames and the heaps of glowing coals.

"I'll venture the prediction," said Pennington, "that our next march is not against an army, but against guerrillas. They say that up there in the Alleghanies Slade and Skelly are doing a lot of harm. They may have to be hunted out and the Winchester men have the best reputation in the army for that sort of work. We earned it by our work against these very fellows in Tennessee."

"For which most of the credit is due to Sergeant Whitley," said Dick. "He's a grand trailer, and he can lead us with certainty, when other regiments can't find the way."

Dick gazed westward beyond the dim blue line of the Alleghanies, and he knew that he would feel no surprise if Pennington's prediction should come true. The nest of difficult mountains was a good shelter for outlaws, and the Winchesters, with the sergeant picking up the trail, were the very men to hunt them.

He knew too that, unless the task was begun soon, it would prove a supreme test of endurance, and there would be dangers in plenty. Snow would be falling before long on the mountains, and they would become a frozen wilderness, almost as wild and savage as they were before the white man came.

But it seemed for a while that the intuition of both Dick and Pennington had failed. They spent many days in the valley trying to catch the evasive Mosby and his men, although they had little success. Mosby's rangers knowing the country thoroughly made many daring raids, although they could not become a serious menace.

When they returned through Winchester from the last of these expeditions the Winchester men were wrapped in heavy army cloaks, for the wind from the mountains could now cut through uniforms alone. Dick, glancing toward the Alleghanies, saw a ribbon of white above their blue line.

"Look, fellows! The first snow!" he said.

"I see," said Warner. "It snows on the just and the unjust, the unjust being Slade and Skelly, who are surely up there."

"Just before we went out," sad Pennington, "the news of some fresh and special atrocity of theirs came in. I'm thinking the time is near when we'll be sent after them."

"We'll need snow shoes," said Warner, shivering as he looked. "I can see that the snow is increasing. Which way is the wind blowing, Dick?"

"Toward us."

"Then we're likely to get a little of that snow. The clouds will blow off the mountains and sprinkle us with flakes in the valley."

"I like winter in peace, but not in war," said Pennington. "It makes campaigning hard. It's no fun marching at night in a driving storm of snow or hail."

"But what we can't help we must stand," said Warner with resignation.

Both predictions, the one about the snow and the other concerning the duty that would be assigned to them, quickly came to pass. Before sunset the blue line of the Alleghanies was lost wholly in mist and vapor. Then great flakes began to fall on the camp, and the young officers were glad to find refuge in their tents.

It was not a heavy snow fall where they were, but it blew down at intervals all through the night, and the next morning it lay upon the ground to the depth of an inch or so. Then the second part of the prophecy was justified. Colonel Winchester himself aroused all his staff and heads of companies.

"A fine crisp winter morning for us to take a ride," he said cheerfully. "General Sheridan has become vexed beyond endurance over the doings of Slade and Skelly, and he has chosen his best band of guerrilla-hunters to seek 'em out in their lairs and annihilate 'em."

"I knew it," groaned Pennington in an undertone to Dick. "I was as certain of it as if I had read the order already." But aloud he said as he saluted: "We're glad we're chosen for the honor, sir. I speak for Mr. Mason, Mr. Warner and myself."

"I'm glad you're thankful," laughed the colonel. "A grateful and resolute heart always prepares one for hardships, and we'll have plenty of them over there in the high mountains, where the snow lies deep. But we have new horses, furnished especially for this expedition, and Sergeant Whitley and Mr. Shepard will guide us. The sergeant can hear or see anything within a quarter of a mile of him, and Mr. Shepard, being a native of the valley, knows also all the mountains that close it in."

The young lieutenants were sincerely glad the sergeant and Shepard were to go along, as with them they felt comparatively safe from ambush, a danger to be dreaded where Slade and Skelly were concerned.

"We agreed that General Sheridan was worth ten thousand men," said Warner, "and I believe that the battle of Cedar Creek proved it. Now if Sheridan is worth ten thousand, the sergeant and Shepard are certainly worth a thousand each. It's a simple algebraic problem which I could demonstrate to you by the liberal use of x and y, but in your case it's not necessary. You must accept my word for it."

"We'll do it! We'll do it! say no more!" exclaimed Pennington hastily.

It was a splendid column of men that rode out from the Union camp and General Sheridan himself saw them off. Colonel Winchester at their head was a man of fine face and figure, and he had never looked more martial. The hardships of war had left no mark upon him. His face was tanned a deep red by the winds of summer and winter, and although a year or two over forty he seemed to be several years less. Behind him came Dick, Pennington and Warner, hardy and well knit, who had passed through the most terrible of all schools, three and a half years of incessant war, and who although youths were nevertheless stronger and more resourceful than most men.

Near them rode the sergeant, happy in his capacity as scout and guide, and welcoming the responsibility that he knew would be his, as soon as they reached the mountains, looming so near and white. He felt as if he were back upon the plains, leading a troop in a great blizzard, and guarding it with eye and ear and all his five senses against Sioux or Cheyenne ambush. He was not a mere trainer of a squad of men, he was, in a real sense, a leader of an army.

Shepard, the spy, also felt a great uplift of the spirits. He was a man of high ideals, whose real nature the people about him were just beginning to learn. He did not like his trade of a spy, but being aware that he was peculiarly fitted for it intense patriotism had caused him to accept its duties. Now he felt that most of his work in such a capacity was over. He could freely ride with the other men and fight openly as they did. But if emergency demanded that he renew his secret service he would do so instantly and without hesitation.

Colonel Winchester looked back with pride at his column. Like most of the regiments at that period of the war it was small, three hundred sinewy well-mounted young men, who had endured every kind of hardship and who could endure the like again. All of them were wrapped in heavy overcoats over their uniforms, and they rode the best of horses, animals that Colonel Winchester had been allowed to choose.

The colonel felt so good that he took out his little silver whistle, and blew upon it a mellow hunting call. The column broke into a trot and the snow flew behind the beating hoofs in a long white trail. Spontaneously the men burst into a cheer, and the cold wind blowing past them merely whipped their blood into high exaltation.

But as they rode across the valley Dick could not help feeling some depression over its ruined and desolate appearance, worse now in winter than in summer. No friendly smoke rose from any chimney, there were no horses nor cattle in the fields, the rails of the fences had gone long since to make fires for the soldiers and the roads rutted deep by the rains had been untouched. Silence and loneliness were supreme everywhere.

He was glad when they left it all behind, and entered the mountains through a pass fairly broad and sufficient for horsemen. He did not feel so much oppression here. It was natural for mountains to be lonely and silent also, particularly in winter, and his spirits rose again as they rode between the white ridges.

At the entrance to the pass a mountaineer named Reed met them. It was he who had brought the news of the latest exploit by Slade and Skelly, but he had returned quickly to warn some friends of his in the foothills and was back again in time to meet the soldiers. He was a long thin man of middle age, riding a large black mule. An immense gray shawl was pinned about his shoulders, and woollen leggings came high over his trousers. As he talked much he chewed tobacco vigorously. But Dick saw at once that like many of the mountaineers he was a shrewd man, and, despite lack of education, was able to look, see and judge.

Reed glanced over the column, showed his teeth, yellowed by the constant use of tobacco, and the glint of a smile appeared in his eyes.

"Look like good men. I couldn't hev picked 'em better myself, colonel," he said, with the easy familiarity of the hills.

"They've been in many battles, and they've never failed," said the colonel with some pride.

"You'll hev to do somethin' more than fight up thar on the high ridges," said the mountaineer, showing his yellow teeth again. "You'll hev to look out fur traps, snares an' ambushes. Slade an' Skelly ain't soldiers that come out an' fight fa'r an' squar' in the open. No, sirree, they're rattlesnakes, a pair uv 'em an' full uv p'ison. We've got to find our rattlesnakes an' ketch 'em. Ef we don't, they'll be stingin' jest the same after you've gone."

"That's just the way I look at it, Mr. Reed. Sergeant Whitley here is a specialist in rattlesnakes. He used to hunt down and kill the big bloated ones on the plains, and even the snow won't keep him from tracing 'em to their dens here in the mountains."

Reed, after the custom of his kind, looked the sergeant up and down with a frank stare.

"'Pears to be a good man," he said, "hefty in build an' quick in the eye. Glad to know you, Mr. Whitley. You an' me may take part in a shootin' bee together an' this old long-barreled firearm uv mine kin give a good account uv herself."

He patted his rifle affectionately, a weapon of ancient type, with a long slender barrel of blue steel, and a heavy carved stock. It was just such a rifle as the frontiersmen used. Dick's mind, in an instant, traveled back into the wilderness and he was once more with the great hunters and scouts who fought for the fair land of Kain-tuck-ee. His imagination was so vivid that it required only a touch to stir it into life, and the aspect of the mountains, wild and lonely and clothed in snow, heightened the illusion.

"I s'pose from what you tell us that you'll have the chance to use it, Mr. Reed," said the sergeant.

"I reckon so," replied the mountaineer emphatically. "'Bout five miles up this pass you'll come to a cove in which Jim Johnson's house stood. Some uv them gorillers attacked it, three nights ago. Jim held 'em off with his double-barreled shotgun, 'til his wife an' children could git out the back way. Then he skedaddled hisself. They plundered the house uv everythin' wuth carryin' off an' then they burned it plum' to the groun'. Jim an' his people near froze to death on the mounting, but they got at last to the cabin uv some uv their kin, whar they are now. Then they've carried off all the hosses an' cattle they kin find in the valleys an' besides robbin' everybody they've shot some good men. Thar is shorely a good dose uv lead comin' to every feller in that band."

The mountaineer's face for a moment contracted violently. Dick saw that he was fairly burning for revenge. Among his people the code of an eye for an eye and a tooth for a tooth still prevailed, unquestioned, and there would be no pity for the guerrilla who might come under the muzzle of his rifle. But his feelings were shown only for the moment. In another instant, he was a stoic like the Indians whom he had displaced. After a little silence he added:

"That man Slade, who is the brains uv the outfit, is plum' devil. So fur ez his doin's in these mountings are concerned he ain't human at all. He hez no mercy fur nuthin' at no time."

His words found an echo in Dick's own mind. He remembered how venomously Slade had hunted for his own life in the Southern marshes, and chance, since then, had brought them into opposition more than once. Just as Harry had felt that there was a long contest between Shepard and himself, Dick felt that Slade and he were now to be pitted in a long and mortal combat. But Shepard was a patriot, while Slade was a demon, if ever a man was. If he were to have a particular enemy he was willing that it should be Slade, as he could see in him no redeeming quality that would cause him to stay his hand, if his own chance came.

"Have you any idea where the guerrillas are camped now?" asked Colonel Winchester.

"When we last heard uv 'em they wuz in Burton's Cove," replied the mountaineer, "though uv course they may hev moved sence then. Still, the snow may hev held 'em. It's a-layin' right deep on the mountings, an' even the gorillers ain't so anxious to plough thar way through it."

"How long will it take us to reach Burton's Cove?"

"It's jest ez the weather sez, colonel. Ef the snow holds off we might make it tomorrow afore dark, but ef the snow makes up its mind to come tumblin' down ag'in, it's the day after that, fur shore."

"At any rate, another fall of snow is no harder for us than it is for them," said the colonel, who showed the spirit of a true leader. "Now, Mr. Reed, do you think we can find anybody on this road who will tell us where the band has gone?"

"It ain't much uv a road an' thar ain't many people to ride on it in the best uv times, so I reckon our chance uv meetin' a traveler who knows much is jest about ez good as our chance uv findin' a peck uv gold in the next snowdrift."

"Which means there's no chance at all."

"I reckon that's 'bout the size uv it. But, colonel, we don't hev to look to the road fur the word."

"What do you mean?"

"We'll turn our eyes upward, to the mounting heights. Some uv us who are jest bound to save the Union are settin' up on top uv high ridges, whar that p'ison band can't go, waitin' to tell us whar _we_ ought to go. They've got some home-made flags, an' they'll wave 'em to me."

"Mr. Reed, you're a man of foresight and perception."

"Foresight? I know what that is. It's the opposite uv hindsight, but I ain't made the acquaintance uv perception."

"Perception is what you see after you think, and I know that you're a man who thinks."

"Thank you, colonel, but I reckon that in sech a war ez this a man hez jest got to set right plum' down, an' think sometimes. It's naterally forced upon him. Them that starts a war mebbe don't do much thinkin', but them that fights it hev to do a power uv it."

"Your logic is sound, Mr. Reed."

"I hev a pow'ful good eye, colonel, an' I think I see a man on top uv that high ridge to the right. But my eye ain't ez good ez your glasses, an' would you min' takin' a look through 'em? Foller a line from that little bunch of cedars to the crest."

"Yes, it's a man. I can see him quite plainly. He has a big, gray shawl like your own, wrapped around his shoulders. Perhaps he's one of your friends."

"I reckon so, but sence he ain't makin' no signs he ain't got nuthin' to tell. It wuz agreed that them that didn't know nuthin' wuz to keep it to theirselves while we rode on until we come to them that did. It saves time. Now he's gone, ain't he, colonel?"

"Yes, something has come in between."

"It's the first thin edge uv the mist. Them's clouds out thar in the northwest, floatin' over the mountings. I'm sorry, colonel, but more snow is comin'. The signs is too plain. Look through that gap an' see what big brown clouds are sailin' up! They're just chock full uv millions uv millions uv tons uv snow!"

"You know your own country and its winter ways, Mr. Reed. How long will it be before the snow comes?"

"Lend me your glasses a minute, colonel."

He examined the clouds a long time through the powerful lenses, and when he handed them back he replied:

"Them clouds are movin' up in a hurry, colonel. They hev saw us here ridin' into the mountings, an' they want to pour their snow down on us afore we git whar we want to go."

Colonel Winchester looked anxious.

"I don't like it," he said. "It doesn't suit cavalry to be plunging around in snowdrifts."

"You're right, colonel. Deep snow is shorely hard on hosses. It looks ez ef we'd be holed up. B'ars an' catamounts, how them clouds are a-trottin' 'cross the sky! Here come the fust flakes an' they look ez big ez feathers!"

The colonel's anxiety deepened, turning rapidly to alarm.

"You spoke of our being holed up, Mr. Reed, what did you mean by it?" he asked.

"Shet in by the snow. But I know a place, colonel, that we kin reach, an' whar we kin stay ef the snow gits too deep fur us. These mountings are full uv little valleys an' coves. They say the Alleghanies run more than a thousand miles one way an' mebbe three hundred or so another. I reckon that when the Lord made 'em, an' looked at His job, he wondered how He wuz goin' to hev people live in sech a mass uv mountings. Then He took His fingers an' pressed 'em down into the ground lots an' lots uv times, an' He made all sorts of purty valleys an' ravines through which the rivers an' creeks an' branches could run, an' snug little coves in which men could build thar cabins an' be sheltered by the big cliffs above an' the forest hangin' on 'em. I reckon that He favored us up here, 'cause the mountings jest suit me. Nuthin' on earth could drive me out uv 'em."

He looked up at the lofty ridges hidden now and then by the whirling snow, and his eyes glistened. It was a stern and wild scene, but he knew that it made the snug cove and the log cabins all the snugger. The flakes were increasing now, and an evil wind was driving them hard in the men's faces. The wind, as it came through the gorges, had many voices, too, howling and shrieking in wrath. The young troopers were devoutly grateful for the heavy overcoats and gloves with which a thoughtful general had provided them.

But there was one man in the regiment to whom wind and snow brought a certain pleasure. It took Sergeant Whitley back to earlier days. He was riding once more with his command over the great plains, and the foe they sought was a Cheyenne or Sioux band. Here, they needed him and his wilderness lore, and he felt that a full use for them all would come.

The mountaineer now led them on rapidly, but the snow was increasing with equal rapidity. Fortunately, the road through the pass was level enough to provide good footing for the horses, and they proceeded without fear of falls. Soon the entire column turned into a white procession. Men and horses alike were covered with snow, but, after their first chill, the hardy young riders began to like it. They sang one of their marching songs, and the colonel made no effort to restrain them, knowing that it was raising their spirits.

"It's all rather picturesque," said Warner, when the song was over, "but it'll be a good thing when Reed leads us into one of those heavenly coves that he talks so much about. I think this snow is going to be about forty feet deep, and it will be hard for a column of three hundred men to proceed by means of tunnels."

The mountaineer riding by the side of Colonel Winchester was looking eagerly, whenever a break in the clouds occurred. At length, he asked him for the glasses again and, after looking intently, said:

"Jest between the edges uv two clouds I caught a glimpse uv a man, an' he wuz wavin' a flag, which wuz a sheet from his own bed. It would be Jake Hening, 'cause that wuz his place, an' he told me to go straight on to the cove, ez they wuz now expectin' us thar!"

"Who is expecting us?"

"Friends uv ours. People 'roun' here in the mountings who want to see you make hash uv them gorillers. I reckon they're fixin' things to keep you warm. We oughter see another man an' his sheet afore long. Thar would be no trouble 'bout it, ef this snow wuzn't so thick."

As they advanced farther into the mountains the noise of the wind increased. Confined in the gorges it roared in anger to get out, and then whistled and shrieked as it blew along the slopes. The snow did not cease to fall. The road had long since been covered up, but Reed led them on with sure eye and instinct.

An hour later he was able to detect another figure on the crest of a ridge, this time to their left, and he observed the waving of the signal with great satisfaction.

"It's all right," he said to Colonel Winchester. "They're waitin' for us in the cove, not many uv 'em, uv course, but they'll help."

"Have we much more riding?" asked the colonel. "I don't think the men are suffering, but our horses can't stand it much longer."

"Not more'n an hour."

They passed soon between high cliffs, and faced a fierce wind which almost blinded them for the time, but, when they emerged they found better shelter and, presently, Reed led them off the main road, then through another narrow gorge and into the cove. They had passed around a curving wall of the mountain and, as it burst upon them suddenly, the spectacle was all the more pleasant.

Before them, like a sunken garden, lay a space of twenty or thirty acres, hemmed in by the high mountains, which seemed fairly to overhang its level spaces. A small creek flowed down from a ravine on one side, and dashed out of a ravine on the other. Splendid oaks, elms and maples grew in parts of the valley, and there was an orchard and a garden, but the greater part of it was cleared, and so well protected by the lofty mountains that most of the snow seemed to blow over it. In the snuggest corner of the cove stood a stout double log cabin and, in the open space around, great fires were roaring and sending up lofty flames, a welcome sight to the stiff and cold horsemen. Fully twenty mountaineers, long and lank like Reed, were gathered around them, and were feeding them constantly.

"What's this I see?" exclaimed Warner. "A little section of heaven?"

"Not heaven, perhaps," said Dick, "but the next door to it."

"This wuz Dick Snyder's home an' place, colonel," said Reed. "On account uv the gorillers he found it convenient to light out with his folks three or four days ago, but he's come back hisself, an' he's here to he'p welcome you. Thar's room in the house, an' the stable, which you can't see 'cause uv the trees, fur all the officers, an' they're buildin' lean-tos here to protect the soldiers an' the hosses. A lot uv the fellers hev brought forage down on thar own hosses fur yourn."

"Mr. Reed," said the colonel, gratefully, "you and your men are true friends. But there's no danger of an ambush here?"

"Nary a chance, colonel. We've got watchers on the mountings, men that hev lived here all thar lives, an' them gorillers hev about ez much chance to steal up on us ez the snowflakes hev to live in the fires thar."

"That being so, we'll all alight and prepare for the night."

When Dick sprang from his horse he staggered at first, not realizing how much the cold had affected him, but a little vigorous flexing of the muscles restored the circulation, and, when an orderly had taken their mounts, his comrades and he went to one of the fires, where they spread out their hands and basked in the glow.

They had brought food on extra horses, and expert cooks were at work at once. Colonel Winchester knew that if his men had plenty to eat and good shelter they would be better fitted for the fierce work before them, and he spared nothing. Bacon and ham were soon frying on the coals and the pots of coffee were bubbling.

The horses were put behind the high trees which formed a kind of windrow, and there they ate their forage, and raised their heads now and then to neigh in content. Around the fires the hardy youths were jesting with one another, and were dragging up logs, on which they could sit before the fires, while they ate their food and drank their coffee. Far over their heads the wind was screaming among the ridges, but they did not heed it nor did they pay any attention to the flakes falling around them. The sheltered cove caused such a rebound after the long cold ride that they were boys again, although veterans of a hundred battles large and small.

Dick shared the exaltation of the rest, and had words of praise for the mountaineer who had guided them to so sheltered a haven. He had no doubt that his famous ancestor, Paul Cotter, and the great Henry Ware had often found refuge in such cosy nooks as this, and it pleased him to think that he was following in their steps. But he was surrounded by comrades and the great fires shed warmth and light throughout the whole basin.

"It's a good log house," said Warner, who had been investigating, "and as it's two stories, with two rooms on each floor, a lot of us can sleep there. The stable and the corn crib will hold many more, but, as for me, I think I'll sleep against one of these lean-tos the mountaineers are throwing up. With that behind me, a big fire before me, two heavy blankets around me, and dead leaves under me, I ought to fare well. It will at least have better air than those sod houses in which some of the best families of Nebraska live, Frank Pennington."

"Never mind about the sod houses," rejoined Pennington, cheerfully. "They're mighty good places in a blizzard. But I think I'll stay outside too, if Colonel Winchester will let us."

The colonel soon disposed his force. The younger officers were to sleep before a fire as they wished, although about half way between midnight and morning they were to join the watch, which he intended to be strong and vigilant. Meanwhile they ate supper and their spirits were so high that they almost made a festival of it. The aroma of the ham and bacon, broiled in the winter open, would have made a jaded epicure hungry. They had sardines and oysters, in tins, and plenty of coffee, with army biscuits which were not hard to them. Some of them wanted to sing, but the colonel would not allow it in the cove, although they could chatter as much as they pleased around the fires.

"We don't need to sing," said Dick. "The wind is doing it for us. Just listen to it, will you?"

All the mountain winds were blowing that night, coming from every direction, and then circling swiftly in vast whirlwinds, while the ridges and peaks and gorges made them sing their songs in many keys. Now it was a shriek, then a whistle, and then a deep full tone like an organ. Blended, it had a majestic effect which was not lost on the young soldiers.

"I've heard it in the Green Mountains," said Warner, "but not under such conditions as we have here. I'm glad I have so much company. I think it would give me the creeps to be in the cove alone, with that storm howling over my head."

"Not to mention Slade and Skelly hunting through the snowdrifts for you," said Pennington. "They'd take a good long look for you, George, knowing what a tremendous fellow you are, and then Dick and I would be compelled to take the trouble and danger of rescuing you."

"I hold you to that," said Warner. "You do hereby promise and solemnly pledge yourselves in case of my capture by Slade, Skelly or anybody else, to come at once through any hardship and danger to my rescue."

"We do," they said together, and they meant it.

Their situation was uncommon, and their pleasure in it deepened. The snow still fell, but the lean-tos, built with so much skill by soldiers and mountaineers, protected them, and the fires before them sank to great beds of gleaming coals that gave out a grateful warmth. Far overhead the wind still shrieked and howled, as if in anger because it could not get at them in the deep cleft. But for Dick all these shrieks and howls were transformed into a soothing song by his feeling of comfort, even of luxury. The cove was full of warmth and light and he basked in it.

Pennington and Warner fell asleep, but Dick lay a while in a happy, dreaming state. He felt as he looked up at the cloudy sky and driving snow that, after all, there was something wild in every man that no amount of civilization could drive out. An ordinary bed and an ordinary roof would be just as warm and better sheltered, but they seldom gave him the same sense of physical pleasure that he felt as he lay there with the storm driving by.

His dreamy state deepened, and with it the wilderness effect which the little valley, the high mountains around it and the raging winter made. His mind traveled far back once more and he easily imagined himself his great ancestor, Paul Cotter, sleeping in the woods with his comrades and hidden from Indian attack. While the feeling was still strong upon him he too fell asleep, and he did not awaken until it was time for him to take the watch with Pennington and Warner.

It was then about two o'clock in the morning, and the snow had ceased to fall, but it lay deep in all places not sheltered, while the wind had heaped it up many feet in all the gorges and ravines of the mountains. Dick thought he had never beheld a more majestic world. All the clouds were gone and hosts of stars glittered in a sky of brilliant blue. On every side of them rose the lofty peaks and ridges, clothed in gleaming white, the forests themselves a vast, white tracery. The air was cold but pure and stimulating. The wind had ceased to blow, but from far points came the faint swish of sliding snow.

Dick folded his blankets, laid them away carefully, put on his heavy overcoat and gloves, and was ready. Colonel Winchester maintained a heavy watch, knowing its need, fully fifty men, rifle on shoulder and pistol at belt, patrolling all the ways by which a foe could come.

Dick and his comrades were with a picket at the farther end of the valley, where the creek made its exit, rushing through a narrow and winding gorge. There was a level space on either side of the creek, but it was too narrow for horsemen, and, clogged as it was with snow, it looked dangerous now for those on foot too. Nevertheless, the picket kept a close watch. Dick and his friends were aware that guerrillas knew much of the craft and lore of the wilderness, else they could never have maintained themselves, and they did not cease for an instant to watch the watery pass.

They were joined very soon by Shepard, upon whose high boots snow was clinging to the very tops, and he said when Dick looked at him inquiringly:

"I see that you're an observer, Mr. Mason. Yes, I've been out on the mountainside. Colonel Winchester suggested it, and I was glad to do as he wished. It was difficult work in the snow, but Mr. Reed, our guide, was with me part of the time, and we climbed pretty high."

"Did you see anything?"

"No footsteps. That was impossible, because of the falling snow, but I think our friends, the enemy, are abroad in the mountains. The heavy snow may have kept them from coming much nearer to us than they are now."

"What makes you think so?"

Shepard smiled.

"We heard sounds, odd sounds," he replied.

"Were they made by a whistle?" Dick asked eagerly. Shepard smiled again.

"It was natural for you to ask that question, Mr. Mason," he replied, "but it was not a whistle. It was a deeper note, and it carried much farther, many times farther. Mr. Reed explained it to me. Somebody with powerful lungs was blowing on a cow's horn."

"I've heard 'em. They use 'em in the hills back of us at home. The sound will carry a tremendous distance on a still night like this. Do you think it was intended as a signal?"

"It's impossible to say, but I think so. I think, too, that the bands — there were two of them, one replying to the other — belong to the Slade and Skelly outfit. Skelly has lived all his life in the mountains and Slade is learning 'em fast."

"Then it behooves us to be watchful, and yet more watchful."

"It does. Maybe they're attempting an ambush, with which they might succeed against an ordinary troop, but not against such a troop as this, led by such a man as Colonel Winchester. Hark, did you hear that noise?"

All of them listened. It sounded at first like the cow's horn, but they concluded that it was the rumble, made by sliding snow, which would be sending avalanches down the slopes all through the night.

"Are you going out again, Mr. Shepard?" Dick asked.

"I think not, sir. Colonel Winchester wants me to stay here, and, even if the enemy should come, we'll be ready for him."

They did not speak again for a while and they heard several times the noise of the sliding snow. Then they heard a note, low and deep, which they were sure was that of the cow's horn, or its echo. It was multiplied and repeated, however, so much by the gorges that it was impossible to tell from what point of the compass it came.

But it struck upon Dick's ears like a signal of alarm, and he and all the others of the picket stiffened to attention.

CHAPTER XIII
DICK'S GREAT EXPLOIT

It was a singular and weird sound, the blowing of the great cow's horn on the mountain, and then the distant reply from another horn as great. It was both significant and sinister, such an extraordinary note that, despite Dick's experience and courage, his hair lifted a little. He was compelled to look back at the camp and the coals of the fire yet glowing to reassure himself that everything was normal and real.

"I wish there wasn't so much snow," said Shepard, "then the sergeant, Mr. Reed and myself could scout all over the country around here, mountains or no mountains."

They were joined at that moment by Reed, the long mountaineer, who had also been listening to the big horns.

"That means them gorillers, shore," he said. "We've got some p'ison people uv our own, an' when the gorillers come in here they j'ined 'em, and knowin' ev'ry inch uv the country, they kin guide the gorillers wherever they please."

"You agree then with Mr. Shepard that these signals are made by Slade and Skelly's men?" asked Dick.

"Shorely," replied the mountaineer, "an' I think they're up to some sort uv trick. It pesters me too, 'cause I can't guess it nohow. I done told the colonel that we'd better look out."

Colonel Winchester joined them as he was speaking, and listened to the double signal which was repeated later. But it did not come again, although they waited some time. Instead they heard, as they had heard all through the night, the occasional swish of the soft snow sliding down the slopes. But Dick saw that the colonel was uneasy, and that his apprehensions were shared both by Shepard and the mountaineer.

"Do you know how many men these brigands have?" Colonel Winchester asked of Reed.

"I reckon thar are five hundred uv them gorillers," replied the mountaineer. "Some uv our people spied on 'em in Burton's Cove an' counted 'bout that number."

Colonel Winchester glanced at his sleeping camp.

"I have three hundred," he said, "but they're the very flower of our youth. In the open they could take care of a thousand guerrillas and have something to spare. Still in here—"

He stopped short, but the shrewd mountaineer read his meaning.

"In the mountings it ain't sech plain sailin'," he said, "an' you've got to watch fur tricks. I reckon that when it comes to fightin' here, it's somethin' like the old Injun days."

"I can't see how they can get at us here," said Colonel Winchester, more to himself than to the others. "A dozen men could hold the exit by the creek, and fifty could hold the entrance."

Despite his words, his uneasiness continued and he sent for the sergeant, upon whose knowledge and instincts he relied greatly in such a situation. The sergeant, who had been watching at the other end of the valley, came quickly and, when the colonel looked at him with eyes of inquiry, he said promptly:

"Yes, sir; I think there's mischief a-foot. I can't rightly make out where it's going to be started, but I can hear it, smell it an' feel it. It's like waitin' in a dip on the prairies for a rush by the wild Sioux or Cheyenne horsemen. The signs seem to come through the air."

Dick's oppression increased. A mysterious danger was the worst of all, and his nerves were on edge. Think as he might, he could not conceive how or where the attack would be made. The only sound in the valley was the occasional stamp of the horses in the woods and behind the windrows. The soldiers themselves made no noise. The steps of the sentinels were softened in the snow, and the fires, having sunk to beds of coals, gave forth no crackling sounds.

He stared down the gap, and then up at the white world of walls circling them about. The sky seemed to have become a more dazzling blue than ever, and the great stars with the hosts of their smaller brethren around them gleamed and quivered. The stamp of a horse came again, and then a loud shrill neigh, a piercing sound and full of menace in the still night.

"What was that?" exclaimed the sergeant in alarm. "A horse does not neigh at such a time without good reason!"

And then the storm broke loose in the valley. There was a series of short, fierce shouts. Torches were suddenly waved in the air. Many horses neighed in the wildest terror and, all of them breaking through the forest and windrows, poured in a confused and frightened stream toward the entrance of the valley.

Then the experience of the sergeant in wild Indian warfare was worth more than gold and diamonds. He knew at once what was occurring and he shouted:

"It's a stampede! There have been traitors here, and they've driven the horses with fire!"

"And maybe some of them have managed to slip down the mountain side!" said Shepard.

It was well for them all that they were men of decision and supreme courage. The terrible tumult in the valley was increasing. The horses, a stampeded mass, were driving directly for the entrance. Only one thing could stop them and that the guards then did. They snatched many burning brands from the nearest fire and waved them furiously in the face of the frightened herd, which turned and ran back the other way, only to be confronted by other waving brands that filled them with terror. Then the horses, instinctively following some leader, turned again and ran back to their old places among the trees and behind the windrows, where they stood, quivering with terror.

A crackling of rifles had begun before the horses were driven back, and bullets pattered in the valley. Dark figures appeared crouched against the slopes, and jets of fire ran like a red ribbon upon the white of the snow.

"The gorillers!" cried Reed. "They've crep' over the ridges, spite uv all our watchin'."

Colonel Winchester did not lose his head for an instant, nor did any of his young soldiers, who had been trained to think as well as obey. Without waiting for orders they had already won an important victory by turning the horses back with fire, and the colonel, with the help of his officers, formed them rapidly to meet the attack. The house, the stable and the corn crib were filled with sharpshooters and others lay down among the trees or behind any shelter they could find. A number were detailed rapidly to tether the horses, and make them secure against a second fright. Warner was sent to the men guarding the entrance, Pennington to those at the exit, while Dick was kept with the colonel, who crouched, after his arrangements were made, in a little clump of trees near the center of the valley.

Colonel Winchester was willing enough to risk his life but knowing that it was of the highest importance now to preserve it he did not take any risks through false pride. Besides Dick he kept Reed, Shepard and the sergeant with him.

The ring of fire on the slopes had been increasing fast, and the assailants found much shelter there among the dwarf pines and cedars. Bullets were pattering all over the valley. Several of the Winchesters had been slain in the early firing, and they lay where they had fallen. Others were wounded, but they bound up their own hurts and used their rifles, whenever they could pick out a figure on the slopes.

"You spoke of traitors, Mr. Reed," said the colonel. "Did you know well all the men who came to help in the preparations for us?"

"All but two," replied the mountaineer. "One was named Leonard and the other Bosley. They come from the other side uv the mounting with some uv the boys an' we thought they wuz all right, but I reckon they must be the traitors, an' I reckon too they must hev helped some uv the gorillers into the camp. I ain't seed a sign uv either sence them hosses wuz headed back. I guess we wuz took in, an' I'm pow'ful sorry, colonel."

"You're not to blame, Mr. Reed. It's not always possible to guard against treachery, but since we've defeated their attempt to stampede our horses we'll defeat all other efforts of theirs."

"Colonel, would you mind lendin' me them glasses uv yourn fur a look? The night's so bright I guess I kin use 'em nigh ez well ez in the day."

"Certainly you can have them, Mr. Reed. Here they are."

The mountaineer took a long look through them, and when he handed them back he uttered a clucking sound, significant of satisfaction.

"I 'lowed it was him, when I saw him crawlin' behind that bush," he said, "an' now I know."

"Who is who?" said Dick.

"It's that feller Bosley what came with the rest uv the boys. I know that gray comfort what's tied 'roun' his neck, an' the 'coonskin cap what's on his head. He jest crawled behind that little twisted pine up thar, an' took a pot shot at some uv us down here."

"I wish I could reach him," said Shepard.

"Ef you could I wouldn't let you," said the mountaineer grimly.

"Why?"

"'Cause he's my meat. He come here with my people, an' played a trick on us, a trick that might hev wiped out all uv Colonel Winchester's men. No man kin do that with me an git away. He's piled up a pow'ful big score an' I'm goin' to settle it myself."

"How?"

"See this rifle uv mine? I reckon it ain't got all the fancy tricks that some uv the new repeatin' breech-loadin' rifles hev. It's jest a cap an' ball rifle, but it's got a long, straight barrel an' a delicate trigger, an' it sends a bullet wherever you p'int it. It's killed squirrels, an' rabbits, an' wil' turkeys an' catamounts, an' b'ars, an' now I reckon it's goin' to hunt higher game."

The man was talking very quietly, but when Dick caught the light in his eye he knew that he meant every word. It was a cold, implacable look, and the face of the mountaineer was like that of an avenging fate.

"I loaded it with uncommon care," he continued, looking affectionately at his rifle, and then looking up again, "an' now that the colonel's glasses hev showed the way I kin see that feller peepin' from roun' his bush, tryin' to git another shot, mebbe at me an' mebbe at you. It's a long carry, but I'm shore to hit. I had a chance at him then, but I 'low to wait a little!"

"Why do you wait?" asked Dick curiously.

"I'm givin' him time to say his prayers."

"Why, he doesn't know that you're going to shoot at him, and he wouldn't pray, even if he did."

"Mebbe not, but I was raised right, an' I know my duty. I ain't goin' to send no man to kingdom without givin' him _time_ to pray. Ef he won't use it the blame is his'n, but that ain't no reason why I oughtn't to give him the _time_."

"How long?"

"Wa'al, I reckon 'bout three minutes is 'nough fur a right good prayer. Thar, he's shot ag'in, but I don't know whar his bullet went. He's usin' up his prayin' time fast."

Reed never altered his quiet, assured tone. He reminded Dick of Warner, talking about his algebra, and the lad was impressed so much by his manner that he believed he was going to do as he said. He began unconsciously to count the seconds.

"Time's up," said Reed at length, "an' that traitor is pokin' his head 'roun' fur another shot."

He raised suddenly his long-barreled rifle, took a quick aim, and pulled the trigger. A stream of fire poured from the muzzle, the figure of a man leaped from the bush and then rolled down the snowy slope.

"I give him plenty uv time," said Reed as he reloaded. "Now I reckon I'll look fur that other feller, Leonard. I'll know him when I see him, an' this old cap-an'-ball rifle uv mine knows too how to talk to traitors."

Dick left presently with a message to a captain who was in command of the force detached to hold the entrance to the valley. He ran part of the way in the shelter of the trees and crept the rest, reaching the captain in safety. Warner was there also, and the fire upon them from the slopes was hot.

"There has been no attempt to force the gate-way here," said Warner. "Since they failed with the horses they wouldn't dare try it. Besides, our sharpshooters are doing execution. Those in the upper story of the house have an especially good chance. Look at the black dots in the snow high up on the slopes. Those are dead guerrillas. There, two men fell! Perhaps if they had known the kind of regiment it was they were coming after they wouldn't have been in such a hurry to attack us."

He spoke with pride, but Dick felt some chagrin.

"That's true," he said, "though I don't like our regiment to be besieged here by a lot of guerrillas. It's an ignominy. It's not enough for us to hold our own against 'em, because they're the people we came to get, and we ought to get 'em."

"I dare say the colonel thinks as you do and he's already planning how to do it. This is a smart little battle, as it is. Those sharpshooters of ours in the houses are certainly making it warm for the enemy!"

The firing was now very fast, and, as long as the brilliancy of the night remained unobscured, much of it was deadly, but a great amount of smoke gathered, and, as it rose, it formed a cloud. The showers of bullets then decreased in volume and a comparative lull came. But the men of Slade and Skelly could yet be seen on the crests and slopes, and there was no indication that they would draw off.

Dick made his way back to Colonel Winchester, who was still in the clump of trees, a central point, from which he could direct the defense. The colonel, as Dick clearly saw, felt chagrin. While they had prevented the stampede of the horses, and were holding off Slade and Skelly, the roles which he had intended for the forces to play were reversed. They had come forth to destroy the guerrillas, and now they had to fight hard to keep the guerrillas from destroying them. Despite their shelter, about fifteen of the Winchester men had been slain, and perhaps twenty-five wounded, a loss over which the colonel grieved. Doubtless as many of the guerrillas had fallen or had been hurt, but that was a poor consolation.

It was obvious too that Slade and Skelly were handling their forces with much skill, utilizing for shelter every bush and dwarfed tree on the slopes, and never exposing themselves, except for a moment or two. Had there not been so many sharpshooters among the Winchester men they might have escaped almost without any damage, but for some of the deadly riflemen in the valley a single glimpse was enough. Nevertheless Colonel Winchester's dissatisfaction remained. He felt that a force such as his, which had come forth to do so much, should do it, and he ransacked his brain for a plan.

"Mr. Reed," he said to the mountaineer, who had remained with him, "do you think we could send a detachment through the pass down the stream and take them in the rear? That is, this force might climb the slopes behind them, and attack from above?"

The mountaineer chewed his tobacco thoughtfully, looked up at the ridges, and then at the gorge down which they could hear the waters of the little creek rushing.

"It's a big risk," he replied, "but I 'low it kin be done, though you'll hev to pick your men, colonel. You let me be guide and be shore to send the sergeant, 'cause he's a full fo'-hoss team all by hisself. An' Mr. Shepard ought to go along too. All the others ought to be youngsters, an' spose you let Mr. Mason here lead 'em."

Colonel Winchester did not resent at all these suggestions, which he knew to be excellent, and, while at first, for personal reasons of his own, he hesitated about sending Dick on so perilous an errand, he knew that he was better fitted for it than any other young officer in his command, and so he chose him. The plan, too, appealed to him strongly. He had taken lessons from the grand tactics of Lee and Jackson. Lee would keep up a great demonstration in front, while Jackson, circling in silence, would strike a tremendous and deadly blow on the flank. The longer he thought about it the more he was pleased with it. If the flanking force could cut through the gorge the prospect of success was good, and fortunately the night had turned darker, the snow clouds reappearing.

The colonel picked one hundred and fifty of his best men, with Shepard, Reed and Whitley to guide, and Dick to lead them. Warner and Pennington protested when they were not allowed to go, but the colonel quieted them with the assurance that they would soon have plenty of dangerous work to do in the valley. To Dick he said gravely:

"Before now you've nearly always been a staff officer and messenger, and this is the most important command you've ever held. I know you'll acquit yourself well, but trust a lot to your guides."

"I will, sir," said Dick earnestly. He felt the full weight of his responsibility, but his courage rose to meet it. It was the largest task yet confided to him, and he was resolved to make it a success. He noticed also that fortune, as if determined to help the brave, was already giving him aid. More stars were withdrawing into the void, and the clouds were increasing. The night had grown much darker, and a few flakes of snow wandered lazily down, messengers of the multitude that might follow.

The increasing dusk did not diminish the activity of the brigands on the slopes. It was obvious that they had an unlimited supply of ammunition, as they sent an unbroken stream of bullets into the valley, and pink dots ran like ribbons around its entire snowy rim. But in the valley itself all the fires had been put out, and it was fairly dark there, enabling Dick's command to gather unseen by the enemy.

"Now, Dick," said Colonel Winchester, "I trust you. Go, and may luck go with you."

He led his men away, the three guides by his side, and they used every particle of cover they could find, in order that the movement might remain invisible until the last possible moment. They hugged the fringe of forest, and when they reached the gorge he felt sure they were still unseen, although it was only the easy part of their task that had yet been done. But the lazy flakes had increased in number, and the canopy of cloud was still being drawn across the heavens. He gave the word to his men to be as silent as possible, not to let any weapon rattle or fall, and then they entered the gorge in two files separated by the creek, the narrow ledges affording room for only one man on either side.

Dick kept his outward calm, but the great pulses in his throat and temples were beating hard. Reed was just ahead of him, and on the other side of the creek the sergeant led, with Shepard following. Large flakes of snow fell on his face and melted there, but they were welcome messengers, telling him that the cloak for the movement would not only remain, but would increase in extent.

After the first curve the stream took a sharp descent, but the land on either side widened a little, permitting two to walk abreast. The valley and the slopes encircling it were now entirely shut out from their view, but they heard the crackling of the rifles in greater volume than ever. Colonel Winchester, true to Lee and Jackson's plan of grand tactics, had opened an extremely heavy fire on the enemy, as soon as his flanking column had disappeared in the gorge.

"I 'low the signs are good," whispered Reed. "Them that lay an ambush sometimes git laid in an ambush theirselves. I felt pow'ful bad at bein' held in a trap here in my own mountings by them gorillers, but mebbe we'll do some trap-layin' uv our own."

"I feel sure of it," said Dick. "Look! the stream ahead of us is lined with bushes which will afford concealment for our march, and the slopes beyond are covered with scrub forest."

"Like ez not the gorillers come that way, an' when we circle about we kin foller in thar tracks."

Dick felt that fortune was showering her favors upon him. The last star was now gone, and the entire sky was veiled. The big flakes of snow were falling fast enough to help their concealment, but not fast enough to impede their movements. A mile down the gorge and they halted, still unseen by the enemy, due doubtless to the heavy firing in the valley which was engrossing all the attention of the guerrillas. They could hear it very distinctly where they were, and they were quite sure that it would not permit Slade and Skelly to detach any part of their force for purposes of observation. So Dick gave orders for his men to turn and begin the ascent of the slope, under shelter of the scrub forest of cedars. They were to go in a column four abreast, carefully treading in the tracks of one another, in order that they might not start a slide of snow.

Dick's pulses beat hard, until they reached the shelter of the cedars, but no lurking guerrilla or posted sentinel saw them and they drew into the forest in silence and unobserved. Here they paused a few minutes and listened to the heavy rifle fire in the valley.

"It looks like a success, sir," said Shepard. "If we catch 'em between two fires victory is surely ours."

"Besides beatin' 'em, thar's one thing I hope fur," said Reed. "Ef that traitor Leonard hasn't fell already I'm prayin' that I git a look at him. My old cap-an'-ball rifle here is jest ez true ez ever."

The mountaineer's eyes glittered again, and Dick did not feel that Leonard's fate was in any doubt. But there was little time for talk, as the column began the march again and pressed on under cover of the cedars until they came without interruption and triumphantly to the very crest of the slope. The firing was still distinctly audible here, and the other half of the army was undoubtedly keeping the guerrillas busy.

On the summit Dick gave his men another brief breathing spell, and then they began their advance toward the battle. He threw in advance the best of the sharpshooters and scouts, including Whitley,

Shepard and Reed, and then followed swiftly with the others. Half the distance and a man behind a tree saw them, shouted, fired and ran toward the guerrillas.

Dick, knowing that concealment was no longer possible, cried to his men to rush forward at full speed. A light, scattering fire met them. Two or three were wounded but none fell, and the entire column swept on at as much speed as the deep snow would allow, sending in shot after shot from their own rifles at the guerrillas clustered along the crests and slopes. The light was sufficient for them to take aim, and as they were sharpshooters the fire was accurate and deadly.

Their shout of victory rose and swelled, and the mountain gave it back in many echoes. Dick, feeling his responsibility, managed to keep cool, but he continually shouted to his men to press on, knowing how full advantage should be taken of a surprise. But they needed no urging. Aflame with fire and zeal they charged upon the guerrillas, pulling the trigger as fast as they could slip in the cartridges, and Slade and Skelly, despite all their cunning and quickness, were unable to make a stand against them.

A great shout came up from the valley. The moment Colonel Winchester heard the fire on the flank he knew that his plan, executed with skill by one of his lieutenants, was a success, and, gathering up his own force, he crept up the slopes, his men sending their fire into the guerrillas, who were already breaking.

Dick's troop was doing great damage. The guerrillas in their rovings and robberies had never before faced such a fire and they fell fast, the deep snow making flight difficult. Reed, who was at Dick's side, suddenly uttered a cry.

"I see him! I see him!" he shouted.

The long-barreled cap-and-ball rifle leaped to his shoulder, and when the stream of fire gushed from the muzzle, Leonard, the mountaineer, fell in the snow and would never betray anybody else. Most of the guerrillas were now fleeing in panic, and Dick heard the shrill, piercing notes of Slade's whistle as he tried to draw his men off in order. For a moment or two he forgot his duties as a leader as, pistol in hand, he looked for the little man under the enormous slouch hat. Once more the feeling seized him that it was a long duel between Slade and himself that must end in the death of one or the other, and he meant to end it now. Despite the fierce notes of the whistle, coming from one point and then another, he did not see him. He caught a glimpse of the gigantic form of Skelly, but he too was soon gone, and then when he felt the restraining hand of Shepard upon his arm he came out of his rage.

"Look there!" cried Shepard.

About a score of the guerrillas had been cut off from their comrades and were driven toward the valley, where they remained on its edge, crouched down, and firing. The deep snow in which they knelt was quivering. Dick shouted to his men to draw back. Then the huge bank of snow gave way and slid down the slope, carrying the guerrillas, and gathering volume and force as it went. A terrified shouting came from the thick of it, as the avalanche hurled itself into the valley, where the bruised and broken guerrillas were taken prisoners without resistance.

Dick, after one glance at their fate, continued the pursuit of the main band down the other slope. He knew that they were robbers and murderers, and he felt little scruple. His sharpshooters fairly mowed them down as they fled in terror, but all who threw up their hands or signified otherwise that they wished to surrender were spared.

Still bearing in mind that it was their duty not merely to scatter but to destroy, he urged on the pursuit continually, and Shepard and the sergeant aided him. They gave Slade and Skelly no time to reform their men, driving them from every clump of trees, when they attempted it, and continually reducing their numbers.

The rout was complete, and Dick's heart beat high with triumph, because he knew that his force had been the striking arm. They were nearly at the foot of the far side of the mountain, when he saw Slade among the bushes. He shouted to him to surrender, but the outlaw, suddenly aiming a pistol, fired pointblank at the young lieutenant's face. Dick felt the bullet grazing his head, and he raised his own pistol to fire, but Slade was gone, and, although they trailed him a long distance in the snow, they did not find him.

CHAPTER XIV
THE MOUNTAIN SHARPSHOOTER

Colonel Winchester's own mellow whistle finally recalled his men, as he did not wish them to become scattered among the mountains in pursuit of detached guerrillas. Although the escape of both Slade and Skelly was a great disappointment the victory nevertheless was complete. The two leaders could not rally the brigand force again, because it had ceased to exist. Nearly half, caught between the jaws of the Union vise, had fallen, and most of the others were taken. Perhaps not more than fifty had got away, and they would be lucky if they were not captured by the mountaineers.

Dick's head was bound up hastily but skillfully by Sergeant Whitley and Shepard. Slade's bullet had merely cut under the hair a little, and the bandage stopped the flow of blood. The sting, too, left, or in his triumph he did not notice it. His elation, in truth, was great, as he had succeeded in carrying out the hardest part of a difficult and delicate operation.

As he led his men back toward the valley, their prisoners driven before them, he felt no weariness from his great exertions, and both his head and his feet were light. At the rim of the valley Colonel Winchester met him, shook his hand with great heartiness, and congratulated him on his success, and Warner and Pennington, who were wholly without envy, added their own praise.

"I think it will be Captain Mason before long," said Warner. "Lots of boys under twenty are captains and some are colonels. Your right to promotion is a mathematical certainty, and I can demonstrate it with numerous formulae from the little algebra which even now is in the inside pocket of my tunic."

"Don't draw the algebra!" exclaimed Pennington. "We take your word for it, of course."

"I shouldn't want to be a captain," said Dick sincerely, "unless you fellows became captains too."

Further talk was interrupted by the necessity for care in making the steep descent into the valley, where the fires were blazing anew from the fresh wood which the young soldiers in their triumph had thrown upon the coals. Nor did Colonel Winchester and his senior officers make any effort to restrain them, knowing that a little exultation was good for youth, after deeds well done.

It was still snowing lazily, but the flames from a dozen big fires filled the valley with light and warmth and illuminated the sullen faces of the captives. They were a sinister lot, arrayed in faded Union or Confederate uniforms, the refuse of highland and lowland, gathered together for robbery and murder, under the protecting shadow of war. Their hair was long and unkempt, their faces unshaven and dirty, and they watched their captors with the restless, evasive eyes of guilt. They were herded in the center of the valley, and Colonel Winchester did not hesitate to bind the arms of the most evil looking.

"What are you going to do with us?" asked one bold, black-browed villain.

"I'm going to take you to General Sheridan," replied the colonel. "I'm glad I don't have the responsibility of deciding your fate, but I think it very likely that he'll hang some of you, and that all of you richly deserve it."

The man muttered savage oaths under his breath and the colonel added:

"Meanwhile you'll be surrounded by at least fifty guards with rifles of the latest style, rifles that they can shoot very fast, and they are instructed to use them if you make the slightest sign of an attempt to escape. I warn you that they will obey with eagerness."

The man ceased his mutterings and he and the other captives cowered by the fire, as if their blood had suddenly grown so thin that they must almost touch the coals to secure warmth. Then Colonel Winchester ordered the cooks to prepare food and coffee again for his troopers, who had done so well, while a surgeon, with amateur but competent assistants, attended to the hurt.

While they ate and drank and basked in the heat, the mountaineer, Reed, came again to Colonel Winchester. Dick, who was standing by, observed his air of deep satisfaction, and he wondered again at the curious mixture of mountain character, its strong religious strain, mingled with its merciless hatred of a foe. He knew that much of Reed's great content came from his slaying of the two traitors, but he did not feel that he had a right, at such a time, to question the man's motives and actions.

"Colonel," said Reed, "it's lucky that my men brought along plenty of axes, an' that your men ez well ez mine know how to use 'em."

"Why so, Mr. Reed?"

"'Cause it's growin' warmer."

"But that doesn't hurt us. We're certainly not asking for more cold."

"It will hurt us, ef we don't take some shelter ag'in it. It's snowin' now, colonel, an' ef it gits a little warmer it'll turn to rain, an' it kin rain pow'ful hard in these mountings."

"Thank you for calling my attention to it, Mr. Reed. I can't afford to have the troops soaked by winter rains. Not knowing what we had to expect in the mountains I fortunately ordered about twenty of my own men to bring axes at their saddlebows. We'll put 'em all at work."

In a few minutes thirty good axmen were cutting down trees, saplings and bushes, and more than a hundred others were strengthening the lean-tos, thatching roofs, and making rude but serviceable floors. Dick, owing to his slight wound, but much against his wish, was ordered into the house, where he spread his blankets near a window, although he could not yet sleep, all the heat of the battle and pursuit not yet having left him. His nerves still tingling with excitement, he stood at the window and looked out.

He saw the great fire blazing and many persons passing and repassing before the red glow. He saw the captives crouching together, and the red gleam on the bayonets of the men who guarded them. He saw Warner and Pendleton go into one of the lean-tos, and he saw Colonel Winchester, accompanied by Shepard and the sergeant, go down the valley toward the exit.

After a while the prisoners moved to the lean-tos, and then everybody took shelter. The crackle of the big fires changed to a hiss, and more smoke arose from them. The reason was obvious. The big flakes of snow had ceased to fall, and big drops of rain were falling in their place. Reed had been a true prophet, and he had not given his warning too soon.

The rain increased. Dick heard it driving on the window panes and beating on the roof. All the fires in the valley were out now, and rising mists and vapors hid nearly everything. The faint, sliding sound of more snow-falls precipitated by the rain came to his ears. He realized suddenly how fine a thing it was to be inside four walls, and with it came a great feeling of comfort. It was the same feeling that he had known often in childhood, when he lay in his bed and heard the storm beat against the house.

There were others in the room—the floor was almost covered with them—but all of them were asleep already, and Dick, wrapping himself in his blanket, joined them, the last thing that he remembered being the swish of the rain against the glass. He slept heavily and was not awakened until nearly noon, when he saw through the window a world entirely changed. The rain had melted only a portion of the snow, and when it ceased after sunrise the day had turned much colder, freezing every thing hard and tight. The surface of valley, slopes and ridges was covered with a thick armor of ice, smooth as glass, and giving back the rays of a brilliant sun in colors as vivid and varied as those of a rainbow. Every tree and bush, to the last little twig, was sheathed also in silver, and along the slopes the forests of dwarfed cedar and pines were a vast field of delicate and complex tracery.

It was a glittering and beautiful world, but cold and merciless. Dick saw at once that the whole force, captors and captured, was shut in for the time. It was impossible for horses to advance over a field of ice, and it was too difficult even for men to be considered seriously. There was nothing to do but remain in the valley until circumstances allowed them to move, and reflection told him they would not lose much by it. They had done the errand on which they were sent, and there was little work left in the great valley itself.

The big fires had been lighted again, the cove furnishing wood enough for many days, and within its limited area they brought back glow and cheeriness. Dick went outside and found all the men in high spirits. They expected to be held there until a thaw came, but there would be no difficulty, except to obtain forage for the horses, which they must dig from under the snow, or which some of the surest footed mountaineers must bring over the ridge. He heard that Colonel Winchester was already making arrangements with Reed, and he was too light-hearted to bother himself any more about it.

Warner and Pennington saluted him with bows as a coming captain, and declared that he looked extremely interesting with a white bandage around his head.

"It's merely to prevent bleeding," said Dick. "The bullet didn't really hurt me, and it won't leave a scar under the hair."

"Then since you're not even an invalid," said Pennington, "come on and take your bath. The boys have broken the ice for a long distance on the creek and all of us early risers have gone there for a plunge, and a short swim. It'll do you a world of good, Dick, but don't stay in too long."

"Not over a half hour," said Warner.

"O, a quarter of an hour will be long enough," said Pennington, "but I'd advise you to rub yourself down thoroughly, Dick."

"I'll do just as you did," laughed Dick.

"And what's that?"

"I'll go to the edge of the creek, look at it, and shiver when I see how cold its waters are. Then I'll kneel down on the bank, bathe my face, and come away."

"You've estimated him correctly, Dick," said Warner, "but you don't have to shiver as much as Frank did."

The cold bath, although it was confined to the face only, made his blood leap and sparkle. He was not a coming captain but a boy again, and he began to think about pleasant ways of passing the time while the ice held them. After his breakfast he joined Colonel Winchester, who debated the question further with a group of officers. But there was only one conclusion to which they could come, and that had presented itself already to Dick's mind, namely, to wait as patiently as they could for a thaw, while Shepard, the sergeant and two or three others made their way on foot into the Shenandoah valley to inform Sheridan of what had transpired.

The messengers departed as soon as the conference closed, and the little army was left to pass the time as it chose in the cove. But time did not weigh heavily upon the young troops. As it grew colder and colder they added to the walls and roofs of their improvised shelters. There was scarcely a man among them who had not been bred to the ax, and the forest in the valley rang continually with their skillful strokes. Then the logs were notched and in a day or two rude but real cabins were raised, in which they slept, dry and warm.

The fires outside were never permitted to die down, the flames always leaped up from great beds of coals, and warmth and the comforts that follow were diffused everywhere. The lads, when they were not working on the houses, mended their saddles and bridles or their clothes, and when they had nothing else to do they sang war songs or the sentimental ballads of home. It was a fine place for singing—Warner described the acoustics of the valley as perfect—and the ridges and gorges gave back the greatest series of echoes any of them had ever heard.

"If this place didn't have a name already," said Pennington, "I'd call it Echo Cove, and the echoes are flattering, too. Whenever George sings his voice always comes back in highly improved tones, something that we can stand very well."

"My voice may not be as mellow as Mario's," said Warner calmly, "but my technique is perfect. Music is chiefly an affair of mathematics, as everybody knows, or at least it is eighty per cent, the rest being voice, a mere gift of birth. So, as I am unassailable in mathematics, I'm a much better singer than the common and vulgar lot who merely have voice."

"That being the case," said Pennington, "you should sing for yourself only and admire your own wonderful technique."

"I never sing unless I'm asked to do so," said Warner, with his old invincible calm, "and then the competent few who have made an exhaustive study of this most complex science appreciate my achievement. As I said, I should consider it a mark of cheapness if I pleased the low, vulgar and common herd."

"With that iron face and satisfied mind of yours you ought to go far, George," said Pennington.

"Everything is arranged already. I will go far," said Warner in even tones.

"I wonder what's happening outside in the big valley," said Dick.

"Whatever it is it's happening without us," said Warner. "But I fancy that General Sheridan will be more uneasy about us than we are about him. We know what we have done, that our task is finished, but for all he knows we may have been trapped and destroyed."

"But Shepard or the sergeant will get through to him."

"Not for three or four days anyhow. Not even men on foot can travel fast on a glassy sheet of ice. Every time I look at it on the mountain it seems to grow smoother. If I were standing on top of that ridge and were to slip I'd come like a catapult clear into the camp."

"Nothing could tempt me to go up there now," said Dick.

"Maybe not, nor me either, but as I live somebody is on top of that ridge now."

Dick's eyes followed his pointing finger, saw a black dot on the utmost summit, and then he snatched up his glasses.

"It's Slade, his very self!" he exclaimed in excitement. "I'd know that hat anywhere. Now, how under the sun did he come there!"

"It's more important to know why he has come," said Warner, using his own glasses. "I see him clearly and there is no doubt that it's the same robber, traitor and assassin who, unfortunately, escaped when we shot his horde to pieces."

"He has a rifle with him, and as sure as we live he's sitting down on the ice, and picking out a target here in the valley."

"A risky business for Slade. Shooting upward we can take better aim at him than he can at us."

There was a great stir in the valley, as others saw the figure on the mountain and read Slade's intentions. Fifty men sprang to their feet and seized their rifles. But the guerrilla moved swiftly along the knife-edge of the ridge, obviously sure of his footing, and before any of them could fire, dropped down behind a little group of cedars. Every stem and bough was cased in a sheath of silver mail, but they hid him well. Dick, with his glasses, could not discern a single outline of the man behind the glittering tracery.

But as they looked, a head of red appeared suddenly in the silver, smoke floated away, and a bullet knocked up the ice near them. They scattered in lively fashion, and from shelter watched the silver bush. A second bullet came from its foliage and wounded slightly a man who was carrying wood to one of the fires. But the annoying sharpshooter remained invisible.

"He's lying down on the ice like a Sioux or Cheyenne in a gully," said Pennington.

"Maybe he has a gully in the ice," said Dick, "and he can crouch here and shoot at us all day, almost in perfect safety."

But Colonel Winchester appeared and ordered a score of the men, with the heaviest rifles, to shoot away the entire clump of cedars. They did it with a method and a regard for mathematics that filled Warner's soul with delight, firing in turn and planting their bullets in a line along the front of the clump, cutting down everything like a mower with a scythe.

Dick with the glasses saw the ice fly into the air in a silver spray as bush after bush fell. Presently they were all cut away by that stream of heavy bullets, but no human being was disclosed.

"He's just gone over the other side of the ridge," said Warner in disgust, "and is waiting there until we finish. We couldn't shoot through a mountain, even if we had one of our biggest cannon here. He'll find another clump of bushes soon and be potting us from it."

"But we can shoot that away too," said Dick hopefully.

"We can't shoot down all the forests on the mountain. He must have heavy hobnails, or, like the mountaineers, he has drawn thick yarn socks over his boots, else he couldn't scoot about on the ice the way he does."

"Ah, there goes his rifle, behind the clump of bushes to the right of the one that we shot away!"

A second man was wounded by the bullet, and then an extraordinary siege ensued, a siege of three hundred men by a single sharpshooter on top of a mountain as smooth as glass. Whenever they shot his refuge away he moved to another, and, while they were shooting at it he had nothing to do but drop down a few feet on the far side of the ridge and remain in entire safety until he chose another ambush.

"I suppose this was visited upon us because we were puffed up with pride over our exploits," said Pennington, "but it's an awful jolt to us to have the whole Winchester regiment penned up here and driven to hiding by a single brigand."

"It's not a jolt," said Warner, "it's a tragedy. Unless we get him we can never live it down. We may win another Gettysburg all by ourselves, but history and also the voice of legend and ironic song will tell first of the time when Slade, the outlaw, held us all in the cove at the muzzle of his rifle."

Colonel Winchester, although he did not show it, raged the most of them all. The great taunt would be for him rather than his young officers and troopers, and the blood burned in his veins as he watched the operations of the sharpshooter on the ridges. One of his men had been killed, three had been wounded, and all of them were compelled to seek shelter for their lives as none knew where Slade's bullet would strike next. In his perplexity he called in Reed, the mountaineer, who fortunately was in camp, and he suggested that they send out a group of men through the entrance, who might stalk him from the far side in the same way that they had crushed his band.

"But how are they to climb on the smooth ice?" asked the colonel.

"Wrap the feet uv the men in blankets, an' let 'em use their bayonets for a grip in the ice," replied the mountaineer, "an' ef you don't mind, colonel, I'd like to go along with the party. Mebbe I'd git a shot at that big hat uv Slade's."

The idea appealed to the colonel, especially as none other offered, and Warner, to his great delight, received command of the party detailed for the difficult and dangerous duty. Several of the coarsest and heaviest blankets were cut up, and the feet of the men were wrapped in them in such manner that they would not slip on the ice, although retaining full freedom of movement. They tried their "snow shoes" behind the house, where they were sheltered from Slade's bullets, and found that they could make good speed over the ice.

"Now be careful, Warner," said Colonel Winchester. "Remember that your party also may present a fair target to him, and we don't wish to lose another man."

"I'll use every precaution possible, sir," replied Warner, "and I thank you for giving me this responsibility."

Then keeping to the shelter of trees he led his men out through the pass, and the soul of Warner, despite his calm exterior, was aflame. Dick had achieved his great task with success, and, in the lesser one, he wished to do as well. It was not jealousy of his comrade, but emulation, and also a desire to meet his own exacting standards. As he disappeared with his picked sharpshooters and turned the shoulder of the mountain his blood was still hot, but his Vermont head was as cool as the ice upon which he trod.

Warner heard the distant reports of Slade's rifle, and also the crackle of the firing in reply. He knew the colonel would keep Slade so busy that he was not likely to notice the flank movement, and he pressed forward with all the energy of himself and his men. The heavy cloth around their shoes gave them a secure foothold until they reached the steeper slopes, and there, in accordance with Reed's suggestion, they used their bayonets as alpenstocks.

A third of the way up the slope, and they reached one of the clumps of cedars, into which they crawled. Although a glittering network of silver it was a cold covert, but they lay on the ice there and watched for Slade's next shot. They heard it a minute later, and then saw him behind a pine about five hundred yards away. After sending his bullet into the valley he had withdrawn a little and was slipping another cartridge into the fine breech-loading rifle that he carried, the most modern and highly improved weapon then used, as Warner could clearly see.

"Would you let me take a look at him through your glasses?" asked Reed.

"Certainly," replied Warner, handing them to him.

"Jest as I thought," said Reed, as he took a long look. "He's done gone plum' mad with the wish to kill. It strikes them evil-minded critters that way sometimes, an' he's had so much luck shootin' down at us, an' keepin' a whole little army besieged that it's mounted to his head. Ef he had his way he'd jest wipe us all out."

"A sanguinary and savage mind," said Warner. "It's the spirit of the rattlesnake or the cobra, and we must exterminate him. He's moving further along the ridge, and he's exactly between us and that clump of cedars, higher up and about three hundred yards away. If we could make those cedars we would bring him within range. It's a pretty steep climb, but I want to try it."

"We kin do it shore by stabbin' our bayonets into the ice and hangin' on to 'em ez we edge up," said Reed optimistically. "The clump itself will help hide us, an' Slade ain't likely to look this way.

Ez I told you he hez gone plum' mad with the blood fever, an' he ain't got eyes for anythin' except the soldiers in the valley what he wants to shoot."

"Poison, nothing but poison," said Warner. "We must remove him as speedily as possible for the sake of the universe. Come on! I mean to lead."

He emerged from the clump and took his way toward the second cluster, digging a heavy hunting knife into the ice whenever he felt that he was about to slip. Reed was just behind him, breathing hard from the climb, and then came the whole detachment. Warner felt a momentary shiver lest the guerrilla see them. If he caught them on the steep ice between the two cedar clumps he could decimate them with ease.

But fortune was kind and they breathed mighty sighs of relief as they drew into the second network of silver, where they lay close watching for Slade, who had fired three times into the valley while they were on the way.

He had gone farther down the ridge, but they saw him partially as he kneeled for another shot. If he moved again in the same direction after firing they would not be able to reach him, and Warner, Reed agreeing with him, decided that they must make the attempt to remove him now or never. It was a hard target, not much of Slade's body showing, but the entire party took aim and fired together at the leader's word.

Slade threw up his arms, fell back on their side of the mountain and then slid down the slippery slope. Warner watched him with a kind of horrified fascination as he shot over the clear ice. His body struck a small pine presently and shattered it, the broken pieces of the icy sheath flying in the air like crystals. After a momentary pause from the resistance Slade went on, slid over a shelf, and disappeared in a deep drift.

"He's out o' business," said Reed. "I reckon we'd better go down thar, an' see ef he's all broke to pieces."

They climbed down slowly and painfully, reaching the drift, but to their amazement Slade was not there. They found his rifle and spots of blood, but the outlaw was gone, a thin red trail that led down a rift showing the way he went.

"We hit our b'ar an' took the bite out uv him," said Reed philosophically, "but we ain't got his hide to show. Still he's all broke up, jest the same, 'cause he didn't even think to take his gun, an' this red trail shows that we won't be bothered by him ag'in fur a long time."

Warner would have preferred the annihilation or capture of Slade, whom he truly called a rattlesnake or cobra, but he was satisfied, nevertheless. He had destroyed the guerrilla's power to harm for a long time, at least, and not a man of his had been hurt. He was sure to receive Colonel Winchester's words of approval, and he felt the swell of pride, but did not show it by word or manner.

Carrying the rifle, as the visible proof of victory, they returned to the cove, and received from Colonel Winchester the words for which they were grateful. Further proof was the failure of Slade to return and the lifting of the terrible weight which a single man had put upon them. They could now go about in the open, as they pleased, the big fires were built up again, and cheerfulness returned.

The mountaineers brought in more food the next day, and the following night Reed and another mountaineer crossed the ridge and were lucky enough to shoot a fat bear in a ravine. They dressed it there, and, between them, managed to bring the body back to the camp. A day later they secured another, and there was a great feast of fresh meat.

That night the weather rapidly turned warmer and all knew the big thaw was at hand. A long heavy rain that lasted almost until daylight hastened it and great floods roared down the slopes. Tons and tons of melting snow also slid into the valley, and the creek became a booming torrent. They were more thankful than ever for their huts and lean-tos, and all except the sentinels clung closely to their shelter.

Throughout the day the mountains were veiled in vapors from the rain and the melting snow, and, after another night, the troop saddled and departed, the horses treading ankle deep in mud, but their riders eager to get away.

"We overstayed our time," said Dick, looking back, "but it was a good cove for us. Our presence there tempted the enemy to battle, and we destroyed him. Then we had shelter and a home when the great storm came."

"A good cove, truly," said Pennington, "and we sha'n't forget it."

When they reached the main pass they found it also deep in mud and melting snow, and their progress was slow and painful. But before noon they met Shepard and the sergeant returning with news that they had carried an account of the victory to General Sheridan, but that nothing had happened in the main valley save a few raids by Mosby. Shepard, who acted as spokesman, was too tactful to say much, but he indicated very clearly that the commander-in-chief was highly pleased with the destruction of the Slade and Skelly band, the maraudings of which had become a great annoyance and danger. Dick was eager to hear more, and, when the opportunity presented itself, he questioned the sergeant privately.

"What do we hear from Petersburg?" he asked. "Is the deadlock there broken?"

"Not yet, sir," replied the sergeant. "The winter being so very severe the troops are not able to do much. General Lee still holds his lines."

"I suppose that General Grant doesn't care to risk another Cold Harbor, but what has been done here in the Valley of Virginia should enable him to turn Lee's flank in the spring."

"I take it that you're right, sir. General Lee is a hard nut to crack, as we all know, but his army is wearing away. In the spring the shell of the nut will be so thin that we'll smash it."

The column, after its exploit, reported to Sheridan at Winchester, the little city around which and through which the war rolled for four long years, and where two great commanders, one of the gray and the other of the blue, had their headquarters at times. But Colonel Winchester and his young staff officers rode through streets that were faced by closed shutters and windows. Nowhere was the hostility to the Northern troops more bitter and intense than in Winchester, the beloved city of the great Stonewall which had seen with its own eyes so many of his triumphs.

Dick and his comrades had learned long since not to speak to the women and girls for fear of their sharp tongues, and in his heart he could not blame them. Youth did not keep him from having a philosophical and discerning mind, and he knew that in the strongest of people the emotions often triumph over logic and reason. Warner's little algebra was all right, when the question was algebraic, but sentiment and passion had a great deal to do with the affairs of the world, and, where they were concerned, the book was of no value at all.

Dick's new rank of captain was conferred upon him by General Sheridan himself, and it was accompanied by a compliment which though true made him blush in his modesty. A few days later Warner received the same rank for his achievement in driving away Slade, and it was conferred upon Pennington too for general excellence. The three were supremely happy and longed for more enemies to conquer, but a long period of comparative idleness ensued. The winter continued of unexampled severity, and they spent most of the time in camp, although they did not waste it. Several books of mathematics came from the North to Warner and he spent many happy evenings in their study. Dick got hold of a German grammar and exercise book, and, several others joining him, they made a little class, which though it met irregularly, learned much. Pennington was a wonder among the horses. When the veterinarians were at a loss they sent for him and he rarely failed of a cure. He modestly ascribed his merit to his father who taught him everything about horses on the great plains, where a man's horse was so often the sole barrier between him and death.

Thus the winter went on, and they longed eagerly for spring, the breaking up of the great cold, and the last campaign.

CHAPTER XV
BACK WITH GRANT

Despite the inevitable hostility of the people their stay at Winchester was pleasant and fruitful. All three of the new young captains experienced a mental growth, and their outlook upon the enemy was tempered greatly. They had been through so many battles and they had measured their strength and courage against the foe so often that all hatred and malice had departed. North and South, knowing too little of each other before the war, had now learned mutual respect upon the field of combat. And Dick, Warner and Pennington, feeling certain that the end was at hand, could understand the loss and sorrow of the South, and sympathize with the fallen. Their generous young hearts did not exult over a foe whom they expected soon to conquer.

Late in January of the fateful year 1865 Dick was walking through the streets of Winchester one cold day. The wind from the mountains had a fierce edge, and, as he bent his head to protect his face from it, he did not see a stout, heavily built man of middle age coming toward him, and did not stop until the stranger, standing squarely in his way, hailed him.

"Does the fact that you've become a captain keep you from seeing anything in your path, Mr. Mason?" asked the man in a deep bass, but wholly good-natured voice.

Dick looked up in surprise, because the tones were familiar. He saw a ruddy face, with keen, twinkling eyes and a massive chin, a face in which shrewdness and a humorous view of the world were combined. He hesitated a moment, then he remembered and held out his hand.

"It's Mr. Watson, the contractor," he said.

"So it is, lad," said John Watson, grasping the outstretched hand and shaking it heartily. "Don't mind my calling you lad, even if you are a captain. All things are comparative, and to me, a much older man, you're just a lad. I've heard of your deed in the mountains, in fact, I keep track of all of you, even of General Sheridan himself. It's my business to know men and what they do."

"I hope you're still making money," said Dick, smiling.

"I am. That's part of a merchant's duty. If he doesn't make money he oughtn't to be a merchant. Oh, I know that a lot of you soldiers look down upon us traders and contractors."

"I don't and I never did, Mr. Watson."

"I know it, Captain Mason, because you're a lad of intelligence. The first time I saw you I noticed that the reasoning quality was strong in you, and that was why I made you an offer to enter my employ after the war. That offer is still open and will remain open at all times."

"I thank you very much, Mr. Watson, but I can't accept it, as I have other ambitions."

"I was sure you wouldn't take it, but I like to feel it's always waiting for you. It's well to look ahead. This war, vast and terrible as it has been, will be over before the year is. Two or three million men who have done nothing but fighting for four years will be out of employment. Vast numbers of them will not know which way to turn. They will be wholly unfit, until they have trained themselves anew, for the pursuits of peace. Captains, majors, colonels and, yes, generals, will be besieging me for jobs, as zealously as they're now besieging Lee's army in the trenches before Petersburg, and with as much cause. When the war is over the soldier will not be of so much value, and the man of peace will regain his own. I hope you've thought of these things, Captain Mason."

"I've thought of them many times, Mr. Watson, and I've thought of them oftener than ever this winter. My comrades and I have agreed that as soon as the last battle is fought we'll plunge at once into the task of rebuilding our country. We amount to little, of course, in such a multitude, but one can do only what one can."

"That's so, but if a million feel like you and push all together, they can roll mountains away."

"You're not a man to come to Winchester for nothing. You've been doing business with the army?"

"I've been shoeing, clothing and bedding you. I deliver within two weeks thirty thousand pairs of shoes, thirty thousand uniforms, and sixty thousand blankets. They are all honest goods and the price is not too high, although I make the solid and substantial profit to which I am entitled. You soldiers on the battle line don't win a war alone. We who feed and clothe you achieve at least half. I regret again, Captain Mason, that you can't join me later. Mine's a noble calling. It's a great thing to be a merchant prince, and it's we, as much as any other class of people, who spread civilization over the earth."

"I know it," said Dick earnestly. "I'm not blind to the great arts of peace. Now, here come my closest friends, Captain Warner and Captain Pennington, who have understanding. I want you to meet them."

Dick's hearty introduction was enough to recommend the contractor to his comrades, but Warner already knew him well by reputation.

"I've heard of you often from some of our officers, Mr. Watson," he said. "You deliver good goods and you're a New Englander, like myself. Ten years from now you'll be an extremely rich man, a millionaire, twenty years from now you'll be several times a millionaire. About that time I'll become president of Harvard, and we'll need money—a great university always needs money—and I'll come to you for a donation of one hundred thousand dollars to Harvard, and you'll give it to me promptly."

John Watson looked at him fixedly, and slowly a look of great admiration spread over his face.

"Of course you're a New Englander," he said. "It was not necessary for you to say so. I could have told it by looking at you and hearing you talk. But from what state do you come?"

"Vermont."

"I might have known that, too, and I'm glad and proud to meet you, Captain Warner. I'm glad and proud to know a young man who looks ahead twenty years. Nothing can keep you from being president of Harvard, and that hundred thousand dollars is as good as given. Your hand again!"

The hands of the two New Englanders met a second time in the touch of kinship and understanding. Theirs was the clan feeling, and they had supreme confidence in each other. Neither doubted that the promise would be fulfilled, and fulfilled it was and fourfold more.

"You New Englanders certainly stand together," said Dick.

"Not more than you Kentuckians," replied the contractor. "I was in Kentucky several times before the war, and you seemed to be one big family there."

"But in the war we've not been one big family," said Dick, somewhat sadly. "I suppose that no state has been more terribly divided than Kentucky. Nowhere has kin fought more fiercely against kin."

"But you'll come together again after the war," said Watson cheerfully. "That great bond of kinship will prove more powerful than anything else."

"I hope so," said Dick earnestly.

They had the contractor to dinner with them, and he opened new worlds of interest and endeavor for all of them. He was a mighty captain of industry, a term that came into much use later, and mentally they followed him as he led the way into fields of immense industrial achievement. They were fascinated as he talked with truthful eloquence of what the country could become, the vast network of railroads to be built, the limitless fields of wheat and corn to be grown, the mines of the richest mineral continent to be opened, and a trade to be acquired, that would spread all over the world. They forgot the war while he talked, and their souls were filled and stirred with the romance of peace.

"I leave for Washington tonight," said the contractor, when the dinner was finished. "My work here is done. Our next meeting will be in Richmond."

All three of the young men took it as prophetic and when John Watson started north they waved him a friendly farewell. Another long wait followed, while the iron winter, one of the fiercest in the memory of man, still gripped both North and South. But late in February there was a great bustle, portending movement. Supplies were gathered, horses were examined critically, men looked to their arms and ammunition, and the talk was all of high anticipation. An electric thrill ran through the men. They had tasted deep of victory since the previous summer, and they were eager to ride to new triumphs.

"It's to be an affair of cavalry altogether," said Warner, who obtained the first definite news. "We're to go toward Staunton, where Early and his remnants have been hanging out, and clean 'em up. Although it's to be done by cavalry alone, as I told you, it'll be the finest cavalry you ever saw."

And when Sheridan gathered his horsemen for the march Warner's words came true. Ten thousand Union men, all hardy troopers now, were in the saddle, and the great Sheridan led them. The eyes of Little Phil glinted as he looked upon his matchless command, bold youths who had learned in the long hard training of war itself, to be the equals of Stuart's own famous riders. And the eyes of Sheridan glinted again when they passed over the Winchesters, the peerless regiment, the bravest of the brave, with the colonel and the three youthful captains in their proper places.

The weather was extremely cold, but they were prepared for it, and when they swung up the valley, and forty thousand hoofs beat on the hard road, giving back a sound like thunder, their pulses leaped, and they took with delight deep draughts of the keen frosty air.

While they carried food for the entire march, the rest of their equipment was light, four cannon, ammunition wagons, some ambulances and pontoon boats. Dick thought they would make fast time, but fortune for awhile was against them. The very morning the great column started the weather rapidly turned warmer, and then a heavy rain began to fall. The hard road upon which the forty thousand hoofs had beat their marching song turned to mud, and forty thousand hoofs made a new sound, as they sank deep in it, and were then pulled out again.

"If it keeps us from going fast," said the philosophical sergeant, "it'll keep them that we're goin' after from gettin' away. We're as good mud horses as they are."

"Do you think we'll go through to Staunton?" asked Dick of Warner.

"I've heard that we will, and that we'll go on and take Lynchburg too. Then we're to curve about and in North Carolina join Sherman who has smashed the Confederacy in the west."

"I don't like the North Carolina part," said Dick. "I hope we'll go to Grant and march with him on Richmond, because that's where the death blow will be dealt, if it's dealt at all."

"And that it will be dealt we don't doubt, neither you, nor I nor any of us."

"Yes, that's so."

While mud and rain could impede the progress of the great column they could not stop it. Neither could they dampen the spirits of the young troopers who rode knee to knee, and who looked forward to new victories. Through the floods of rain the ten thousand, scouts and skirmishers on their flanks, swept southward, and they encountered no foe. A few Southern horsemen would watch them at a great distance and then ride sadly away. There was nothing in the valley that could oppose Sheridan.

Dick's leggings, and his overcoat with an extremely high collar, kept him dry and warm and he was too seasoned to mind the flying mud which thousands of hoofs sent up, and which soon covered them. The swift movement and the expectation of achieving something were exhilarating in spite of every hardship and obstacle.

That night they reached the village of Woodstock, and the next day they crossed the north fork of the Shenandoah, already swollen by the heavy rains. The engineers rapidly and dexterously made a bridge of the pontoon boats, and the ten thousand thundered over in safety.

The next night they were at a little place called Lacy's Springs, sixty miles from Winchester, a wonderful march for two days, considering the heavy rains and deep mud, and they had not yet encountered an enemy. How different it would have been in Stonewall Jackson's time! Then, not a mile of the road would have been safe for them. It was ample proof of the extremities to which the Confederacy was reduced. Lee, at Petersburg, could not reinforce Early, and Early, at Staunton, could not reinforce Lee!

They intended to move on the next day, and they heard that night that Rosser, a brave Confederate general, had gathered a small Confederate force and was hastening forward to burn all the bridges over the middle fork of the Shenandoah, in order that he might impede Sheridan's progress. Then it was the call of the trumpet and boots and saddles early in the morning in order that they might beat Rosser to the bridges.

"I hope for their own sake that they won't try to fight us," said Dick.

"I'm with you on that," said Pennington. "They can't be more than a few hundreds, and it would take thousands, even with a river to help, to stop an army like ours."

It was not raining now and the roads growing dryer thundered with the hoofs of ten thousand horses. The Winchesters had an honored place in the van, and, as they approached the middle fork of the Shenandoah, the three young captains raised themselves in their saddles to see if the bridge yet stood. It was there, but on the other side of the stream a small body of cavalrymen in gray were galloping forward, and some had already dismounted for the attempt to destroy it. The arrival of the two forces was almost simultaneous, but the Union army, overwhelming in numbers, exulting in victory, swept forward to the call of the trumpets.

"They're not more than five or six hundred over there," said Warner, "too few to put up a fight against us. I feel sorry for 'em, and wish they'd go away."

The Southerners nevertheless were sweeping the narrow bridge with a heavy rifle fire, and Sheridan drew back his men for a few minutes. Then followed a series of mighty splashes, as two West Virginia regiments sent their horses into the river, swam it, and, as they emerged dripping on the farther shore, charged the little Confederate force in flank, compelling it to retreat so swiftly that it left behind prisoners and its wagons.

It was all over in a few minutes, and the whole army, crossing the river, moved steadily on toward Staunton, where Early had been in camp, and where Sheridan hoped to find him. The little victory did not bring Dick any joy. He knew that the Confederacy could now make no stand in the Valley of Virginia, and it was like beating down those who were already beaten. He sincerely hoped that Early would not await them at Staunton or anywhere else, but would take his futile forces out of the valley and join Lee.

The heavy rains began again. Winter was breaking up and its transition into spring was accompanied by floods. The last snow on the mountains melted and rushed down in torrents. The roads, already ruined by war, became vast ruts of mud, but Sheridan was never daunted by physical obstacles. The great army of cavalry, scarcely slacking speed, pressed forward continually, and Dick knew that Early did not have the shadow of a chance to withstand such an army.

The next day they entered Staunton, another of the neat little Virginia cities devoted solidly and passionately to the Southern cause. Here, they were faced again by blind doors and windows, but Early and his force were gone. Shepard brought news that he had prepared for a stand at Waynesborough, although he had only two thousand men.

"Our general will attack him at once," said Warner, when he heard of it. "He sweeps like a hurricane."

"He is surely the general for us at such a time," said Pennington, who began to feel himself a military authority.

"It's humane, at least," said Dick. "The quicker it's over the smaller the toll of ruin and death."

Nor had they judged Sheridan wrongly. His men advanced with speed, hunting Early, and they found him fortified with his scanty forces on a ridge near the little town of Waynesborough. The daring young leader, Custer, and Colonel Winchester, riding forward, found his flank exposed, and it was enough for Sheridan. He formed his plan with rapidity and executed it with precision. The Custer and Winchester men were dismounted and assailed the exposed flank at once, while the remainder of the army made a direct and violent charge in front.

It seemed to Dick that Early was swept away in an instant, and the attack was so swift and overwhelming that there was but little loss of life on either side. Four fifths of the Southern men and their cannon were captured, while Early, several of his generals and a few hundred soldiers escaped to the woods. His army, however, had ceased to exist, and Sheridan and his muddy victors rode on to the ancient town of Charlottesville, which, having no forces to defend it, the mayor and the leading citizens surrendered.

Dick, Warner and Pennington walked through the silent halls of the University of Virginia, the South's most famous institution of learning, founded by Thomas Jefferson, one of the republic's greatest men.

"I hope they will re-open it next year," said Warner generously, "and that it will grow and grow, until it becomes a rival of Harvard. We want to defeat the South, but not to destroy it. Since it is to be a part of the Union again, and loyal forever I hope and believe, we want it strong and prosperous."

"I'm with you in that," said Dick, "and I feel it with particular strength while I am here. There have been many great Virginians and I hope there'll be many more."

They also visited Monticello, the famous colonial mansion which the great Jefferson had built, and in which he had lived and planned for the republic. They trod there with light steps, feeling that his spirit was still present. Virginia was the greatest of the border states, but it seemed to Dick that here he was in the very heart of the South. Virginia was the greatest of the Southern fighting states too, and it had furnished most of the great Southern leaders, at least two of her sons ranking among the foremost military geniuses of modern times. For nearly four years they had barred the way to every Northern advance, and had won great victories over numbers, but Dick was sure as he stood on a portico at Monticello, in the very heart of valiant Virginia, that the fate of the South was sealed.

They did not stay long at Charlottesville and Monticello, but a portion of the army, including the Winchester men, went on, tearing up the railroad, while another column demolished a canal used for military purposes. Then the two forces united at a town called New Market, but they could go no farther. The heavy rains and the melting snows had swollen the rivers enormously, all the bridges before them were destroyed, and their own pontoons proved inadequate in face of the great rushing streams. Then they turned back.

Dick and his comrades were secretly glad. The rising of the waters had prevented them from going into North Carolina and joining Sherman. Hence, they deduced that so active a man as Sheridan would march for a junction with Grant, and that was where they wanted to go. They did not believe that the Confederacy was to be finished in North Carolina, but at Richmond. They knew that Lee's army yet stood between Grant and the Southern capital, and, there, would be the heart of great affairs.

Spring was now opening and Sheridan's army marched eastward. Men and horses were covered with mud, but they still had the flush of victories won, and the incentive of others expected. They were even yet worn by hard marching and some fighting, but it was a healthy leanness, making their muscles as tough as whipcord, while their eyes were keen like those of hawks.

Dick did not rejoice now in the work they were doing, although he saw its need. Theirs was a task of destruction. For a distance of more than fifty miles they ruined a canal important to the Confederacy. Boats, locks, everything went, and they also made cuts by which the swollen James poured into the canal, flooding it and thrusting it out of its banks. They met no resistance save a few distant shots, and Sheridan rejoiced over his plan to join the Army of the Potomac, although he had not yet been able to send word of it to Grant.

But the omens remained propitious. They saw now that there were no walls in the rear of the Confederacy and they had little to do but march. The heavy rains followed them, roads disappeared, and it seemed to the young captains that they lived in eternal showers of mud. Horses and riders alike were caked with it, and they ceased to make any effort to clean themselves.

"This is not a white army," said Warner, looking down a long column, "it's brown, although it would be hard to name the shade of brown."

"It's not always brown," said Pennington. "Lots of the Virginia mud is a rich, ripe red. Bet you anything that before tomorrow night we will have turned to some hue of scarlet."

"We won't take the wager," said Dick, "because you bet on a certainty."

That afternoon the scouts surprised a telegraph station on the railroad, and found in it a dispatch from General Early. To the great amazement of Sheridan, Early was not far away. He had only two hundred men, but with them the grim old fighter prepared to attack the Union army. Sheridan himself felt a certain pity for his desperate opponent, but he promptly sent Custer in search of him. The young cavalryman quickly found him and scattered or captured the entire band.

Early escaped from the fight with a lone orderly as his comrade, and the next day the general who had lost all through no fault of his own, rode into Richmond with his single companion, and from him Jefferson Davis, President of the Confederacy, heard the full tale of Southern disaster in the Valley of Virginia.

Meanwhile Sheridan and his victorious army rode on to a place called White House, where they found plenty of stores, and where they halted for a long rest, and also to secure new mounts, if they could. Their horses were worn out completely by the great campaign and were wholly unfit for further service. But it was hard to obtain fresh ones and the delay was longer than the general had intended. Nevertheless his troops profited by it. They had not realized until they stopped how near they too had come to utter exhaustion, and for several days they were in a kind of physical torpor while their strength came back gradually.

"I think I've removed the last trace of the Virginia mud from my clothes and myself," said Warner on the morning of the second day, "but I've had to work hard to do it, as time seemed to have made it almost a part of my being."

"I've spent most of my time learning to walk again, and getting the bows out of my legs," said Dick. "I've been a-horse so long that I felt like a sailor coming ashore from a three years' cruise."

"Agreed with me pretty well, all except the mud, since I was born on horseback," said Pennington. "But I don't like to ride in a brown plaster suit of armor. What do you think is ahead, boys?"

"Junction with General Grant," said Dick. "They say, also, that General Sherman, after completing his great work in Georgia and North Carolina, is coming to join them too. It will be a great meeting, that of the three successful generals who have destroyed the Confederacy, because there's nothing of it left now but Lee's army, and that they say is mighty small."

It was in reality a triumphant march that they began after they left White House, refreshed, remounted and ready for new conquests. They soon came into touch with the Army of the Potomac, and the great meeting between Grant, Sherman and Sheridan took place, Sherman having come north especially for the purpose. Then Sheridan's force became attached to the Army of the Potomac, and his cavalry columns advanced into the marshes about Petersburg. All fear that they would be sent to cooperate with Sherman passed, and Dick knew that the

Winchester men would be in the final struggle with Lee, a struggle the success of which he felt assured.

April was not far away. The fierce winter was broken up completely, but the spring rains were uncommonly heavy and much of the low country about Petersburg was flooded, making it difficult for cavalry and impossible for infantry. Nevertheless the army of Grant, with Sheridan now as a striking arm, began to close in on the beleaguered men in gray. Lee had held the trenches before Petersburg many months, keeping at bay a resolute and powerful army, led by an able and tenacious general, but it was evident now that he could not continue to hold them. Sheridan's victorious force on his flank made it impossible.

The Winchester men were in a skirmish or two, but for a few days most of their work was maneuvering, that is, they were continually riding in search of better positions. At times, the rain still poured, but the three young captains were so full of expectancy that they scarcely noticed it. Dick often heard the trumpets singing across the marshes, and now and then he saw the Confederate skirmishers and the roofs of Petersburg. He beheld too with his own eyes the circle of steel closing about the last hope of the Confederacy, and he felt every day, with increasing strength, that the end was near.

But the outside world did not realize that the great war was to close so suddenly. It had raged with the utmost violence for four years and it seemed the normal condition in America. Huge battles had been fought, and they had ended in nothing. Three years before, McClellan had been nearer to Richmond than Grant now was, and yet he had been driven away. Lee and Jackson had won brilliant victories or had held the Union numbers to a draw, and to those looking from far away the end seemed as distant as ever. At that very moment, they were saying in Europe that the Confederacy was invincible, and that it was stronger than it had been a year or two years earlier.

Dick, all unconscious of distant opinion, watched the tightening of the steel belt, and helped in the task. He and his comrades never doubted. They knew that Sherman had crushed the Southeast, and that Thomas, that stern old Rock of Chickamauga, had annihilated the Southern army of Hood at Nashville. Dick was glad that the triumph there had gone to Thomas, whom he always held in the greatest respect and admiration.

He often saw Grant in those days, a silent, resolute man, thinner than of old and stooped a little with care and responsibility. Dick, like the others, felt with all the power of conviction that Grant would never go back, and Shepard, who had entered Petersburg twice at the imminent risk of his life, assured him that Lee's force was wearing away. There was left only a fraction of the great Army of Northern Virginia that had fought so brilliantly at Chancellorsville, Gettysburg, the Wilderness and on many another battlefield.

"Only we who are here and who can see with our own eyes know what is about to happen," said the spy. "Even our own Northern states, so long deluded by false hopes, can't yet believe, but we know."

"Did you hear anything of the Invincibles when you were in Petersburg?" asked Dick.

"I heard of them, and I also saw them, although they did not know I was near. I suppose Harry Kenton could scarcely have contained himself had he known it was my sister who filched that map from the Curtis house in Richmond and that it was to me she gave it."

"But he was all right? He escaped unhurt from the Valley?"

"Yes, or if he took a hurt it was but a slight one, from which he soon recovered. He and his comrades, Dalton, St. Clair and Langdon, and the two Colonels, Talbot and St. Hilaire, are back with Lee, and they've organized another regiment called the Invincibles, which Talbot and St. Hilaire lead, although your cousin and Dalton are on Lee's staff again."

"I suppose we'll come face to face again, and this time at the very last," said Dick. "I hope they'll be reasonable about it, and won't insist on fighting until they're all killed. Have you heard anything of those two robbers and murderers, Slade and Skelly?"

"Not a thing. But I didn't expect it. They'd never leave the mountains. Instead they'll go farther into 'em."

That night many messengers rode with dispatches, and the lines of the Northern army were tightened. Dick saw all the signs that portended a great movement, signs with which he had long since grown familiar. The big batteries were pushed forward, and heavy masses of infantry were moved closer to the Confederate trenches. He felt quite sure that the final grapple was at hand.

CHAPTER XVI
THE CLOSING DAYS

Within the Southern lines and just beyond the range of the Northern guns, two men sat playing chess. They were elderly, gray and thin, but never had the faces of the two colonels been more defiant. With the Confederacy crumbling about them it was characteristic of both that they should show no despair, if in truth they felt it. Their confidence in Lee was sublime. He could still move mountains, although he had no tools with which to move them, and the younger officers, mere boys many of them, would come back to them again and again for encouragement. Spies had brought word that Grant, after nine months of waiting, and with Sheridan and a huge cavalry force on his flank, was about to make his great attack. But the dauntless souls of Colonel Leonidas Talbot and Lieutenant Colonel Hector St. Hilaire remained unmoved.

"I'm glad the rains are apparently about to cease, Hector," said Colonel Talbot. "When the ground grows firmer it will give General Lee a chance to make one of his great circling swoops, and rout the Yankee army."

"So it will, Leonidas. We've been waiting for it a long time, but the chance is here at last. We've had enough of the trenches. It's a monotonous life at best. Ah, I take your pawn, the one for which I've been lying in ambush more than a month."

"But that pawn dies in a good cause, Hector. When he fell, he uncovered the path to your remaining knight, as a dozen more moves will show you. What is it, Harry?"

Harry Kenton, thin, but hardy and strong, saluted.

"We have news, sir," he replied, "that the portion of the Union army under General Sheridan is moving. I bring you a dispatch from

General Lee to march and meet them. Other regiments, of course, will go with you."

They put away the chessmen and with St. Clair and Langdon marshaled the troops in line of battle. Harry felt a sinking of the heart when he saw how thin their ranks were, but the valiant colonels made no complaint. Then he went back to General Lee, whose manner was calm in face of the storm that was so obviously impending. The information had come that Grant and the bulk of his army were marching to the attack on the White Oak road, and, if he broke through there, nothing could save the Army of Northern Virginia.

Harry, after taking the dispatch to the Invincibles, carried orders to another regiment, while Dalton was engaged on similar errands. It was obvious to him that Lee was gathering his men for a great effort, and his heart sank. There was not much to gather. Throughout all that long autumn and winter the Army of Northern Virginia had disintegrated steadily. Nobody came to take the place of the slain, the wounded and the sick. All the regiments were skeletons. Many of them could not muster a hundred men apiece.

But Harry saw no sign of discouragement on the face of the chief whom he respected and admired so much. Lee was thinner and his hair was whiter, but his figure was as erect and vigorous as ever, and his face retained its ruddy color. Yet he knew the odds against him. Grant outside his works mustered a hundred thousand trained fighters, not raw levies, and the seasoned Army of the Potomac, that had persisted alike through victory and defeat, and proof now against any adversity, saw its prize almost in its hand. And the worn veterans whom the Southern leader could marshal against Grant were not one third his numbers.

The orderly who usually brought Lee's horse was missing on another errand, and Harry himself was proud to bring Traveler. The general was absorbed in deep thought, and he did not notice until he was in the saddle who held the bridle.

"Ah, it is you, Lieutenant Kenton!" he said. "You are always where you are needed. You have been a good soldier."

Harry flushed deeply with pleasure at such a compliment from such a source.

"I've tried to do my best, sir," he replied modestly.

"No one can do any more. You and Mr. Dalton keep close to me. We must go and deal with those people, once more."

His calm, steady tones brought Harry's courage back. To the young hero-worshiper Lee himself was at least fifty thousand men, and even with his scanty numbers he would pluck victory from the very heart of defeat.

There could no longer be any possible doubt that Grant was about to attack, and Lee made his dispositions rapidly. While he led the bulk of his army in person to battle, Longstreet was left to face the army north of the James, while Gordon at the head of Ewell's old corps stood in front of Petersburg. Then Lee turned away to the right with less than twenty thousand men to meet Grant, and fortified himself along the White Oak Road. Here he waited for the Union general, who had not yet brought up his masses, but Harry and Dalton felt quite sure that despite the disparity of numbers Lee was the one who would attack. It had been so all through the war, and they knew that in the offensive lay the best defensive. The event soon proved that they read their general's mind aright.

It was the last day of March when Lee suddenly gave the order for his gaunt veterans to advance, and they obeyed without faltering. The rains had ceased, a bright sun was shining, and the Southern trumpets sang the charge as bravely as at the Second Manassas or Chancellorsville. They had only two thousand cavalry on their flank, under Fitz Lee, but the veteran infantry advanced with steadiness and precision. Colonel Leonidas Talbot and Lieutenant Colonel Hector St. Hilaire were on foot now, having lost their horses long since, but, waving their small swords, they walked dauntlessly at the head of their little regiment, St. Clair and Langdon, a bit farther back, showing equal courage.

The speed of the Southern charge increased and they were met at first by only a scattering fire. The Northern generals, not expecting Lee to move out of his works, were surprised. Before they could take the proper precautions Lee was upon them and once more the rebel yell that had swelled in victory on so many fields rang out in triumph. The front lines of the men in blue were driven in, then whole brigades were thrown back, and Harry felt a wild thrill of delight when he beheld success where success had not seemed possible.

He saw near him the Invincibles charging home, and the two colonels still waving their swords as they led them, and he saw also the worn faces of the veterans about him suffused once more with the fire of battle. He watched with glowing eyes as the fierce charge drove the Northern masses back farther and farther.

But the Union leaders, though taken by surprise, did not permit themselves and their troops to fall into a panic. They had come too far and had fought too many battles to lose the prize at the very last moment. Their own trumpets sounded on a long line, calling back the regiments and brigades. Although the South had gained much ground Harry saw that the resistance was hardening rapidly. Grant and Sheridan were pouring in their masses. Heavy columns of infantry gathered in their front, and Sheridan's numerous and powerful cavalry began to cut away their flanks. The Southern advance became slow and then ceased entirely.

Harry felt again that dreadful sinking of the heart. Leadership, valor and sacrifice were of no avail, when they were faced by leadership, valor and sacrifice also added to overwhelming numbers.

The battle was long and fierce, the men in gray throwing away their lives freely in charge after charge, but they were gradually borne back. Lee showed all his old skill and generalship, marshaling his men with coolness and precision, but Grant and Sheridan would not be denied. They too were cool and skillful, and when night came the Southern army was driven back at all points, although it had displayed a valor never surpassed in any of the great battles of the war. But Lee's face had not yet shown any signs of despair, when he gathered his men again in his old works.

It was to Harry, however, one of the gloomiest nights that he had ever known. As a staff officer, he knew the desperate position of the Southern force, and his heart was very heavy within him. He saw across the swamps and fields the innumerable Northern campfires, and he heard the Northern bugles calling to one another in the dusk. But as the night advanced and he had duties to do his courage rose once more. Since their great commander-in-chief was steady and calm he would try to be so too.

The opposing sentinels were very close to one another in the dark and as usual they often talked. Harry, as he went on one errand or another, heard them sometimes, but he never interfered, knowing that nothing was to be gained by stopping them. Deep in the night, when he was passing through a small wood very close to the Union lines, a figure rose up before him. It was so dark that he did not know the man at first, but at the second look he recognized him.

"Shepard!" he exclaimed. "You here!"

"Yes, Mr. Kenton," replied the spy, "it's Shepard, and you will not try to harm me. Why should you at such a moment? I am within the Confederate lines for the last time."

"So, you mean to give up your trade?"

"It's going to give me up. Chance has made you and me antagonists, Mr. Kenton, but our own little war, as well as the great war in which we both fight, is about over. I will not come within the Southern lines again because there is no need for me to do so. In a few days there will be no Southern lines. Don't think that I'm trying to exult over you, but remember what I told you four years ago in Montgomery. The South has made a great and wonderful fight, but it was never possible for her to win."

"We are not beaten yet, Mr. Shepard."

"No, but you will be. I suppose you'll fight to the last, but the end is sure as the rising of tomorrow's sun. We have generals now who can't be driven back."

Harry was silent because he had no answer to make, and Shepard resumed:

"I'm willing to tell you, Mr. Kenton, that your cousin, Mr. Mason, a captain now, is here with General Sheridan, and that he went through today's battle uninjured."

"I'm glad at any rate that Dick is now a captain."

"He has earned the rank. He is my good friend, as I hope you will be after the war."

"I see no reason why we shouldn't. You've served the North in your own way and I've served the South in mine. I want to say to you, Mr. Shepard, that if in our long personal struggle I held any malice against you it's all gone now, and I hope that you hold none against me."

"I never felt any. Good-by!"

"Good-by!"

Shepard was gone so quickly and with so little noise that he seemed to vanish in the air, and Harry turned back to his work, resolved not to believe the man's assertion that the war was over. He slept a little, and so did Dalton, but both were awake, when a red dawn came alive with the crash of cannon and rifles.

Shepard had spoken truly, when he said that the North now had generals who would not be driven back. Nor would they cease to attack. As soon as the light was sufficient, Grant and Sheridan began to press Lee with all their might. Pickett, who had led the great charge at Gettysburg, and Johnson, who held a place called Five Forks, were assailed fiercely by overpowering numbers, and, despite a long and desperate resistance, their command was cut in pieces and the fragments scattered, leaving Lee's right flank uncovered.

The day, like the one before it, ended in defeat and confusion, and, at the next dawn, Grant, silent, tenacious, came anew to the attack, his dense columns now assailing the front before Petersburg, and carrying the trenches that had held them so long. The thin Confederate lines there fought in vain to hold them, but the Union brigades, exultant and cheering, burst through everything, flung aside those of their foes whom they did not overthrow, and advanced toward the city. Here fell the famous Lieutenant General A. P. Hill, a man of frail body and valiant soul, beloved of Lee and the whole army.

The next noon came, somber to Harry beyond all description. The youngest officer knew that while General Lee was still in Petersburg he could no longer hold it, and that they were nearly surrounded by the victorious and powerful Union host. The break in the lines had been made just after sunrise, and had been widened in the later hours of the morning. Now there was a momentary lull in the firing, but the lifting clouds of smoke enabled them to see vast masses of men in blue advancing and already in the suburbs of the town.

Lee's headquarters were about a mile and a half west of Petersburg, where he stood on a lawn and watched the progress of the combat. Nearly opposite him was a tall observatory that the Union men had erected, and from its summit the Northern generals also were watching. Harry and Dalton stood near Lee, awaiting with others his call, and every detail he saw that day always remained impressed upon Harry Kenton's mind.

He intently watched his general. Feeling that the Southern army was so near destruction he thought that the face of Lee would show agitation. But it was not so. His calm and grave demeanor was unchanged. He was in full uniform of fine gray, and had even buckled to his belt his dress sword which he seldom carried. It was told of him that he said that morning if he were compelled to surrender he would do so in his best. But he had not yet given up hope.

Harry turned his eyes away from Lee to the enemy. Without the aid of glasses now, he saw the great columns in blue advancing, preceded by a tremendous fire of artillery that filled the air with bursting shells. The infantry themselves were advancing with the bayonet, the sunlight gleaming on the polished metal. As far as he could see the ring of fire and steel extended. One heavy column was advancing toward the very lawn on which they stood.

"Looks as if they were going to trample us under foot," said Dalton.

"Yes, but the general may still find a way out of it," said Harry.

"They are still coming," said Dalton.

The shells were bursting about them and bullets too soon began to strike upon the lawn. A battery that sought to drive back the advancing column was exposed to such a heavy fire that it was compelled to limber up and retreat. The officers urged Lee to withdraw and at length, mounting Traveler, he rode back slowly and deliberately to his inner line. Harry often wondered what his feelings were on that day, but whatever they were his face expressed nothing. When he stopped in his new position he said to one of his staff, but without raising his voice:

"This is a bad business, colonel."

Harry heard him say a little later to another officer:

"Well, colonel, it has happened as I told them it would at Richmond. The line has stretched until it has broken."

But the general and his staff were not permitted to remain long at their second stop. The Union columns never ceased to press the shattered Southern army. Their great artillery, served with the rapidity and accuracy that had marked it all through the war, poured showers of shell and grape and canister upon the thin ranks in gray, and the rifles were close enough to add their own stream of missiles to the irresistible fire.

Harry was in great fear for his general. It seemed as if the Northern gunners had recognized him and his staff. Perhaps they knew his famous war horse, Traveler, as he rode slowly away, but in any event, the shells began to strike on all sides of the little group. One burst just behind Lee. Another killed the horse of an officer close to him, and the bursting fragments inflicted slight wounds upon members of the staff. Lee, for the first time, showed emotion. Looking back over his shoulder his eyes blazed, and his cheeks flushed. Harry knew that he wished to turn and order a charge, but there was nothing with which to charge, and, withdrawing his gaze from the threatening artillery, he rode steadily on.

The general's destination now was an earthwork in the suburbs of the city, manned by a reserve force, small but ardent and defiant. It welcomed Lee and his staff with resounding cheers, and Harry's heart sprang up again. Here, at least, was confidence, and as they rode behind them the guns replied fiercely to the advancing Northern batteries, checking them for a little while, and giving the retreating troops a chance to rest.

Now came a lull in the fighting, but Harry knew well that it was only a lull. Presently Grant and Sheridan would press harder than ever. They were fully aware of the condition of the Southern army, its smallness and exhaustion, and they would never cease to hurl upon it their columns of cavalry and infantry, and to rake it with the numerous batteries of great guns, served so well. Once more his heart sank low, as he thought of what the next night might bring forth. He knew that General Lee had sent in the morning a messenger to the capital with the statement that Petersburg could be held no longer and that he would retreat in the night.

Every effort was made to gather the remaining portion of the Southern army into one strong, cohesive body. Longstreet, at the order of Lee, left his position north of the James River, while Gordon took charge of the lines to the east of Petersburg. It was when they gathered for this last stand that Harry realized fully how many of the great Confederate officers were gone. It was here that he first heard of the death of A. P. Hill, of whom he had seen so much at Gettysburg. And he choked as he thought of Stonewall Jackson, Jeb Stuart, Turner

Ashby and all the long roll of the illustrious fallen, who were heroes to him.

The Northern infantry and cavalry did not charge now, but the cannon continued their work. Battery after battery poured its fire upon the earthworks, although the men there, sheltered by the trenches, did not suffer so much for the present.

Harry found time to look up his friends, and discovered the Invincibles in a single trench, about sixty of them left, but all showing a cheerfulness, extraordinary in such a situation. It was characteristic of both Colonel Talbot and Lieutenant Colonel St. Hilaire that they should present a bolder front, the more desperate their case. Nor were the younger officers less assured. Captain Arthur St. Clair was carefully dusting from his clothing dirt that had been thrown there by bursting shells, and Lieutenant Thomas Langdon was contemplating with satisfaction the track of a bullet that had gone through his left sleeve without touching the arm.

"The sight of you is welcome, Harry," said Colonel Leonidas Talbot in even tones. "It is pleasant to know at such a time that one's friend is alive, because the possibilities are always against it. Still, Harry, I've always felt that you bear a charmed life, and so do St. Clair and Langdon. Tell me, is it true that we evacuate Petersburg tonight?"

"It's no secret, sir. The orders have been issued and we do."

"If we must go, we must, and it's no time for repining. Well, the town has been defended long and valiantly against overwhelming numbers. If we lose it, we lose with glory. It can never be said of the South that we were not as brave and tenacious as any people that ever lived."

"The Northern armies that fight us will be the first to give us that credit, sir."

"That is true. Soldiers who have tested the mettle of one another on innumerable desperate fields do not bear malice and are always ready to acknowledge the merits of the foe. Ah, see how closely that shell burst to us! And another! And a third! And a fourth! Hector, you read the message, do you not?"

"Certainly, Leonidas, it's as plain as print to you and me. John Carrington—good old John! honest old John!—is now in command of that group of batteries on the right. He has been in charge of guns elsewhere, and has been suddenly shifted to this point. The great increase in volume and accuracy of fire proves it."

"Right, Hector! He's as surely there as we are here. The voice of those cannon is the voice of John Carrington. Well, if we're to be crushed I prefer for good old John to do it."

"But we're not crushed, Leonidas. We'll go out of Petersburg tonight, beating off every attack of the enemy, and then if we can't hold Richmond we'll march into North Carolina, gather together all the remaining forces of the Confederacy, and, directed by the incomparable genius of our great commander, we'll yet win the victory."

"Right, Hector! Right! Pardon me my moment of depression, but it was only a moment, remember, and it will not occur again. The loss of a capital—even if it should come to that—does not necessarily mean the loss of a cause. Among the hills and mountains of North Carolina we can hold out forever."

Harry was cheered by them, but he did not fully share their hopes and beliefs.

"Aren't they two of the greatest men you've ever known?" whispered St. Clair to him.

"If honesty and grandeur of soul make greatness they surely are," replied Harry feelingly.

He returned now to his general's side, and watched the great bombardment. Scores of guns in a vast half circle were raining shells upon the slender Confederate lines. The blaze was continuous on a long front, and huge clouds of smoke gathered above. Harry believed that the entire Union army would move forward and attack their works, but the charge did not come. Evidently Grant remembered Cold Harbor, and, feeling that his enemy was in his grasp, he refrained from useless sacrifices.

Another terrible night, lighted up by the flash of cannon and thundering with the crash of the batteries came, and Lee, collecting his army of less than twenty thousand men, moved out of Petersburg. It tore Harry's heart to leave the city, where they had held Grant at bay so long, but he knew the necessity. They could not live another day under that concentrated and awful fire. They might stay and surrender or retreat and fight again, and valiant souls would surely choose the latter.

The march began just after twilight turned to night, and the darkness and clouds of skirmishers hid it from the enemy. They crossed the Appomattox, and then advanced on the Hickory road on the north side of the river. General Lee stood on foot, but with the bridle of Traveler in his hand and his staff about him, at the entrance to the road, and watched the troops as they marched past.

His composure and steadiness seemed to Harry as great as ever, and his voice never broke, as he spoke now and then to the marching men. Nor was the spirit of the men crushed. Again and again they cheered as they saw the strong figure of the gray commander who had led them so often to victory. Nor were they shaken by the booming of the cannon behind them, nor by the tremendous crashes that marked the explosions of the magazines in Petersburg.

When the last soldier had passed, General Lee and his staff mounted their horses and followed the army in the dusk and gloom. Behind them lofty fires shed a glaring light over fallen Petersburg.

CHAPTER XVII
APPOMATTOX

The morning after Lee's retreat the Winchester regiment rode into Petersburg and looked curiously at the smoldering fires and what was left of the town. They had been before it so long it seemed almost incredible to Dick Mason that they were in it now. But the Southern leader and his army were not yet taken. They were gone, and they still existed as a fighting power.

"We have Petersburg at last," he said, "but it's only a scorched and empty shell."

"We've more than that," said Warner.

"What do you mean?"

"We've Richmond, too. The capital of the Confederacy, inviolate for four years, has fallen, and our troops have entered it. Jefferson Davis, his government and its garrison have fled, burning the army buildings and stores as they went. A part of the city was burned also, but our troops helped to put out the fires and saved the rest. Dick, do you realize it? Do you understand that we have captured the city over which we have fought for four years, and which has cost more than a half million lives?"

Dick was silent, because he had no answer to make. Neither he nor Warner nor Pennington could yet comprehend it fully. They had talked often of the end of the war, they had looked forward to the great event, they had hoped for the taking of Richmond, but now that it was taken it scarcely seemed real.

"Tell it over, George," he said, "was it Richmond you were speaking of, and did you say that it was taken?"

"Yes, Dick, and it's the truth. Of course it doesn't look like it to you or to me or to Frank, but it's a fact. Today or tomorrow we may go there and see it with our own eyes, and then if we don't believe the sight we can read an account of it in the newspapers."

It was a process of saturation, but in the next hour or two they believed it and understood it fully. On the following day they rode into the desolate and partly burned capital, now garrisoned heavily by the North, and looked with curiosity at the little city for which such torrents of blood had been shed. But as at Winchester and Petersburg, they gazed upon blind doors and windows. Nor did they expect anything else. It was only natural, and they refrained carefully from any outward show of exultation.

Richmond was to hold them only a few hours, as Grant and Sheridan continued hot on the trail of Lee. They knew that he was marching along the Appomattox, intending to concentrate at Amelia Court House, and they were resolved that he should not escape. Sheridan's cavalry, with the Winchester regiment in the van, advanced swiftly and began to press hard upon the retreating army. The firing was almost continuous. Many prisoners and five guns were taken, but at the crossing of a creek near nightfall the men in gray, still resolute, turned and beat off their assailants for the time.

The pursuit was resumed before the next daylight, and both Grant and Sheridan pressed it with the utmost severity. In the next few days Dick felt both pity and sympathy for the little army that was defending itself so valiantly against extermination or capture. It was almost like the chase of a fox now, and the hounds were always growing in number and power.

The Northern cavalry spread out and formed a great net. The Southern communications were cut off, their scouts were taken, and all the provision trains intended for Lee were captured. The prisoners reported that the Southern army was starving, and the condition of their own bodies proved the truth of their words. As Dick looked upon these ragged and famished men his feeling of pity increased, and he sincerely hoped that the hour of Lee's surrender would be hastened.

During these days and most of the nights too Dick lived in the saddle. Once more he and his comrades were clothed in the Virginia mud, and all the time the Winchester regiment brought in prisoners or wagons. They knew now that Lee was seeking to turn toward the

South and effect a junction with Johnston in North Carolina, but Dick, his thoughts being his own, did not see how it was possible. When the Confederacy began to fall it fell fast. It was only after they passed through Richmond that he saw how frail the structure had become, and how its supporting timbers had been shot away. It was great cause of wonder to him that Lee should still be able to hold out, and to fight off cavalry raids, as he was doing.

And the Army of Northern Virginia, although but a fragment, was dangerous. In these its last hours, reduced almost to starvation and pitiful in numbers, it fought with a courage and tenacity worthy of its greatest days. It gave to Lee a devotion that would have melted a heart of stone. Whenever he commanded, it turned fiercely upon its remorseless pursuers, and compelled them to give ground for a time. But when it sought to march on again the cavalry of Sheridan and the infantry of Grant followed closely once more, continually cutting off the fringe of the dwindling army.

Dick saw Lee himself on a hill near Sailor's Creek, as Sheridan pressed forward against him. The gray leader had turned. The troops of Ewell and Anderson were gathered at the edge of a forest, and other infantry masses stood near. Lee on Traveler sat just in front of them, and was surveying the enemy through his glasses. Dick used his own glasses, and he looked long, and with the most intense curiosity, mingled with admiration, at the Lion of the South, whom they were about to bring to the ground. The sun was just setting, and Lee was defined sharply against the red blaze. Dick saw his features, his gray hair, and he could imagine the defiant blaze of his eyes. It was an unforgettable picture, the one drawn there by circumstances at the closing of an era.

Then he took notice of a figure, also on horseback, not far behind Lee, a youthful figure, the face thin and worn, none other than his cousin, Harry Kenton. Dick's heart took a glad leap. Harry still rode with his chief, and Dick's belief that he would survive the war was almost justified.

Then followed a scattering fire to which sunset and following darkness put an end, and once more the Southern leader retreated, with Sheridan and his cavalry forever at his heels, giving him no rest, keeping food from reaching him, and capturing more of his men. The wounded lion turned again, and, in a fierce attack drove back

Sheridan and his men, but, when the battle closed, and Lee resumed his march, Sheridan was at his heels as before, seeking to pull him down, and refusing to be driven off.

Grant also dispatched Custer in a cavalry raid far around Lee, and the daring young leader not only seized the last wagon train that could possibly reach the Confederate commander, but also captured twenty-five of his guns that had been sent on ahead. Dick knew now that the end, protracted as it had been by desperate courage, was almost at hand, and that not even a miracle could prevent it.

The column with which he rode was almost continually in sight of the Army of Northern Virginia, and the field guns never ceased to pour shot and shell upon it. The sight was tragic to the last degree, as the worn men in gray retreated sullenly along the muddy roads, in rags, blackened with mire, stained with wounds, their horses falling dead of exhaustion, while the pursuing artillery cut down their ranks. Then the news of Custer's exploit came to Grant and Sheridan, and the circle of steel, now complete, closed in on the doomed army.

It was the seventh of April when the Winchester men rested their weary horses, not far from the headquarters of General Grant, and also gave their own aching bones and muscles a chance to recover their strength. Dick, after his food and coffee, watched the general, who was walking back and forth before his tent.

"He looks expectant," said Dick.

"He has the right to look so," said Warner. "He may have news of earth-shaking importance."

"What do you mean?"

"I know that he sent a messenger to Lee this morning, asking him to surrender in order to stop the further effusion of blood."

"I wish Lee would accept. The end is inevitable."

"Remember that they don't see with our eyes."

"I know it, George, but the war ought to stop. The Confederacy is gone forever."

"We shall see what we shall see."

They didn't see, but they heard, which was the same thing. To the polite request of Grant, Lee sent the polite reply that his means of resistance were not yet exhausted, and the Union leader took another hitch in the steel girdle. The second morning afterward, Lee made a desperate effort to break through at Appomattox Court House, but crushing numbers drove him back, and when the short fierce combat ceased, the Army of Northern Virginia had fired its last shot.

The Winchester men had borne a gallant part in the struggle, and presently when the smoke cleared away Dick uttered a shout.

"What is it?" exclaimed Colonel Winchester.

"A white flag! A white flag!" cried Dick in excitement. "See it waving over the Southern lines."

"Yes, I see it!" shouted the colonel, Warner and Pennington all together. Then they stood breathless, and Dick uttered the words:

"The end!"

"Yes," said Colonel Winchester, more to himself than to the others. "The end! The end at last!"

Thousands now beheld the flag, and, after the first shouts and cheers, a deep intense silence followed. The soldiers felt the immensity of the event, but as at the taking of Richmond, they could not comprehend it all at once. It yet seemed incredible that the enemy, who for four terrible years had held them at bay, was about to lay down his arms. But it was true. The messenger, bearing the flag, was now coming toward the Union lines.

The herald was received within the Northern ranks, bearing a request that hostilities be suspended in order that the commanders might have time to talk over terms of surrender, and, at the same time, General Grant, who was seven or eight miles from Appomattox Court House in a pine wood, received a note of a similar tenor, the nature of which he disclosed to his staff amid much cheering. The Union chief at once wrote to General Lee:

> Your note of this date is but at this moment (11:50 A. M.) received,
> in consequence of my having passed from the Richmond and Lynchburg
> road to the Farmville and Lynchburg road. I am at this writing about four miles west of Walker's Church, and will push forward to
> the front for the purpose of meeting you. Notice sent to me on this road where you wish the interview
> to take place will meet me.

It was a characteristic and modest letter, and yet the heart under the plain blue blouse must have beat with elation at the knowledge that he had brought, what was then the greatest war of modern times, to a successful conclusion. The dispatch was given to Colonel Babcock of his staff, who was instructed to ride in haste to Lee and arrange the interview. The general and his staff followed, but missing the way, narrowly escaped capture by Confederate troops, who did not yet know of the proposal to suspend hostilities. But they at last reached Sheridan about a half mile west of Appomattox Court House.

Dick and his comrades meanwhile spent a momentous morning. It would have been impossible for him afterward to have described his own feelings, they were such an extraordinary compound of relief, elation, pity and sympathy. The two armies faced each other, and, for the first time, in absolute peace. The men in blue were already slipping food and tobacco to their brethren in gray whom they had fought so long and so hard, and at many points along the lines they were talking freely with one another. The officers made no effort to restrain them, all alike feeling sure that the bayonets would now be rusting.

The Winchester men were dismounted, their horses being tethered in a grove, and Dick with the colonel, Warner and Pennington were at the front, eagerly watching the ragged little army that faced them. He saw soon a small band of soldiers, at the head of whom stood two elderly men in patched but neat uniforms, their figures very erect, and their faces bearing no trace of depression. Close by them were two tall youths whom Dick recognized at once as St. Clair and Langdon. He waved his hand to them repeatedly, and, at last, caught the eye of St. Clair, who at once waved back and then called Langdon's attention. Langdon not only waved also, but walked forward, as if to meet him, bringing St. Clair with him, and Dick, responding at once, advanced with Warner and Pennington.

They shook hands under the boughs of an old oak, and were unaffectedly glad to see one another, although the three youths in blue felt awkwardness at first, being on the triumphant side, and fearing lest some act or word of theirs might betray exultation over a conquered foe. But St. Clair, precise, smiling, and trim in his attire, put them at ease.

"General Lee will be here presently," he said, "and you, as well as we, know that the war is over. You are the victors and our cause is lost."

"But you have lost with honor," said Dick, won by his manner. "The odds were greatly against you. It's wonderful to me that you were able to fight so long and with so much success."

"It was a matter of mathematics, Captain St. Clair," said Warner. "The numbers, the big guns and the resources were on our side, If we held on we were bound to win, as anyone could demonstrate. It's certainly no fault of yours to have been defeated by mathematics, a science that governs the world."

St. Clair and Langdon smiled, and Langdon said lightly:

"It would perhaps be more just to say, Mr. Warner, that we have not been beaten, but that we've worn ourselves out, fighting. Besides, the spring is here, a lot of us are homesick, and it's time to put in the crops."

"I think that's a good way to leave it," said Dick. "Do you know where my cousin, Harry Kenton, is?"

"I saw him this morning," replied St. Clair, "and I can assure you that he's taken no harm. He's riding ahead of the commander-in-chief, and he should be here soon."

A trumpet sounded and they separated, returning respectively to their own lines. Standing on a low hill, Dick saw Harry Kenton and Dalton dismount and then stand on one side, as if in expectancy. Dick knew for whom they were waiting, and his own heart beat hard. A great hum and murmur arose, when the gray figure of an elderly man riding the famous war horse, Traveler, appeared.

It was Lee, and in this moment, when his heart must have bled, his bearing was proud and high. He was worn somewhat, and he had lost strength from the great privations and anxieties of the retreat, but he held himself erect. He was clothed in a fine new uniform, and he wore buckled at his side a splendid new sword, recently sent to him as a present.

Near by stood a farm house belonging to Wilmer McLean, but, Grant not yet having come, the Southern commander-in-chief dismounted, and, as the air was close and hot, he remained a little while under the shade of an apple tree, the famous apple tree of Appomattox, around which truth and legend have played so much.

Dick was fully conscious of everything now. He realized the greatness of the moment, and he would not miss any detail of any movement on the part of the principals. It was nearly three o'clock in the afternoon when Grant and his staff rode up, the Union leader still wearing his plain blue blouse, no sword at his side, his shoulder straps alone signifying his rank.

The two generals who had faced each other with such resolution in that terrible conflict shook hands, and Dick saw them talking pleasantly as if they were chance acquaintances who had just met once more. Presently they went into the McLean house, several of General Grant's staff accompanying him, but Lee taking with him only Colonel Thomas Marshall.

Before the day was over Dick learned all that had occurred inside that unpretentious but celebrated farm house. The two great commanders, at first did not allude to the civil war, but spoke of the old war in Mexico, where Lee, the elder, had been General Winfield Scott's chief of staff, and the head of his engineer corps, with Grant, the younger, as a lieutenant and quartermaster. It never entered the wildest dreams of either then that they should lead the armies of a divided nation engaged in mortal combat. Now they had only pleasant recollections of each other, and they talked of the old days, of Contreras, Molino del Rey, and other battles in the Valley of Mexico.

They sat down at a plain table, and then came in the straightforward manner characteristic of both to the great business in hand. Colonel Marshall supplied the paper for the historic documents now about to be written and signed.

General Grant, humane, and never greater or more humane than in the hour of victory, made the terms easy. All the officers of the Army of Northern Virginia were to give their parole not to take up arms against the United States, until properly exchanged, and the company or regimental commanders were to sign a like parole for their men. The artillery, other arms and public property were to be turned over to the Union army, although the officers were permitted to retain their side arms and their own horses and baggage. Then officers and men alike could go to their homes.

It was truly the supreme moment of Grant's greatness, of a humanity and greatness of soul the value of which to his nation can never be overestimated. Surrenders in Europe at the end of a civil war had always been followed by confiscations, executions and a reign of terror for the beaten. Here the man who had compelled the surrender merely told the defeated to go to their homes.

Lee looked at the terms and said:

"Many of the artillerymen and cavalrymen in our army own their horses, will the provisions allowing the officers to retain their horses apply to them also?"

"No, it will not as it is written," replied Grant, "but as I think this will be the last battle of the war, and as I suppose most of the men in the ranks are small farmers who without their horses would find it difficult to put in their crops, the country having been swept of everything movable, and as the United States does not want them, I will instruct the officers who are to receive the paroles of your troops to let every man who claims to own a horse or mule take the animal to his home."

"It will have a pleasant effect," said Lee, and then he wrote a formal letter accepting the capitulations. The two generals, rising, bowed to each other, but as Lee turned away he said that his men had eaten no food for several days, except parched corn, and he would have to ask that rations, and forage for their horses, be given to them.

"Certainly, general," replied Grant. "For how many men do you need them?"

"About twenty-five thousand," was Lee's reply.

Then General Grant requested him to send his own officers to Appomattox Station for the food and forage. Lee thanked him. They bowed to each other again, and the Southern leader who no longer had an army, but who retained always the love and veneration of the South, left the McLean house. Thus and in this simple fashion — the small detached fighting elsewhere did not count — did the great civil war in America, which had cost six or seven hundred thousand lives, and the temporary ruin of one section, come to an end.

Dick saw Lee come out of the house, mount Traveler and, followed by Colonel Marshall, ride back toward his own men who already had divined the occurrences in the house. The army saluted him with undivided affection, the troops crowding around him, cheering him, and, whenever they had a chance, shaking his hand. The demonstration became so great that Lee was moved deeply and showed it. The water rose in his eyes and his voice trembled as he said, though with pride:

"My lads, we have fought through the war together. I have done the best I could for you. My heart is too full to say more."

He could not be induced to speak further, although the great demonstration continued, but rode in silence to his headquarters in a wood, where he entered his tent and sat alone, no one ever knowing what his thoughts were in that hour.

Twenty-six thousand men who were left of the Army of Northern Virginia surrendered the next day, and the blue and the gray fraternized. The Union soldiers did not wait for the rations ordered by Grant, but gave of their own to the starved men who were so lately their foes. Dick and his friends hastened at once to find Harry Kenton and his comrades, and presently they saw them all sitting together on a log, thin and pale, but with no abatement of pride. Harry rose nevertheless, and received his cousin joyfully.

"Dick," he said as their hands met, "the war is over, and over forever. But you and I were never enemies."

"That's so, Harry," said Dick Mason, "and the thing for us to do now is to go back to Kentucky, and begin life where we left it off."

"But you don't start this minute," said Warner. "There is a small matter of business to be transacted first. We know all of you, but just the same we've brought our visiting cards with us."

"I don't understand," said Harry.

"We'll show you. Frank Pennington, remove that large protuberance from beneath your blouse. Behold it! A small ham, my friends, and it's for you. That's Frank's card. And here I take from my own blouse the half of a cheese, which I beg you to accept with my compliments. Dick, you rascal, what's that you have under your arm?"

"It's a jar of prime bacon that I've brought along for the party, George."

"I thought so. We're going to have the pleasure of dining with our friends here. We've heard, Captain Kenton, that you people haven't eaten anything for a month."

"It's not that bad," laughed Harry. "We had parched corn yesterday."

"Well, parched corn is none too filling, and we're going to prepare the banquet at once. A certain Sergeant Whitley will arrive presently with a basket of food, such as you rebels haven't tasted since you raided our wagon trains at the Second Manassas, and with him will come one William Shepard, whom you have met often, Mr. Kenton."

"Yes," said Harry, "we've met often and under varying circumstances, but we're going to be friends now."

"Will you tell me, Captain St. Clair," said Dick, "what has become of the two colonels of your regiment, which I believe you call the Invincibles?"

St. Clair led them silently to a little wood, and there, sitting on logs, Colonel Leonidas Talbot and Lieutenant Colonel Hector St. Hilaire were bent intently over the chess board that lay between them.

"Now that the war is over we'll have a chance to finish our game, eh, Hector?" said Colonel Talbot.

"A just observation, Leonidas. It's a difficult task to pursue a game to a perfect conclusion amid the distractions of war, but soon I shall checkmate you in the brilliant fashion in which General Lee always snares and destroys his enemy."

"But General Lee has yielded, Hector."

"Pshaw, Leonidas! General Lee would never yield to anybody. He has merely quit!"

"Ahem!" said Harry loudly, and, as the colonels glanced up, they saw the little group looking down at them.

"Our friends, the enemy, have come to pay you their respects," said Harry.

The two colonels rose and bowed profoundly.

"And to invite you to a banquet that is now being prepared not far from here," continued Harry. "It's very tempting, ham, cheese, and other solids, surrounded by many delicacies."

The two colonels looked at each other, and then nodded approval.

"You are to be the personal guests of our army," said Dick, "and we act as the proxies of General Grant."

"I shall always speak most highly of General Grant," said Colonel Leonidas Talbot. "His conduct has been marked by the greatest humanity, and is a credit to our common country, which has been reunited so suddenly."

"But reunited with our consent, Leonidas," said Lieutenant Colonel St. Hilaire. "Don't forget that I, for one, am tired of this war, and so is our whole army. It was a perfect waste of life to prolong it, and with the North reannexed, the Union will soon be stronger and more prosperous than ever."

"Well spoken, Hector! Well spoken. It is perhaps better that North and South should remain together. I thought otherwise for four years, but now I seem to have another point of view. Come, lads, we shall dine with these good Yankee boys and we'll make them drink toasts of their own excellent coffee to the health and safety of our common country."

The group returned to a little hollow, in which Sergeant Whitley and Shepard had built a fire, and where they were already frying strips of bacon and slices of ham over the coals. Shepard and Harry shook hands.

"I may as well tell you now, Mr. Kenton," said Shepard, "that Miss Henrietta Carden, whom you met in Richmond, is my sister, and that it was she who hid in the court at the Curtis house and took the map. Then it was I who gave you the blow."

"It was done in war," said Harry, "and I have no right to complain. It was clever and I hope that I shall be able to give your sister my compliments some day. Now, if you don't mind, I'll take a strip of that wonderful bacon. It is bacon, isn't it? It's so long since I've seen any that I'm not sure of its identity, but whatever it is its odor is enticing."

"Bacon it surely is, Mr. Kenton. Here are three pieces that I broiled myself and a broad slice of bread for them. Go ahead, there's plenty more. And see this dark brown liquid foaming in this stout tin pot! Smell it! Isn't it wonderful! Well, that's coffee! You've heard of coffee, and maybe you remember it."

"I do remember tasting it some years ago and finding it good. I'd like to try it again. Yes, thank you. It's fine."

"Here's another cup, and try the ham also."

Harry tried it, not once but several times. Langdon sat on the ground before the fire, and his delight was unalloyed and unashamed.

"We have raided a Yankee wagon train again," he said, "and the looting is splendid. Arthur, I thought yesterday that I should never eat again. Food and I were such strangers that I believed we should never know each other, any more, or if knowing, we could never assimilate. And yet we seem to get on good terms at once."

While they talked a tall thin youth of clear dark complexion, carrying a long bundle under his arm, approached the fire and Lieutenant Colonel St. Hilaire welcomed him with joy.

"Julien! Julien de Langeais, my young relative!" he cried. "And you are indeed alive! I thought you lost!"

"I'm very much alive, sir," said young De Langeais, "but I'm starved."

"Then this is the place to come," said Dick, putting before him food, which he strove to eat slowly, although the effort at restraint was manifestly great. Lieutenant Colonel St. Hilaire introduced him to the Union men, and then asked him what was the long black bag that he carried under his arm.

"That, sir," replied De Langeais, smiling pathetically, "is my violin. I've no further use for my rifle and sword, but now that peace is coming I may be able to earn my bread with the fiddle."

"And so you will! You'll become one of the world's great musicians. And as soon as we've finished with General Grant's hospitality, which will be some time yet, you shall play for us."

De Langeais looked affectionately at the black bag.

"You're very good to me, sir," he said, "to encourage me at such a time, and, if you and the others care for me to play, I'll do my best."

"Paganini himself could do no more, but, for the present, we must pay due attention to the hospitality of General Grant. He would not like it, if it should come to his ears that we did not show due appreciation, and since, in the course of events, and in order to prevent the mutual destruction of the sections, it became necessary for General Lee to arrange with someone to stop this suicidal war, I am glad the man was General Grant, a leader whose heart does him infinite credit."

"General Grant is a very great man, and he has never proved it more fully than today," said Dick, who sat near the colonels—his first inclination had been to smile, but he restrained it.

"Truly spoken, young sir," said Colonel Leonidas Talbot. "General Lee and General Grant together could hold this continent against the world, and, now that we have quit killing one another, America is safe in their hands. Harry, do you think I've eaten too much? I wouldn't go beyond the exploits of a gentleman, but this food has a wonderful savor, and I can't say that I have dined before in months."

"Not at all, sir, you have just fairly begun. As Lieutenant Colonel St. Hilaire pointed out, General Grant would be displeased if we didn't fully appreciate his hospitality and prove it by our deeds. Here are some sardines, sir. You haven't tasted 'em yet, but you'll find 'em wonderfully fine."

Colonel Leonidas Talbot took the sardines, and then he and Lieutenant Colonel St. Hilaire rose suddenly and simultaneously to their feet, a look of wonder and joy spreading over their faces.

"Is it really he?" exclaimed Colonel Talbot.

"It's he and none other," said Lieutenant Colonel St. Hilaire.

A tall, powerfully built, gray-haired man was coming toward them, his hands extended. Colonel Talbot and Lieutenant Colonel St. Hilaire stepped forward, and each grasped a hand.

"Good old John!"

"Why, John, it's worth a victory to shake your hand again!"

"Leonidas, I've been inquiring, an hour or two, for you and Hector."

"John Carrington, you've fulfilled your promise and more. We always said at West Point that you'd become the greatest artilleryman in the world, and in this war you've proved it on fifty battle fields. We've often watched your work from the other side, and we've always admired the accuracy with which you sent the shells flying about us. It was wonderful, John, wonderful, and it did more than anything else to save the North from complete defeat!"

A smile passed over John Carrington's strong face, and he patted his old comrade on the shoulder.

"It's good to know, Leonidas, that neither you nor Hector has been killed," he said, "and that we can dine together again."

"Truly, truly, John! Sit down! It's the hospitality of your own general that you share when you join us. General Lee would never make terms with men like McClellan, Burnside and Hooker. No, sir, he preferred to defeat them, much as it cost our Union in blood and treasure, but with a man of genius like General Grant he could agree. Really great souls always recognize one another. Is it not so, John?"

"Beyond a doubt, Leonidas. We fully admit the greatness and lofty character of General Lee, as you admit the greatness and humanity of General Grant. One nation is proud to have produced two such men."

"I agree with you, John. All of us agree with you. The soldiers of General Lee's army who are here today will never dispute what you say. Now fall on, and join us at this board which, though rustic, is indeed a most luxurious and festive one. As I remember at West Point, you were a first-class trencherman."

"And I am yet," said John Carrington, as he took his share. They were joined a little later by a gallant young Southern colonel, Philip Sherburne, who had led in many a cavalry attack, and then the equally gallant Northern colonel, Alan Hertford, came also, and as everybody was introduced to everybody else the good feeling grew. At last the hunger that had been increasing so long was satisfied, and as they leaned back, Lieutenant Colonel St. Hilaire turned to Julien de Langeais:

"Julien," he said, "take out your violin. There is no more fitting time than this to play. Julien, John, is a young relative of mine from Louisiana who has a gift. He is a great musician who is going to become much greater. Perhaps it was wrong to let a lad of his genius enter this war, but at any rate he has survived it, and now he will show us what he can do."

De Langeais, after modest deprecations, took out his violin and played. Upon his sensitive soul the war had made such a deep impression that his spirit spoke through his instrument. He had never before played so well. His strings sang of the march, the camp, of victory and defeat, and defeat and victory, and as he played he became absorbed in his music. The people around him, although they were rapidly increasing in numbers, were not visible to him. Yet he played upon their hearts. There was not one among them who did not see visions and dream dreams as he listened. At last his bow turned into the old and ever young, "Home Sweet Home."

> 'Mid pleasures and palaces though we may roam,
> Be it ever so humble, there's no place like home.
> An exile from home, splendor dazzles in vain,
> Oh! give me my lowly, thatched cottage again.

Into the song he poured all his skill and all his heart, and as he played he saw the house in which he was born on the far Louisiana plantation. And those who listened saw also, in spirit, the homes which many of them had not seen in fact for four years. Stern souls were softened, and water rose to eyes which had looked fearlessly and so often upon the charging bayonets of the foe.

He stopped suddenly and put away his violin. There was a hush, and then a long roll of applause, not loud, but very deep.

"I hear Pendleton calling," said Harry to Dick.

"So do I," said Dick. "I wonder what they're doing there. Have you heard from your father?"

"Not for several months. I think he's in North Carolina with Johnston, and I mean to go home that way. I've a good horse, and he'll carry me through the mountains. I think I'll find father there. An hour or two ago, Dick, I felt like a man and I was a man, but since De Langeais played I've become a boy again, and I'm longing for Pendleton, and its green hills, and the little river in which we used to swim."

"So am I, Harry, and it's likely that I'll go with you. The war is over and I can get leave at once. I want to see my mother."

They stayed together until night came over Appomattox and its famous apple tree, and a few days later Harry Kenton was ready to start on horseback for Kentucky. But he was far from being alone. The two colonels, St. Clair, Langdon, Dick, De Langeais, Colonel Winchester and Sergeant Whitley were to ride with him. Warner was to go north and Pennington west as soon as they were mustered out. Dick wrung their hands.

"Good-by, George! Good-by, Frank! Old comrades!" he said. "But remember that we are to see a good deal of one another all through our lives!"

"Which I can reduce to a mathematical problem and demonstrate by means of my little algebra here," said Warner, fumbling for his book to hide his emotion.

"I may come through Kentucky to see you and Harry," said Pennington, "when I start back to Nebraska."

"Be sure to come," said Dick with enthusiasm, "and remember that the latch string is hanging out on both doors."

Then, carrying their arms, and well equipped with ammunition, food and blankets, the little party rode away. They knew that the mountains were still extremely unsettled, much infested by guerrillas, but they believed themselves strong enough to deal with any difficulty, and, as the April country was fair and green, their hearts, despite everything, were light.

CHAPTER XVIII
THE FINAL RECKONING

They rode a long time through a war-torn country, and the days bound the young men together so closely that, at times, it seemed to them they had fought on the same side all through the war. Sergeant Whitley was usually their guide and he was an expert to bargain for food and forage. He exhibited then all the qualities that afterward raised him so high in the commercial world.

Although they were saddened often by the spectacle of the ruin the long war had made, they kept their spirits, on the whole, wonderfully well. The two colonels, excellent horsemen, were an unfailing source of cheerfulness. When they alluded to the war they remembered only the great victories the South had won, and invariably they spoke of its end as a compromise. They also began to talk of Charleston, toward which their hearts now turned, and a certain handsome Madame Delaunay whom Harry Kenton remembered well.

As they left Virginia and entered North Carolina they heard that the Confederate troops everywhere were surrendering. The war, which had been so terrible and sanguinary only two or three months before, ended absolutely with the South's complete exhaustion. Already the troops were going home by the scores of thousands. They saw men who had just taken off their uniforms guiding the ploughs in the furrows. Smoke rose once more from the chimneys of the abandoned homes, and the boys who had faced the cannon's mouth were rebuilding rail fences. The odor of grass and newly turned earth was poignant and pleasant. The two colonels expanded.

"Though my years have been devoted to military pursuits, Hector," said Colonel Leonidas Talbot, "the agricultural life is noble, and many of the hardy virtues of the South are due to the fact that we are chiefly a rural population."

"Truly spoken, Leonidas, but for four years agriculture has not had much chance with us, and perhaps agriculture is not all. It was the mechanical genius of the North that kept us from taking New York and Boston."

"Which reminds me, Happy," said St. Clair to Langdon, "that, after all, you didn't sleep in the White House at Washington with your boots on."

"I changed my mind," replied Happy easily. "I didn't want to hurt anybody's feelings."

Soon they entered the mountains, and they met many Confederate soldiers returning to their homes. Harry always sought from them news of his father, and he learned at last that he was somewhere in the western part of the state. Then he heard, a day or two later, that a band of guerrillas to the south of them were plundering and sometimes murdering. They believed from what details they could gather that it was Slade and Skelly with a new force, and they thought it advisable to turn much farther toward the west.

"The longest way 'round is sometimes the shortest way through," said Sergeant Whitley, and the others agreed with him. They came into a country settled then but little. The mountains were clothed in deep forest, now in the full glory of early spring, and the log cabins were few. Usually they slept, the nights through, in the forest, and they helped out their food supply with game. The sergeant shot two deer, and they secured wild turkeys and quantities of smaller game.

Although they heard that the guerrillas were moving farther west, which necessitated the continuation of their own course in that direction, they seemed to have entered another world. Where they were, at least, there was nothing but peace, the peace of the wilderness which made a strong appeal to all of them. In the evenings by their campfire in the forest De Langeais would often play for them on his violin, and the great trees about them seemed to rustle with approval, as a haunting melody came back in echoes from the valleys.

They had been riding a week through a wilderness almost unbroken when, just before sunset, they heard a distant singing sound, singularly like that of De Langeais' violin.

"It is a violin," said De Langeais, "but it's not mine. The sound comes from a point at the head of the cove before us."

They rode into the little valley and the song of the violin grew louder. It was somebody vigorously playing "Old Dan Tucker," and as the woods opened they saw a stout log cabin, a brook and some fields. The musician, a stalwart young man, sat in the doorway of the house. A handsome young woman was cooking outside, and a little child was playing happily on the grass.

"I'll ride forward and speak to them," said Harry Kenton. "That man and I are old friends."

The violin ceased, as the thud of hoofs drew near, but Harry, springing from his horse, held out his hand to the man and said:

"How are you, Dick Jones? I see that the prophecy has come true!"

The man stared at him a moment or two in astonishment, and then grasped his hand.

"It's Mr. Kenton!" he cried, "an' them's your friends behind you. 'Light, strangers, 'light! Yes, Mr. Kenton, it's come true. I've been back home a week, an' not a scratch on me, though I've fit into nigh onto a thousand battles. I reckon my wife, that's Mandy there, wished so hard fur me to come back that the Lord let her have her way. But 'light, strangers! 'Light an' hev supper!"

"We will," said Harry, "but we're not going to crowd you out of your house. We've plenty of food with us, and we're accustomed to sleeping out of doors."

Nevertheless the hospitality of Dick Jones and his wife, Mandy, was unbounded. It was arranged that the two colonels should sleep inside, while the others took to the grass with their blankets. Liberal contributions were made to the common larder by the travelers, and they had an abundant supper, after which the men sat outside, the colonels smoking good old North Carolina weed, and Mrs. Jones knitting in the dusk.

"Don't you and your family get lonesome here sometimes, Mr. Jones?" asked Harry.

"Never," replied the mountaineer. "You see I've had enough o' noise an' multitudes. More than once I've seen two hundred thousand men fightin', and I've heard the cannon roarin', days without stoppin'. I still git to dreamin' at night 'bout all them battles, an' when I awake, an' set up sudden like an' hear nothin' outside but the tricklin' o' the branch an' the wind in the leaves, I'm thankful that them four years are over, an' nobody is shootin' at nobody else. An' it's hard now an' then to b'lieve that they're really an' truly over."

"But how about Mrs. Jones?"

"She an' the baby stayed here four whole years without me, but we've got neighbors, though you can't see 'em fur the trees. Jest over the ridge lives her mother, an' down Jones' Creek, into which the branch runs, lives her married sister, an' my own father ain't more'n four miles away. The settlements are right thick 'roun' here, an' we hev good times."

Mrs. Jones nodded her emphatic assent.

"Which way do you-all 'low to be goin' tomorrow?" asked Jones.

"We think we'd better keep to the west," replied Colonel Talbot. "We've heard of a guerrilla band under two men, Slade and Skelly, who are making trouble to the southward."

"I've heard of 'em too," said Jones, "an' I reckon they're 'bout the meanest scum the war hez throwed up. The troops will be after 'em afore long, an' will clean 'em out, but I guess they'll do a lot o' damage afore then. You gen'lemen will be wise to stick to your plan, an' keep on toward the west."

They departed the next morning, taking with them the memory of a very pleasant meeting, and once more pursued their way through the wilderness. Harry, despite inquiries at every possible place, heard nothing more of his father, and concluded that, after the surrender, he must have gone at once to Kentucky, expecting his son to come there by another way.

But the reports of Slade and Skelly were so numerous and so sinister that they made a complete change of plan. The colonels, St. Clair and Langdon, would not try to go direct to South Carolina, but the whole party would cling together, ride to Kentucky, and then those who lived farther south could return home chiefly by rail. It seemed, on the whole, much the wiser way, and, curving back a little to the north, they entered by and by the high mountains on the line between Virginia and Kentucky. Other returning soldiers had joined them and their party now numbered thirty brave, well-armed men.

They entered Kentucky at a point near the old Wilderness Road, and, from a lofty crest, looked down upon a sea of ridges, heavy with green forest, and narrow valleys between, in which sparkled brooks or little rivers. The hearts of Harry and Dick beat high. They were going home. What awaited them at Pendleton? Neither had heard from the town or anybody in it for a long time. Anticipation was not unmingled with anxiety.

Two days later they entered a valley, and when they stopped at noon for their usual rest Harry Kenton rode some distance up a creek, thinking that he might rouse a deer out of the underbrush. Although the country looked extremely wild and particularly suited to game, he found none, but unwilling to give up he continued the hunt, riding much farther than he was aware.

He was just thinking of the return, when he heard a rustling in a thicket to his right, and paused, thinking that it might be the deer he wanted. Instead, a gigantic figure with thick black hair and beard rose up in the bush. Harry uttered a startled exclamation. It was Skelly, and beside him stood a little man with an evil face, hidden partly by an enormous flap-brimmed hat. Both carried rifles, and before Harry could take his own weapon from his shoulder Skelly fired. Harry's horse threw up his head in alarm, and the bullet, instead of hitting the rider, took the poor animal in the brain.

As the horse fell, Harry sprang instinctively and alighted upon his feet, although he staggered. Then Slade pulled trigger, and a searing, burning pain shot through his left shoulder. Dizzy and weak he raised his rifle, nevertheless, and fired at the hairy face of the big man. He saw the huge figure topple and fall; he heard another shot, and again felt the thrill of pain, this time in the head, heard a shrill whistle repeated over and over, and did not remember anything definite until some time afterward.

When his head became clear once more Harry believed that he had wandered a long distance from that brief but fierce combat, but he did not know in what direction his steps had taken him. Nearly all his strength was gone, and his head ached fearfully. He had dropped his rifle, but where he did not know nor care. He sat down on the ground with his back against a tree, and put his right hand to his head. The wound there had quit bleeding, clogged up with its own blood. He was experienced enough to know that it was merely a flesh wound, and that any possible scar would be hidden by his hair.

But the wound in his left shoulder was more serious. The bullet had gone entirely through, for which he was glad, but the hurt was still bleeding. He made shift to bandage it with strips torn from his underclothing, and, after a long rest, he undertook to walk back to the camp. He was not sure of the way, and after two or three hundred yards he grew dizzy and sat down again. Then he shouted for help, but his voice sounded so weak that he gave it up.

He was never sure, but he thought another period of unconsciousness followed, because when he aroused himself the sun seemed to be much farther down in the west. His head was still aching, though not quite so badly as before, and he made a new effort to walk. He did not know where he was going, but he must go somewhere. If he remained there in the wilderness, and his comrades could not find him, he would die of weakness and starvation. He shuddered. It would be the very irony of fate that one who had gone through Chancellorsville, Gettysburg and all the great battles in the East should be slain on his way home by a roving guerrilla.

He rested again and summoned all his strength and courage, and he was able to go several hundred yards farther. As he advanced the forest seemed to thin and he was quite sure that he saw through it a valley and open fields. The effect upon him was that of a great stimulant, and he found increased strength. He tottered on, but stopped soon and leaned against a tree. He dimly saw the valley, the fields, and a distant roof, and then came something that gave him new strength. It was a man's voice singing, a voice clear, powerful and wonderfully mellow:

> They bore him away when the day had fled,
>   And the storm was rolling high,
> And they laid him down in his lonely bed
>   By the light of an angry sky.
> The lightning flashed and the wild sea lashed
>   The shore with its foaming wave,
> And the thunder passed on the rushing blast
>   As it howled o'er the rover's grave.

He knew that voice. He had heard it years ago, a century it seemed. It was the voice of a friend, the voice of Sam Jarvis, the singer of the mountains. He rushed forward, but overtaxing his strength, fell. He pulled himself up by a bush and stood, trembling with weakness and anxiety. Still came the voice, but the song had changed:

> Soft o'er the fountain, lingering falls the Southern moon,
> Far o'er the mountain breaks the day too soon,

> In thy dark eyes' splendor, where the warm light loves to dwell,
> Weary looks yet tender speak their fond farewell,
> Nita! Juanita! Ask thy soul if we should part,
> Nita! Juanita! Lean thou on my heart!

It was an old song of pathos and longing, but Harry remembered well that mellow, golden voice. If he could reach Sam Jarvis he would secure help, and there was the happy valley in which he lived. As he steadied himself anew fresh strength and courage poured into his veins, and leaving the fringe of forest he entered a field, at the far end of which Jarvis was ploughing.

The singer was happy. He drove a stout bay horse, and as he walked along in the furrow he watched the rich black earth turn up before the ploughshare. He hated no man, and no man hated him. The war had never invaded his valley, and he sang from the sheer pleasure of living. The world about him was green and growing, and the season was good. His nephew, Ike Simmons, was ploughing in another field, and whenever he chose he could see the smoke rising from the chimney of the strong log house in which he lived.

Harry thought at first that he would go down the end of the long field to Jarvis, but the ploughed land pulled at his feet, and made him very weak again. So he walked straight across it, though he staggered, and approached the house, the doors of which stood wide open.

He was not thinking very clearly now, but he knew that rest and help were at hand. He opened the gate that led to the little lawn, went up the walk and, scarcely conscious of what he was doing, stood in the doorway, and stared into the dim interior. As his eyes grew used to the dusk the figure of an old, old woman, lean and wrinkled, past a hundred, suddenly rose from a chair, stood erect, and regarded him with startled, burning eyes.

"Ah, it's the governor, the great governor, Henry Ware!" she exclaimed. "Didn't I say to you long ago: 'You will come again, and you will be thin and pale and in rags, and you will fall at the door.' I see you coming with these two eyes of mine!"

As she spoke, the young man in the tattered Southern uniform, stained with the blood of two wounds, reeled and fell unconscious in the doorway.

When Harry came back to the world he was lying in a very comfortable bed, and all the pain had gone from his head. A comfortable, motherly woman, whom he recognized as Mrs. Simmons, was sitting beside him, and Colonel Leonidas Talbot, looking very tall, very spare and very precise, was standing at a window.

"Good morning, Mrs. Simmons," said Harry in a clear, full voice.

She uttered an exclamation of joy, and Colonel Talbot turned from the window.

"So you've come back to us, Harry," he said. "We knew that it was only a matter of time, although you did lose a lot of blood from that wound in the shoulder."

"I never intended to stay away, sir."

"But you remained in the shadowy world three days."

"That long, sir?"

"Yes, Harry, three days, and a great deal of water has flowed under the bridge in those three days."

"What do you mean, colonel?"

"There was a military operation of a very sharp and decisive character. When you fell in the doorway here, Mrs. Simmons, who happened to be in the kitchen, ran at once for her brother, Mr. Jarvis, a most excellent and intelligent man. You were past telling anybody anything just then, but he followed your trail, and met some of us, led by Sergeant Whitley, who were also trailing you."

"And Slade and Skelly, what of them?"

"They'll never plunder or murder more. We divined much that had happened. You were ambushed, were you not?"

"Yes, Slade and Skelly fired upon me from the bushes. I shot back and saw Skelly fall."

"You shot straight and true. We found him there in the bushes, where your bullet had cut short his murderous life. Then we organized, pursued and surrounded the others. They were desperate criminals, who knew the rope awaited them, and all of them died with their boots on. Slade made a daring attempt to escape, but the sergeant shot him through the head at long range, and a worse villain never fell."

"And our people, colonel, where are all of them?"

"Most of the soldiers have gone on, but the members of our own immediate group are scattered about the valley, engaged chiefly in agricultural or other homely pursuits, while they await your recovery, and incidentally earn their bread. Sergeant Whitley, Captain St. Clair and Captain Mason are putting a new roof on the barn, and, as I inspected it myself, I can certify that they are performing the task in a most workmanlike manner. Captain Thomas Langdon is ploughing in the far field, by the side of that stalwart youth, Isaac Simmons, and each is striving in a spirit of great friendliness to surpass the other. My associate and second in command, Lieutenant Colonel Hector St. Hilaire, has gone down the creek fishing, a pursuit in which he has had much success, contributing greatly to the larder of our hostess, Mrs. Simmons."

"And where is Sam Jarvis?"

The colonel raised the window.

"Listen!" he said:

Up from the valley floated the far mellow notes:

> I'm dreaming now of Hallie, sweet Hallie,
> > For the thought of her is one that never dies.
> She's sleeping in the valley
> > And the mocking bird is singing where she lies.
> Listen to the mocking bird singing o'er her grave,
> Listen to the mocking bird, where the weeping willows wave.

"The words of the song are sad," said Colonel Talbot, "but sad music does not necessarily make one feel sad. On the contrary we are all very cheerful here, and Mr. Jarvis is the happiest man I have ever known. I think it's because his nature is so kindly. A heart of gold, pure gold, Harry, and that extraordinary old woman, Aunt Suse, insists that you are your own greatgrandfather, the famous governor of Kentucky."

"I was here before in the first year of the war, colonel, and she foretold that I would return just as I did. How do you account for that, sir?"

"I don't try to account for it. A great deal of energy is wasted in trying to account for the unknowable. I shall take it as it is."

"What has become of Colonel Winchester, sir?"

"He rode yesterday to a tiny hamlet about twenty miles away. We had heard from a mountaineer that an officer returning from the war was there, and since we old soldiers like to foregather, we decided to have him come and join our party. They are due here, and unless my eyes deceive me—and I know they don't—they're at the bead of the valley now, riding toward this house."

Harry detected a peculiar note in Colonel Talbot's voice, and his mind leaped at once to a conclusion.

"That officer is my father!" he exclaimed.

"According to all the descriptions, it is he, and now you can sit up and welcome him."

The meeting between father and son was not demonstrative, but both felt deep emotion.

"Fortune has been kind to us, Harry, to bring us both safely out of the long war," said Colonel Kenton.

"Kinder than we had a right to hope," said Harry.

The entire group rode together to Pendleton, and Dick was welcomed like one risen from the dead by his mother, who told him a few weeks later that he was to have a step-father, the brave colonel, Arthur Winchester.

"He's the very man I'd have picked for you, mother," said Dick gallantly.

The little town of Pendleton was unharmed by the war, and, since bitter feeling had never been aroused in it, the reunion of North and South began there at once. In an incredibly short period everything went on as before.

The two colonels and their younger comrades remained a while as the guests of Colonel Kenton and his son, and then they started for the farther south where St. Clair and Langdon were to begin the careers in which they achieved importance.

Harry and Dick in Pendleton entered upon their own life work, which they were destined to do so well, but often, in their dreams and for many years, they rode again with Stonewall in the Valley, charged with Pickett at Gettysburg, stood with the Rock of Chickamauga, or advanced with Grant to the thunder of the guns through the shades of the Wilderness.